Carol Ericson is a bestselling, award-winning author of more than forty books. She has an eerie fascination for true-crime stories, a love of film noir and a weakness for reality TV, all of which fuel her imagination to create her own tales of murder, mayhem and mystery. To find out more about Carol and her current projects, please visit her website at www.carolericson.com, 'where romance flirts with danger.'

Julie Anne Lindsey is a multigenre author who writes the stories that keep her up at night. She's a self-proclaimed nerd with a penchant for words and proclivity for fun. Julie lives in rural Ohio with her husband and three small children. Today she hopes to make someone smile. One day she plans to change the world. Julie is a member of International Thriller Writers and Sisters in Crime. Learn more about Julie Anne Lindsey at julieannelindsey.com

Also by Carol Ericson

Enemy Infiltration
Undercover Accomplice
Delta Force Defender
Delta Force Daddy
Delta Force Die Hard
Locked, Loaded and SEALed
Alpha Bravo SEAL
Bullseye: SEAL
Point Blank SEAL
Secured by the SEAL

Also by Julie Anne Lindsey

Shadow Point Deputy
Marked by the Marshal
Federal Agent Under Fire
The Sheriff's Secret

Discover more at millsandboon.co.uk

CODE CONSPIRACY

CAROL ERICSON

DEADLY COVER-UP

JULIE ANNE LINDSEY

MILLS & BOON

First Published in Great Britain 2020
by Mills & Boon, an imprint of HarperCollins*Publishers*
1 London Bridge Street, London, SE1 9GF

Code Conspiracy © 2019 Carol Ericson
Deadly Cover-Up © 2019 Julie Anne Lindsey

ISBN: 978-0-263-28014-2

0120

MIX
Paper from
responsible sources
FSC™ C007454

This book is produced from independently certified FSC™
paper to ensure responsible forest management.

For more information visit: www.harpercollins.co.uk/green

Printed and bound in Spain
by CPI, Barcelona

CODE CONSPIRACY

CAROL ERICSON

Prologue

"Dreadworm."

The speaker, slouching behind a post on the tracks of the central Berlin train station, drew out the last syllable of the word and it reverberated in Rex Denver's chest like an omen. He coughed as if to dislodge it from his throat.

"Dreadworm? You mean the hacking group?"

"Only they can break into the CIA's computer system." The man drew the hood of his gray sweatshirt more tightly around his face with a pair of gloved hands. "Rumor has it they've already been successful."

Denver had a side view only, but he didn't care. The identity of the informant held no interest for him, but his words acted like an electric prod.

"You're sure the CIA is behind this setup? In league with an international band of terrorists?" Denver's gut roiled and tumbled, bitter bile clawing its way up his throat.

"The entire Central Intelligence Agency?" The man jerked his head from side to side, his hood moving with it. "No, but forces within that agency…and others…are actively working against US interests and that means holding the government hostage with the threat of some kind of terrorist attack."

Denver swore and spit the sour taste in his mouth onto

the train tracks. "Why are you telling *me* this? Reaching out to me in this secretive way?"

"Call me a concerned citizen."

Denver snorted. "Most concerned citizens don't risk their lives and livelihood on what could be a conspiracy hoax."

"Was the attack on you, your Delta Force teammate and that army ranger a hoax? Is the campaign to discredit you and label you a traitor a hoax?"

"Hell, no. That's real."

"So is this."

"Why not go to the director? I'm just gonna assume here that you're CIA."

"Don't assume anything, Major Denver. I have no solid proof that this is happening." The informant lifted a pair of narrow shoulders. "And I don't know whom to trust."

"The director?" A cold chill seeped into Denver's bones and it had nothing to do with the empty tracks he was straddling in the dank tunnel, his hand flattened against the damp wall.

"It could be anyone. That's why you need Dreadworm. They can cross all boundaries. They *have* crossed all boundaries."

"Their leader, Olaf, is in hiding."

"So are you, Major Denver. Tell me. How did you get from Afghanistan to the streets of Berlin without showing up on anyone's radar?"

"You know that thing you said about trust?" Denver shoved his cold hands into his pockets. "Right about now, I trust no one—except my Delta Force team."

"That's wise. They're the only ones who have been actively working to clear your name…and they're getting close." The man stepped back against the wall as the tracks beneath them vibrated. "You don't have to explain—dark-haired man with a beard slipping across borders with the other refugees. Who would stop to think the mass of people contained an American Delta Force soldier?"

Denver didn't plan to reveal his secrets to anyone—not even a shadow in the night with his *own* secrets. "I know someone who works with Dreadworm."

"Then I suggest you start pulling in favors, major."

The informant stepped forward, and Denver jerked back, gripping the weapon in his pocket.

"Stay where you are."

"Your contacts at Dreadworm might be interested in this." He held up a cardboard wheel in his gloved hand. "Go ahead. Take it."

Denver snatched the circular object and shoved it into his pocket. "I should pass this on to Dreadworm?"

"That would be advisable." The informant pulled the collar of his jacket close around his neck. "Because Dreadworm is your only hope right now. Dreadworm is *our* only hope—I never thought I'd hear myself say those words."

"Wait." Denver peered into the blackness, as the man stepped back. "How am I going to contact you again?"

"I'll find you when I need to." He laughed, a hollow sound that echoed in the tunnel. "After all, we need to save the world."

A light appeared at the end of the tunnel, outlining the slim figure hugging the wall, and Denver prayed it was a metaphor for his current situation. Could Dreadworm really be the light at the end of *his* tunnel?

The shrill train whistle made his teeth ache. Denver climbed off the tracks, his head cranked over his shoulder, his eyeballs throbbing with the effort to pick out his informant, still on the tracks in the path of the oncoming train.

Denver shouted. "Get out of the way!"

The light from the train flooded the tunnel, the empty tunnel, and as Denver stepped back onto the platform, the train whooshed past him, lifting the ends of his long hair and shaking the buttons on his shirt.

His informant had melted away, but his words rang in Denver's ears.

Pulling his watch cap over those ears and hunching his shoulders, Denver put his head down and made for the stairs.

He had to get word to Gray Prescott to make contact with his ex-girlfriend. Things had ended badly between Gray and his ex, but Gray would have to suck it up and make nice with the hacker with the chip on her shoulder—she just might hold the fate of the world in her hands.

Chapter One

Jerrica turned her head and sucked in a quick breath as the man behind her ducked into a doorway. She hitched her backpack over her shoulders and darted into the street.

A taxi blared at her, and she smacked her hand on its hood, yelling. "Watch where you're goin'!"

She crouched behind another taxi, the heat from the exhaust pipe burning her leg as the car lurched forward.

For a half a block, she stayed in the middle of the street, navigating a straight path between two lines of cars. Drivers yelled at her from their windows, the obscenities pinging her coat of armor but never piercing it. What did she care about a few dirty words tossed her way? She'd endured worse—a lot worse.

She twirled around and negotiated the traffic while walking backward, keeping her gaze pinned to the surging crowd on the sidewalk, trying to pick out her tail.

She'd lost him. Damn, she'd gotten good at losing people.

She threaded her way through the cars back to the sidewalk and slipped down a small alley. Two doors down, she formed a fist and banged on the metal. She had the access card that would gain her entry, but she knew Amit would be working away and she preferred not to surprise him by slipping in unannounced.

He really needed to adjust his schedule every once in a while—predictability could be dangerous in their line of work.

A lock clicked from the inside, and Jerrica eased open the door just widely enough to insert her body through the space. She placed both hands against the cold surface to make sure the door closed with a snap. Then she glanced at the video display above the door—the alley remained empty.

Her heavy boots clomped on the stairs as she made her way up to the work area.

Amit looked up from his computer monitor, adjusting his glasses. "I thought you were coming in earlier."

Jerrica swung her pack from her back and settled into a chair in front of a scrolling display of numbers and letters. "Did Dreadworm turn into a nine-to-five gig while I was busy programming?"

"Don't bite my head off." Amit ducked behind his screen. "I was just asking."

"I think I was being followed." She held her breath, waiting for Amit's outburst.

He sniffed and wiped his nose with a tissue. "What else is new?"

"What's that supposed to mean?" She leveled a finger at the crumpled tissue in his hand. "Do *not* leave that thing lying around. Nobody wants your germs…or your judgment."

"I'm not sick. I have allergies."

"Whatever. I'm getting tired of picking them up."

"All right. All right." Amit stuffed the thing into his front pocket.

She narrowed her eyes. "You didn't answer me. You're not worried that someone was on my tail?"

"You *think* someone was on your tail. When is someone *not* on your tail, Jerrica? Or trying to hack into your computer? Or peeping in your window at night?"

Blinking her lashes, she cocked her head. "They caught onto Olaf, didn't they? Do you want to go into hiding like him? I don't."

Amit slumped in his chair and pushed his glasses to the top of his head, making his hair stick up. "What did you uncover last week that has you looking over your shoulder again?"

"I'm not ready to reveal it yet." She double-clicked on the screen to stop the scrolling and entered another command.

"You don't have to reveal it publicly, but you can tell me, Kiera and Cedar in the other office." He circled his index finger in the air. "We work together. We're coworkers, remember?"

"Coworkers?" She brushed her bangs out of her eyes. "We're hackers. Olaf always wanted us to work on our own stuff. That's why the two of us are here and Kiera and Cedar are…somewhere else. I'll reveal it when I'm ready."

Amit shook his head and attacked his keyboard. "You and Olaf are two of a kind. Do you know where he is?"

"Why would he tell me? Why would he tell anyone? It's safer to keep to yourself." She turned away and stashed her backpack under her desk.

"It might be safer, Jerrica, but there's more to life than safety." His long fingers hovered over the keyboard. "You wanna go to a party tonight with me and Kelly?"

"I have work to do." She batted her lashes at him. "And, as you so kindly pointed out, I came in late."

"I'm going to take off in about two hours. Are you sure you want to stay here by yourself?"

"I thought you weren't concerned about safety? You were here by yourself." She wiggled her fingers above the keys. "Besides, this is one of the most secure places in Manhattan—cameras, locks, motion sensors. I'm good."

"The person supposedly following you didn't see you come into this building, did he?"

"There was no *supposedly* about it, but no, he didn't follow me here. I lost him." She wrinkled her nose. "I gotta get back to what I was working on."

"I can take a hint."

The steady clicking from Amit's keyboard indicated a dogged determination and concerted commitment. Amit might pretend that it was Jerrica who was the obsessed one, but the fire blazed in his gut just as hotly as it did in hers.

They each had their own reasons for their dedication to hacking into government systems and exposing the lies and corruption. Amit just did a better job of functioning in society.

She'd had a life once. She'd even had a boyfriend. Her nose stung and she swiped it with the back of her hand.

As if *that* was ever gonna work out.

After a few hours of companionable tapping, Amit pushed his chair away from the desk and reached both arms up to the ceiling that was crisscrossed with pipes. "I'm calling it a night. You sure you don't want to hit that party with me and Kelly?"

"I'm on a trail, so close." She grabbed the bottle of water she'd pulled out of her backpack earlier and chugged some. "But say hi to Kelly for me."

"Yeah, yeah. She's gonna give me hell for leaving you here by yourself."

Jerrica choked on her next sip of water. "She doesn't know we're Dreadworm, does she?"

"Who do you think I am?" Amit yanked a flash drive out of the computer. "You?"

"That's not fair." She wound her hair around her hand and tossed it over her shoulder. "I didn't tell anyone anything. He figured it out."

"Yeah, the last person who needs to know about Dreadworm—someone in the military."

Jerrica's cheeks blazed and she pressed the water bottle against her face. "Maybe that's why he was able to figure it out. He was Special Forces...*is* Special Forces."

Amit crammed some personal items into his bag. "And he never told anyone?"

"He wouldn't do that."

"Dude must've been crazy about you to keep that to himself."

"Crazy about me?" Jerrica snorted. "Yeah, so crazy about me he dumped me."

"Kinda hard for a guy in Delta Force to hang with someone who's trying to expose all the secrets of the federal government." Amit slipped his bag's strap across his body. "Dumping you is the least he could've done. It could've been a lot worse."

Jerrica pressed a hand over her heart and the dull ache centered there. "Don't you have a party to go to?"

"Outta here." Amit saluted and then tapped the monitor of the desktop computer. "Leave this running, please. I'm looking for some files connected to the attack on the embassy outpost in Nigeria. I know we didn't get the full story on that one, and I programmed a little worm that's chewing through some data right now."

She eyed the flickering display on Amit's computer. "See you later."

When the metal door downstairs slammed behind him, she shifted her gaze to the TV monitors to make sure nobody slipped into the building before the door closed.

Could she help it if paranoia sat beside her and whispered in her ear day and night? She'd been raised on conspiracy theories—and so far nothing in her life had belied that upbringing, nothing had stilled those dark undercurrents that bubbled beneath the surface of every encounter she had—even the most personal ones.

Amit disappeared from the security cam and Jerrica jumped from her chair and hunched over Amit's, folding her arms across the back and studying the data marching across the display. The attack on the embassy outpost in Nigeria had been on her radar, too. And not only because it involved someone she knew, peripherally, anyway.

Delta Force Major Rex Denver had played a significant role in the Nigeria debacle, as he'd visited the outpost days before the attack. He'd also, allegedly, played a role in the bombing at the Syrian refugee center, although the witnesses in Syria had been walking back that narrative for a few months now.

She drummed her fingers against her chin. And Denver's name had come up again as she scurried down the rabbit hole of her current hunch—or maybe she'd been scurrying down a mole hole, if moles even burrowed into holes. Because she'd bet all the settlement money sitting in her bank account that the intel she'd been tracking was going to lead to a mole—possibly in the CIA itself.

Rubbing her hands together, she returned to her own chair and continued inputting data to dig deeper into the CIA system she'd already compromised.

After a few hours of work, she rubbed her eyes and took a swig of water. As she watched her screen, a blurry message popped up in the lower-left corner of her display.

She blinked and the words came into focus. She read them aloud to the room where all sounds of human intercourse had been replaced by the whirs and clicks of computer interaction. "Who are you?"

She huffed out a breath and growled. "You show me yours first, buddy."

So, someone at the other end had detected an intruder. She entered her reply, whispering the words as she typed them.

Who are you?

Not terribly clever, but she had no intention of showing her hand. She fastened her gaze on the blinking cursor, waiting for the response.

Her eyeballs dried up watching that cursor, so she set the program's command to keep running in her absence, just as Amit had done on his computer. If Amit came back to the Dreadworm offices, he would know to leave the program running, but just in case, she plastered a sticky note to her screen before packing up for the night.

Jerrica scanned the video feed showing the alley while she scooped up her backpack and hitched it over one shoulder. She swept up her black fedora, which she'd left here the other night, and clapped it on her head.

Flipping up the collar of her black leather jacket, she jogged down the steps from the work area. She tipped her head back to check the video from outside and then, pausing at the door, she pressed her ear against the cold metal, not that she could hear anything through it.

She took a final glance at the monitor above the door before easing the door open. She looked both ways up and down the alley. She shimmied through the space, the zipper and metal studs on her jacket scraping against the doorjamb, and pulled the heavy slab of metal shut behind her.

This alley had just a few doorways and a couple of fire escapes, so it didn't attract much traffic. Olaf, Dreadworm's founder, had searched high and low in Manhattan to find just the right locations, and then had secured those locations—but he hadn't been able to secure himself.

Someone outed him and his residence and he'd had to go on the run or face federal prosecution. She didn't want to be criminally charged, but she couldn't give up this job...mission...especially now that she'd hacked into the CIA databases.

She emerged from the alley onto the crowded sidewalk and joined the surge of people. Darkness hadn't descended yet on this cool spring evening. Summer with its heat and humidity waited right around the corner, and Jerrica wanted to soak up the last bits of May with its hint of freshness still on the cusp of the air. She closed her eyes and inhaled, getting a lungful of exhaust fumes and some guy's over-ambitious aftershave.

She headed underground to catch the subway to her neighborhood. Just as she plopped down in her seat, an old man with a cane scraping beside him shuffled onto the train.

Jerrica's gaze swept the other passengers in the car, their heads buried in their phones, earbuds shoved in their ears, noses dipped into tablets, reading devices and portable game consoles. Nobody budged, nobody stirred from the online, electronic worlds sucking up their attention and their humanity.

Jerrica hoisted her backpack from her lap and pushed up from her seat. She tapped the old man's arm and pointed to the empty spot.

He nodded and smiled, the light reaching his faded blue eyes.

The train lurched around a bend, and Jerrica grabbed the bar above her head, swaying with the motion of the car. Maybe she should've accepted Amit's invitation to the party. She didn't even have her cat to greet her at home. Puck had disappeared last month without a trace just as seamlessly as he'd entered her realm. Even cats had a way of passing through her life, perhaps recognizing her rootless existence and most likely identifying with it.

With both of her hands holding on for dear life, she shook her hair from her face. Yeah, she definitely needed to get out and socialize. She'd call Amit once she got home and had some dinner and put on her best party face.

The train rumbled into her station and she jumped off. She emerged into the fresh air but hung back at the top of the steps.

If someone had been following her this afternoon, they must've picked up her trail around here—her neighborhood, her subway stop. No way someone just started tracking her in the middle of Manhattan. She took a different route to Dreadworm every time she went there. This place, this neighborhood, comprised her only constants.

She zeroed in on a few faces, attuned to sudden stops, starts and reversals. She moved forward by putting one foot in front of the other because she had to start somewhere. Sometimes the fear and uncertainty paralyzed her.

She ducked into her favorite noodle shop and ordered a spicy vegetarian pho with tofu, inhaling the aroma of the rich broth while she waited for her order.

Kevin, the shop's owner, placed the bag in her hands. "Special for Jerrica. You find your cat yet?"

"No, I'm afraid he's gone for good, Kevin."

"I look out for him." He tapped his cheekbone beneath his eye with the tip of his finger. "Cats come and go."

So did people.

"If you do see Puck, give him some chicken and call me." She waved as she shoved through the door, sending the little bell into a frenzy.

She loped to her apartment, her pack bouncing against her back and the plastic bag containing the soup swinging from her fingertips. She could've afforded fancier digs, but this neighborhood on the Lower East Side suited her—and she'd found a secure building without a nosy doorman watching her comings and goings.

She made it up to her apartment, got through the triple locks and shut the door behind her. Her gaze flicked about the room, and a shot of adrenaline lanced her system.

She dropped her dinner, plunged her hand into the front pocket of her backpack and pulled out her .22.

"Get out here with your hands up or I swear to God I'll shoot you through the bathroom wall."

The door to the bathroom inched open and a pair of hands poked through the opening, fingers wiggling. "Don't shoot. I even brought a bottle of wine."

Jerrica lowered her weapon with unsteady hands and closed her eyes as she braced one hand against the wall.

Just like that, Gray Prescott had slipped past her best defenses...like he always did.

Chapter Two

Heavy breathing came at him from the other room, but he ducked his head anyway. He never could tell about Jerrica West. The woman didn't play by any rules.

Leaning back, he stuck one leg out the door. If she started shooting, he'd rather she take out a kneecap than his eyeball. "It's me, Gray… Gray Prescott."

For all he knew Jerrica could've wiped him from that databank she called a brain. When he'd ended their relationship over her hacking, she hadn't even blinked an eye as she showed him the door.

"I'm unarmed, and I need to talk to you, Jerrica."

A clunk resounded down the hallway. "C'mon out. I won't shoot…yet."

He poked his head out the bathroom door and whistled through his teeth. "I guess that was stupid to be in the bathroom when you came home, but I was washing my hands. I didn't know what time to expect you since I remembered you work late."

As he rambled on, he approached Jerrica as if stalking a wildcat. Her green eyes narrowed as he got closer, her heavy, black boots planted on the floor in a shooter's stance. He'd taught her that.

"What are you doing here and how the hell did you get

in?" Her gaze flicked to the window that he'd left open a crack after climbing through.

"Yeah, well, I did come through that window, but the security for this building is good—better than most." He'd added that last part because he knew how important safety was for her, and he didn't want Jerrica freaking out right now.

"We're on the third floor." She pushed her black hair out of her eyes. "Oh, that's right, you're a hotshot Delta Force soldier able to leap tall buildings in a single bound."

"There was a fire escape, a ledge…and…forget it. I'm here now."

"What are you doing here? You said you wanted to talk—about what?" She crossed her arms over her chest not looking like she wanted to talk at all.

"Can we sit down and get comfortable? I wasn't kidding about the bottle of wine, and it took a lot of effort to get it up here. I left it in the kitchen." He pointed to the sofa with colorful pillows strewn across it. "You first."

"Where are my manners? I guess they went *out* the window, when you came *in* the window. It's not every day someone breaks into my apartment."

"It's not like I'm a stranger. I've even been to this inner sanctum before."

"Have a seat, and I'll get us a glass of wine." She finally uprooted her feet from the floor, and her heavy boots clomped across the hardwood to the kitchen. She grabbed the bottle of wine by its neck and raised it in the air. "How did you manage to break in here while carrying this bottle of wine?"

He wiggled his eyebrows up and down. "You have your secrets and I have mine."

"You don't have any secrets Gray. Nobody does." She jabbed a corkscrew into the cork, twisted and eased it from the bottle. The glasses clinked together as she pulled them out of the cupboard. "You use a computer? The internet? Social media? Buy online? Nothing is sacred. They know all about you."

"I know. You've told me before." He kicked his feet up onto her coffee table. "And after that cheery reminder, I'm gonna need a glass of wine more than ever."

She marched back into the living room, cupping a glass of wine in each hand. The ruby-red liquid sloshed with her jerky steps. She held a wine glass out to him. "You always did prefer red, didn't you?"

His gaze locked onto her lips, the color of the wine in her glass. "Yeah, I always did like red better."

Her cheeks flushed, matching her lips. She backed away from him and plopped down in the chair across from the sofa, pulling a pillow into her lap with one hand. "Now, what's so important that you need to scale a three-story building and break into my place, all while carrying a killer bottle of pinot noir?"

"I need your help, Jerrica." Damn, this was going to be harder than he'd expected. He'd better ease into it. "The kind of help only you can give me."

She swirled her wine in the glass before taking a sip. Raising her eyes to the ceiling, she swished the liquid around in her mouth as if at a wine tasting. "That's...interesting. What kind of help would that be?"

Gray gulped back a mouthful of wine. She was just trying to make this harder on him. Could he blame her? With a little more liquid courage warming his belly, he said, "You know. That hacking thing you do."

Her eyebrows disappeared into her bangs. "What was that? Hacking? You told me that was illegal, immoral and un-American."

He snorted and the wine he'd just downed came up his nose. "I never said immoral."

"Whatever." She flicked her short, unpolished nails in the air, and the tattoo of the bird between her thumb and forefinger took flight—she also had one on her wrist. "The words and the accusations were coming so hot and heavy I couldn't keep track of them."

That hadn't been the only thing hot and heavy between them. He did his best to keep his gaze pinned to her eyes. If they wandered below her chin, he could expect one of those boots planted against his leg.

He spread his hands. "Give me a break, Jerrica. When we first started dating, I thought you were a generic computer programmer. Then you dropped the bombshell that you worked for one of the most notorious hackers out there, Dreadworm."

"I didn't drop any bombshell. You went snooping through my stuff." She rolled her eyes. "You really believed I was using you to get military secrets to post on Dreadworm?"

"Can you blame me?" He jumped up from the sofa and his wine came dangerously close to spilling over the rim. "If you had discovered I'd been lying to you, you would have gone underground and cut off all communications. Your reaction to my suspicion was laughable coming from one of the most paranoid people I know."

She bent forward at the waist and undid the laces on her right boot, hiding her face and buying time. He knew her well.

She pulled off the boot and got to work on the second one. She looked up, her bangs tangled in her long dark lashes. "You know now I never would've done that to you. You should've known it then."

He stopped his pacing to walk toward her, resting a

hand on her shoulder, his fingers tangling in her silky hair. He rubbed a lock between his thumb and forefinger. "I knew it then, too, Jerrica. You just took me by surprise."

She shifted her head away from his touch and the diamond in the side of her nose glinted in the light. "Even if you weren't Delta Force, even if you didn't believe that I was using you, you're not a big fan of hacking, are you?"

"It seems...wrong." He stepped away from her and went back to his seat. "These are private government systems you're hacking. In some cases, these are classified systems. Communications not meant for the general public."

"All government systems should be for the general public." She tossed back her hair and raised her chin.

Gray took up the challenge. "Not if that exposure is going to result in outing people, putting their lives in danger, compromising their safety."

"Dreadworm never did that, and if you'd stuck around long enough to let me explain you would've known that."

"Maybe you're right. I admit I jumped the gun." He stretched his legs out in front of him. Now he had to get to the rest of his request. He tossed off the last of his wine.

"Looks like you need another." Jerrica pointed at his empty glass. "Maybe that'll help you get to the point."

"That obvious huh?" He pushed to his feet and held his hand out for her glass. "You, too?"

"I think I may need a few more to hear your request." She scrambled out of the chair and shoved her glass into his hand. "I brought some pho home for my dinner. Do you wanna share it with me? When I dropped the bag, the container even landed upright."

"Yeah, breaking and entering always makes me hungry." He took the wine glasses into the kitchen and filled them halfway. As he turned he almost plowed right into Jerrica. He lifted the glasses over her head. "Whoa."

The bag of food swung from her fingertips. "You're too big for this kitchen."

He surveyed the small space. "A jockey would be too big for this kitchen. I thought you were going to move to a bigger place, a safer neighborhood. It's not like you can't afford it."

"I like this place. I feel secure here."

"I was able to break in." He set her wine glass on the counter at her elbow.

Nudging him with her hip she said, "You just told me my place was safer than most and it was your mad Delta Force skills that allowed you to break in here."

"I said safer than *most*, but you have the money to get into a much better neighborhood than this one with a doorman, twenty-four-hour security, the works. I don't know why you don't make the move." She picked up her glass and he clinked his against hers.

"You know I don't like using that money. Blood money." She took a quick sip of wine.

"You must use the money for living expenses, anyway. I can't imagine Dreadworm pays you the kind of salary to live in a Manhattan apartment without roommates. Didn't you tell me once that most of the other hackers have day jobs?"

"And didn't you tell me you came to Manhattan to ask me a favor?" She ladled the pho into two bowls.

As the savory steam rose, his eyes watered and he blinked, his nose already running from the spices. "Did I say it was a favor?"

"If it weren't a favor, Prescott, we wouldn't be standing around drinking wine and eating pho together. You're a man who likes to get to the point. You've been doing a lot of waffling." She slid a bowl closer to him and the tofu bobbed in the liquid like square life preservers.

He stirred the broth, chockful of health, with a spoon. "Figures you got tofu in here."

"Waffler." She puckered her lips and slurped up a spoonful.

This time, he allowed his gaze to linger on her mouth. If she wanted to see waffling, he could show her waffling by kissing her.

She wiped her nose with a paper towel, covering the bottom half of her face. "What's going on with you? What do you want me to do?"

He dropped his spoon in the broth and took a deep breath. "It's my commander, Major Rex Denver. He's in trouble."

"What kind of trouble?"

"He's AWOL, but that's not the worst of his problems."

"If going AWOL isn't the worst, it must be bad."

"He went AWOL because someone's trying to set him up."

Jerrica flinched and her eye twitched.

He hadn't even thought that Jerrica's own experience might make her more apt to help him, but here they were. She'd probably accuse him of using her again.

"I know."

His head jerked up. "You know about Major Denver?"

"Syrian refugee camp? Weapons stash at an embassy outpost in Nigeria? Fake emails?"

"Dreadworm really does know it all." He hunched forward on his forearms, pushing the bowl of soup aside. "That's why I'm asking for your help, Jerrica. You already know this info because you guys have access to all kinds of computer systems. We think there's someone on the inside manipulating data, emails, people to set up Denver and discredit him."

"Discredit him? Why?"

"Because he was onto something. Our Delta Force team was always operating one level beyond our special ops assignments. Denver was hot on the trail of some terrorist activity and someone was afraid he knew too much…or was on the verge of knowing too much." He reached out and grabbed her hand. "You understand more than anyone the government doesn't always operate on the up-and-up."

She withdrew her hand from his and sucked her bottom lip between her teeth.

Had he gone too far? He held his breath.

Her cell phone buzzed on the counter where she'd plugged it in to charge.

"Hold that thought." She raised her index finger.

Hold the thought? His appeal had gotten a better reception than he'd thought it would. He let out a noisy breath and picked up his pho again as she answered the phone.

"What is it? Thought you were at a party."

He almost spit out the pho he'd just put in his mouth. Did she have a boyfriend now? Just because he hadn't been able to move on after their breakup didn't mean *she* hadn't found someone to keep her warm at night.

"Wait, wait. Slow down. Who's following you? Did you get a look at him?"

This time he almost choked on some noodles. Listening in on Jerrica's phone conversations was proving hazardous to his health.

"Where are you now? Is Kelly with you?" She snapped her fingers at him and pointed to a pen and an envelope on the counter.

Maybe *not* a boyfriend. He shoved the pen and paper toward her and then went back to his soup, trying to concentrate on avoiding the slimy-looking veggies floating back and forth and to tune out Jerrica's escalating tone of voice.

"Stay right there. I'm serious. I'm coming." She glanced up at Gray. "*We're* coming."

He raised his eyebrows and tapped the handle of the spoon against his chest.

Jerrica nodded and ended the call, stuffing the envelope into her back pocket. "You wanted inside information on Denver? Here's your chance."

"What's this all about? Who was on the phone?"

"That was one of my coworkers at Dreadworm." She downed the rest of her wine. "He thinks he's being followed."

"What does that have to do with Denver?"

"Amit was working on delving into some classified correspondence regarding that weapons stash at the embassy outpost in Nigeria." She grabbed her backpack and slung it over one shoulder. "Denver was on that, wasn't he?"

"He was, and now your coworker is being followed." Gray cocked his head. "He's not...like you, is he?"

She wrinkled her nose. "What exactly does that mean?"

"You know, slightly paranoid."

She punched his shoulder with a right jab that made him flinch. "Get your stuff. We're meeting him in twenty minutes at a coffeehouse in the Village."

He grabbed his flannel and rubbed his shoulder. "Can we walk?"

"Subway. I'll make a New Yorker out of you yet."

As they raced down the building's stairs, Gray poked

her back. "Why are we running to meet Amit? If you need to talk to him in person, why doesn't he come here?"

"He's scared. I could hear it in his voice. That's the best time to get them talking."

"Dreadworm shares information with the world. Are you telling me that its employees don't share with each other?"

"Employees? We're not really employees."

She hiked up her pack and strode down the sidewalk of her Lower East Side neighborhood where people still milled around after their dinners and ducked in and out of shops. Gray kept pace with her.

Jerrica made a sharp right turn to head down the stairs to a subway station.

He followed her down and grabbed her arm as she started to push through the turnstile. "I need a Metro-card."

"Oh, I forgot." She led him to a machine and he purchased a single ride.

If Jerrica planned to dart around the city dragging him along with her, he'd better get a pass next time. But really, the woman had enough money stashed away to hire a car service. He did, too, but he felt about as disconnected from his money as she did from hers—probably for similar reasons. Neither one of them had earned the money on their own.

The subway swallowed them up and spit them out somewhere on the edge of Greenwich Village.

"Do you know where you're going? You haven't looked at the address since you wrote it down in your kitchen." He lengthened his stride to match her smaller but more numerous steps.

She patted the back pocket of her jeans. "It's right here if you wanna have a look, but I memorized it."

His gaze darted to her backside, shapely in her tight jeans, and his knees weakened for a second before he stuffed his hand in his own pocket. "That's okay. I trust that brain of yours."

"It's not much farther. Probably just around the next corner."

He didn't even bother asking her how she knew that. He'd accepted her calculating mind. What he couldn't accept was her guarded heart, but then he'd exceeded her distrustful expectations by dumping her once he'd found out she worked for Dreadworm. She'd fully gotten and relished the irony of his asking for her help, using the same skills he'd lambasted before.

He could live with eating crow—a lot of it—if it meant clearing Denver and getting to the bottom of this terrorist plot.

Jerrica tugged on his sleeve. "This way. You were about to pass it right by."

He veered to the right, dodging oncoming pedestrians. How could Amit know anyone was following him with all these people coming and going?

"This is it." Jerrica tipped her chin toward a building with a blue-and-white striped awning over the front door. "I hope he's still here and didn't get spooked."

Gray lunged past her to open the door, and the soft strains of a guitar melody curled around them, drawing them into a dark space where he caught a whiff of roasted coffee beans. He couldn't drink coffee at this time of night, but the smells took him back to late-night conversations with Jerrica, who seemed to run on the stuff when she was working on a gnarly hacking job for Dreadworm—when he'd believed she was just a programmer dedicated to her clients.

He glanced at her, eyes closed and nostrils flaring, getting a caffeine buzz off the fumes.

Her lids flew open and she scanned the room. "Damn, I don't see Amit."

"Do you want to get something and wait?" He gestured toward the counter. "I could go for a chocolate croissant."

"You go ahead." She swung her backpack around and dipped into the front zippered pouch, pulling out her phone. "I'm going to text him."

As Gray joined the line of mostly college students ordering complicated caffeinated concoctions, Jerrica hunched over her phone.

He reached the counter and ordered his croissant and a slice of lemon cake for Jerrica, even though she didn't know she wanted it yet. He dipped into his pocket for his wallet and twisted around. "Did he…?"

The strange woman behind him folded her arms and looked him up and down, a pair of pencil-thin eyebrows raised above her tortoiseshell glasses.

"Sorry. I thought you were my…friend. Did you see where she went? Black hair, about yea big?" He held his hand just beneath his chin.

She shook her head and went back to her phone.

"Sir, that's $6.75." The barista waited, a patient but trained smile on her face.

He handed her a crumpled ten. "Did you see where my friend went?"

"I didn't notice." She lifted her shoulders. "Maybe the restroom? They're around the corner."

"Thanks." Gray stepped out of line and waved his hand at the change on the counter, his heart beating an uncomfortable rhythm in his chest that didn't at all complement the strains of the folk music from the small stage.

He took the corner to the bathrooms at such high speed, he nearly plowed into a woman on crutches.

"I'm sorry." He pointed to one of the restrooms. "Anyone in there?"

The woman readjusted her crutch under her arm. "It's all yours. Good thing since you're in such a big hurry."

Gray maneuvered past her and tried the other door. "Jerrica?"

A gruff male voice answered him. "Nope."

Gray poked his head into the other restroom and confirmed what the woman on crutches had told him— empty.

He peered down the short hallway at a back door with a glowing Exit sign above it. Could Jerrica have gone out there to meet Amit?

He strode down the short, dark length of the hallway and pushed against the metal bar. He stepped into the alley, and held his breath against the odor of garbage coming from the overflowing dumpster to his left.

As he huffed the smell from his nose, a scraping, shuffling noise from beyond the dumpster made him cock his head. Adrenaline pumped through his body with a whoosh that left him light-headed...but just for a second.

His body shifted into gear and he launched past the dumpster.

Jerrica's face appeared to him as a white oval in the darkness for a split second before the lump crouching at her feet took human form, rose and slammed her body against the wall.

Chapter Three

The man drove his shoulder into her ribs as he smashed against her, pushing the air from her lungs. Her attention had been distracted by the appearance of Gray in the alley, but she couldn't wait for him to come to the rescue.

Her gaze shifted to the glint of steel on the ground. At least she'd knocked the knife from his hand when she bashed her fist against his nose.

She sucked in some air, coiled her thigh muscles and kneed her attacker between the legs. She didn't get as high or as much power as she'd wanted, but her lips twisted into a smile when he grunted.

The grunt turned into a wheeze when Gray materialized behind him and physically and forcibly removed him from her sphere.

Her assailant's body seemed to fly through the air, and his eyes bugged out of his skull. He yelled an expletive when he landed with a sickening thud, but he had enough strength or determination to extend his fingers toward his knife.

"Gray! The knife!" She panted as she slid down the wall into a crouch, all the strength seeping from her body.

Gray whipped around and stomped on the man's wrist with his boot.

The guy let out a howl that echoed down the alleyway and some shouting answered from the street on one end.

Gray scooped up the knife and turned his back to the broken man writhing on the ground. He kneeled in front of her. "Are you hurt? Do you need an ambulance?"

"No. No police or ambulance." She clutched at Gray's shirt with both hands. "He's getting away. Don't let him get away. He has Amit."

He cupped her sore face with one hand. "I'm not leaving you in this alley by yourself. He might have an accomplice."

She struggled to stand as her attacker staggered to his feet and limped off at a surprising clip, holding his arm.

"Is there a problem? What's going on?" Two men peered over Gray's shoulder, and he slipped the switchblade into his pocket.

"That guy was assaulting this woman." Gray jerked his thumb over his shoulder, but her attacker had already made it out of the alley and had turned the corner. "Now get lost."

The men immediately drew back in unison and muttered to each other as they took a hike.

Gray helped her to her feet. "Are you sure you're okay? I can take you to the emergency room and you can tell them you had a fall. You're good at covering up."

She hopped up on one foot, hanging onto his shirt. "I'm not okay. You just let the guy who was following Amit and attacked me escape. He has Amit and we let him walk away."

"He was limping away and how do you know he has Amit?" He rubbed her arms, brushing the dirt from her jacket.

"He texted me from Amit's phone. How do you think I wound up out here?" She gestured with her arm and winced.

"What I'm wondering is why the hell you scurried out to a dark alley based on a text without telling me." He ran his fingers through the hair hanging over her shoulder. "Dirt."

"I did tell you I was going outside. I guess you didn't hear me because you were so focused on ordering your chocolate croissant." She started toward the street, pressing one hand against her midsection.

"Where are you going and where are you injured?"

She leveled a finger at the street, teeming with traffic just beyond the alley. "I'm gonna look for the guy who bruised my ribs."

"You're not going to find him now, Jerrica." He patted the pocket of his shirt. "But I have his fingerprints. He wasn't wearing gloves."

She stopped and leaned against Gray's shoulder. "You're right. I'm not going to find him out there."

His arm came around her, and she put more pressure against his body, soaking in his warmth and power.

He squeezed her and his voice roughened as he said, "He had that knife. How'd you get out of it? When I got here, you had the upper hand."

"My senses were already on high alert. When I saw him out here instead of Amit, I knew something was wrong, so when he came at me I was ready. All those years of martial arts paid off. I gave him a quick shot to the face, and it startled him into dropping the knife."

Gray kissed the side of her head. "Ever think of trying out for Delta Force?"

She closed her eyes for a few seconds just to inhale the scent of him, all that clean masculinity making her feel soft and protected—even though she'd just kicked some guy's ass—almost. Feeling soft and protected was a dangerous place to be. The last time she felt soft and protected, her whole world had blown up.

She stepped back and shook her head. "They'd never have me."

"Let's go back inside. There's a slice of lemon loaf in there with your name on it."

He tugged on her arm and she went willingly, even though she couldn't stop looking over her shoulder.

She asked, "What do you think he did with Amit and why?"

Gray opened the back door of the coffeehouse and ushered her inside, the smell of coffee replacing the stench of garbage and fear that permeated the alley.

"I don't know. What did he want with you? Did he say anything? Was he trying to get you to go with him or was he trying to...kill you?"

"I'm not sure." She flipped her hair over one shoulder. "I didn't stop to ask him."

Gray seated her at a table, and keeping one eye on her, he retrieved two plates from the counter. He slipped the piece of lemon cake in front of her. "Eat."

She sawed off a corner. "This all has something to do with Amit looking into that arms stash in Nigeria. I'm sure of it."

"Which means it probably has to do with Major Denver. But why come after you?"

"Maybe because Amit called me, so they had my number. Maybe Amit didn't give them anything, and they thought they'd try me. They'd want to stop whatever hacking Amit is doing into that system."

"Stop how?"

"Get into Dreadworm's space and shut it all down. If the government is behind this, they've been wanting to shut down Dreadworm for years." She popped the bite of cake into her mouth and the taste of the sweet, tart lemon on her tongue almost erased the ashes left there by the conversation.

Had Amit divulged Dreadworm's location? If so, she'd have to mobilize Olaf's army to back up all the programs and data and physically move the computers before they were destroyed.

"Why don't you call Amit again—just for fun. Let's see what happens."

Jerrica caught a crumb of lemon cake from the corner of her mouth with her tongue and pulled out her phone. She scrolled to her recent calls and tapped Amit's name. Her stomach churned as she listened to the ringing on the other end. "No voice mail coming up. They must've turned off his phone. Do you think…?"

"No." Gray dabbed a flake of chocolate from his plate and sucked it off his finger. "They can't get anything out of a dead man."

"They can make him stop what he's doing. If they know he hacked into this classified system, Amit's death ensures that stops immediately."

"But it doesn't, does it?" Gray planted his elbows on the table on either side of his half-eaten croissant. "If he wrote a program to get into this secret database, that's going to keep running whether or not Amit is there to monitor it. Am I wrong?"

"You surprise me, Gray Prescott." She hunched forward and rubbed her thumb across a chocolate smudge on his chin. "You really *were* listening to me."

"I always listened to what you had to say, Jerrica. You're one of the most fascinating people I know. Why wouldn't I?" He placed the tip of his finger against his chin where she'd just cleaned it off.

"Because you hated everything I did, everything it implied."

"Hate?" He rubbed his knuckles against his jaw. "That's a strong word. I didn't believe what you were doing was right…or necessary."

"And now?" She folded her hands, prim as a school-girl, waiting for her absolution.

"I'm still not sure it's right, but it sure as hell is necessary. If people within the government are actively working against the interests of the US, those people need to be outed and stopped. Dreadworm can do that."

"It's worse than that, Gray, and you know it. These moles in our government aren't just working against us, they're working with terrorists to kill our fellow citizens. It's happening. We have all the pieces. Major Denver has all the pieces. We just need to fit them together to discover the who, what and when." She swiped a napkin across her mouth and crumpled it in her fist. "And we need to save Amit."

"Amit's going to have to save himself. Does Dread-worm have some sort of protocol in place that tells you what to do if one of you is…captured like this?"

"For communicating, but nothing for an abduction." She tossed the mangled napkin onto her plate. "You know Olaf went into hiding when he felt the snare tightening."

"It was worldwide news. Of course, I know." He reached across the table and entwined his fingers with hers. "When I heard that, all I could think of was you and your safety, and now here I am contributing to the danger."

Her heart fluttered when Gray said things like that

to her, but pretty words didn't mean much. She hadn't been able to count on him before. He'd bolted once and he might do so again when he got what he wanted from her. It might be even worse this time if he felt guilty over his complicity in hacking into secure systems, but this time those systems belonged to rogue government employees, not the good guys as Gray had assumed.

Just because his family was so plugged into government service didn't mean all those nameless, faceless bureaucrats roaming the halls of Washington had the best interests of this country as their number one priority... or as any priority.

She disentangled her fingers from his. "You're not endangering me. I was onto this conspiracy before you arrived in New York, although I have to admit the data I stumbled on piqued my curiosity even more when I realized the person at the center of this swirling controversy was none other than your commander, Major Denver."

Gray cocked his head to the side. "You surprise me, Jerrica West."

"Why?" She slid her hands from the table and tucked them between her bouncing knees. Had she revealed how crazy attracted she still was to him?

"You remembered my Delta Force commander's name. I guess you *were* listening to me." He brushed his fingers together over his plate, a smug little smile playing about his lips.

Listening? She'd hung on to every word out of his mouth, never quite believing he was truly hers or would stick around. And she'd been right.

"You had some interesting stories, yourself."

"I thought..." He shrugged his broad shoulders, and a tide of color rushed into his face.

She narrowed her eyes. "You thought what?"

"Once I learned about your line of work, I thought your interest in me had more to do with what I could reveal about our defense than me personally." He thumped his fist against his chest.

"You said something like that before and it's idiotic." She grabbed her purse and shot up from her chair. "Let's go."

He followed her toward the door so closely she could feel his warm breath stirring her hair. For a good-looking guy, Gray had a surprising number of insecurities. His well-connected family had mega bucks, and she'd figured it always had him wondering if women wanted him or his family's wealth and connections.

With her own stash of cash in the bank from the settlement and the modest way she lived, he'd never been able to accuse her of going for the gold, so he'd made up another reason that she'd be interested in him.

She tossed her head and flicked her gaze at the many women tracking his progress out of the coffeehouse. Did the man have a mirror?

When they hit the sidewalk, she took his arm. "I'm worried about Amit. We have to find him before they hurt him."

"Or break him."

"That's not going to happen." She pulled him toward the subway station. "Olaf's army is loyal. We don't break."

"You may not break under the gentle, monitored, *legal* questioning of the government, but that's not what we're dealing with here. If these are government agents, they're not your mother's government agents."

She tripped to a stop at the top of the stairs leading to the platform. "*Your* mother's, maybe. They're exactly my mother's and my father's."

As she trotted downstairs, tears blurred her eyes and Gray put a steadying hand on her back.

He ducked his head to hers. "Sorry. Stupid thing to say."

When they boarded the train, she gripped the pole and swayed toward him as the car moved forward, her eyes locking onto his dark blue ones.

She shuffled closer to Gray, almost whispering in his ear. "Amit's in danger, isn't he?"

"You're *both* in danger."

"I have to tell Olaf. Maybe we should go to the Dreadworm offices now." She chewed on her bottom lip, all the sweetness of the lemon cake gone.

"And get followed? Not a good idea." He pinched her chin between his thumb and forefinger. "Stop doing that. You'll make it bleed."

"You're right. Now is not the time to go running off to Dreadworm. That's what they'd expect." She slid a gaze to the side. "Someone could be on our tail now."

The train squealed as it rolled into their stop and the force threw her against Gray's chest. She rested there for a few seconds, long enough for Gray to balance his chin on top of her head.

"We'll figure this out. We'll find Amit."

As she pulled away from him, strands of her hair clung to the scruff on his jaw, connecting them for seconds longer, seconds she needed to collect herself.

They hustled down the sidewalk, shoulders bumping, and she'd never felt so safe—except for the last time Gray had been with her in New York—before he found out what she did.

When they reached her building, one of the other residents pushed through the door and held it open for them, nodding at Jerrica. She gave him a hard stare.

The door closed behind them and Gray watched her curiously. "You don't know him?"

"I do, but he's never seen you before in his life. How'd he know you were with me?"

Gray raised his hand clasping hers. "Maybe this is a hint."

"You never know. I could be your captive." She studied Gray's face, but he didn't even roll one eye. That attack had scared him as much as it had her.

They clumped up the stairs, their boots filling the staircase with noise. Jerrica placed her hand against her door and turned the first lock.

She froze as icy fingers played up her spine. Then she hissed between her teeth. "Someone's been here."

Chapter Four

Gray's muscles tensed and he stepped between Jerrica and the door. He bent his head to hers, his lips brushing her ear. "How do you know?"

"This lock." She circled a piece of tarnished metal with her fingertip. "It locks from the outside with a key. I locked it when we left, and now it's not locked. The other two lock automatically when the door closes."

"Unlock the rest and stand back." He hovered over her shoulder as she shoved her key into two more locks, clicking them open.

Earlier, he'd taken one look at that line of locks on Jerrica's door and figured he'd have better luck coming through the window. Had someone else come to the same conclusion and then left through the front door?

Or was that someone else still waiting inside?

As he pushed into the room, he clutched the gun in his pocket and tensed his muscles. A breeze ruffled the curtains at the window—the same window he used earlier.

"You didn't leave a window open a slice, did you?"

"Absolutely not."

"Stay back." Nobody had jumped out at them or appeared with guns blazing, but that didn't seem to be their style. The guy in the alley had had an opportunity to stab

Jerrica when she first went out there, but he'd wanted something else.

He pulled the gun from his pocket and followed it into the room, raking his gaze from side to side. Jerrica's possessions, in place and undisturbed, belied the presence of an intruder.

Tipping back his head, he scanned the loft. From his vantage point, nobody had disturbed Jerrica's neat space. If it weren't for that lock and the window open a crack, they'd have no reason to believe anyone had compromised her apartment.

Together, they walked into the guest bedroom downstairs and Gray checked the closet and the bathroom.

Jerrica gasped and his finger tightened on the trigger.

"My laptop's upstairs."

Lunging after her, he reached out to grab her but she twisted away from him and stomped up the rest of the stairs. He had no choice but to follow her, his panic causing him to pant.

As Jerrica dove for the laptop on the nightstand, Gray threw open the closet doors. The mostly dark-colored clothes shimmied on their hangers. His hands plowed through the materials, skimming leather and denim and soft cotton, but no intruders crouched in the recesses of the closet.

He took a step back and bumped into the foot of Jerrica's bed where she was sitting cross-legged, hunched over her computer.

"They didn't take your laptop? That's weird." His eyes darted around the neat, bare room, as impersonal as a jail cell, and he took a deep breath. "Are you sure someone broke in?"

She raised her gaze from the laptop and her green eyes narrowed. "I knew right away. I always secure that lock.

They underestimated me if they thought I wouldn't notice that, the window…or other things."

"Such as?" Again, his gaze wandered around the spare room.

"I can't explain it to you—it's the placement of a book, the angle of a cushion. They didn't want to leave a mess. Didn't want me to think they'd been here." She dug her fingers into her black hair, and pulled it back from her face with one hand. "That's why they left my laptop."

"If they didn't take anything and didn't want to scare you by tossing your place, then what?"

She flicked her fingers at the computer. "They're going to track me through this."

Gray's heart jumped. "How would they do that? *Can* they do that?"

"Keystrokes."

"You lost me, just like you always do with this stuff." He sank to the bed and an unexpected flash of desire scorched his flesh as he remembered the last time they'd been on this bed, in this room.

Jerrica gave no sign that the memory had crept into her databank. She ducked her head, her straight hair creating a curtain around her face as her fingers flew across the keys.

"The intruders probably loaded a program on my laptop that's going to send anything I do straight to them—anything I look up, any emails, any programs I run. That's what I'd do. It'll be like they're looking over my shoulder while I work."

"You think you can find it?"

She peeked at him through the strands of her hair and snorted, causing the black curtain to flutter about her face. "No problem."

As Jerrica sank farther into the zone, Gray slid from

the bed and jerked his thumb over his shoulder. "I'm going to head downstairs and see about securing that window so nobody, including me, can get into your place that way again."

Jerrica murmured without looking up.

He'd been in this situation with her before and knew better than to disturb her.

Jogging downstairs, he skimmed his hand along the bannister and jumped off the last step. He curled his fingers under the window and shoved it open the rest of the way. He leaned out, looking down into the street from the third-floor drop.

The tree abutting the building offered wily climbers, like him, access to the ledge running along the side of the apartment building. He couldn't get rid of the tree, but he could do something about the ledge and the window itself.

He pivoted away from the window and into the kitchen. He threw open a few cupboard doors until he found a bottle of olive oil. Too bad Jerrica didn't have cooking spray, but he didn't expect to find anything that unnatural in her kitchen.

He unscrewed the lid of the bottle as he walked back to the window and then drizzled the contents along the ledge below. A slick surface wouldn't allow someone the grip he needed to hang onto the side of the building. He set the empty bottle on the counter and tipped back his head, calling up to the loft.

"Do you have a hammer and some nails?" He had to yell twice before Jerrica emerged from her fog.

"What?"

"Hammer and nails? Where do you keep your tools… if you have any?"

"Toolbox on the floor of the front closet. Why? Never mind. Carry on."

Crouching before the closet, he clawed through the coats and scarves hanging to the floor and wrapped his fingers around the handle of a metal toolbox. He dragged it out and flipped open the lid.

Jerrica kept the toolbox as neat as everything else in her life—every nut and bolt had its place. He messed them up before selecting several long nails and a hammer, wrapping his fingers around the black rubber encasing the handle.

He returned to the window and nailed it shut. As he tapped the final nail into place, Jerrica appeared behind him, her hands on her slim hips.

He met her gaze in the window's reflection.

"You just nailed my window shut."

"That's right. Nobody can get through it."

She reached over his arm and traced a nailhead with her fingertip. "Someone could smash it."

"And crawl through jagged glass? I don't think so." He turned to face her and they stood chest to chest, neither of them moving or pulling away. "Besides, I poured oil on the ledge. Nobody is going to be able to hang on it or stand outside the window long enough to be able to break it or cut it."

Her eyes widened and he got the full effect of those green orbs. "You poured oil on the outside of my building? What is this, 1066 and you're defending the castle?"

"It wasn't *hot* oil. It's an effective method—as long as it doesn't rain several days in a row." He pulled on his earlobe. "Your building manager isn't going to suddenly power wash the building, is he?"

"Did you actually get a look at my building while you were scaling it? I don't think it's been washed in a hundred years. Wait. What kind of oil?" She spun around, her black hair lashing his cheek.

He rested his hand on her shoulder as he pointed to the bottle on the counter. "Olive oil."

"Are you securing my building or making hummus?"

"Hummus?" He sniffed. "Why would I make hummus? It's the only oil I could get my hands on. If you were a normal person, you'd have some cooking spray on hand. That would've been a lot easier to use."

She wrinkled her nose. "Cooking spray has chemicals you don't want anywhere near your food."

"I'm sure it does." He raised his hands. "Don't ruin cooking spray for me like you ruined red meat."

"Does that mean you gave it up?" Turning her head, she raised one hopeful eyebrow.

"Not quite. I just try not to think about you while I'm ripping into a juicy steak." He snapped his mouth shut and sealed his lips. Had he just admitted to her that he thought about her? A lot?

She shifted away from him and reached for the empty bottle. "I guess I'll have to put olive oil on my grocery list."

He cleared his throat. "Did you get done what you needed to get done up there? Did you find the bug or the program or whatever?"

"I did not. Nothing was loaded on my computer." She sucked in her bottom lip. "Maybe they weren't smart enough to do something like that."

Gray methodically surveyed the small, neat space—not a cushion was out of place. "What did they do here, then?"

Shrugging, Jerrica splayed her hands in front of her. "I don't know. I would think they'd want to hit my laptop. They want to know what we know—or what we're going to discover. But they couldn't break into it and didn't want to take it and alert me."

A knot formed in the pit of Gray's stomach as his eyes darted around the room. Maybe the intruder didn't take anything. Maybe he left something behind.

"Gray." Jerrica grabbed his arm. "What are we going to do about Amit?"

His gaze shifted to Jerrica's face, her forehead creased and her mouth turned down. His fingers itched to smooth the lines from her face, to turn up her lips. "Unless you want to call the police, there's not much we can do right now. Do you have his girlfriend's number?"

Her frown deepened. "No. I wish she would call *me*. Maybe we could get some info out of her. Maybe she saw someone or something."

"Would she call the police if she doesn't hear from Amit?"

"I'm not sure. He lives…"

Gray put two fingers against her lips and shook his head.

Her eyes got round but her mouth tightened with understanding. She grabbed his hand. "It's late and I'm tired. I'm going to soak in the tub for a bit before I go to bed. Do you want to join me?"

Even though he knew it to be a ruse, his heart thumped at the thought of sharing a tub with Jerrica. "Lead the way."

She headed for the stairs and he followed her, his gaze dropping to her derriere outlined in a pair of tight black jeans. Jerrica didn't follow the latest fashions, but her urban guerilla style pushed all his buttons. This time his buttons would remain pushed…no release. The sexual tension coiled in his gut until he gave himself a mental shake when Jerrica pushed open the bathroom door.

Remember why you're here. What's at stake.

He slammed the door behind them, and Jerrica hunched over the tub and cranked on the faucets full blast.

"You think that's enough?" The running water almost drowned out her whisper.

"I think that'll do it." He lifted a framed photo of a woman in an old-time swimsuit from the wall, ran his hand along the back of it and around the edges of the frame.

As Jerrica twisted her fingers in front of her, he lifted the lid on the toilet tank and scanned the dry parts. Then he pointed to the mirrored medicine cabinet.

Jerrica swung open the door and studied the inside as if deciding which medicine to take. "I don't see anything. You?"

"No, but we're not talking freely outside of this room until I do a search with my cell phone."

"Your cell phone?"

He plunged his hand into his pocket, pulled out his phone and tapped the display. "I have a program on my phone that will detect audio devices."

"That's handy. How come I don't know about that?" She tipped her head back and her gaze darted to the four corners of the ceiling. "Cameras?"

"I doubt it, but I'm going to check for those, too. I'm pretty sure whoever is tracking you is more interested in what you say than what you do."

"And who I do it with?" She pointed a finger at him.

"Me?" He swiped a hand across the back of his neck as the steam from the hot water swirled around him.

"If these people are aware that Denver's Delta Force team members are the only ones actively working on his behalf, you can bet they know who you all are at this point."

"You're probably right." He reached forward and plucked a strand of hair from Jerrica's moist face. "Yours is exactly the kind of mind needed for this situation."

She cocked her head. "Only for this situation?"

"Hell, I'd be happy to have you by my side in *any* situation, Jerrica West." He ran his thumb along her lower lip. "I'm trying to remember if we said anything revealing out there before it dawned on me that they might have bugged the place."

"As far as I can recall, we spent most of our time talking about olive oil."

He snapped his fingers. "At least they'll know they can't get into your place again."

"We talked about Amit, but they know more about him than we do." She sank to the edge of the tub. "What have they done with him? If they have his phone, they must have him...or worse."

"They're not going to kill someone if they want to get intel from him." He slammed a fist against his chest. "Take it from someone who knows."

"I don't want to hear about what you do." She made a cross with her fingers and held it in front of her face. "But if Amit refused to give them what they wanted, refused to take them to Dreadworm, they'd have no more reason to keep him alive."

"They would if they thought they could change his mind." He sat down on the tub next to her and draped his arm around her shoulders as the water rose behind them. "I know it's hard, but try not to think about Amit right now. When that guy had you cornered in the alley, he could've killed you with the knife, but he didn't."

"I should warn everyone else, send out messages. Olaf has a warning system in place and neither Amit nor I used it. We just panicked."

"That's understandable." He squeezed the back of her neck, and then glanced over his shoulder. "I think we'd better turn off the water before it overflows, but until I do my search of the rest of the house, no talking about anything related to Amit or Olaf or Dreadworm."

"Or Major Denver." She reached around him to turn the faucet, her soft breast momentarily pressing against his arm.

Closing his eyes, he swallowed. "You're not going to waste all that water, are you? You stay here and relax while I do my thing."

"I'm not going to miss this search. I can help." She flicked some water at his chest. "The tub can wait."

Gray left the bathroom first, tapping the display on his phone to bring up the program that could detect radio waves. He headed into Jerrica's bedroom first and waved the phone over her headboard and the framed pictures on the wall above it.

Jerrica joined him and pointed to the closet.

He shook his head. Any sound would be muffled before it reached a mic in the closet. He continued to move around her room, wielding the phone in front of him as if warding off evil spirits.

As he passed the phone in front of the second nightstand, he heard a clicking sound. He brought the phone close to his face and watched the line on the display flicker.

Jerrica tugged on his sleeve and he nodded as he crouched before the nightstand. He felt around the base of a lamp and inside the shade, his fingers stumbling across a disc stuck to the inside.

He picked it off with his fingernail and cupped it in the palm of his hand to show Jerrica. She aimed a rude gesture at the little bug, and he grinned before he strode into her bathroom and dropped it into the toilet. He flushed it down and brushed his hands together.

As Jerrica started to open her mouth, he covered it lightly with his hand and pointed at the floor. Downstairs, he found the same type of listening devices attached to a lampshade next to the sofa and on the underside of a cupboard.

Jerrica sighed as he disposed of the last bug. "Do you think that's it?"

"I hope so. These wouldn't be hidden inside cupboards or closets because that would reduce their efficiency. I'll keep the program up and running on my phone, just in case, and I'll give the spare room and bathroom a once-over before I go to bed."

She whipped her head around. "You're sleeping here tonight?"

"I sure as hell am not leaving you here on your own after everything that happened today, and if there are any more bugs, they'd hear me leave. That's not happening."

"What hotel are you staying at?" She stood at the sink and rinsed out their dishes from earlier this evening, which now seemed days ago. "Wait. Let me guess."

He grabbed her fingers in the stream of water. "Yeah, it's a nice place. And don't act like you couldn't afford to stay there with me, but tonight I'm staying with you."

"Touché." She wriggled her hand free from his and flicked some droplets of water at *his* face this time. "The bed in the second bedroom is made up. Towels in the bathroom closet, unless…"

She pushed away from the counter and grabbed a dish towel from the oven door handle. "Yeah, I'm not gonna let that warm water go to waste. I need to wash the grit from that alley off my body, anyway."

"Toothbrush?" He tipped his head toward the hallway,

reluctant to leave the small enclosure of the kitchen where he felt like he could keep Jerrica close to him.

"There should be some extras in that bathroom closet."

"Try to relax." He nudged Jerrica out of the kitchen and walked with her to the stairs, afraid to let her out of his sight.

She turned at the top of the stairs and held up her hand in a wave. "Thanks."

When she disappeared into the bathroom and clicked the door shut, he rested his head against the wall for a few seconds, almost feeling the warmth course through his body as if he were slipping into the embrace of the water with Jerrica between his legs.

He tapped his jaw with his knuckles. This wasn't the right time to rekindle a relationship with Jerrica…even if she wanted it.

Gray turned the corner into the hallway and entered the second bedroom, waving his phone in front of him. The intruders hadn't bothered bugging this room or the bathroom. He dropped to the made-up bed, kicked off his shoes and peeled off his shirt.

He'd brush his teeth and hit the sack. The only shower he needed right now was a cold one—and he'd rather wallow in his X-rated thoughts about Jerrica for a while longer.

A half hour later, Gray crawled between the sheets, running his tongue along his minty teeth, and pulled the covers up to his chin. When he'd gotten the message from Denver about contacting Jerrica West to ask for Dreadworm's help, he hadn't hesitated for a second. How much of that was due to his desire to clear his commander's name and how much was his desire to see Jerrica again, he didn't know and he didn't want to analyze. He'd call it a draw.

A muffled buzzing noise interrupted his hazy thoughts and he bolted upright in the bed. He cocked his head, and as the sound continued, he threw back the covers, grabbed his weapon from the nightstand and bounded across the room.

He stumbled into the hallway, and Jerrica called from the bathroom upstairs.

"It's the door to the building. Don't let anyone in."

As if he needed her to tell him that. He crept toward the computer display Jerrica had set up in her entryway, his gun dangling at his side, and swiped the mouse.

Hurried footsteps padded down the stairs and Gray looked over his shoulder to take in Jerrica flying down the steps, a white towel wrapped around her slim frame.

He turned back to the display and the image of the street, and the front of the building appeared on the screen…along with a tall figure bent over at the waist, his face hidden.

Gray mumbled. "C'mon buddy. Show yourself."

As Jerrica joined him, her hand resting on his shoulder, the man at the door dropped his head back and peered at the camera, his swollen face distorted and bloodied.

Jerrica dug her fingers into Gray's flesh. "Oh my God. It's Amit."

Chapter Five

Adrenaline pumped through Jerrica's body, and she reached over Gray's shoulder for the release button to unlock the door.

Before she got midway there, Gray snatched her hand. "Wait."

"Wait for what?" She clutched at the slipping towel with her other hand. "Can't you see him? He's been beaten. He needs our help."

"We don't know what they've done to him, Jerrica. It might be a trick. They probably followed him." Gray's jaw hardened and she recognized the look.

She dug her heels into the floor as her fist curled around the terry cloth under her arms, holding the towel in place. "What does it matter? They already know where I live. They've been inside, planted bugs."

"They might've armed him with something. Maybe he's wearing a wire."

She twisted her fingers in his grasp, which he tightened. "They already tried that, and we disrupted their plan. We'll do it again, even if Amit is wired. He's not going to turn on me, anyway."

"You don't know that. You don't know what they're capable of doing to make people bend to their will." A muscle twitched at the corner of Gray's mouth, and the tension radiated off his body.

"I know my…friend's in the street, battered and bloody, and he came to me for help—and you always called *me* the cold one." Maybe she'd never considered Amit a friend before, but they were in this together now. She released the hold on her towel and slammed her thumb against the button to unlock the front door. She leaned toward the speaker. "Come up, Amit…and hurry."

When she'd let go of the towel, it had fallen to her feet, and goosebumps raced across her naked body.

"Stubborn woman." Gray swept her towel from the floor and bunched it against her midsection. "Stay here. The guy can't even make it up the first flight of stairs by himself."

She shook out the towel and twisted it around her body, securing a corner. "A-are you going to help him?"

"Yeah." He leveled a finger at her, nearly touching it to her nose. "Watch the display and make sure nobody slips in behind him or tries to ambush us on our way up."

She nodded as Gray gripped his weapon in front of him and lunged past her to the front door, his boxers hanging on his hips. He slammed the door behind him.

Jerrica's nose stung as she watched Amit sag against the door. He'd been capable of just enough steps to get him inside the building, but he hadn't moved since.

Her heart slammed against her chest as a dark figure moved into view. When she realized it was Gray, she gulped in some air to steady her breathing.

Amit had Gray by a few inches in height, but Gray had the muscle and he used it to good effect as he hitched Amit's arm around his shoulders and wrapped his own arm around Amit's body. He half-dragged, half-carried Amit toward the stairs.

Jerrica's eyes burned as she watched the display for any unusual movement behind them or further attempts to breach the front door. When she heard their thumping and bumbling footsteps in the hallway, she peeled her gaze away from the monitor and clawed at the locks on her door.

She swung it wide and gasped as Gray dragged an unconscious Amit into her apartment. "What happened? Why did he pass out? Is he still alive?"

"He's alive. He lost some blood." He settled Amit onto the floor. "Get some towels—wet and dry. Ice. Whiskey."

Jerrica scurried to the closet in the downstairs bathroom and snatched several hand towels from the shelf. She filled her arms with some first aid supplies and dumped everything next to Gray, crouching beside Amit. Then she bunched one of the towels in her hand and made for the kitchen where she left it under the faucet as she filled a plastic bag with ice and grabbed a bottle of tequila from the cupboard above the fridge.

She dropped to the floor next to Gray, his fingers resting against Amit's pulse, and dabbed his facial wounds with the damp towel. As she wiped away the blood, she blew out a breath.

"It looks worse than it is."

"Stanch the blood flow from the back of his head. That's the deepest cut, the one that's bleeding the most." Gray raised Amit's eyelids with his thumb. "We could take him to the emergency room."

"No." Jerrica pressed a dry towel against the wound on Amit's head and unbuttoned his shirt with trembling fingers. "That would bring cops and questions. Dreadworm has strict protocol about that. Amit knows."

"If he doesn't respond soon, we have no choice. I'm not

going to sit here and watch someone die. What's Dreadworm's protocol on that?"

She ran her hands across Amit's chest and around his back. "No wires. He's not hooked up."

Gray raised an eyebrow. "Any wounds on his body?"

"None of those, either." Heat suffused her cheeks. "You're the one who warned me about wires."

"Relax. I know." He traced some red spots splotched across Amit's chest and abdomen. "Looks like he took a beating to the midsection."

"At least they used fists instead of knives." She replaced the cloth at the back of Amit's head.

"Check his pockets, too." Gray picked up the bottle of booze. "Tequila?"

"I don't drink whiskey. That tequila is the closest thing I have. If you want to clean his wounds, I have antiseptic for that." She shoved one of her hands in the front pocket of Amit's jeans.

"I wanted to try to give him a sip to see if it revives him. Tequila might work." He unscrewed the lid from the bottle and tipped it toward Amit's lips. The clear liquid ran down the side of his face to his neck. "Guess not."

Jerrica dumped the coins she'd dug out of Amit's pocket onto the floor and searched the other one. She held up a scrap of paper. "Just an old receipt."

"Check his back pockets for a wallet." Gray hoisted Amit into a sitting position, placing his back against the foot of the couch. "I'm going to try to wake him up."

Reaching beneath his body, Jerrica patted Amit's back pockets. "Nothing."

"Amit! Wake up." Gray took Amit's jaw between his thumb and forefinger and squeezed as he shook his head back and forth. "Wake up."

"More tequila?" Jerrica doused the corner of a towel

with the alcohol and squeezed a few drops into his mouth while Gray pinched it open.

Amit's dark lashes fluttered, and Jerrica patted him on the cheek. "Amit! It's Jerrica."

He groaned and turned his head to the side to escape Gray's fierce grip.

"Lighten up." She circled her fingers around Gray's wrist. "He's bruised enough."

"I want him conscious." Gray grabbed the bag of ice and applied it to the side of Amit's head.

Amit's eyes flew open and he gasped, as if sucking in air after a near drowning. His eyeballs rolled back in his head for a second and then he focused on her face. "Jerrica?"

"Thank God." She grabbed one of his thin hands and chafed it between her own, even though he wasn't cold in the least. "What do you need?"

Amit sucked in a breath and squeezed his eyes closed. "Everything hurts. Where am I?"

"You're at my place." She exchanged a quick look with Gray. "Do you remember coming here?"

"Yeah." His hazy gaze wandered to Gray. "Who…?"

"He's a friend. He's going to help us. Can you tell me what happened tonight? When we got to the coffeehouse, you were gone."

Amit's head dropped back against the sofa, as he clutched his middle.

"Let's help him onto the bed." Gray rose to his haunches and curled an arm beneath Amit. "Can you get up?"

Amit staggered to his feet with Gray's help, and walked on wobbly legs to the bedroom. "Kelly. I have to call Kelly."

"We'll make sure she knows you're okay." Jerrica

squeezed past the two men into the spare bedroom where the covers were still turned down after Gray's quick exit from the bed. She bunched the pillows against the head-board and patted the mattress. "Put him here."

Gray eased Amit's broken body to the bed and propped him up. "Try to stay alert for a while. We'll get you cleaned up and tend to your wounds. Do you need to go to the hospital?"

"No!" Amit winced with the effort of his yell. "No hospitals. No police."

"Then you'd better not die on us." Gray turned from the bed and left the room.

Jerrica unbuttoned the rest of Amit's shirt and peeled it from his shoulders. "Can you tell me what happened?"

"Like I told you on the phone, I was being followed. I sent Kelly home with friends because I didn't want ei-ther of us to be followed to our place. I ducked into the coffeehouse because I thought I'd be safe in a crowd." He closed his eyes. "I was wrong."

"Did they strong-arm you out of the coffeehouse?" Gray had returned to the bedroom, carrying the first aid supplies.

Amit opened one eye and assessed Gray. "Is he…?"

"He's safe."

"I meant, is he the Navy SEAL?"

Gray cleared his throat. "Delta Force. What happened in the coffeehouse?"

"Ouch." Amit jerked his head back as Jerrica pressed the ice pack against his temple. "Some guy followed me in there with a knife."

"I wonder if he's the same guy who attacked you in the alley, Jerrica. He must've figured you'd come after Amit at the coffeehouse." Gray sat on the edge of the bed and shook a bottle of ibuprofen in the air. "Take a few of these. You'll need them for those ribs."

Amit's eyes widened as much as they could. "Someone attacked you, too?"

"We went out to the coffee place, and I received a text from you. I went out to the alley to meet you and was met by a guy with a knife instead."

"They took my phone." Amit popped the pills and chased them down with a slug of tequila. "You actually went into the alley to meet someone? You?"

"That's what I said." Gray flicked a strand of Jerrica's hair.

"Not the smartest move, but I guess I was desperate to find you, Amit." She brushed her hand across her cheek and the growing warmth there.

"Don't worry. I didn't tell them anything. I didn't lead them to Dreadworm."

Jerrica folded her arms over her stomach. She probably deserved that. Of course, Amit would think she'd be more worried about Dreadworm than his safety. He'd be wrong. She'd learned a thing or two after Gray dumped her. Had learned she could hurt people as much as they'd hurt her. She hadn't liked the realization.

Gray lifted one eyebrow. "How'd you get away from them? Did they let you go in exchange for leading them to more Dreadworm hackers? Leading them to Jerrica?"

"Hey, no." Amit made a grab for the bloody towel against the back of his head as it slipped to his shoulder. "They didn't let me go. A cop saved me."

"You went to the police? You just said no police." Jerrica pursed her lips.

Tapping his bruised forehead, Amit said, "You're not thinking very clearly, Jerrica, which is a first for you. After the guy roughed me up in the alley, he started marching me at knifepoint out to the street to what I guessed was a waiting car and more torture in my future. Luckily, there was a group of unruly drunks on the sidewalk that had caught the attention of two cops. I broke away from my captor a few feet in front of the cop and fell onto the sidewalk. The guy with the knife disappeared into the crowd, taking my wallet and cell with him."

"What did you tell the officer?" Jerrica placed a hand against her chest, trying to tame her galloping heart.

"Told him I'd had an altercation of a personal nature in the alley and didn't want to make a report or press charges." Amit raised one shoulder. "He was only too happy to let it go. I would never lead them here, Jerrica."

"They made it here, anyway." She swept a hand through the air. "In fact, they may be listening to everything we've been saying."

"They broke into your place?" Amit's gaze darted around the room. "What do you mean, listening to us?"

Gray pushed off the foot of the bed and took a turn around the room. "When we got back here, Jerrica insisted someone had broken in. Nothing was missing and she couldn't detect any activity on her computer, though. They wouldn't break in and leave with nothing, so I swept the place for listening devices. We found several and dispatched them. We were just turning in until…"

"Until I showed up and ruined the party." Amit glanced at Jerrica and his gaze dropped to the towel still wrapped around her body. "Aren't you cold?"

"Freezing." She rubbed her bare arms.

As if noticing his own state of undress for the first time, Gray yanked his shirt off the top of the dresser and pulled it on. "Go upstairs and put on some pajamas. I'll finish dressing Amit's wounds."

As Jerrica backed out of the room, she said, "Don't get to any of the good stuff without me."

Upstairs in the loft, Jerrica let the towel fall to her feet. She slipped into a pair of pajama bottoms and a matching top, pulling it over her head with her hands still trembling.

Both she and Amit had been attacked in one night, but their attackers hadn't gotten what they wanted...not yet. She had a feeling they wouldn't stop until they did.

She jogged downstairs and walked in on Gray and Amit talking about the attack. "What's the verdict? Is he gonna live?"

"He took a beating, but he'll be okay." Gray stuffed the last of the bloody towels in a plastic garbage bag. "Some bruised ribs, a few cuts, and he'll have a black eye for sure."

"Why did he pass out?"

"In case you haven't noticed I'm not a doctor, but I'm guessing blood loss and exhaustion. He did try to keep his abductors away from your place, so he was wandering around for a while and riding the subway."

Amit touched the bandage on the back of his head. "For not being a doctor, you did a good job."

"I've had some practice patching wounds." Gray dropped the bag by the door. "Now, let's figure out what these people want."

Jerrica sat cross-legged on the foot of the bed. "The keepers of that shadow government database must've figured out that Dreadworm had compromised it."

"But how do they know who we are? I'm a mild-mannered computer programmer by day. Kelly doesn't even know what I do at night." Amit waved his hand at Jerrica. "You're an independent on-call computer nerd. How are they following us and breaking into our homes?"

Gray asked, "Who are the other Dreadworm people who work here?"

Amit held up two bony fingers. "Cedar and Kiera. I mean, there are others in other locations, but we're the only four in the New York area and only Jerrica and I are in that particular office. Nobody else knows about that location—except Olaf. We don't see much of Cedar or Kiera. If they have a location like we do, we don't know where it is. Olaf tends to keep us separate."

Jerrica said, "We need to send out an SOS to them. We've definitely been compromised. They could be in danger, too."

"Unless they're the ones who outed you." Gray rubbed his chin. "Think about it. They did it or Olaf did it."

"Wait." Jerrica held up her hands. "Those are only the people we know of who know our identities. There could be others—*you* know I work for Dreadworm and you apparently told Major Denver because *he* knew. Who else knows? Where else is it circulating?"

"Guilty, but I know Denver didn't ID you, and I sure as hell didn't."

"Did you tell your other Delta Force team members? You know how that goes. They tell someone innocent and they tell someone innocent, and eventually the intel gets to someone who's not so innocent."

Gray shot her a look of annoyance from beneath a set of scowling eyebrows. "Let's start with the inner circle first."

"For whatever it's worth, the guy who was beating me up didn't ask any specifics about Dreadworm. He warned me to stop meddling. Told me what we were doing was only helping the government."

Jerrica sliced a hand through the air. "Dreadworm

has never been about bringing down the government. It's about making it better, more accountable to the people."

"This guy seemed to think that would be a persuasive argument for me." Amit stifled a yawn. "Did one of those happy pills contain codeine or something?"

"You needed it for the pain." Gray nudged Jerrica in the back. "And now we all need some sleep. We can continue to untangle this in the morning."

Amit shoved a pillow beneath his head. "Is it safe here? You said someone broke in."

"Don't worry. I'll handle the security."

"Kelly." Amit's lids drifted closed. "I need to tell Kelly."

"Keep Kelly ignorant and safe for now, Amit. We'll find some way to get word to her, and I'll send out an alert to the others." Jerrica shut off the light and pulled the door shut.

Kicked out of his bed, Gray veered toward the living room and the smallish sofa.

Jerrica grabbed his hand. "Don't be an idiot. You can share my bed upstairs. I don't bite…anymore."

Gray chuckled, but a look of panic flashed across his face. Did the thought of being in bed with her make him think twice about his motive for being here?

"I don't mind the sofa. I've slept on worse."

"I'm sure you have, tough guy." She placed her hands against his back and gave him a little shove up the stairs. "But you're back in civilization now."

His back and shoulders held military stiff, Gray trod up the stairs as if meeting a firing squad. Maybe she should've let him sleep on the couch.

In the loft, she flicked on the lamp where they'd found the bug and turned down the covers. "I did finally invest in a king-size bed, so there's plenty of room for both of us."

She slipped under the covers and turned off the light.

As he crawled into the bed as far away from her as he could possibly get without falling out, she cleared her throat. "I'm glad you showed up today, Gray. Both Amit and me would've been lost without you."

Rolling onto this back, he pulled the covers up to his chin like a virgin on his wedding night and growled. "Like I said, I'll take care of the security and you can do your hacking thing. We need to uncover this plot and exonerate Denver. At this point, I think you're the only one who can do that."

"Nice of you to think so, anyway."

"Good night, Jerrica."

"Good night, Gray."

She slid a sideways glance at his profile in the darkness, noticing his wide-open eyes staring at the ceiling, his hands at his sides. Maybe he was just keeping alert for safety.

She had to know one way or the other. She wanted him. Needed the comfort of his body.

"Gray?" She stroked his corded forearm with her fingertips, and it was as if she'd brought a statue to life.

Chapter Six

Gray's body shuddered and shifted as he answered her, his voice hoarse and gruff. "Yeah?"

A million words rushed through her brain, formed and discarded. This didn't have to be perfect. It just had to be honest and true. She said the words that had been running through her brain all day.

"I want you."

Gray seemed to burst from the tight cocoon he'd been inhabiting and rolled to his side, reaching for her.

She went willingly into his arms, her head fitting in the crook of his neck as if it belonged there. It did.

He stroked her hair back from her face. "Are you sure?"

"Are you? You're the one who walked out on me." She pressed her lips against the tight skin over his collarbone.

"Dumbest thing I ever did." He skimmed one finger down her spine. "I thought you were using me to get information. It bruised my ego, and I couldn't get over that."

She snorted. "You don't have an ego, Gray. As if any woman wouldn't want to be with you for you— I never cared about your money, your political connections or the military intel you could provide—I knew you'd never go down that road, and I never would've asked you. I thought *I* was the paranoid one."

"I should've known. I *did* know that." He cupped her face with his hand and kissed her hard on the mouth.

She murmured against his lips. "Can we stop talking now?"

He answered with his touch, flattening one palm against her belly and circling up to her breast in a slow, sensuous movement that had her squirming. When he reached her nipple, he traced it with one fingertip. After one gentle pinch, he undid the top few buttons of her pajama top. He then grabbed the hem and pulled the top over her head.

She kissed the firm line of his jaw. "Keep doing what you were doing before, you tease."

"No one's ever accused me of being a tease before, including you." This time he placed both of his hands on her breasts, now aching for attention, and stroked and shaped them to his pleasure...and hers.

She tugged at his T-shirt. "Why are you wearing this?"

"I was trying to be prim and proper and put as much material between me and you as possible." He dragged the shirt from his chest, dispensing with prim and proper.

"Why? D-do you feel guilty for being here in my bed? Is it for the wrong reasons?"

"I'm not sure what the right and wrong reasons are anymore, are you? I just know I've never been able to stop thinking about you, but I didn't know how you'd feel about seeing me again."

"Excited, elated...and very, very turned on."

She pushed away from him to drink in the sight of the hard slabs of muscle shifting across his chest. She outlined the planes with the tips of her fingers, skimming through the dusting of dark hair sprinkled over his flesh.

Brushing her nails across his flat abs, she said, "Is this a twelve-pack now?"

"It's whatever you want it to be." He slipped his hand beneath her pajama bottoms and underwear and smoothed it over the curve of her derriere. "All this time, I've been aching for your touch, and I couldn't even muster the strength to tell you I was sorry for how things ended—for my part in it. I needed my commander to order me to contact you."

"Umm, I don't think I gave you much reason to believe I'd ever accept your apology or want to see you again."

He grabbed her hands as they inched their way down to the waistband of his boxers. "I'm thinking we should've had this talk before we hit the sheets together."

"It's not like we've had time to discuss our relationship." She hitched her thumbs in the elastic of her bottoms and yanked them off, along with her panties. "Besides, I can talk and play at the same time."

"Really?" He made a mocking face. "I dare you to try."

He cinched her around the waist and flipped her onto her back as he straddled her naked body. The kisses he rained on her face, throat, chest and belly had her gasping and arching her body for more.

As he flicked his tongue across her navel, she gritted her teeth and gasped out, "As soon as you accused me of using you for intel, I should've realized you were equating me with all those other women interested in your family's money and power."

Resting his chin on her abdomen, he glanced up at her. "That's quite a mouthful. I'm failing you."

He trailed his hands between her legs and nudged her thighs apart, his hot breath moist against her swollen flesh. "Care to continue your analysis of my insecurities?"

She opened her mouth, but he had moved so he could plunge his tongue inside her and the only thing coming from her throat was a squeak. She felt his smile hot against her skin.

Several words flitted across her brain, but the only one she could manage as his tongue prodded her was, "Oh."

Her fingers curled into his thick hair and her nails dug into his scalp as he brought her closer and closer to her release. For several moments, time stood still as she hung on a precipice of desire, her breath coming out in short puffs, every nerve ending alight with fire.

Gray scooped his hands beneath her bottom, tilting her toward his greedy mouth. As he pinched and kneaded her soft flesh, her passion reached dizzying heights. Her temples throbbed with the tension until she let out a tiny breath.

That small act of submission opened the floodgates, and her orgasm swelled inside her, infusing every pore in her body with sweet release.

Gray kept his mouth locked onto her, riding every wave as it crested and then crashed, teasing her back up again and again until her body opened to him completely.

Satiated and limp, she lacked the energy to even guide his erection into her as he prodded her with its insistent head.

After a few thrusts where he filled her completely and then slid out, she returned to some semblance of sense and reason. His performance deserved an active partner, and she wrapped her legs around his hips, holding him to her. She raised one arm to brace herself against the headboard as he rode her.

He hitched up to his elbows and stared into her face as if committing it to memory. All of her memories came flooding back with the heaviness of him between her legs. She sucked his bottom lip between her teeth, nibbling at the softness.

A drop of sweat rolled down Gray's face, and every part of his body seemed to get harder. His gaze rose to a point above her head, and she knew he was close. By the time they'd split up, she'd been able to read every nuance of his lovemaking. They'd been able to read each other, allowing them to fit together like two pieces of a puzzle.

Her other half released something between a growl and a moan as he plowed into her with quick, sure strokes. A flush rose from his chest and suffused his face as he reached the peak.

She watched the pleasure soften the features of his face, and she brushed her knuckles against the stubble on his chin. Tears pricked the back of her eyes as he lowered his body on top of hers, spent and satiated, the weight of it making her feel protected and secure.

She'd always scoffed at the notion of making love. Sex had been a function just like anything else in life, one partner easily swapped for another—until the day she met Gray Prescott.

He'd swept her off her feet in a way that belonged in movies and fairy tales—ones she'd never believed in before.

Although their backgrounds couldn't be more different— he from a wealthy, politically connected, privileged family, she from an outlaw commune, tracked and raided by the very government his family represented— Gray had felt their similarities almost immediately. He'd known her from the beginning, knew what she needed before she did.

That's why it had hurt so much when he turned from her. He should've known she'd never try to compromise him—not even for Dreadworm.

"Am I crushing you?" He shifted his damp body to the

side and kissed her ear. "You can continue talking now, if you want—if you remember what you were saying."

Rolling toward him, she hitched her leg over his hip and curled her toes in feline satisfaction. "I don't even know if I remember how to talk after that. You leave me speechless."

"You leave me breathless." His heavy hand shaped the curve of her hip. "We weren't under the covers one minute before you made your move. Did I make it that obvious that I wanted back in your bed?"

"I wasn't sure at first. You came off as very professional, forced to see me again because Major Denver demanded it."

He took a lock of her hair and swept the end of it along his jaw. "It was a good cover. I'd been wanting to reconnect with you for a long time—as soon as I realized what an ass I'd been about the whole Dreadworm thing. Denver gave me the perfect opportunity, a chance to reconnect and to prove to you that I trusted you."

"How could you be sure you'd get the response you wanted from me?" She drilled a finger into his chest. "We left on bad terms, throwing accusations like flowerpots at each other."

"And hurting ten times more than flowerpots." He touched her nose with his fingertip. "Even if you didn't want anything to do with me personally, I knew you wouldn't have been able to pass up a chance to use your hacking skills to ferret out a conspiracy. It's your lifeblood."

"Is it?" She rubbed his muscular backside with her hand as he flexed it. "I'm beginning to think something else is my lifeblood because I've felt adrift without you. I mean, adrift was my middle name growing up, but you gave me something different. I missed it when you left. Craved it."

"I never knew any of that when we were together."

"Maybe I didn't, either." She turned her back to him and dragged one of his arms around her waist.

He nuzzled the back of her neck, and a thrill ran down her spine. Who knew the one thing that had driven Gray away would be the catalyst to bring him back into her life?

A pinprick of fear needled her brain. *Unless he's using you and Dreadworm to save Major Denver and plans to disappear just as completely as before.*

JERRICA WOKE UP to an empty bed, as usual, but this time it was unexpected. She swept her hand across the cool sheets beside her, just in case she'd missed the six-foot-tall, muscle-bound man who'd rocked her world last night.

The clinking from the kitchen downstairs brought her upright, and she sniffed the air. The rich smell of coffee swirled its way up to the loft and put a smile on her face. When she heard Amit's voice waft upstairs, her smile grew broader.

They'd just scaled one hurdle in this mess, Amit's safe return, but it was a big one and she'd take it for now.

She dove under the covers to retrieve her discarded pajamas and underwear with a smile twisting her lips. If Gray had thought he could come into her bed and actually fall asleep, he must've forgotten how things were between them.

She hadn't.

Scrambling into her pajamas and hopping on one foot, she called downstairs. "Save some coffee for me."

When she reached the kitchen, Gray was hunching over the small counter that divided the kitchen from the living room, cupping a mug of coffee in his hands. Amit faced him, a bag of ice clutched to his eye.

"How are you feeling?" She poked Amit's arm on her way into the kitchen, and he winced. "Not so good?"

"I feel like a truck ran over me and then reversed to do it all over again." He put the ice down to curl his fingers around the handle of a steaming mug. "And we're trying to figure out how to reach Kelly to let her know I'm okay, without putting anyone in danger."

"I think we should contact the other two New York-based Dreadworm hackers. If you two have been compromised, maybe they have, as well." Gray held up the coffee pot. "You want some?"

"What do you think lured me down here?" Jerrica swung open a cupboard door and snatched a coffee cup from the shelf. As she held the cup out to Gray, she said, "We have procedures to contact Kiera and Cedar. We'll put those in place this morning. Kelly is another matter."

Amit patted the front pocket of his shirt. "If I had my phone I'd call one of her friends, but I don't have any of those numbers memorized."

"What about social media sites?" Jerrica dipped into the fridge and popped up holding a small carton of cream. "Can you get to her friends via social media? Post something or private message them?"

"I can do that." Amit traced the bandage on the back of his head. "Don't know why I didn't think of that before. I'm losing it."

Gray slurped at his coffee and eyed Jerrica over the edge of the cup. "What's the procedure for contacting Kiera and Cedar?"

"Message boards." She dumped some cream into her coffee and watched the white swirls invade the dark liquid. "We're supposed to check a couple of TV message boards daily for information or put an alert on our phones for message replies. That's how Olaf communicates with us, too. I'll put out the SOS that Amit and I have been made."

Amit tipped some cream into his own cup. "We have to check on the equipment."

"You could lead them right to Dreadworm if they're following you." Gray raised his eyebrows. "And it seems as if they are."

"I agree with Amit." Jerrica tapped her fingers on the counter. "We have to try. If those computers have been compromised, we have to shut down our operations."

"Can you do that remotely?" Gray asked.

Jerrica widened her eyes. "You mean do it anyway without checking? No way. We'd lose whatever inroads we've made into this stealth government database—the same database that's been keeping track of Denver's activities."

Gray dumped the rest of his coffee in the sink where it splashed up on the sides of the stainless steel. "We don't even know what these guys look like, which would help in spotting a tail. How are we going to know if they're following you?"

"We do know. We both saw him last night when he attacked me in the alley, and we've already determined he's the same guy who abducted Amit."

"That's one guy, and he could've been wearing a disguise." Gray held up his index finger. "Do you really think he's working on his own? Do you think he's the same one who broke in here? There could be dozens more."

"We'll wear our own disguises—God knows, I have a few. And we can get out of this building without going through the front door." Jerrica folded her arms and leaned against the counter. "We have to get to Dreadworm."

Amit shoved his coffee cup toward her. "And I have to contact Kelly. Can I use your laptop?"

"It's upstairs." Jerrica left the men in the kitchen and took the stairs two at a time up to her loft. She swept the laptop from the nightstand and tucked it under her arm as she jogged back downstairs.

When she hit the bottom step, she crooked her finger at Gray and Amit. "Join me on the couch."

Amit limped across the room with Gray by his side, his hand on his shoulder. Amit lowered himself stiffly to the sofa cushion beside her.

Biting her lip, she turned to him. "I don't think you should leave this apartment, Amit. Gray and I can go to Dreadworm."

Amit sucked in a breath as he pressed his fingers against his temple. "It's my work."

"I get it, but you're going to stand out and if we have to make a quick getaway, you're going to be in trouble."

"She's right." Gray dropped to the sofa on the other side of her. "Jerrica will be able to tell if the Dreadworm space and the work have been compromised."

"All right, all right." Amit collapsed against the back of the sofa and closed his eyes. "Try Becca Landau. She's one of Kelly's best friends."

Jerrica shoved her computer onto Amit's lap. "You'll have to log in with your account. I have a fake one and if I try to private message Becca, she may never see it. If you two are already friends, she'll look at it."

Amit opened one eye. "I have a fake account, too, but Becca knows who I am. She'll recognize the name I use."

As he bent forward, Jerrica put a hand on his back. "They really did a number on you."

"No kidding." Amit logged in under his phony name and clicked on Becca Landau's profile. "This is it. What should I put in the message?"

"Just ask her to tell Kelly you're safe but can't reach out to her right now." She tapped Amit's arm as he began typing. "And tell her not to say anything to anyone else, and Kelly shouldn't, either."

Midway through the message, Amit's fingers froze. "What if they know where we live? They must if they followed us to the party. Is Kelly going to be safe? What if they grab her to get to me?"

"Can she leave town?" Jerrica tugged on Gray's sleeve. "Should she leave town, Gray?"

Gray chewed on the inside of his cheek and Jerrica's pulse jumped because she recognized the look. He was about to deliver news he didn't want to deliver.

"If she has someplace to stay, that might be best." Gray tipped his head toward the laptop. "Add that to the message."

Amit's Adam's apple dipped as he swallowed. "You're not kidding, are you?"

"I'm afraid not. This is not the US government. You've crossed people who have no rules. They are a law unto themselves, and they'll go to any lengths to achieve their results. We already know that and shouldn't take any chances."

Amit's fingers flew over the keyboard. When he finished his message to Kelly's friend, he eased back against the sofa. "I can't believe I dragged Kelly into this."

"It'll be okay, Amit." Jerrica patted his knee in an awkward attempt to soothe him. They'd really never been anything more than coworkers up to this point. She didn't kid herself that Amit had run to her for comfort. He'd come to her because he thought she could help…and that was okay.

Amit's gaze dropped to her hand, and she shifted it. "I'm not like you, Jerrica. You live and breathe this stuff—and I know why."

She snatched her hand away from his leg. "What does that mean?"

"Just because you're the best hacker at Dreadworm doesn't mean the rest of us aren't damned good. I've known about your background for over a year now."

"What do you know?" Jerrica laced her stiff fingers together.

Amit glanced at Gray, who shrugged.

Jerrica waved her hand at Gray. "He knows everything about me." *Almost everything.*

"I know that your father ran that compound down in New Mexico and that the government raided it, he fought back and both of your parents were killed."

Jerrica eased out a breath and loosened the tight grip of her fingers as Gray rubbed a circle on her back. "Good work. Yeah, that's my legacy, but it doesn't mean I want to continue living my life looking over my shoulder."

Amit snorted softly through his nostrils. "Okay. And I definitely don't want to live *my* life looking over my shoulder."

Gray swept the computer from Jerrica's lap and pushed up from the sofa. "Then you're in the wrong line of work, Amit. What you two are doing with Dreadworm invites scrutiny. I don't know what you expect. Olaf is in hiding."

"We don't expect to get killed." Jerrica jumped from the sofa. "Do you want Dreadworm's help or not to get the information about Major Denver?"

"You know I do, but I don't like seeing you in danger—either of you." Gray wagged his finger between her and Amit, still slumped on the sofa.

"Like you said—" Jerrica turned toward the staircase "—we're in the wrong business."

An hour later, they had settled Amit back in bed with a gun beside his right hand, and Jerrica had sent out the SOS codes to their Dreadworm coworkers in the city.

As Jerrica slid the final lock on her apartment door into place, Gray asked, "Are you sure the doors to the utility room and alley are going to be unlocked?"

"I used this exit fairly recently." She jabbed him in the ribs. "You're as nervous as Amit."

"He's right, you know."

"About what?" She hoisted a small backpack over her shoulders and grabbed the bannister on her way down.

"You've always lived your life in a state of paranoia."

She shook her head. "Not you, too. Give it a rest. I didn't grow up behind the white picket fence like you did, with all the comforts and privileges, but I turned out halfway normal, didn't I?"

"Normal enough for a home and kids?"

Jerrica almost tripped and she clutched the bannister for support. "Are you asking?"

"Just wondering." He tugged on her backpack. "I'm not asking anything until I know the answers."

"That's a cowardly way to live your life." She broke away from him and jogged down to the first floor of her building, as much to hide her confusion as to make sure they could escape this way. Was Gray really thinking about marriage and children?

Could she get that close to him without revealing everything?

She tried the handle to the door that led to the basement utility room. "It's open."

Gray followed her down another flight of stairs, breathing heavily.

"Are you out of shape, D-boy?"

He sneezed. "It's dank down here."

"It's where we keep the trash." She pointed to another door past a row of dumpsters. "But it's where the building next door keeps its trash, too, so this is our ticket out."

"What's on the other side?" Gray strode past her and grabbed the handle of the metal door.

"Stairwell landing—in the other building."

As Gray yanked on the handle, Jerrica held her breath, but the door creaked open. Poking his head into the space, he said, "All clear, just as you said."

He held the door wide for her and she brushed past him, strolling into the other building.

"We don't even have to go to the first floor and out the front of this building. There's a door that leads to the side alley, so even if someone is watching the back of my building, we won't be going out that way."

"Perfect." Gray blew out a breath he'd probably been holding since they hit the stairwell. "You've developed the skills you needed for the job you do."

"You can thank Olaf for that."

Gray's eyes flickered in the semidarkness, and Jerrica sealed her lips. Gray had always felt a twinge of jealousy about her relationship with Olaf. The man had recruited her specifically for Dreadworm based on her past. Gray didn't know half of her complicated relationship with Olaf, but not one ounce of that relationship contained anything remotely akin to romance. But she had no intention of revealing any of it to Gray. It might lead to other revelations—ones she wasn't ready to expose.

"Maybe Olaf should've practiced a little of what he preached. He might be a free man right now."

"He's free."

"He's in hiding."

"He's still free."

"If you can call it that." Gray lifted one shoulder and then wedged it against the door. "Okay to open?"

"It's now or never."

"Wait." He pulled his weapon from his pocket and held it close to his body as he eased open the door.

The cool air from the alley flooded the stairwell, and Gray held up his hand. "Stand back for a second."

He stepped outside first and then cupped his hand and motioned her forward.

She joined him in the empty alley and tugged her hat down over her ears. "Quick getaway."

"You're a genius." Gray kissed the side of her head.

"On to Dreadworm."

By playing lookout and bodyguard, Gray made the path to the Dreadworm office easier than ever. They made so many twists and turns to get there, nothing less than a bloodhound could've tracked them.

When they reached the door on the alley, Gray peeked up from beneath the bill of his baseball cap. "Cameras?"

"Cameras, locks, sensors. The works."

They slipped into the building and Jerrica let the heavy door clang behind them. "It's upstairs."

"Nobody should be here, right?"

"That's right. Just Amit and I have access to this site. So, if anyone got to our stuff, they did it remotely."

"And you don't even know where the other Dreadworm site is in the city?"

"Nope. And they don't know the location of ours—not that we don't trust each other." As Jerrica climbed the stairs with Gray behind her, she swept off her cap and tousled her hair. She sighed when she reached the top step. "Everything looks good."

"But you can't tell until you look at the computers, right?"

She tipped her head. "You're learning." She dragged her chair out from her workstation and plopped into it.

Her fingers on the keys woke up the computer and she checked through her processes. "Still working and still making headway into the stealth database."

"Amit works over there?" Gray jerked his thumb toward another bank of computers.

"Yeah, and I have his codes. He didn't have a choice." She sat in Amit's chair and cranked it up so she was eye level with the displays.

"He's coming at the database from another angle, but it's the same database of communications and email traffic. I know he's looking at the weapons stash in Nigeria, but I'm not completely sure where he is with that. We don't necessarily share."

She entered Amit's passwords to access his computer and tapped into the dark government database that they'd both stumbled onto.

With Gray hovering over her shoulder, she flicked her fingernail at the monitor as lines of text scrolled down the screen. "This is it. I think he broke in even further."

"What does it all mean? What are those lines of text?"

"They're entries in the database—emails, files, even text messages."

"And these are the people setting up Denver?" He dragged over a stool and straddled it. "Can't you just enter some search criteria to narrow down the conversations?"

"We can and we have, but most of the text is in code. Even if we search for Denver, for example, nothing will return because his name isn't used in the messages. We would have to crack the code first, and that's not necessarily what we do—even Olaf."

"Then it's a good thing others do it." Gray's hands shook as he scrabbled for the phone in his pocket.

Jerrica pressed a hand against her chest. "What are you saying? Do you have the code deciphered?"

"Some of it." Gray scrolled through his phone. "Try entering these words—fickle, Monday, scope."

Jerrica stopped the scan process and switched to a search mode. "Repeat those words."

Gray said the three words again, and Jerrica entered them into the search field. The words popped up on the screen in yellow highlight.

"Can you print this out?" Gray jabbed a finger at the screen.

"I will, but let's not wait." She swung the monitor toward Gray. "Can you do it online?"

"Yep." He tapped his phone and held it up to the screen, mumbling under his breath, his gaze tracking back and forth between the computer and the phone.

He swore and smacked his phone facedown on the desk. "This is it, Jerrica. This database is outlining the plan."

"What plan?"

"The plan to stage a sarin attack on US soil and blame it on Major Denver."

Chapter Seven

Gray could barely get the words out of his mouth, past his thick tongue. These people, whoever they were, planned to pin this on Denver. How? Why?

Jerrica blinked. "Sarin? This is the plan Denver was uncovering?"

"Who is this, Jerrica?" Gray slammed his fist next to the keyboard. "Who are these people?"

"Can't tell you that yet. All we know is that it's connected to the government, but it's not a standard government database. It's under the radar. There's not a name or a government official we can connect it to."

"We need to find out before this attack is carried out."

A crease formed between Jerrica's eyebrows. "How are they going to blame Denver for this when he's still missing?"

"That'll make it easier for them." He skimmed a hand across his head. "Denver's going to have to come in. If he's under military arrest, he can't be blamed for anything."

"Really?" Jerrica scooted back her chair and crossed her legs at the ankles. "He can still be accused of the setup if not the implementation."

"I wonder if Denver knows any of this?"

She flicked a finger at his phone. "He must, if he's the one who gave you the code."

"He did give me the code, which he got from someone else, but he doesn't have access to the files here." He hunched forward and planted his elbows on his knees. "Nobody but us has access to this. Do you think all this data is going to tell us who's behind the plan? It has to be someone high up."

Jerrica cinched his wrist. "Maybe you can help with that, Gray. You know these people. You rub elbows with them."

He searched her green eyes for the usual signs of disdain reflected there when she spoke of his family. They glinted back at him with hope and enthusiasm.

Her grip on him tightened. "Can you do it? Will you do it?"

"If it means getting to the bottom of this and stopping a terrorist attack, of course. I don't have any loyalty to people who are willing to destroy this country...do you?"

Jerrica's cheeks flushed and the jewel in her nose glinted as she flared her nostrils. "I never did. That's not what my family was about."

"All right. I'm not going to get into a battle of the families here." He brushed a lock of black hair from her hot cheek. "But in case you haven't noticed, we're in New York and my family and my family connections are all in DC."

"Maybe we need to take a trip to DC to visit your family. They know you're stateside? I can't imagine you're here on official business."

"I'm not. I'm on leave, and my family knows it. They did invite me to their annual Memorial Day bash, though. That might be the place to start."

"Then it's time for a family visit."

He cocked his head at her. "You never wanted to meet my family before—when we were together."

"I didn't figure they'd be all that interested in meeting the daughter of Jimmy James. I thought you were keeping me away from them. Did you even tell them you were dating the daughter of the infamous survivalist who got into a shootout with the FBI?"

As Gray answered, he shifted his gaze to his phone and the code Denver had sent. "I told them."

"And?" Jerrica tapped the square toe of her boot on the cement floor.

"They weren't thrilled." Gray shrugged it off. His parents' opinions about the women he dated, even this woman, didn't matter to him.

Jerrica traced the edge of her phone. "Is that why you dumped me?"

"That had more to do with your work at Dreadworm… and your association with Olaf…than any outside opinions. And that was a mutual dumping."

"Only because you were acting like an ass." Her lips pressed into a tight smile. "And now here you are."

"Who's acting like an ass now?" He ruffled her hair. "Don't rub it in."

"I'm glad you're here." She dropped her long lashes and jerked in her chair. "Speaking of codes, I just got an alert from Kiera's message board. I need to check it."

Jerrica sprang up from the chair in front of Amit's computer and scurried to her own desk. As Gray looked over her shoulder, she brought up a website with a discussion board for a popular TV show.

"Zombies? That's appropriate." Gray drew up a chair beside her as she clicked on a message thread.

"What are you looking for?"

She ran her finger down the user names. "A message from Deadgirl."

Gray slapped at a prick of uneasiness on the back of his neck. "Laying it on kinda thick, isn't she?"

"It fits for the venue. Don't read anything into it." She hopped in her seat. "There she is."

Jerrica clicked on a message from Deadgirl and read aloud. "I think they should've blown up the bridge to Bristol to stop the zombies, and my favorite episode this season is five."

"Okay." Gray scratched his chin. "Do we need another cipher decoder to figure this out?"

"No, we have our own code. Bristol stands for Washington Square Park and episode five is the time, so she wants to meet at Washington Square Park at five o'clock. The zombies? You can figure that out. Easy."

"Maybe too easy?"

"Who would know to look for our communications on a discussion board for a TV show?"

"That gives us some time for lunch and to start deciphering the communications from this database. We know the what and where, but we still need the when and the who to stop this thing."

"I suppose the why doesn't matter, does it? The whys are always the same—power, control, probably money."

"You don't really believe what your father built had nothing to do with power and control, do you? He was an autocrat He ruled that compound with an iron fist."

She whipped her head around. "I never defended what he did, but the FBI didn't have the right to come in and kill innocents."

"Jimmy James opened fire first, Jerrica. You told me the story yourself."

"I know, but the women, the children? My mother,

my brother…" She put a hand over her eyes as the pain stabbed her heart.

Gray scooted closer and wrapped his arms around her. "I know. I'm sorry. Everyone knows it could've been handled differently. That's why your lawyers got you such a huge settlement."

"Blood money." She dashed a tear from her face, and then pointed at Amit's computer. "That has to be done printing out soon. When it is, we'll get lunch and bring something for Amit—along with the good news that we can decode the databases we found."

"Deal." He pinched her chin between his thumb and forefinger and kissed her forehead.

Jerrica didn't like talking about the raid on her father's compound, which he'd egotistically and ironically called Jamestown. Jimmy James had been stockpiling weapons and ranting and raving against the government for years, starting to challenge authorities on government lands. The FBI had reacted and then overreacted, and Jerrica had lost her entire family in the shootout.

Lawyers had swooped in on behalf of her and the other survivors, and she'd won a multi-million-dollar settlement and had been sent to her mother's sister, eventually taking her aunt's married name, West.

Jerrica had a reason to be paranoid and he'd hated to further enforce that paranoia, but the world they inhabited was a scary place.

Olaf, who'd once worked for the federal government, had taken advantage of Jerrica's situation. He'd recruited her, groomed her to be a hacker and eventually take over Dreadworm. Gray didn't trust the man or like him.

"Earth to Gray." Jerrica snapped her fingers in his face. "The printer has finally stopped. I'll find a manila envelope and put that tome in my backpack."

"Yeah, okay." He pointed to Amit's computer. "Should we put that back doing the job it was doing before?"

"I'll do it. You grab the printout and check that shelf for an envelope or folder."

"Yes, ma'am." He saluted and crossed the room to the printer. He gathered up the papers that contained what was gibberish for most but pure gold for them. The printout was useless without the code and the code was useless without the printout, but together they told a story of corruption, deceit, betrayal and death—he'd protect both the code and the printout with his life.

GRAY CHOMPED DOWN on the last bite of the taco from the Indian taco place Jerrica had dragged him to.

She dabbed his chin with a napkin. "I can tell you hated it."

"Pretty good for tofu and other healthy junk." He shook the paper bag next to him on the counter. "Are you sure Amit's gonna like this?"

Jerrica slid from her stool and wedged a hand on her hip. "He's a vegetarian."

"A buddy of mine in Delta Force is Indian, and I can assure you he's not a vegetarian."

"If he's in Delta Force, I'm pretty sure he's no pacifist, either."

"At the end of all this, Amit's not going to be a pacifist. If he's going to continue in this line of work, he'd better start packing heat."

Jerrica snatched the bag from the counter. "Maybe he will."

They made it back to Jerrica's apartment building not far from the Indian taco stand on the Lower East Side by the same method they'd used before.

Gray didn't take a breath until they'd reached Jerrica's front door. As they eased it open, they faced Amit, bruised and battered, pointing a gun in their general direction.

Gray poked Jerrica in the back. "What did I tell you?"

"It's just us. Are you all right?" She held out the bag. "We brought you lunch from Goa Taco."

Amit's shoulders dropped. "I slept most of the morning. I feel weak. Maybe the food will help."

"Do you want me to bring it to you in bed?"

"I'll try eating it here." Amit sank to the sofa, the gun still attached to his hand.

"I'll take that, Amit." Gray reached down and loosened the gun from Amit's stiff fingers. "You're going to feel a lot better when we tell you our news."

"I'm ready for some good news—more good news. Kelly's friend messaged me back. Kelly's on her way to Boston—no questions asked."

"That's a relief." Jerrica returned to the living room, two messy tacos on a plate and a glass of water clutched in her other hand. "Do you need more meds?"

"Just some ibuprofen." He held up a trembling hand. "No more stuff to knock me out. I'm groggy enough."

Gray sat in a chair across from Amit and pulled Jerrica's backpack into his lap. Reaching into the pack, he said, "We printed out a chunk of what was coming through on the database you hacked."

Amit swallowed a bit of taco and choked, his dark eyes wide. "Print? You printed out something, Jerrica?"

"I know. Not standard procedure, but we have a code to decipher and the means to do it." She held out her cupped hand containing two gelcaps.

"You're kidding." Amit wiped his nose with the back of his hand and dropped the pills into his mouth.

"Denver sent the code to me, hoping you guys would

have something I could apply it to…and you did. We've already deciphered a few words, so I know we're on the right track."

"And…" Jerrica perched on the sofa next to Amit "…I got a meet message from Kiera."

Amit said, "She must have something important to communicate to you if she wants to see you in person."

"I just hope it's not that they've also been compromised." She dropped a paper towel on Amit's thigh.

He grabbed her hand before she could pull it away. "Have you heard from Olaf yet?"

Gray's jaw tightened as he waited for Jerrica's answer. She hadn't told him she'd contacted Olaf, but of course Dreadworm's founder would have to know if his organization had been compromised.

"I haven't heard from him." She shrugged and wrested her hand from Amit's hold. "He probably wants to keep a low profile. Can you blame him? If the Feds ever catch up to him, they're going to arrest him."

Gray plopped the folder on the coffee table. "And you, too. Aren't you guys worried about arrest? It's not just Olaf who's under the gun."

"If we can help thwart a terrorist attack and save a Delta Force major, we might just be able to talk ourselves out of federal prison." Amit nudged the folder on the table with his toe.

"I wouldn't hold your breath." Gray gathered up the papers. "Should I spread these out on the kitchen table?"

"That's probably the best place." Jerrica beat him there and cleared off a vase of colorful flowers and a few dead petals. She pushed aside a candle and stacked the four woven place mats on the edge of the table. "I'm going to put my laptop over here, too. I can probably write a program that will do the decoding for us, so we don't have to match letter for letter."

Gray shook his head. "I'm in awe."

Amit grabbed the arm of the sofa and staggered to his feet. "I was using your computer in the bedroom. Hope that's okay."

"No problem." She waved her hand at Amit. "Sit down. I'll get it."

When she left the room, Gray sat on the arm of the sofa next to Amit. "Have you ever met Kiera before? Do you even know what she looks like?"

"African-American woman. Small but muscular." Amit held a hand at his shoulder. "Braids about down to here."

"So, if a tall white woman with short hair shows up, we're probably in trouble."

"What are you two whispering about?" Jerrica strode past them and plugged in her laptop at the kitchen table.

"Gray was just asking about Kiera."

Jerrica glanced up from the laptop and puffed a strand of hair from her eyes. "She communicated with me via the message board. This meeting is legit."

"You thought the text Amit sent you was legit, too." Gray pushed up from the sofa and planted himself at the table.

"Cell phones can be stolen. Nobody knows about this message board."

"Except the four of you…and Olaf."

Amit raised a hand. "Leave me out of it. I swear, I didn't reveal anything when they had me. I'm not saying I wouldn't have caved once they got me to their torture chamber, but those cops saved me."

"I'm allowed to be suspicious." Gray flipped open the

file and brought up the code on his phone. "I'm going to try to decipher this first line."

Jerrica grabbed the back of his chair. "Before you start, Sherlock, can you send that code to my email address?"

"Is it safe?"

"My email is encrypted. Only I could break into that." She winked at him.

"Okay, here it comes. The subject is a recipe for buttercream frosting."

Jerrica rolled her eyes. "Anyone who knows me would spot that as a fake right away. Go ahead."

Gray emailed her the attachment Major Denver had forwarded to him and the code wheel, and then grabbed a sharpened pencil. Above each letter in the database transcript, he wrote in the corresponding letter from the code.

After one minute, he squinted at his handiwork. "Houston, we have a problem."

"What's wrong?" Jerrica asked.

"There's another layer to this code." He drilled the tip of the pencil into the stack of papers. "It's not a simple substitution."

"But we did a spot check and it worked. The matched-up letters spelled out real words instead of this gibberish."

"Now it's a different kind of gibberish, featuring real words this time, but words that don't make any sense together." He picked up the first sheet of the paper. "How about this? Eagle Scout has landed, but he didn't bring the bubble gum."

"So, if someone does get the code like we just did, he…or she would still be in the dark. A random search for Denver or sarin gas or Times Square would not yield any results." Jerrica folded one leg beneath her.

Across the room, Amit choked. "They're planning to release sarin gas in Times Square?"

Jerrica clicked her tongue. "Relax over there. That was just an example."

"But you know it's sarin gas and you're pretty sure it's New York, aren't you?"

"Gray had some previous intelligence from his Delta Force team and we already knew one of the code words for sarin, but we need hard facts to nail this down." Jerrica tapped the top of her laptop. "I'm going to get going on a program to at least translate the code to real words. We can work on what those words mean, later."

Gray nodded, but his insides tightened. He didn't know how many laters they had. Denver had gone AWOL almost six months ago, betrayed, set up and forced to go on the run due to information he was going to get from a source in Afghanistan. That plan he was investigating must be close to fruition.

"I have a dumb question." Amit gasped as he struggled to rise from the sofa. "Isn't your father Senator Grayson Prescott?"

Gray shot a sideways glance at Jerrica. "He is."

"Why don't you take all of this to him? You trust your own father, don't you?"

A muscled twitched at the corner of Gray's mouth. "I trust him, but he's part of the system. He's former military himself. He's never going to believe those around him, seemingly dedicated to the same goals as he is, may be actively working against those goals undercover. And if I tell him I'm working with Dreadworm, he'll do his duty. Jerrica…both of you…could be in danger of arrest. I'm not going to take that chance—even with my father."

"I get it." Amit limped to the kitchen and held up a

hand to stop Jerrica who'd jumped to his aid. "I have to start moving around by myself. I plan to join Kelly in Boston as soon as I can…unless you two need me."

"You've done enough." Gray leaned back in the chair and crossed his arms behind his head. "But don't rush it. You lost a lot of blood and if your ribs aren't broken, they're bruised."

"I'll give it a day or two, and I'll help however I can while I'm here." Amit rubbed the back of his skull. "I sure wish Olaf would check in with us."

"Seems like you two have already been doing most of the heavy lifting without Olaf."

"Olaf *is* Dreadworm." Amit turned his dark gaze on Gray. "You don't like Olaf, do you?"

"Let's just say, I think he's caused a lot of trouble."

"Gray's always had a thing against Olaf." Jerrica lodged her tongue in the corner of her mouth.

Gray clenched his teeth. He must've been obvious about his jealousy toward Olaf. "I realize if it weren't for Olaf and Dreadworm, we wouldn't even be close to nailing down this plan. So, I'm feeling kind of warm and fuzzy about the guy now."

"That'll be the day." Jerrica clicked a few more keystrokes. "We'd better start getting ready to meet Kiera."

"There's something special you need to do for the meeting?" Gray's *something special* meant bringing a weapon.

"It's kind of silly, but I'll wear a cap with the TV show's logo on it. That's how she'll pick me out."

"You've never met her before?" The uneasiness churned in his gut again.

"I haven't, but Amit has. I know what she looks like, and she has a description of me. It's fine, Gray."

"Then let's get the cap."

GRAY AND JERRICA set out again, exiting from the building next door. If anyone was watching Jerrica's building, maybe they'd believe they all relocated. Maybe they *should* all relocate.

If Gray hoped to identify any of the government moles, he and Jerrica would have to plan a trip to DC, anyway. And what could be safer than a sitting US senator's home in North Arlington?

His mother was always coming up to DC to throw parties, and their gathering for Memorial Day was legendary with all the movers and shakers in attendance. Dad was always trying to foist him on the political powerbrokers. Maybe it was time for him to show interest.

"We're taking the subway." Jerrica hooked a finger in his belt loop and tugged.

"I'm an expert now. Washington Square Park?" Gray planted himself in front of a map on the wall in the subway station and studied the multicolored lines crisscrossing Manhattan.

He placed his hand on the small of Jerrica's back. "This way."

Gray successfully got them to their location and as they climbed the stairs to fresh air, he tucked his sunglasses into his pocket. He hadn't bothered with a disguise, but Jerrica had that silly hat with the ghoulish logo pulled down to her eyebrows.

As they entered the park, Gray's muscles tensed and his gaze darted around the open space. A kid screamed, causing a hitch in his step.

Jerrica patted his arm. "I know how you feel."

Did she? Gray slipped his hand into his jacket pocket and caressed his gun. Jerrica, usually so careful and on edge, almost had a spring in her step as she approached a bench.

She must trust Olaf so absolutely that she trusted everyone around him. If Olaf had handpicked Kiera, she must be golden.

Jerrica settled on the bench facing the street. "I'll see her coming, and she'll see me."

Gray remained standing and scanned the students with their backpacks, the couples on a stroll to somewhere else and a couple of transients looking for a handout. "I'm going to leave you here to meet Kiera while I play scout."

"Do you want me to send up a smoke signal or something when I see her?" Jerrica crossed one leg over the other and immediately began her nervous habit of kicking her foot back and forth.

The gesture gave him some comfort that she was taking this meeting seriously.

"No. I'm sure I'll know her when I see her—gauzy red scarf, right?"

"Yes. We shouldn't be long. She'll tell me what she needs to, and we'll part ways. I don't owe her any information, and I don't plan to tell her anything about what Amit and I have going on—just that we've been compromised and to watch out."

"Got it." He squeezed her shoulder and sauntered away to people watch.

A few minutes later, a short African-American woman with long braids, a long skirt and a red scarf hanging loosely over her shoulders shuffled into the park area.

She glanced over her shoulder, and Gray narrowed his eyes and peered behind her for any unusual activity. Maybe nerves had gotten the better of her, too, and she was checking for a tail.

She seemed to be dragging her feet, as if meeting Jerrica was the last thing she wanted to do.

Her head jerked to the side, and she pinned Jerrica

with an unrelenting stare. Keeping her focus on Jerrica, Kiera walked toward her as if in a trance.

Gray licked his dry lips. Out of the corner of his eye, he sensed movement and his skin prickled as he watched a previously stationary homeless guy give up his prime spot and mosey toward Jerrica's bench.

Kiera's head shifted slightly toward the transient and the three of them—Jerrica, Kiera and the homeless guy formed a taut triangle that buzzed with electricity.

Gray's head snapped toward Jerrica. Did she sense it?

Her leg kicked back and forth furiously, and she craned her neck like a bird trying to scope out the offerings. She felt something.

The transient picked up the pace, making a beeline toward Jerrica. Kiera waved, keeping Jerrica's attention focused on her trusted Dreadworm coworker.

Gray's brain clicked with every movement of the two people closing in on Jerrica. As if in slow motion, the homeless man reached into one of his bulging bags, keeping his hand planted inside.

Would he kill both of them, or just Jerrica?

Adrenaline pumped through Gray's system and it felt as if he had springs on the bottom of his shoes as he bounded forward.

Kiera whipped her head around toward him, her braids flying through the air, her eyes wide.

It was enough of a signal to the transient, who didn't even turn around to look at Gray. Instead, his hand emerged from the bag, his fingers wrapped around a gun with a silencer attached. He'd probably never meant to shoot Jerrica from this distance, but his plans had clearly just changed.

So had Gray's.

"Jerrica, take cover!" As Gray shouted, the unmistakable whiz of a bullet zipped through the air.

Gray hoped to God it hadn't found its mark, but he had to keep his eye on the gunman who looked ready to take another shot. Gray steadied his own weapon and leveled it at the fake transient.

Before Gray could get off a shot, the man grabbed a child running past in the confusion. Using the boy as a shield, the gunman backed out of the park amid the screaming and chaos.

Then his arm rose and he shot Kiera where she stood.

Chapter Eight

The bullet from the silenced gun cut through the air and the pounding in Jerrica's eardrums. Was it aimed at her? At Gray? God, not the boy. She dug her nails into the dirt beneath the bench where she'd taken cover.

As the gunman pushed the little boy and he fell to his knees, Jerrica opened her mouth in a silent scream. She scrambled forward on her belly to reach the boy, who popped up crying but unscathed and ran to his mother's outstretched arms.

Jerrica collapsed. Thank God the boy hadn't been harmed.

"Jerrica, are you hit?" Gray's voice invaded the fog encompassing her head, and she reached out a hand.

"I'm okay. He didn't shoot that child." If she'd had to bear witness to another child dying from a gunshot wound, it would've been almost impossible for her to get to her feet.

Crouching beside her, Gray put his arm around her waist and helped her up. "Kiera wasn't so lucky."

As her boots hit the ground, Jerrica's legs gave way beneath her and she grabbed Gray's arm. She didn't need to, as he'd kept a firm, steadying hold on her.

She peeked over his shoulder at Kiera splayed in the

dirt, her braids fanning out around her head as a pool of blood inched its way to the ends of the arc they created.

She turned her face into Gray's shoulder and mumbled against the rough denim of his jacket. "Oh my God. Why?"

"I guess he figured if he couldn't shoot one Dreadworm hacker, he'd shoot another."

"But Kiera had nothing to do with the compromised database." She tugged on his sleeve. "Police."

Gray stroked bits of debris from the hair hanging below her cap. "We don't know anything. We don't know Kiera. We were here taking a stroll."

"What if someone saw you pull out your weapon?" She patted the gun Gray had crammed back into his pocket.

"I doubt anyone noticed, but if someone did, I have a concealed-carry permit. I saw the man had a gun, and I was going to try to take him down. Best to stick with the truth as much as possible."

"Why didn't you?"

"Why didn't I what?" Gray nodded at the cop headed their way.

"Take him down."

"He'd grabbed the boy by the time I could take aim. I'm a pretty good shot, but I'm not going to risk a child's life. You were safe, I had cover and I never thought he'd turn on Kiera."

"Why *did* he shoot her?"

"Shh." Gray hissed in her ear at the officer's approach.

"You folks witness what happened here?"

After introducing himself to the officer, Gray kept his story brief and to the point. Nobody must've noticed his gun because the officer didn't question him about it, and he didn't offer it up.

"Ma'am, what did you see?"

"Not much of anything." Jerrica swept the cap from her head and ran her fingers through her tangled hair. "I saw that the transient had a gun, and my...boyfriend saw it, too. He warned me to take cover, and I did. I had my eyes on the child the man grabbed, so I didn't even realize he'd shot the woman. Is she...?"

"Yes, she's deceased." The cop tapped his pencil against his notebook. "Did he seem to be targeting her? Others said he was walking in the direction of this bench."

Gray cleared his throat. "I'm not sure he was targeting anyone. He pulled out his weapon, the people who noticed it screamed and started running out of the park or taking cover. He shot the woman. Then he took off."

"Can you give me a description?"

Jerrica held up her hands. "I can't. I didn't get a good look at him."

"I can help with that."

Gray proceeded to give the officer a description of the transient, and both he and Jerrica gave him their names and phone numbers.

"Thanks. We'll be in touch if we need more information, and call us if you remember anything else." The cop tucked his notebook into his pocket, pivoted and then stopped. "It's weird though. You wouldn't think a homeless guy would have a gun with a silencer attached."

"That is strange." Gray draped his arm around Jerrica's shoulders. "Can we leave now?"

"Sure, and thank you for your service, Lieutenant Prescott."

"Thank you for *yours*."

Gray entwined his fingers with Jerrica's and tugged. They left the park, and she didn't even give a parting glance to Kiera's dead body on the ground.

They kept silent for two long blocks, putting as much space as possible between themselves and the park.

Gray pointed ahead to a street glowing with welcoming lights. "Let's get something to eat."

"Should we tell Amit what happened?"

"He doesn't have a phone and even if he did, I'm not sure I trust your device."

"You have your phone. I'll communicate with him through the message board." She stopped in front of a bistro and grabbed the door handle. "Here."

Gray reached above her and pushed open the door. The whoosh of noise and warmth and savory smells cast an immediate spell on Jerrica, luring her inside the buzzing scene.

She closed her eyes. The longing for normality hit her like a sledgehammer. Why now? With everything in her life coming to a head, she sensed an explosion in her future—and she didn't mean the kind the terrorists had planned.

"Two?" The hostess appeared before them, and Gray nodded.

"We'll take the bar if we have to."

"We just cleared a table by the kitchen." The hostess tried to keep her gaze from wandering over Gray's body but failed.

Jerrica couldn't blame her, but she didn't have to like it. She stepped between the hostess and her view. "That's fine."

The hostess eked out a tight smile and spun around, crooking her finger. "Follow me."

Gray rested a hand on Jerrica's hip and leaned close. "It's crowded in here."

"A good spot in case we were followed, don't you think?"

"We weren't followed." He dug his fingertips into the swell of her hip. "I made sure of that."

The hostess seated them, and Gray slid one of the menus she'd left toward Jerrica. "Please tell me there's something more than veggie stuff here."

"This isn't a vegetarian place. I think they even have—" she whispered "—burgers."

Jerrica grabbed the edge of the menu to flip it open with a hand that still trembled.

Gray didn't miss a thing. He covered her fingers with his own. "You're sure you're okay?"

"Still shaken. If you hadn't warned me to take a dive, I'd be as dead as Kiera—unless he killed her because he couldn't kill me." She finally opened the menu and stared at the words blurring in front of her.

"I think he always intended to kill Kiera."

"You think he made her, too, and intercepted our communication?"

A busboy set two glasses of water down. As soon as he left, Gray reached across the table again.

"Jerrica." Gray placed his hands flat across her menu. "I think Kiera's the one who gave you up. She tried to set you up for him. He must've had something on her."

"No." She took a gulp of water and put down the glass harder than she'd intended. "Why would she do that?"

"Being in military intelligence, I can think of several reasons why." He held up his hand and ticked off his fingers. "Someone threatened her, threatened her family, had something on her for blackmail, paid her off. The reasons are endless."

They ended their conversation again as the waiter approached. Gray ordered a burger and fries and she ordered a veggie burger, although she had little appetite for anything now.

She dug her elbows into the table and buried her chin in her palm. "I can't believe she'd do that."

"Why? You didn't know her. You'd never even seen her before tonight."

"Because she's Dreadworm. Olaf vetted us all thoroughly."

"Even the great Olaf can make mistakes." Gray rolled his eyes.

"I suppose, but that puts him in danger, too."

"The next question is, who outed Kiera?" Gray steepled his fingers and peered at her over the apex. "Where did it all start? If Kiera had to tell them about you and Amit, who told them about her? Who's her coworker? Cedar?"

"Yeah, Cedar."

Gray raised his eyebrows and his lips quirked into a grin.

"Cedar grew up on a commune. You don't want to know his brothers' names."

"You're right. I don't." Gray traced the edge of his water glass. "You seem to know more about him than Kiera."

"About the same. Kiera's father was one of the founding members of the Black Panthers. She has a son who attends Columbia." She sniffled and swirled the ice in her glass before taking a sip. "I know a few salient facts about them."

"The facts that make them ripe for working at Dreadworm."

"I suppose you could say that. What's your point?"

"My point is that Olaf chose wisely. He must've recruited most of you. It's not like you went on an internet job board."

"Food's here." She wanted to cut off this conversation about Olaf and how she knew him. She poked at her burger. "Mustard, please."

The waiter answered, "Absolutely. Anything else?"

"Actually, I'd like a beer. Jerrica? I think we both could use one."

"Sure. Make it two, and I'll have whatever he's having."

Gray made a selection from the beer menu and then doused his fries with ketchup. "Don't worry. I'm not going to drink to the point where I can't get us back to your place safely."

"I know that." She held her hand out over the table and it was mostly steady. "I'm almost calm."

"How do we reach Cedar?"

"Ugh, I knew that was going to be your next question." She thanked the waiter for the mustard and squirted some on her bun. "We have our own message board with another TV show."

"Then it's time we either warn him or kill him."

Jerrica flicked a napkin in his face.

"I'm just kidding—sort of. For all we know, he could be dead already."

"Okay, just stop." She pointed a knife at him. "I sent out the SOS to Cedar, too, but he didn't respond."

"Even if he does, you're not going to any more secret meetings. Communicate with him via the message board, and that's it." He picked up a fry and waved it at her. "I'm not allowing you to be an easy target again."

"Once Cedar sees the news and learns Kiera is dead, he's either going to contact me or he's going to run."

The waiter placed their beers in front of them. Gray finished chewing his french fry and then took a long pull from his mug.

"I needed that." He clinked his glass with hers. "Here's to finding out who's exposing Dreadworm...and why."

"And why." Jerrica took a sip of beer through the thick head of foam and closed her eyes as the alcohol sent warm, soothing waves to her frazzled nerve endings.

Gray interrupted her happy place. "I think we know the why. They know Dreadworm has compromised their clandestine database, and they want to keep you out before you can discover anything of substance...or turn it over to someone who can."

"I know." Jerrica opened her eyes and nibbled at the edge of her veggie burger, her appetite still lying in the dirt with Kiera's body. "But that's Amit and I. Kiera and Cedar have no knowledge of this database. Why go after them?"

"To get to you. If Amit didn't rat you out, and it doesn't sound like he did, and you didn't give him up, how did these people know where to find the two of you? How'd they know to pick up Amit's trail at that party? How'd they find out where you live? Kiera led one of them straight to you. They got to her somehow, turned her somehow—and killed her when she'd served her purpose."

Jerrica dropped her burger. "This time he was willing to kill me. What changed? The first attempt on Amit and me was abduction. That guy with the gun in the park looked intent on murder...not kidnapping."

"We don't know what he would've done. Maybe he squeezed off the shot to wound you and would've taken you captive after that. Kiera he had no use for."

"If Amit and I are dead, our programs die with us and we won't have the opportunity to send anything to Olaf."

Gray glanced up sharply from his plate. "Is that what you intend to do? Send this info to Olaf?"

"W-we always do."

"Have you told him about this, yet?"

"How could we?" Jerrica wrapped her hands around the mug, sweating beads of moisture. "We didn't really know what we had until you showed up with the code."

"You knew you had a black ops database inside the government."

"I knew that, and I communicated it to Olaf. Whether or not Amit did the same, I'm not sure."

Gray swiped a napkin across the lower half of his face. "Dreadworm really is a case of the right hand not knowing what the left is doing."

"Olaf designed it that way. It cuts down on the type of situation we find ourselves in now. I was surprised that Olaf even told us about each other and that Amit and I work in the same office." Jerrica traced a finger around the base of her mug. "Look at us now."

"Strange."

"We have to get back to Amit. I have to tell him what happened. If he's watching TV or going through news sites online, he may already know. He's going to be worried."

"You barely touched your dinner."

She poked at her burger on the plate. "I suppose I can take it home, and Amit can have the uneaten half."

"Get the waiter over here while I finish my food— and my beer." Gray dug into his burger while she waved at the server.

"Can I get this to go, please, and the check?"

"Sure. Anything else?"

Jerrica shook her head. "Not unless you have an armored car."

"Excuse me?"

"Just the check, thanks."

Gray studied her over his mug. "Let's take a taxi back. We can get dropped off around the corner and come through the other building."

"I guess we can do that. It'll be safer."

Gray polished off the last of his fries by dragging them through the puddle of ketchup on his plate and popping them in his mouth. "With your money, you could hire a car and a bodyguard."

"I could hire a car and a driver, but I already have my bodyguard." She grabbed his wrist. "I never said thank you for saving my life."

"I didn't do much. I was too slow. I should've shot him."

"For all my security measures and heightened senses, I didn't even notice the guy coming at me. I didn't see the gun until you yelled—saving my life." She squeezed his arm. "Can you imagine the mess if you'd shot him? The police? The questions?"

"I would've been within my rights. He had a gun out." Gray crumpled his napkin and tossed it onto the table. "I could've taken out the bastard. Sent a message."

"It didn't work out that way, but we're both safe." She put her hands together as if in prayer and pressed the tips of her fingers against her lips to stifle the sob bubbling from her throat. "Kiera. Her son."

"These people are out of control, Jerrica. Scares the hell out of me. They're desperate."

"And that's just how we want them. They know we're in the database. Imagine how they'd react if they knew we had the first part of the code to decipher their gibberish."

He hunched his shoulders. "I hope they never find that out. As long as they think you're scrabbling around with meaningless words, maybe this group, whatever and whoever it is, won't bring their full forces down on you—because those forces must be awful if they can set up a man like Denver and keep dismissing all evidence that would exonerate him."

"Okay, now you've really ruined my evening. Let's head back to my place and check on Amit."

After settling the check, they stepped onto the street and walked a half a block before grabbing a taxi. Gray sat sideways the entire ride back to her neighborhood to keep an eye out the rear window. Occasionally, he'd tell the puzzled driver to take a quick right or left.

When the taxi pulled up to the curb around the block from her apartment building, Gray leaned over and whispered in her ear. "Didn't notice anyone following us."

He paid the driver, and they turned down the alley that led to the building next to hers.

By default, Jerrica stuck close to the wall and the shadows, and Gray gravitated toward her, matching her step for stealthy step. Even with Gray's solid presence beside her, the cold that had seeped under her skin, and had receded only with the beer and the company, crept back, needling her flesh.

Gray curled an arm around her waist, fitting her against his body, as if sensing her unease. Or maybe he felt it, too.

"Do we need a key for this door?"

"Not this one. Remember, it leads to the stairwell and the two doors—one leading to each building." She dragged her keychain from her pocket. "I *do* have a key for that door."

Gray reached around her and pushed down on the handle. The squeak it made had her grinding her back teeth. He eased open the door wide enough to accommodate his bulky frame but no more.

She tripped in ahead of him, pinching the key in her

fingers. She waited until Gray pulled the door closed behind them, then pivoted to the door that led to her building's basement.

The yellow light from the bare bulb above them cast a weak glow over the metal door. Suddenly Jerrica gasped and threw out her hands in front of her. The icy prickles she'd felt in the alley stabbed the back of her neck as she stretched out her fingers to trace over the chalk letters scribbled on the door to her building.

In a voice that quavered just a little, she read aloud, "It's Olaf."

Chapter Nine

Gray caught Jerrica around the shoulders as she listed to one side. He narrowed his eyes as he read the message on the door. "What the hell does that mean? What's Olaf?"

"Cedar wrote this."

"Cedar?" He asked as if he knew more than one Cedar. "How do you know that?"

She leveled a finger at a drawing of a tree near the corner of the message. "That's his signature. Cedar, tree. Get it?"

"Okay, but why did he leave this message and what does it mean? What's he trying to say about Olaf?"

"I'm not sure, but I don't want to stand here all night while we figure it out." She shoved the key in the lock and pushed on the door.

"Wait." Gray grabbed the edge of the door. "Let's get rid of it. I'm pretty sure he meant that for your eyes only."

"If you're getting rid of it, I want proof that it existed." She dug her phone from her pocket and took a picture of the words. "It's all yours."

Gray erased the chalk with the sleeve of his jacket, and prodded her through the open door. "I just hope nobody else saw it."

"Who would see it? Nobody knows about this entrance

into my building, except the residents, and I'm not even sure some of them know you can go from one building to the other."

Gray covered his nose and mouth with his hand as they made their way through the foul-smelling basement. "How did Cedar know about the connected buildings?"

"He dropped something off for me one night, and I told him about it because I didn't want him coming to my front door. I guess he remembered, and realized now is the time to lay low."

They maneuvered their way back to Jerrica's place, and Gray tensed his muscles while she released the locks. He didn't know what to expect on the other side.

Jerrica swung open the door and sang out, "It's just us."

Amit met them from the other side of a gun. "What the hell happened out there?"

"Put the gun down, Amit." Gray raised his hands. "We're the good guys, remember?"

"Just taking precautions after what happened in Washington Square Park." He placed the weapon on the coffee table, and then collapsed on the sofa as if the effort of raising and pointing that gun had been too much for him. "That was you, right? The shooting? The dead body? That was Kiera, wasn't it? I read a report online."

Jerrica sat beside him and put a hand on his bouncing knee. "It was. Our meeting was blown. Some guy with a gun, dressed as a transient, crashed our party."

"Oh, God." Amit pressed his palm against his forehead. "Was it like last time? Did he try to abduct you... or did he want to kill you this time?"

"We're not sure." Gray scooped up the gun from the table. "He was there panhandling when we got to the park. Kiera walked up, spotted Jerrica and made her move, but she looked scared. It raised my hackles—even more than they already were. That's when I noticed the homeless guy walking in a trajectory toward Jerrica."

"I was so focused on Kiera, I didn't even notice him. Gray shouted out a warning when he saw the guy's gun, and I dove under the bench."

"How did Kiera end up getting shot?" Amit's dark skin had a decidedly pale cast to it.

"When Gray foiled the gunman's attack on him, the guy grabbed a child as a shield and then shot Kiera on his way out of the park."

"The kid?" Amit's eyes bugged out like a cartoon character's.

Gray answered, "The boy's fine. You didn't read about anyone else getting hurt, did you?"

"No." Amit wiped his brow with the back of his hand and repeated his question. "Was the man going to shoot Jerrica or abduct her at gunpoint?"

"We're not sure." Gray snatched the cap from Jerrica's head and kissed her messy hair. "I wasn't gonna wait to find out."

"How was the meeting compromised? Do you think Kiera ratted you out, Jerrica?"

"You're asking all the same questions we did. You know about as much as we do now about what happened in the park, but there's more." She slid a quick glance at Gray, and he nodded.

Amit was in the thick of it as much as they were.

Jerrica licked her lips as she pulled out her phone. "When we got back here, Cedar had left a message in chalk on the door to the building's basement."

Amit dragged a pillow into his lap as if for security and hugged it against his bruised ribs. "A message? Cedar?"

Jerrica tapped her phone and brought up the photo she'd taken of the words on the door. She zoomed in. "Look."

"There's his stupid tree. It had to be him, right? Unless someone knows how he signs off." Amit dug his fingers into the pillow in his lap. "How'd he know where you live, and how'd he know about the alley entrance?"

"He came through my building that way once when he delivered something to me—that was even before I was really being followed."

"What is Cedar talking about? Olaf? What about Olaf? What does Cedar mean that Olaf is *it*?"

"Slow down." Jerrica grabbed her bag of food from the table. "Have you eaten anything? I brought you my leftover veggie burger."

Amit downed half the sandwich before he came up for air. "Cedar must be communicating with you with chalk messages because he's afraid to use the message board. You used the message board with Kiera and look what happened."

Gray sat on the edge of the chair across from Amit and Jerrica. "Is there any way someone could've found out or figured out the message board thing on his own?"

Both Amit and Jerrica shook their heads in unison.

Jerrica said, "There's no way. There's no rhyme or reason to the message board or our user names. It's not something someone could figure out. Someone might guess the fan boards as a mode of secret communication—I'm sure it's done all the time—but there are hundreds of these boards, hundreds of shows, thousands of users with all kinds of screen monikers."

Gray rubbed his chin. "Could someone have broken

into—or whatever you call that—Kiera's computer? You're sure nobody got into yours?"

"We sweep our computers daily for threats. I'm sure Cedar and Kiera do the same—it's part of our training." Jerrica stuffed the empty foam container into the bag and pushed up from the sofa. On her way to the kitchen, she called over her shoulder. "And after the break-in, I did a thorough scan. Nobody was in my computer."

Amit put a hand to the back of his head and toyed with the bandage. "If nobody compromised the computers, and I believe Jerrica's right about that, then somebody compromised Kiera. You said she looked nervous. She knew someone would be there. She knew what was going down, but she probably hadn't counted on getting killed herself."

"And if they got to Kiera, who's to say they haven't gotten to Cedar, too?" Jerrica returned to the living room and hovered behind Amit.

He turned and stared at her. "Are you questioning me now? You searched me when I collapsed on your doorstep, barely able to take a breath, and didn't find any bugs on me. Is that what you think?"

"Why would you come here?" Jerrica folded her arms. "We're not besties or anything."

"Excuse me for thinking you might have a heart beneath the computer chips." Amit tried to rise in a huff but only made it halfway before falling back against the cushion.

"Hang on." Gray sliced a hand through the air. "Don't start cannibalizing each other."

Jerrica dropped her hands to Amit's shoulders and he flinched beneath her touch. "I'm sorry, Amit. I don't think for a minute you're the Dreadworm mole. I'm just jumpy. Can you blame me? I just saw a woman die in front of me, a child grabbed as a hostage."

Jerrica's voice hung in the room, and she flushed. She'd never use her past to garner sympathy, but there it was. That scene in the park must've brought back memories for her. She'd witnessed the murder of her mother and her brother. Her father had died a fiery death when the FBI had blown up the place where Jimmy James had kept his stash of weapons. Jerrica didn't even have her father's body to bury. She'd had to ID him through a necklace he'd always worn.

Amit must've heard her tone, too. He grabbed Jerrica's fingers and said, "I'm sorry. You had every right to suspect me, especially as I was stupid enough to get caught and then even more stupid to potentially lead my abductors to your place. But you know what?"

"What?" She blinked her eyes rapidly and swiped her hand across her nose.

"Even though we're not…besties, I came to you because you're badass, and that was even before I knew you'd partnered with a Delta Force badass."

Gray clapped his hands to defuse the awkwardness. "Now that you've eliminated each other as suspects… again…let's get back to Cedar's message. What is he trying to tell you about Olaf? Has Olaf gotten back to your SOS, Jerrica?"

"No, but that's not unusual. Sometimes it takes him days to respond."

"Cedar left that message after Kiera's murder. Would Olaf have any reason to want Kiera dead?"

"What? No." Jerrica shot up, pulling back her shoulders. "Olaf wouldn't harm one of his own people."

Amit traced the lump beneath his eye. "Are you sure? What if he found out Kiera had betrayed you?"

"How could he find out that quickly? Gray and I didn't even realize Kiera had betrayed me until the so-called transient pulled out his gun—and I'm still not sure she did double-cross me. How could Olaf have known that?"

"Maybe he saw something before. The man may be in hiding, but he knows and sees more than most people on the ground—us included." Hunching forward, Amit grabbed the arm of the sofa.

"Where do you think you're going?" Jerrica circled the couch to stand in front of her captive guest.

"I need to get up and move before I sink into that sofa. Do you have any tea? I'll make myself a cup."

Jerrica held out her hand, Amit grabbed it and she helped him to his feet. "Get me one, too, please."

Amit straightened slowly, pressing one arm across his midsection. "You want one, Gray?"

"Me? Tea?" Gray poked a finger at his own chest. "No, thanks, but if she's got a beer in there, I'll take that."

"I have a couple of bottles." She smacked a hand against the pocket of the jacket she hadn't removed when they walked into the apartment. "My phone."

"Someone's calling?" Gray's pulse ticked up. "Could it be Cedar following up?"

Jerrica squinted at her phone's display. "I don't know. It's a message notification. Someone responded to my message on the zombie-show board, after my original message."

Amit clanged a pot and then limped out of the kitchen. "That can't be. That's Kiera's board."

Gray circled his finger in the air. "Do what you have to do."

Jerrica dropped to her knees in front of the laptop Amit had left on the coffee table. She tapped on the keyboard. "I'll check it."

Amit perched on the edge of the sofa behind Jerrica, and Gray crouched beside her.

She brought up the message board and scrolled down to the thread that contained her post. "It's a new message under Kiera's user name, Deadgirl."

Amit choked. "She must've had a premonition."

Gray rubbed his eyes as the small letters kept blurring in and out of focus. "What does it say, Jerrica?"

"It says, 'I think the Forest is a better setting. They could do stories for the eleven new characters in the Forest.'"

"Okay, what the hell does that mean?" Gray trailed his fingers through his short hair.

"The Forest is Times Square, and she wants to meet at eleven o'clock. The meeting place is the discount ticket kiosk."

"She? She's dead, Jerrica." Gray jumped as the tea kettle whistled. "You're not meeting anyone tonight."

Amit hobbled back to the kitchen. "I agree with Gray. Looks like the impossible happened and someone figured out our communication system—or Kiera told someone."

"That's impossible, and why would Kiera tell anyone? She gave them what they wanted, leading them to me. There would be no reason for her to reveal our method of communication. The people who got to her figured I'd be dead or captured by now. They wouldn't have thought they'd need a way to communicate with me going forward."

Her jaw formed a hard line, and Gray's stomach sank. "You're going to Times Square, aren't you?"

She grabbed the cap she'd discarded on the sofa and bunched it up in her fist. "Broadway tickets, anyone?"

GRAY HAD CONVINCED her to keep the cap in her pocket until they could figure out what was what and who was who. He'd also convinced her to take a taxi to Times Square, but he hadn't convinced her not to go.

As he slid into the taxi beside her, he said, "Why would Cedar send you two messages? He scrawled one on the door. Why send another through a message board, Kiera's message board?"

"I don't know, but keep your eye out for a scraggly dude with shoulder-length hair, maybe a man bun, and a backpack. Cedar always carries a backpack."

"In Times Square? Easy." He bent his head close to hers and whispered. "It's the ones we can't identify that worry me."

The taxi crawled through the traffic until Jerrica couldn't stand it anymore. She rapped on the divider. "You can pull over up here."

As the car rolled to a stop, she jumped out while Gray handed the driver some cash.

She elbowed Gray in the ribs. "Don't look so worried. If someone were following us, he would stand out like a sore thumb now, right? He'd be getting out of his taxi, too."

Gray walked backward for a few steps, and then turned around. "Nobody's following us—they're probably waiting at the ticket booth instead."

"This time I'm not going to be a sitting duck." A few blocks later, Jerrica grabbed Gray's hand and pulled him across the street toward the pedestrian area of Times Square. "We can hang out behind the bleachers and have a clear view of the kiosk."

They stationed themselves at the corner of the stands where people scattered, taking seats to watch the carnival unfold before them.

Jerrica hoped to God she and Gray wouldn't be providing any more excitement. A figure moved through the crowd wearing a cap like the one in her pocket. Jerrica's heart skipped a beat.

She plucked at Gray's sleeve. "I see someone with the cap. Three o'clock from the Spider-Man character."

Gray moved closer to her and tucked an arm around her waist. "Skinny black kid with the earbuds?"

"Yes."

"No man bun, no backpack. That's not Cedar, is it?"

"Cedar's a white guy. That is definitely not Cedar."

"Then we leave. If you don't know who that is, we get the hell out of here."

"Even if we can take him in and get some intel out of him?"

"Take him in? Here?" Gray's eyes widened. "That's not gonna happen."

"Wait." Jerrica pulled the cap from her pocket. "I know him."

"Are you sure?"

"I'm pretty sure, and it would make total sense right now."

"*Pretty sure* is not good enough when it comes to your safety, Jerrica." Gray slipped his fingers into the waistband of her jeans from behind as if to hold her back. "Who do you *think* it is?"

"That's Russell Cramer—Kiera's son."

She moved forward and jerked to a stop as Gray pulled on her pants.

"Wait. If Kiera was compromised, how do we know they didn't send out her son to lure you in again?"

"Really? He just lost his mother." She twisted away from Gray and plunged into the crowd as she pulled the cap onto her head.

With Gray dogging her steps, she approached Russell and touched his elbow. "I like your cap."

He jumped and spun around, his fists clenched.

Gray moved between them smoothly and growled through his teeth. "You touch her and I'll flatten you."

The young man clutched his stomach and spluttered. "A-are you Jerrica?"

"Yes." She slipped the cap from her head and shoved it back into her pocket. No sense in announcing to the world that she and Russell shared some kind of connection. She dropped her gaze to the skinny arm pressed against his belly. "Are you okay, Russell?"

"Not really." He swiped at a bead of sweat rolling down his face and missed. "You know my name?"

"I do. Let's talk."

"Did anyone follow you?" Gray had shifted to the side, but his body radiated menace and it had poor Russell quaking in his sneakers.

"No. After posting that message, I snuck out of the... hospital." His voice caught on a sob. "I left through the loading dock. If anyone was watching the hospital entrance or the waiting room, they never would've seen me."

Jerrica felt a stab of pain. Russell had just lost his mother, and he wasn't much older than she'd been when she lost hers. But Kiera must've taught him well.

"Sorry, man." Gray patted down Russell's thin frame anyway. "Let's head to that fast food place and talk."

Russell's grief had obviously taken a toll on him. As they crossed the street to the hamburger place, he lurched and tripped beside them. Gray had to grab his arm a few times to keep him upright.

They squeezed into the restaurant, and Jerrica grabbed a table with Russell while Gray ordered some food and drinks to buy their spot.

Jerrica patted Russell's hand. "Are you hungry?"

"Not really. No. I can't eat." Russell's head dropped and he kept it down until Gray returned with a tray full of paper-wrapped burgers and empty cups.

After he placed the tray on the table, he held up the cups. "Do you want something to drink?"

"Ginger ale if they have it. My stomach feels bad." Russell slouched back and for the first time, Jerrica saw that the whites of his eyes had a yellow cast to them.

She sucked in a breath. "You don't look well, Russell."

"That's because I—I've been poisoned."

Chapter Ten

Chapter Ten

Jerrica put a hand to her throat. "You need to get help."

"No." Russell pounded a weak fist against the table. "I can't tell anyone. They said not to tell."

"Who, Russell?" Gray hunched over the table, squeezing the paper cups in his hand. "Who poisoned you? Was it to get to your mother?"

"Of course. Someone poisoned me and when I came home sick, a man and a woman dropped in on my mother and threatened her. I-I didn't understand that much because whatever they gave me made me fade in and out. I just know they threatened her."

"How'd you make it here? How'd you get to the hospital?" Jerrica folded her arms on the table, her fingers digging into her biceps.

"The man and my mother left. The woman stayed behind with me. I think she got a call or a text, and then she gave me a shot. As soon as I started feeling better, she left, but not before she warned me not to tell anyone anything."

"And yet here you are." A muscle ticked at the corner of Gray's jaw.

Jerrica shot him a look from the corner of her eye. She was supposed to be the cold one. "The shot was supposed to make you better? Counteract the poison?"

"Yeah, but how can I trust them? They killed my mom." Russell rubbed his eyes. "I still feel bad, but I'd recovered enough to answer the phone when the police called to tell me my mom had been shot in Washington Square Park."

"Eat something. It might help you feel better." Gray shoved a burger toward Russell. "How did you know to post that message on the fan board?"

"Before the man took Mom away, she tucked a note in the waistband of my sweats when they weren't looking. After the woman left and I could move, I pulled it out. She left instructions that if anything happened to her, I was supposed to post that message on the board and to come to Times Square at eleven o'clock." He shook his head and pulled off the cap. "I thought it was some kind of joke until the cops called."

Jerrica traced a pattern on the table top. "She wanted me to know that she hadn't betrayed me."

"Betrayed you? What's going on? My mom was a computer programmer. I don't understand any of this."

"Eat." Gray held up the cups. "I'm going to get you some water."

As Gray walked away, Russell peeled the waxy paper from the burger. "Did you work with my mom?"

"We worked at the same place—Dreadworm."

Russell choked and went into a coughing fit.

Gray returned with the drinks and pushed a cup of water toward Russell. "Is he okay?"

"I just told him his mother and I worked for Dreadworm."

"Why would you tell him that? You might be endangering his life even more."

"He deserves to know. Nobody has seen us together. They have no idea Kiera left her son that note, and I've told you before that message board is secure. They probably think he's still at the hospital filling out forms. Why would they follow him, anyway?"

"To make sure he doesn't go to the police."

Russell had recovered and gulped down some water. "I'm not going to the police. I thought about it after I found out that they killed my mom, but then I figured they could get to me if they wanted to. They poisoned me without my even knowing about it."

"Going to the police would be pointless, Russell. The people who poisoned you and killed your mother are not going to be caught or stopped by the police."

Toying with the burger, Russell asked, "Dreadworm? You mean that Olaf guy?"

"Yes, your mother was a hacker for Dreadworm, as I am. My coworker and I hacked into a secret database. Someone found out, and they're trying to get us to stop."

"By killing my mom?"

"They used your mother to get to me. She allowed it because she was trying to protect you, and now we're going to make sure you stay safe."

"How are you going to do that?" Russell looked around wildly. "Nobody's safe."

Jerrica sucked in her bottom lip. Another paranoid conspiracy theorist had just been born.

"The first step is to stay away from the police. Accept the official version of events that your mother was randomly gunned down by a transient. Bury your mother and go about your business. You know nothing. Your mother told you nothing, and they have no reason to fear you." Gray plunged a straw into one of the soda cups. "Can you do that?"

"They have to pay for what they did to my mother, to me. I want them to pay."

"Don't worry, kid. They have a lot to pay for, and we're gonna make sure they do."

Once he started eating, Russell couldn't stop. He finished all three burgers, all the fries, downed a couple of cups of water and then got a soda for the road.

She and Gray saw him into a taxi. As he ducked in, Jerrica put her lips close to his ear. "Olaf will pay for all your mother's funeral expenses and the rest of your education at Columbia. Don't worry about that."

Russell didn't have time to respond, as Gray slammed the door of the taxi.

He shoved his hands in his pockets and spit at the ground. "Poison. They were slowly murdering her kid to make her do their bidding."

"And their bidding was to find *me*, so they know Kiera and Cedar don't know anything about the government database."

"Cedar *does* know something, though. He knows something about Olaf."

"I don't know why he left me that message. Am I supposed to figure out what it means? It's Olaf. So, what?"

"Think about it." Gray bumped her shoulder as they merged with the pedestrians on the sidewalk. "Cedar left that message right after Kiera was shot and an attempt was made to either abduct or kill you. It's Olaf."

A chill zigzagged down Jerrica's back and she tripped over a crack in the sidewalk. "You mean, as in, it's Olaf who had Kiera killed? No way."

"I know you worship the man, but why not? He's always been anti-government, and the people who are plotting this attack and framing Denver are nothing if not anti-government."

"I don't worship Olaf." Jerrica pursed her lips. "And I know he's anti-government, but that doesn't mean he's willing to kill innocent Americans to make the government look bad. He wouldn't do that."

"It might explain why nobody has orders to kill you. Olaf still has a soft spot for you and while he wants to stop what you're investigating, he's not willing to kill you to do it."

Jerrica punched Gray's shoulder. "Just stop. You have a distorted image of my relationship with Olaf—and you always have. He's almost twice my age for one thing."

"There's about a twenty-year age difference between you. People have those relationships all the time. It's not unusual."

She stopped, turned to face him and grabbed both of his sleeves. "Do you really think Olaf and I are lovers or even want to be?"

"Maybe not on your side. On your side it's more hero worship, but why wouldn't he be in love with you?"

"I can think of a million reasons why. For one, I'm not particularly lovable." She shook him. "You've given me several more reasons."

"That's because I'm an ass. We already established that." He kissed her right there on the sidewalk. "You're lovable in so many ways, I don't have enough fingers and toes to count them."

Leaning into him, she wrapped her arms around his waist and rested her head on his chest. "I'm glad you're on my side…but you're wrong about Olaf. He loves himself."

He propped his chin on top of her head. "We're impeding traffic. Are we going to walk all the way back to your place or are we going to grab a taxi?"

"Subway stop's right ahead."

As they swayed on the subway in unison, Jerrica tucked a hand into Gray's pocket. "I'm glad Kelly got out of the city. If these people are willing to poison Kiera's son, they wouldn't hesitate to do the same to Amit's girlfriend. I'm lucky. I don't have anyone close to me they can threaten."

"You have me." He kissed the curve of her ear.

She curled her fingers in his pocket. "I'm not worried about you. You can take care of yourself."

"I wish I could say the same about you."

"What do you mean?" She tipped her head back. "I can take care of myself. You know that."

"You're street savvy. I'll give you that." He tugged on a lock of her hair sticking out of the bottom of the cap. "And you know how to take security measures…usually…but these people are different. They're not government, or if they are, they're not playing by any rules."

She snorted softly. "When did the government ever play by any rules?"

"Okay, you have a right to say that." His hand crept to the back of her neck. "When do you think you'll have a handle on the program that can decode the transmissions?"

"I am a super hacker, but I'm not that good. It's going to take a little time. In the meantime, maybe we lure these government moles out of their hiding places."

The train slowed to a stop and rocked back and forth, throwing them together.

Gray put his hands on her waist. "You're going to use yourself as bait?"

"That's the point of going to DC to visit your very well-connected family, right? Memorial Day barbecue to rub elbows with the movers and shakers on the Hill. You know they'll all be there if the Prescotts call. We also know whoever is at the crux of this scheme is a mover and shaker. Has to be."

"You're right." He drilled a knuckle into her back to

propel her off the subway. "I'll start setting that plan in motion."

They sneaked into her building through the alley, and Gray brushed his fist against the chalk dust left by Cedar's message. "I wonder where he went?"

"I wonder *why* he went? He must be afraid of something."

"It's Olaf."

"That makes no sense at all." Jerrica pressed her lips together as she charged up the stairs ahead of Gray.

There was another reason Olaf wouldn't betray her, but she couldn't reveal that to Gray...yet. If they were going to get back together, she'd have to tell him at some point. Or would she? That family of his.

She held her breath as they entered her apartment until she saw Amit asleep on the sofa, the blanket across his chest rising and falling with every breath. This feeling of worrying about someone besides herself was alien.

She'd never worried about Gray, even when he was deployed. The man was solid, impenetrable. She couldn't imagine anything or anyone getting the better of Gray Prescott.

But someone like Amit? She'd never worried about him before, but having him here in her place, dependent on her to help him, caused a whole different strain of feelings in her breast.

She hadn't decided yet whether or not she liked it.

She put her finger to her lips. "Shh. He's out."

Gray picked up a pill bottle and shook it. "Looks like he took a little something for the pain."

"Can you blame him?"

"Not at all, but he's going to have to pull himself together and get out of here. He can join his girlfriend. We can't leave him here alone when we go to DC."

"I know." She pulled the blanket up to Amit's chin. "He's going to lose it when we tell him about Kiera's son and what they did to him."

Folding his arms, Gray leaned against the kitchen counter. "Are you going to check the Cedar message board for anything?"

"I will." Jerrica stifled a yawn. "I don't think he'll use it, though."

"You should set up one of those alerts like you did on the message board you used with Kiera. Then you don't have to keep checking it, right?"

"Yeah. I didn't do it with his because he didn't respond and Kiera did."

"Now we know why she did."

Jerrica rubbed her arms and rose from the sofa. "It's been a terrible night. Imagine how Russell felt—to go through that poisoning all for nothing—they killed his mother anyway."

"We're going to put a stop to all of it, including their sarin gas attack."

Jerrica slid her laptop from the coffee table and placed it on the counter. She accessed the TV message board they used for Cedar's communications and she searched for any posts from Cruz, Cedar's user name.

"Nothing." She snapped the laptop closed. "To be continued tomorrow. I'm exhausted."

"I am, too."

Jerrica gathered her computer, phone and chargers and trailed after Gray up the stairs. She wouldn't mind a repeat performance of last night's escapades, but it didn't feel right to have sex after someone had been murdered in front of you.

When would it feel right? How long would it take to

get back to normal life? It had taken her years to even feel anything at all after the FBI killed her family.

If she were honest with herself, she'd been numb until she met Gray. He'd touched something inside her because he hadn't been afraid of her or what she had to say. He hadn't been afraid of her feelings and so for the first time she'd allowed them to spill out in all their ugliness. He hadn't flinched—not once.

As Gray brushed his teeth in her bathroom, she settled cross-legged on the bed with her devices. She checked her phone for messages, and then plugged it in to the charger.

She flipped open her laptop and scanned her email. Her finger froze as she rolled across a message from a Guatemalan coffee company. She double-clicked on the message, and the words jumped from the screen.

I'm okay. Are you okay?

Chapter Eleven

Gray swiped the hand towel across his face and stared at himself in the mirror. He wanted to take Jerrica into his arms and comfort her. Kiera's death had shaken her to the core, and Russell's experience had skewered her heart.

His girl needed a shoulder and a secure place to land, but he didn't want her to think he was making a move on her after the stressful and upsetting day she'd had. That didn't feel right.

As he walked into the bedroom, Jerrica slammed down the lid of her laptop and pushed it onto the nightstand, knocking her phone to the floor. She leaned over the edge of the bed, trailing a hand across the throw rug.

"It went under the bed. I'll get it." He strode across the room on his bare feet, crouched down and retrieved the phone.

"Thanks." She snatched it from him and placed it on top of her computer. Then she sank under the covers, pulling a pillow beneath her head, her face flushed.

Gray cocked his head, shrugged and circled around to his side of the bed. He clicked off the overhead light and crawled between the sheets. "Any news from Cedar or anyone else?"

Jerrica's body stiffened. "No."

"Are you all right?" He placed a hand on her shoulder.

She rolled away from his touch. "What do you think? Kiera's dead. Her son is recovering from a poisoning. Cedar's on the run. Amit's lying on my sofa, battered and weak. Nothing's all right."

"I'm here for you, Jerrica." Gray reached out in the darkness, his hand hovering over her hair. "If you need… anything. I'm right here."

"I just need sleep. Good night, Gray."

He snatched back his hand and buried it beneath the covers. He'd handled that all wrong, but then Jerrica was like a feral animal sometimes. One wrong move and she could scratch your eyes out.

She'd been different on the subway home, leaning into him, seeking comfort he was only too willing to give. What had changed?

His gaze slid to the laptop on the bedside table, just visible over Jerrica's slim outline in the bed. She'd been on her computer when he came out of the bathroom. Had she gotten more bad news?

If so, why would she keep it from him? They were in this together. But then, the woman had kept secrets from him in the past. She'd been raised on secrets and lies… and leopards didn't change their spots.

Not even leopards you loved.

THE FOLLOWING MORNING, Gray woke with a start, sitting upright in the bed, his heart pounding. He reached across the sheets, and he gulped back the panic as his hand swept the smooth emptiness.

When Jerrica's voice floated upstairs, Gray clenched a fist and pressed it against his chest until his heart returned to its normal rhythm. He must've had a bad dream.

He rubbed his eyes and peered at Jerrica's nightstand, now empty of her phone and laptop. He scratched the stubble on his chin. He'd been imagining things last night just because Jerrica had withdrawn from him. He should know her moods by now.

Rolling from the bed, he called downstairs. "Coffee ready?"

"It's alive!" Jerrica called back up to him.

Gray leaned over the railing and peered down at Jerrica's smiling, fresh-scrubbed face. Whatever mood had possessed her last night that led to her shutting him out had passed.

She whistled. "While I sure enjoy the view, I'm almost certain Amit will not appreciate your nakedness. Put some clothes on and come down here for some coffee. I'd offer you breakfast, but I don't have anything— unless you'd like some oatmeal."

He narrowed his eyes at her long-windedness—almost as if she were trying to distract him from something.

He cleared his throat. "Yeah, about those clothes. They're the same ones I've had on for two days now. I need to drop by my hotel and get my suitcase if I'm going to camp out at your place."

"And you still manage to smell great."

Okay, now she was just buttering him up, and he decided to pop her bubble of effusiveness. "Any news? Get any messages…from anyone?"

"Nope. Cedar is being as elusive as he was yesterday." She wandered out of his view, back into the kitchen.

"And Olaf?" He held his breath and listened for the tiniest exhalation of air or the slightest hitch in her voice.

"Nothing. Nada. Zilch."

He retreated into the bedroom and pulled on his boxers and jeans from yesterday. He sniffed the T-shirt, shook it out and pulled it over his head in resignation.

Heading down the stairs, he almost collided with Amit

at the bottom, which would've been a bad thing. The guy could barely walk upright without wincing with each step.

"Whoa." Gray grabbed the bannister and backtracked up a step. "You feeling better? You're up and about."

Amit tried to raise one shoulder and gave up. "My ribs still hurt like hell, but my head is now just a dull, throbbing mass of pain."

"That sounds…great."

"But I'm determined to get out of here today. I can't stay holed up like a rat clutching a gun in Jerrica's apartment while you two run around and try to save the world."

Jerrica poked her head around the corner, coffee pot in hand. "I told Amit we could get him to Kelly in Boston safely. We can do that, right?"

"Sure." Gray eyed Amit's lanky form as he folded it into a chair at the kitchen table. "But we need to send him off with a decent breakfast. We hardly fed him last night. Man does not live by veggie burger alone."

"Jerrica, I don't know where you got the idea I was vegetarian. Just because I'm Indian?" Amit wrapped his hand around the coffee mug Jerrica had placed before him. "Man, I could use some bacon and sausage."

Jerrica put a hand on her hip. "I'm sticking to my oatmeal, but there's a bodega down the street, on the corner. Maybe Gray could run over there and pick up some groceries for breakfast—if you think it's safe."

"Sure." Gray pulled his socks from inside his boots and sat down. "I can use the alley entrance—and check for more messages."

Jerrica opened a cupboard and stuck her head inside. "You do that, and Amit and I will plot out his escape to Boston."

Gray left the two hackers, heads together over Jerrica's

laptop. It looked like they were doing more than making travel plans. He hoped to God they were figuring out a program to decipher the code. They needed answers.

He followed the now-familiar path down to the basement and checked the metal door where Cedar had left his message yesterday. What did Cedar know about Olaf that Jerrica refused to consider?

The sun blinded him as he stepped outside, and he blinked against the light. He made a quick trip to the store and picked up eggs, bacon, potatoes, milk and orange juice, the entire time his head on a swivel.

Had the enemy given up stalking Jerrica's apartment building? They hadn't given up trying to get to her, but an abduction off the street might be too much—even for them. Or would it? The gunman in the park had been willing to whip out a weapon and...do what? Had he intended to shoot to kill, or to snatch her?

Gray bagged his own groceries and headed outside. He stood on the sidewalk for several seconds to assess his surroundings and the people around him. Nobody hesitated. Nobody looked his way.

It was not *him* they wanted, but the bad guys played dirty and they wouldn't be above using him to get to Jerrica, just like they'd used Russell. They'd be barking up the wrong tree on that one—Jerrica wouldn't give up anything to protect him and he wouldn't allow it, even if she wanted to save him.

He ducked into the alley and waited by the door to make sure nobody had followed him. When he returned to the apartment, Jerrica and Amit had good news.

"The translation program just finished. We now have real words in place of the gobbledygook. We just have to figure out what these words mean." She and Amit high-fived.

"You can't write a computer program for that, can you?"

"Not exactly, and we can't turn it over to people who might be able to do it. Hello, I work for Dreadworm. I've been hacking into your computers illegally for years. Can you do some decoding for me now?" She shook her head. "How can we turn this over to someone without getting into trouble?"

"I'll feel out my dad this weekend."

"In the meantime…" She swooped toward him and snatched a bag from his hand. "We'd better get on this— breakfast, I mean. Amit's starving and he has a flight to Boston to catch."

"Is that going to be safe for him? Any ticket purchased in his name might trigger a response from these people."

"Terrorists." Jerrica pulled the eggs from the bag and held them in the air. "These are terrorists, Gray, whether or not they're members of the government."

"You're right. Even more reason to be concerned about Amit's safety."

Amit waved his hand. "I have my alternate ID at the Dreadworm office. I kept it there because I never believed I'd need it."

"Alternate ID?" Gray joined Jerrica in her small kitchen and asked for a skillet.

Amit wedged his hip against the sofa. "Olaf insisted. We all have fake IDs in different names—driver's licenses, social security cards, even birth certificates. We can get bank accounts, credit cards, passports and airline tickets. Luckily I remembered my fake name, and we booked a flight to Boston for my alter ego."

Jerrica opened the package of bacon and handed it to Gray. "Now we just have to go to Dreadworm and pick up his ID."

Gray asked Jerrica, "You have one of those alternate IDs, too?"

"Of course. Haven't used it yet."

"Hope you never have to."

Jerrica packed a small bag for Amit with a few essentials to take on the plane, so he wouldn't be traveling and arriving in Boston empty-handed. They sneaked him out the back way and traveled a few blocks before ordering a car from Jerrica's phone.

Gray insisted on stopping by his hotel so he could pick up some clothes of his own, and he ended up stuffing a few of his shirts into Amit's bag.

When they reached the general neighborhood of the Dreadworm office, Jerrica ordered the driver to pull over. The three of them navigated their way to the office in broad daylight, and the lack of a tail worried Gray almost as much as having to lose one.

Jerrica flashed her card at the card reader and waited for the click.

Gray opened the door and hustled Jerrica and Amit into the small area at the bottom of the stairs. He pulled the door shut and kept an eye on the video of the alley.

"Me first." He tugged on Jerrica's shirttail and squeezed past her and Amit on the staircase. He didn't need the jacket today, but he'd worn it to stash his weapon in the pocket. He traced the gun's comforting outline of smooth wood inlaid in cold, hard metal and clumped up the rest of the steps.

If someone were waiting for them they would've come out with guns blazing long before now, so no need for stealth. But he still felt the desire to stand between Jerrica and the unexpected.

As Gray reached the office floor, the whirring and buzzing of the computers greeted him. Then his heart slammed against his ribcage, and he jerked the gun from his pocket.

"Stay right where you are. Make a move and you're dead."

Chapter Twelve

Jerrica drew in a breath and almost plowed into Gray's back. She dropped to a crouch and put her hand behind her to grab Amit's ankle.

The wheels on one of the chairs squeaked as it spun around, and then a smooth, low voice drilled through the hum of the computers. "Don't shoot. I own the place."

Jerrica dropped to her knees in relief and peeked out from behind Gray's broad frame. She choked. "Olaf."

Gray's back stiffened. He stepped to the side but didn't lower his weapon. "This is the world-famous Olaf?"

Amit stamped his feet behind her. "My God. I almost tumbled backward down the stairs."

"You don't need any more injuries, my boy. Come in and rest your bones." Olaf flicked the end of his long scarf at Gray. "You can put the gun away."

Gray shoved the gun back in his jacket, but Jerrica could see his hand in his pocket still holding it.

She scrambled to her feet and crossed the room in three long strides, hitching her purse over her shoulder. Olaf stood to greet her, wrapping her in a bear hug, the scent of his favorite tobacco engulfing her.

"What are you doing here? Is it safe for you?"

"Apparently, it's not safe for you." He pinched her

shoulders and set her away from him as his eyes narrowed. "You're traveling with an armed body guard now?"

Turning, Jerrica reached out a hand to Gray. "I'm sorry. This is Gray Prescott. Gray, this is Olaf, Dreadworm's founder."

Gray's jaw visibly tensed, and for a few seconds Jerrica feared the two men would have a standoff, neither approaching the other.

Gray's gaze flicked toward her, and then he made the first move. He approached Olaf as if staking out a poisonous snake, but he held out his hand, the one that had previously been fondling his gun.

"Aren't you supposed to be in hiding?"

Olaf's icy blue eyes crinkled at the corners, but his lips tightened briefly. "I had to come back to rescue my empire, it would seem. One of my New York team dead, one on the run, one beaten and one…stalked."

"Not much of an empire." Gray gave Olaf's hand one last squeeze before he released it, almost tossing it away.

"Ah, you're the Delta Force boyfriend—the one who left Jerrica in the lurch."

Jerrica forced a laugh from her throat. "That's ridiculous. I wasn't in any lurch, and Gray has been our savior these past few days."

"I'll second that." Amit hobbled past the three of them and sank into a chair. "In fact, we just came to the office so I could pick up my fake ID."

"Heading out of town, Amit?" Olaf wrapped his scarf around one hand.

He always had liked to dress dramatically, but Jerrica couldn't help feeling his flamboyance was inappropriate right now. Although technically no longer hiding outside of the country, he still needed to hide.

Jerrica stepped between Amit and Olaf. "Amit is on

his way out, but even we don't know where. I figure it's best if we all just keep ourselves to ourselves right now."

Gray had made a sharp move behind her, and she ducked toward Amit's desk drawer to avoid Gray's stare drilling the back of her head.

Amit coughed and grabbed his ribs. "Yeah, totally incognito. Isn't that what you always taught us? I don't plan to show anyone my ID, either, except at the airport."

"Which is where?" Jerrica tugged on the locked drawer.

"It's not in there." Amit struggled to his feet and crossed to the bathroom in the corner. "Give me a little credit. I'm not that obvious. I had instructions to keep it in a secret location, and that's exactly what I did."

Amit emerged from the bathroom with nothing in his hands. Wherever he'd stashed his ID, he now had it concealed on his person. He'd picked up on her direction quickly. She'd never realized how completely she could count on Amit—and now he was leaving.

Amit clapped Olaf on the shoulder. "It's good to see you again, Olaf, but I have to run. I'm a programmer, a hacker. I'm not cut out for danger. I can work on...other things while I'm away. I'll leave the super-secret stuff to Jerrica."

"Where are you staying, Olaf?" Jerrica slipped one strap of her backpack over her shoulder.

"In the spirit of secrecy, I'm going to keep that to myself...for now. Just know I'm safe, and I'll help you as much as I can with this current situation." His light-colored eyes, which gave him an otherworldly look, shifted briefly to Gray. "Can you tell me any more about what you've found in that database?"

The air in the room stilled and if a paperclip had

dropped to the floor right then, it would have sounded like a lead weight.

Jerrica shook her head. "Nothing yet, but someone out there thinks we're onto something—and it must be pretty important."

"Deadly important. It's the database itself and the fact that you breached it...good work." Olaf aimed a tight smile at Gray. "At least some of us think this is good work."

Gray finally moved after holding himself in a tense bundle ever since entering the room. "We have to get Amit to the airport."

"We do, Olaf." Jerrica leaned in and kissed his cheek. "I'm glad you're here, but you'll have to tell me later why and how. If the Feds get wind of your presence, they'll pick you up in a flash."

"They aren't going to get wind of anything. You're the only ones who know I'm here, the only ones who have seen me without my disguise." He squeezed her hand. "We'll talk later and catch up...on everything. Regular channels, my dear."

"Got it." Jerrica took Amit's arm. "Be careful, Olaf. You have no idea what we've been dealing with here."

Gray dipped his head once in Olaf's direction. "Don't do anything to put Jerrica in further danger."

"Seems like you've done a fine job of that already, Lieutenant Prescott."

Clenching his fists at his side, Gray took a step toward Olaf.

Amit put a hand on Gray's chest. "Are you going to help me get out of this city or what?"

Jerrica swallowed. "Let's go."

The three of them left the Dreadworm office in silence, and walked a few blocks before Jerrica ordered a car to take them to the airport.

As Gray stood on the curb, he folded his arms and hunched his shoulders. "So, that's Olaf. Why didn't you tell him everything? Why didn't you tell him Amit was going to Boston?"

"I'm not sure." Jerrica swung her foot off the curb and tapped the heel of her boot against it on the back swing.

Gray lifted one eyebrow. "You finally believe me about Cedar's message?"

"I don't know. It didn't feel right to tell Olaf everything." She poked Amit's arm. "I'm glad you didn't reveal your ID to him…or us."

Amit replied. "I agree. Something doesn't feel right. Why is he here? He knows if he steps foot in this country, he's subject to immediate arrest."

"Maybe what you two are onto is too big for him to pass up. Maybe he wants the credit himself." Gray nudged her shoulder. "Is that the car?"

"It is." She picked up Amit's bag and handed it to him. "That doesn't make sense, Gray. No one hacker gets credit for a data breach. It's all Dreadworm. We're all Dreadworm."

Gray waved at the oncoming sedan. "And right now, that's not a good thing to be."

They saw Amit safely to the airport and returned to her apartment. As they went through the basement door, Jerrica shook her head at the remnants of chalk dust.

"I don't think Cedar is coming back, but if he never planned to follow up, I wish he hadn't left such a cryptic message." She hooked her thumbs in the front pockets of her jeans, feigning a nonchalance she didn't exactly feel.

With the door closed behind them, Gray turned to

her in the stairwell. "Do you really think it was cryptic? Something about Cedar's message must've rung a bell with you. You weren't exactly forthcoming with Olaf when you saw him at Dreadworm…or that surprised to see him."

She flattened a hand against her chest. "I didn't know he was coming back, if that's what you mean, and something about that message *did* make me uneasy. *It's Olaf.* What else could it mean except that he's involved somehow?"

After they entered her apartment, Gray pulled his suitcase toward the stairs. "I'm going to shower and put on some clean clothes. I'm sick of this shirt."

"I kinda like it." She looked him up and down. "Now that we have everything translated, I'm going to take a crack at the code, or at least see if there's some kind of program I can write to decipher it."

As Gray trudged up the stairs with his suitcase in tow, Jerrica released a long sigh. The tension between him and Olaf had set her on edge, but had Gray acted any differently toward Olaf her boss might have been more suspicious than usual.

Olaf knew Gray's family background, knew Gray held him and Dreadworm in low esteem. Olaf hadn't seemed surprised to see Gray at her side, although neither she nor Amit had revealed to Olaf the nature of the data they'd uncovered. As far as Olaf knew, she and Amit had stumbled onto a dark database linked to the government's information banks, suggesting a government employee had access to set something up on the sly. They hadn't told Olaf about Major Denver or even about the terrorist plot.

Now she was keeping secrets from both Olaf and Gray.

She swept her laptop from the counter and settled on the sofa, tucking one leg beneath her and balancing the computer on her knee. She studied the messages back and forth, discussions of mundane office work but obviously filled with code words—words that stood for something else—much like the codes Dreadworm used on the TV message boards.

Their codes on the fan sites had been predetermined between them on the phone—no way to track down any key. Had these people done the same? Most likely. They wouldn't want to leave a blueprint to deciphering their communications.

"That feels better." Gray jumped from the last step, spreading his arms. "You can come in for a hug now that I'm not wearing the same shirt."

She lifted her laptop. "Love to, but I'm otherwise engaged."

He sat beside her and flicked a strand of hair from her neck. "Are you going to be ready to head to my parents' place in DC?"

"You contacted them?"

"I did. I figured if we're going to stop this thing, we need to be closer to the halls of power."

"Are you going to tell your father what we know so far? It would be good to get someone in government on our side, someone who could make discreet inquiries in the right quarters, someone who can help decode what we have."

"Once we do turn it over, you'll be safe."

"Unless I'm arrested."

Rubbing a circle on her back, he said, "I'm not going to let that happen. I'd like to tell my father what we know without telling him how we know it."

She drummed her fingertips on her chest. "You can blame it all on me."

"I'm not going to do that." He ran a knuckle along the

edge of her collarbone. "I want to introduce you to them as my girlfriend, not a Dreadworm hacker."

A little thrill ran down her back. "Are you sure? You told them about me before, and they were not encouraging. I guess they don't want Jimmy James as an in-law."

"They weren't encouraging because they hadn't met you. And your father died almost ten years ago." He caressed the indentation on her throat with his thumb.

She swallowed. "You have to be sure, Gray. I don't want you thinking this is some sexy adventure where we'll catch the bad guys together and then, when we go back to our regular lives, you're stuck with the hacker girl."

"But I love the hacker girl." He cupped her face with the palm of his hand. "I don't think I can live without the hacker girl. Tried it—didn't like it."

Her nose tingled and the words on the screen blurred in front of her. "What if your family hates me?"

"Impossible."

"'Cuz I'm not changing to gain their approval." She swiped her hand beneath her nose.

"Do I look like the kind of guy who needs parental approval for my dates?" He squared his shoulders and puffed out his chest.

"So, you're bringing me home to, what? Prove to your parents that you won't toe the line?"

He grunted, snatched the laptop from her leg and shoved it onto the coffee table. Then he pulled her into his lap, forcing her to straddle him. He took her face in his hands and kissed her so thoroughly, all thoughts of code, Olaf, her father and his parents fled to the hazy corners of her mind.

When she came up for air, she traced the line of his

jaw with her finger. "You look like the kind of guy who would protect me at all costs and damn the torpedoes."

"And don't you forget that—ever. I'm never going to let you down again, Jerrica."

Her cheeks caught fire, and she shifted off his lap and scooped up the computer. "I just started working on inputting similar words in this program—names, places, numbers. I think I can get somewhere with this."

He tilted his head, and she could feel his eyes boring into the side of her face. Would he feel so protective of her if he knew the truth about her father?

She had to come clean. He'd just told her he loved her, and she couldn't say it back even though she wanted to... and did with all her heart.

She had to break this code and save Major Denver for him. Then maybe nothing she had to confess would change his mind about her. He'd be so indebted to her, he'd forgive her anything.

"If anyone can do it, you can." His hand skimmed down her back. "While you're working on that, I'll see about getting my parents' private jet up here to take us down to DC."

"Really?" Her fingers paused over the keyboard. "Do you think it's necessary? Amit flew under his fake ID because he didn't have his own personal bodyguard. As long as you're with me, I think I'll be okay."

"You weren't okay in that alley behind the coffee-house. You weren't okay in the park. Besides, it's easier this way, and my parents will insist when they realize I'm bringing my girlfriend home." He shrugged. "They like to show off, and they'll want to make a good impression on you."

"Even Jimmy James' daughter?" She wrinkled her

nose. "Make sure they know I have beaucoup bucks of my own, and that I'm not interested in you for your money."

"Already told them all about your multi-million-dollar settlement from the government when we were together before. Believe me, the minute I mentioned your name my father probably had a background check done on you."

"That's exactly the kind of thing Dreadworm fights against—government intrusion into our lives." She ground her back teeth.

"I know. I don't care if you and my parents agree on anything, just that you don't kill each other." He kissed the side of her head. "I'm going to work on our transportation, and then we should think about dinner."

Gray left her to her own tortured thoughts and the repetitive work of scanning the coded messages, finding similar words and plucking them from the text—a perfect complement to those tortured thoughts.

She jumped when Gray placed a hand on her shoulder. "Sorry, hacker girl. Did I scare you?"

"Can you blame me for being on edge?"

His fingers dug into her flesh briefly. "Is that what it is? Stress? You're up and down, back and forth."

"I'm all right." She toyed with his fingers resting on her shoulder. "I couldn't do this without you here, Gray."

"I couldn't do this—" he flicked his fingers at her computer screen "—without you. And I can't do any of it without food. Let's go out and get something to eat."

"Do you think it's safe?" She slid her laptop onto the sofa cushion and stretched her arms above her head, reaching for the ceiling.

"They haven't been able to track us out of this apartment yet. I don't know if they gave up…or they're planning something else. Does Olaf know where you live?"

"Yes, he does."

"Did Kiera?"

"No." She craned her head around to look at his face. "What are you getting at?"

"These people located you before Amit showed up on your doorstep. They were squeezing info out of Kiera, but they couldn't have gotten your address out of her because she didn't know it. They didn't get it from Cedar."

"How do you know they didn't get it from Cedar? Maybe they followed him here." She rubbed the edge of the tattoo that snaked onto her wrist.

"If they'd done that, they would've been waiting for us in that alley a long time ago. So, where'd they get your address?"

"Maybe it *is* Olaf." She raked a hand through her hair. "But we're back to the motive. Why would Olaf betray the people in his own organization? This type of database, it's Dreadworm's lifeblood. I don't know why he'd jeopardize it."

"Is it Dreadworm's lifeblood? What you and Amit are working on will blow the cover off a covert operation. Covert. This is not government-sanctioned. Dreadworm likes to stick it to the Feds."

"Is that what you believe?" She chewed on her bottom lip. No wonder Dreadworm was a sore spot for Gray.

"Of course it's what I believe." He swept an arm through the air. "You have blinders on, Jerrica. Olaf has brainwashed you."

A knot twisted in her gut. "That's ridiculous. You know why I don't trust the government."

"I do, and I understand that, but what we're dealing with now has nothing to do with the government. It's antigovernment. These are rogue operatives within the government, using their positions of power to cause chaos, disrupt our foreign policy, perhaps forge alliances with our enemies."

"I don't want that, Gray. I really, really don't." She yanked on the sleeve of his shirt. "You don't believe that of me, do you?"

"No. I just don't want you to trust Olaf—and it's not because I'm jealous of the influence he has over you."

"Influence." She swept her tongue across her bottom lip. "It's not influence. H-he's my boss."

He held up his hands in surrender. "Okay. Whatever you say. Let's eat."

With Amit gone, Jerrica secured her laptop beneath the floorboards in the spare room and grabbed her purse from the back of a chair. "I'm not sure we need jackets. It's starting to warm up."

Gray stuffed his arms into his and patted a pocket. "I'd wear it if it were a hundred degrees out there. Easier to carry my weapon."

She led the way down to the basement, and they slipped into the alley. This time, they shot across the alley and ducked between two buildings to make their way out to a different street. Each time they had used a different route. If someone circled her building around to the back, they'd find an exit door on the side of the building but only the building next to hers had a door to the alley, and nobody would know to watch that door unless he or she knew about the connection between the two buildings.

This time they exited onto the street next to a dry cleaner.

"Someplace nearby?" Gray took her hand, lacing his fingers with hers as he glanced over his shoulder.

"There's a Mediterranean place about three blocks down. Sound okay?"

"As long as I can get some meat." They walked for a couple of minutes, then he steered her close to a building to get out of the stream of pedestrian traffic and leaned over to tie his shoe…which was already tied.

"What do you see?" She pressed her shoulders against the brick wall, her knees suddenly weak.

"A guy who's been behind us for a block—meandering but always following our path. He just ducked into a shop."

"What does he look like?" Jerrica slid her gaze to the left without moving her head.

"Medium height, baseball cap, jeans, Chucks."

As Gray straightened to his full height, Jerrica pushed off the wall. "What kind of baseball cap? What team?"

Gray jerked his head to the side. "I can't tell from this distance—dark color, blue maybe. Why?"

"Cedar's signature is a Dodgers baseball cap."

"He might be following us to talk to us…or kill us." Gray took her arm and steered her through the crowd.

"That wouldn't be easy if we're in a crowded restaurant." She bumped his shoulder. "Besides, if he's warning me about Olaf, I don't think Cedar is working with him."

"And if it's not Cedar, someone else is following us." Gray brushed some imaginary debris from his shoulder and twisted his head, peering behind them. "Dodgers."

"It's Cedar. Too much of a coincidence." Jerrica wiped her sweaty palms on the thighs of her black pants. "He's not going to approach us out here, so let's keep walking and leave the ball in his court."

"He'd better not make any suspicious moves—or any *more* suspicious moves—than he has already." Gray released her hand and stuck his own in the pocket of his jacket. "Why doesn't he contact you through the normal channels?"

"He heard what happened to Kiera. He probably thinks someone compromised our mode of communication."

"Someone or Olaf?"

"I guess he'll tell us, won't he?" She tipped her head in Cedar's general direction. "Or he's following us to see if anyone else is following us."

"You're giving me a headache. How much farther is this restaurant?"

"A half a block up and to the right."

They trudged on in silence, Gray throwing discreet glances behind them every few seconds to keep tabs on Cedar. "He's still with us."

"Just as long as nobody else is." She poked his ribs. "You've been so fixated on Cedar, have you been paying attention to the rest of our surroundings? We don't have any other tails, do we?"

"That's why Cedar stuck out. I've been scanning behind us ever since we popped out from between those two buildings. We're still good. Like I said before, maybe they gave up getting to you outside your apartment."

They turned the corner, and Jerrica plucked at Gray's sleeve. "It's up there, on the right, blue awning."

Gray opened the door for her, and she stepped into the noise. Someone would have to be bold to take a shot at them in here—or try to abduct her. Maybe they could enjoy a meal in peace—at least until Cedar got here.

Would he really point the finger at Olaf? She couldn't believe Olaf would ever hurt her, but she hadn't been hurt. That man in the alley had had ample opportunity to knife her. The guy in Washington Square Park had had a clear shot at her. She'd escaped both times, thanks to Gray. But if Gray hadn't been there, would she be dead right now or secreted away somewhere?

She even had an idea of where. She shivered, and Gray entwined his fingers with hers.

He asked, "Are you all right?"

"Hungry and tired. I'll be fine."

The host showed them to a table near the bar. "Is this okay?"

"Yes." Gray pulled out a chair for her and then took the seat facing the door, his back to the bar.

Jerrica leaned in. "You're watching for Cedar?"

"I wanna see his demeanor when he comes through that door. I wanna see his hands."

She ran her tongue around the inside of her dry mouth. "I hope, for his sake, he doesn't do anything stupid."

"You and me both."

Cedar took his time getting there. She and Gray got water, tea and pita bread, and had placed their order before Gray's eyes narrowed.

Jerrica swiveled her head to the side and watched Cedar, his Dodgers baseball cap pulled low on his forehead, navigate his way through the tables on his way to the bar. His hands swung freely at his sides, and he never even glanced their way.

"So far, so good." Gray's eye twitched and he took a gulp of water from his glass. "What's his plan?"

"Your guess is as good as mine, but as long as he doesn't pull out a knife, a gun or a needle, I'm good."

"A needle?" Gray's eyebrows shot up to his tousled hair.

"I think that's how they poisoned Russell. How else? He'd been at school all day. Someone bumped into him and did something—needle, skin poison."

"All Cedar has is a beer."

Jerrica glanced up as the bartender placed a mug in front of Cedar, who then crooked his finger at a waitress. Jerrica dropped her gaze to her iced tea, stirring it with her straw.

Her cautious coworker wanted to keep their connection a secret. Who was she to blow his cover?

When their food came, Jerrica pointed her fork at Gray's lamb kebab. "Let me know what you think."

A waitress approached their table with two beers and tossed down a couple of cocktail napkins. "Compliments of your friend at the bar, but he doesn't want any thanks. That's what he told me to say, anyway."

"Okay, well, thank you, then." Gray curled his fingers around the handle and raised the glass to her before she turned away.

"What does this mean?" Jerrica flicked some foam from the top of the mug.

"The waitress placed an extra napkin on the table, right in front of you." Gray tapped it with his finger. "Take a look at it."

Jerrica pinched the edge of the napkin and turned it over. A black scrawl covered the square. She smoothed her thumb across the paper and read aloud in a low voice. "Be careful. Olaf is back. He must be the one who outed Kiera, all of us. I was being followed."

Jerrica's heart fluttered in her chest, and she gulped in a few breaths. "I'm going to reply."

"Go ahead. He's still at the bar."

Jerrica dipped her hand into her purse, pulled out a pen and put the point to the napkin. It scratched the paper. She shook the pen. "No ink."

She dropped the pen on the table and dug through her purse for another. "This one works. What should I write?"

"Ask him how he knows it's Olaf and why?"

Jerrica scribbled the questions on the napkin and asked their waiter to send over the cocktail waitress.

When the waitress arrived, Jerrica crumpled the napkin in her hand. "Can you please take this back to the bar?"

The waitress rolled her eyes, but she took the napkin from Jerrica and walked back to the bar with her empty tray. She dropped the balled-up paper in front of Cedar and returned to work.

Jerrica tried to concentrate on her food, but her stomach churned. Why would Olaf betray them? It didn't make sense. Had these people bought him off, or had Dreadworm always put their interests first? The thought sickened her even more. She pressed a hand against her belly.

"What's wrong?" Gray shoved a water glass toward her. "You look green."

"I don't feel well." She scooted her chair away from the table. "Watch for Cedar's reply. I'm going to the ladies' room."

Gray stood up when she did, his gaze scanning the room.

"It's okay." She patted his arm. "We know we weren't followed—except by Cedar. I'm just humoring him because I know what it's like to be in a state of paranoia."

She threaded her way through the tables to the hallway to the left of the bar. When she reached the restroom, she went into one of the stalls. At the table, she'd felt nauseous, but getting up and moving had helped. As she ripped off a short length of toilet paper to blow her nose, someone entered the bathroom and she leaned to the side to peer beneath the stall door.

A pair of sensible low-heeled shoes planted themselves in front of the vanity, and Jerrica eased out a breath.

She blew her nose and dropped the tissue into the toilet. As she exited the stall, she traded gazes in the mirror with a middle-aged woman washing her hands.

The woman smiled and rinsed her hands while Jerrica pumped the soap dispenser at the sink next to her.

The woman passed behind her on her way to the paper towels, and Jerrica felt a sharp stab in her side.

As she gasped and spun around, she raised her fist to bash the woman in the face but her limbs turned to warm jelly.

The woman's smile broadened as Jerrica slid to the floor.

Chapter Thirteen

Gray picked up the pen on the table and tapped it against the side of his glass. Maybe Cedar just had a feeling about Olaf and no proof at all. Feelings didn't do them much good.

The pen rattled and Gray wrinkled his brow. He shook the pen again. His pulse ticked up a notch. He pulled the cap from the pen and dragged the point across a napkin, ripping it to shreds.

The blood roared in his ears. He unscrewed the top of the pen and tipped out a black device onto the table. He slammed his fist against the GPS and jumped up.

Out of the corner of his eye, he saw Cedar spin around on the barstool, but Gray didn't have time to explain. He charged toward the restrooms, his heart pounding out of his chest.

Jerrica hadn't been in there long, and he'd seen just one middle-aged woman head into the hallway after her.

Gray slammed his shoulder against the ladies' room door, but it didn't budge. He banged on the door with his fist. "Open up. Jerrica?"

Cedar drew up behind him and panted. "What's wrong?"

"Someone tracked us here. A pen in Jerrica's purse had a GPS device in it."

Cedar cursed. "I knew it. I knew they'd find a way. I knew Olaf would find a way."

Gray kicked the door with his boot. "Open it now."

A woman's voice answered. "Move out of the way, or she's dead."

"Jerrica?" Gray croaked her name from a throat parched with fear. "I want to hear her speak."

"She can't speak."

Gray dug his fingers into his scalp. "Why not? What did you do to her?"

Cedar touched Gray's shoulder and pointed to a wide-eyed woman at the end of the hallway. He called to her. "Sorry, ma'am. Just a little domestic altercation. My sister got tipsy and locked herself in the bathroom."

"Sh-should I get the manager?"

"Not yet. We'll be out of your way soon."

"Move away from the door." The woman hissed from the bathroom. "Or I swear, I'll end it here."

Cedar pulled at Gray's arm. "Give her space so we can see Jerrica—see that she's okay."

Against every instinct in his body, Gray stepped away from the door, his muscles aching from tension.

A click resounded from inside the ladies' room and the door eased open. The woman he'd seen earlier wedged her body against the door and pulled Jerrica's limp form in front of her, placing a gun against her temple. "She's just drugged. We won't hurt her. We just need information. That's what she does, anyway, exposes data. We want her to expose it to us."

Cedar growled behind Gray. "Why has Olaf turned on us?"

"Everyone has a price." The woman's lips tightened. "Now move and nobody gets hurt."

Gray took another step back, his fingers curling around a fake inhaler he'd packed earlier.

Jerrica's abductor inched into the hallway, one hand gripping the gun at Jerrica's head, the other arm wrapped around Jerrica's waist to keep her upright.

Jerrica's lashes fluttered, and she formed an O with her lips as if trying to speak. Thank God she was alive—and Gray had to keep her that way.

The woman began to half-drag, half-carry Jerrica in the other direction, to what must be a back exit.

"Wait!" Gray pulled the inhaler from his pocket. "Jerrica has asthma. She's going to need her inhaler if you want her to live through this. That's what Olaf wants, isn't it? He wants Jerrica to live and if she doesn't, he might stop cooperating with you."

The woman's eyes darted from Cedar, well behind Gray, back to Gray's face. She adjusted Jerrica's body so that it leaned against her own, and then stretched out her left hand. "Put it in my palm. If you grab me or try anything, she's dead."

Gray doubted this woman had authority to shoot to kill, but his hand trembled slightly as he extended his hand holding the fake inhaler. As he leaned in closer, he signaled Cedar behind him to get ready

The woman ducked her head, and Gray tipped up the inhaler and depressed the button on the bottom of the container, releasing tear gas into the woman's face.

He kept his gaze pinned to the gun in her hand and as she gasped and stumbled back, the gun slipped down from Jerrica's head.

Holding his breath, Gray swung his arm, knocking the gun up to the ceiling.

Cedar dropped to the floor and scrambled toward the woman's legs, throwing himself at her knees.

Her body buckled and she squeezed off a shot.

Panic coursed through Gray's body as Jerrica slumped, but when plaster rained down on them, he grabbed her ragdoll-like form and tossed her over one shoulder.

"We can get out the back. You okay?"

His eyes watering, Cedar choked out some response but he kept low and crawled past the flailing woman, now hugging the wall and gasping for breath.

Gray turned left and ran toward the exit sign down the dark hallway, Jerrica's body bouncing on his shoulder.

Cedar reached the door before he did and shoved it open. Cedar staggered into the alley, gulping breaths of air.

A car idling in the darkness shot forward and squealed from the alley.

"There goes the getaway car." Gray pointed to a dumpster. "Behind here for a minute."

They took refuge behind a dumpster, and Gray thumped a coughing Cedar on the back. "Can you breathe?"

"Barely. How's Jerrica?"

"Conscious but out of it. I don't think the gas affected her that much because she wasn't taking deep breaths to begin with." He thumbed up one of her eyelids. "I can see it affected her eyes, though. We need to get out of here before the police show up. At least the lady had a silencer on her gun, so the shot isn't going to cause immediate panic but someone will discover her soon. I don't know what management is going to make of that scene in the hallway, but I don't want to try to explain it."

"That bitch was no lady." Cedar wiped his own eyes with the hem of his T-shirt. "You can't very well stagger through the Lower East Side with a woman over your shoulder without drawing attention to yourself."

"She can walk. Like you said. She's tipsy. Had a little too much to drink." He pointed to the end of the alley. "Go hail a taxi like only a New Yorker can. I'll get Jerrica in a position to walk her out to the street and the cab."

Cedar took off in a sprint. The kid had guts.

Gray slid Jerrica off his body and patted her face. "Jerrica, can you hear me? Can you walk? You're safe now. I've got you."

She moaned and shook her head.

"I know." He steadied her on her feet. Hanging his arm around her shoulders, he propped her up against his side. "Just move your feet, hacker girl. You got this."

He walked and she stumbled beside him, but she was upright.

When he got to the street, his estimation of Cedar rose again. A taxi waited at the curb, its back door flung open.

Gray poured Jerrica onto the bench seat and gave the driver the name of his hotel while sliding in after her.

Cedar stepped back from the curb. "I can see she's gonna be okay with you."

"Oh, no you don't." Gray made a grab for Cedar's arm, but the hacker slipped from his grasp. "You're going to tell us everything you know."

"I don't know anything but what I already told you." Cedar put his finger to his lips. "Find out who brought Olaf in from the cold and you'll have your culprit. I do better on my own."

Cedar plucked the baseball cap from his head, shook out his long hair and flipped up the hood of his sweat-shirt, melting into the crowd.

The driver barked, "Are you done, man?"

"Yeah, yeah." Gray slammed the door. "Get going."

He kept his eye on the back window, but for all he knew Jerrica might have another GPS planted on her person and whoever Olaf was working with could be tracking them right to his hotel.

He'd have to figure that out later. He needed to get some water into Jerrica, keep her awake. But if she'd been poisoned with the same substance that had been running through Russell's veins, she'd need more than water to come around.

The driver pulled up in front of the hotel and met Gray's eyes in the rearview mirror. "She okay? This ain't one of those roofie things, is it?"

"My girlfriend can't hold her booze. She'll be okay." Gray almost tipped the guy extra, but figured that might look too much like hush money. He added twenty percent to the fare and left it at that.

As he stood Jerrica up on the sidewalk, he whispered in her ear. "C'mon, love. You can do this. Let's get to my room. It's not far."

Her chin dropped to her chest and his heart sank, but then she lifted her head and he could've sworn her spine straightened.

As they walked into the hotel, her head lolled against his shoulder but she kept her body erect and stumbled only once or twice. When they got into the elevator, she slumped against him as her knees buckled.

"You're doing fine. We're almost there."

The door opened on his floor, and he poked his head into the hallway, looking both ways. The empty hallway beckoned.

When they stepped out of the elevator, Gray swept Jerrica up in his arms and cradled her against his chest as he strode toward his room.

Once inside, he sat her on the edge of the bed. "Don't lie down, Jerrica. Not yet. Don't go to sleep."

She blinked her red eyes at him, and he dove for the

credenza where two five-dollar bottles of water waited. He cracked open one bottle and sat beside her on the bed.

"Drink this, all of it, even if you don't want to, even if it makes you feel sick. It won't help if you throw up because I doubt she gave you something to eat or drink, so the poison's not in your stomach. I'm thinking maybe the water can dilute its effectiveness in your blood stream, though."

Whether she understood anything he'd just said, she parted her lips, anyway, and he tipped the bottle into her mouth. Some of the liquid ran out the side of her mouth and down the slender column of her throat, but her Adam's apple bobbed as she gulped down what she could.

When she finished the first bottle, he put her to work on the second. She gulped even more of this one down, gagging a few times.

He smoothed her hair back from her damp brow. "How are you? Can you talk?"

She nodded. "Hard to move."

"Maybe she gave you a super-accelerated muscle relaxer, something to make you compliant and keep you quiet, but not to knock you out." He squeezed her knee. "I knew she wasn't going to shoot you. We surprised her. You weren't in there that long, and she probably figured she had time to drag you out the back door to the car waiting in the alley."

"How?" She dug her fist into one eye where the gas had irritated her.

He jogged into the bathroom and soaked a washcloth with cool water. He squeezed it out, folded it into a square and returned to Jerrica.

"I'm going to hold this against your eye. Is it stinging?"

"Uh-huh. How?"

"It was the pen, Jerrica."

She tilted her head to the side, and he pulled the pieces of the pen, minus the GPS, from his shirt pocket and bobbled them in his palm. "The pen you pulled out first, the one that didn't work, had a GPS device in it. You know who put it there, right? They've never been able to track our whereabouts before—not until we ran into Olaf at Dreadworm. He slipped it into your purse when he gave you that hug. I should've never let him near you."

A tear rolled down her cheek from her other eye, but he couldn't tell if it was from the news of Olaf's betrayal or the tear gas he'd sprayed at her abductor.

She dashed away the tear with the back of her hand. "Must've been. Cedar?"

"He's okay. Took off after we got you into the taxi."

She smoothed her hand across the bedspread. "Your hotel?"

"Yeah. Ironic, isn't it? Just when I moved my clothes to your place, I'm back here." He made a half-turn to the credenza. "Coffee? Do you think coffee would help?"

"I do." She switched the washcloth to the other eye.

He measured out the coffee for a single cup and sat beside Jerrica on the bed while it brewed. "Can you tell me what happened in there? Did she say anything to you?"

"Nothing. Said more in the hallway." She cleared her throat. "Came in after me. Washed her hands. Passed behind me. Jabbed me with a needle."

"Unbelievable. Then she planned to walk you out of there and into the waiting car."

"It's Olaf."

The words from Cedar's chalk message took on a whole new meaning now.

"She told us as much in the hallway. Said he didn't want

to hurt you, just wants you to stop doing what you're doing." He toyed with the edge of the bedspread. "You could."

She dropped the washcloth from her eye. "No. Major Denver. The terrorist attack. It's real."

"I could take it from here. I have the decoded transmissions. Maybe I could get my father to turn it over to the CIA for further analysis."

"CIA?" She sniffed. "Could be them. Could be someone there."

"I know." He gathered the bedspread in his fist. "This whole thing would've been unimaginable to me six months ago, until I saw how Denver was being railroaded. Even with proof that the initial emails implicating him were false, the narrative about him working with terrorists continued."

"To you." She closed one eye in what could've been a wink.

"What does that mean?"

"Unimaginable to you—not me."

"I know." He jumped up when the buzzer went off on the coffee pot. He slid the glass cup from the coffee maker and wiped the rim with a napkin. He dumped a few of the little creamers into the dark liquid and stirred it with a stick. It would probably be more effective black, but Jerrica wouldn't touch a cup of coffee without a bunch of cream in it.

He brought it to her and slid to the floor next to the bed. "We're going to have to return to your place and get your laptop. Then I think we'd better leave for my folks' place. Do you think Olaf will try to break in? Does he know where you hide your computer?"

She slurped the coffee. "He'll know that I have a backup. Won't do any good to take what I have in my apartment."

"I'm sorry it's Olaf." He circled her ankle lightly with his fingers. "I know he means…something to you."

"He fed my paranoia for sure." She dropped her lashes. "And…"

He waited. When she didn't continue, he glanced up at her. "How are you doing?"

"I'm feeling more in control of my faculties."

"You're talking better. She gave you just enough to incapacitate you to get you out of that restaurant." He unzipped her boot and pulled it from her foot. "I should've never let you out of my sight."

"We were *both* making fun of Cedar for being so careful." She swirled her coffee. "I think I let my guard down because I was with you. You make me feel safe."

"Yeah, and I failed." He stripped off her sock, and she wiggled her toes at him.

"We had no idea I had a GPS in my purse."

"We should've guessed something like that might happen. We were already suspicious of Olaf. Cedar left that message, and there he was in the Dreadworm office. I should've never let him near you." He removed her second boot and sock. "Do you think he was in there trying to disrupt your and Amit's programs?"

"Probably, but even he can't do that. Even if he takes a hammer to the computer, that program is still running somewhere. He can destroy the hardware, but not the process."

"I'll bet he's cursing all the precautions he put in place when first establishing Dreadworm." Gray rubbed his chin. "What's his endgame? I'm sure he wouldn't mind bringing down the government."

"Maybe. I couldn't tell you." Jerrica swung her feet up onto the bed and crossed her legs. "I knew he was no fan, but to be a party to killing innocent people? I didn't see that one coming. Still can't get my mind around it."

"He had Kiera killed, or at least allowed it to happen."

"Had Amit tortured, poisoned Russell."

"And encouraged and abetted your kidnapping—three times."

"Should I meet with him and find out what he's doing?"

He sprang up from the floor and took her empty coffee cup from her. "Absolutely not. We know what he's doing—working with government insiders and terrorists to plot an attack to undermine this country."

She fell back on the bed, her legs hanging off the edge. "I'm so tired. Do you think it's safe for me to sleep now?"

"Sleep?" He stretched out next to her and slipped his hand beneath her shirt, flattening it against her belly. "I don't recommend it."

She released a sigh and yanked her shirt over her head. "I suddenly have all my senses back, but I want to make sure touch is still working."

She unbuttoned his jeans, and tucked her hand inside his briefs.

He sucked in a breath. "Can we try taste now?"

He rolled on top of her and kissed her sweet, coffee-flavored mouth. "I don't know about you, but my taste is just fine. Only problem is, it makes me want more and more."

His phone, stashed in his shirt pocket, buzzed, tickling his chest. He plucked it out, intending to toss it on the bedside table...until he saw his father's number.

He held the display in front of Jerrica's face. "I'd better take this. It might be about the plane."

"Go for it. I'm going rinse out my mouth since neither one of us has a toothbrush here." She shimmied out from under him.

Gray answered the phone. "Hey, Dad. I booked the plane for tomorrow. Is there a problem?"

"No problem. I just wanted to let you know that Keith will be piloting tomorrow. Randy got called away unexpectedly. You know Keith?"

"I don't think so. Always flew with Randy."

"Keith's reliable. Good pilot. Navy man."

"I'll take your word for it." Gray grabbed a few pillows and shoved them up against the headboard, and then sank against them. "I have a question for you."

"Fire away." The clinking of ice carried over the phone, and Gray hoped his old man hadn't had enough drinks to fog his mind.

"What do you know about Olaf from Dreadworm?"

Silence answered him on the other end of the phone. Had he caught his father at the tail end of one too many Scotches?

"Dad?"

"Why are you asking about him now? Did you see something on the news?"

"The news?" Gray sat upright. "Olaf's in the news?"

"Not yet. That was the agreement, anyway. He shouldn't be in the news, but that's just it. You can't trust a guy like that."

"Agreement? What are you talking about, Dad?" Gray raised his eyebrows at Jerrica, who sashayed back into the room wearing a black bra and panties.

Sensing his mood, she yanked a white robe from a hanger in the closet and stuffed her arms into the sleeves as she sat on the edge of the bed.

His father's voice came through the line, roughened by the whiskey. "Why are you asking about Olaf?"

"I heard something about him. I'd rather not say how. You first."

"Dammit. If he went to the press and defaulted on the arrangement, I'll have his ass in federal prison so fast his teeth will rattle in that big head of his."

"Agreements. Arrangements. What the hell is going on?"

"As you already seem to know something and you have top secret clearance, I suppose I can tell you."

"And I'm your son." Gray rolled his eyes at Jerrica.

"The government made a deal with Olaf to allow him to come out of hiding and back to the US."

Gray's mouth got dry and he ran his tongue over his teeth before answering. "What kind of deal?"

Jerrica bumped his shoulder and he put a finger to his lips. The booze had loosened his father's lips, making him uncharacteristically chatty but if he knew he had an audience besides Gray, he'd clam up.

His father coughed. "He's going to stop hacking government databases and turn over everything he has right now."

"You're kidding." Gray's pulse thumped erratically in his temple, giving him a headache.

"I am not."

With Cedar's words ringing in his ears, Gray jabbed two fingers against the side of his head. "Who approved that, Dad?"

"I did."

Chapter Fourteen

Gray's face drained of color, and he white-knuckled his phone. His blue eyes blazed for a second, kindling in his pale face.

Jerrica grabbed his thigh, digging her nails into the denim of his jeans. She mouthed the word *what*.

He choked out one word. "You?"

His lips tightened as he listened to whatever his father had to say on the other end of the line. "Okay, okay. We'll talk then."

Gray ended the call and sat motionless, cupping the phone between his two hands.

"What is it? What did he say?"

Gray swallowed as if he had a lump lodged in his throat. "Olaf is back in the US courtesy of the US government."

"What?" Jerrica crossed her hands over her heart. "How? Why?"

"He made some deal with the government that he would halt all hacking activities and turn over any active projects. In exchange, I guess, he avoids federal prison."

"Wait." Jerrica pinched the bridge of her nose. "Do you think that's why Olaf is trying to stop me?"

"If that were the case, why wouldn't he just tell you?

Ask you all to stop your activities so he could return and avoid prosecution."

"Because he knows we wouldn't do it—even to save him." She rubbed his leg. "But it's more than that, isn't it? You looked kinda sick there for a minute."

He stopped fiddling with his phone and put it down on the nightstand. "It's my father, Jerrica."

"What's your father?"

"He's the one who approved the agreement with Olaf." Gray punched the pillow beside him, leaving a fist-sized indentation. "Cedar and I both agreed that the person responsible for Olaf's return was probably the one behind the scramble to shut down your investigation."

Jerrica's jaw dropped. "Your father? You think Senator Grayson Elliot Prescott the Third is actively working against the US government, setting up Major Rex Denver and plotting a terrorist attack? No way."

A little color washed back into Gray's face. "Why else would he authorize this…clemency for Olaf? He hates the guy."

"Did he give you an explanation?" She reclined against the pillows next to Gray and hooked one leg over his thigh.

"He said we'd discuss it when I got home, which is tomorrow, by the way."

"It could be anything, any reason, Gray. You're jumping to conclusions—to the worst conclusion." She reached over and pinched his chin. "Give your father a chance to explain what happened."

He caught her hand and kissed her fingertips. "If the queen of conspiracy theories is willing to give him a chance, I guess I can, too. What is going on? Do you think Olaf is so desperate to deliver on his promise to the government, he'd go to any measures to stop his own employees from getting to the bottom of these secret communications?"

"Doesn't make sense. Olaf made a deal with the government. You'd think he'd be eager to unearth this plot and hand it to the FBI on a silver platter. What better way to get into their good graces? Instead, he wants to make sure it stays secret…and on track. But—" she held up one finger "—if someone in government, someone responsible for this database wants Olaf to put an end to our nosing around, maybe this person offered him a deal. Come in from the cold with no repercussions but make sure your people back off."

"Then he should've just asked." Gray rolled out of the bed. "He had Kiera killed, Jerrica. There's something very wrong with Olaf, but by tomorrow he's not going to be able to get to you."

Jerrica shrugged out of the hotel robe and crawled into bed to wait for Gray while he rinsed out his mouth.

When he slid into bed next to her, his naked body cool to her touch, she wrapped herself around him and got lost in his kisses.

Little did Gray know, Olaf would always be able to get to her.

THE FOLLOWING MORNING, they couldn't wait to get out of the hotel to make sure nobody had broken into her place. She'd been preparing for her security to be breached for as long as she'd worked for Dreadworm, but she'd never dealt with an enemy that actually had the founder of Dreadworm on its side.

She finally let out a breath after quickly checking her apartment and retrieving her laptop from its hiding place. "Nothing's been disturbed."

"What do you think Olaf's next move will be?" Gray

wheeled her packed bag next to his by the front door. "I think we should be prepared for the worst, Jerrica."

"The worst?" She wedged a carry-on bag on top of her suitcase. "He's not going to kill me, Gray. I think we've established that."

"I'm talking about blackmail."

Jerrica's hand jerked and her bag slipped to the floor. "Blackmail? What do you mean?"

"You work for Dreadworm. What you do is illegal. He just might make that deal to save his skin and keep the data hidden—report you to the authorities."

Her hands shook as she reached for her carry-on. "Let him try. If I'm going to be exposed, anyway, I'll reveal the whole sorry mess. Let the CIA figure it out, and if they do have a mole that's their problem."

"Let's see what my father has to say first." Gray clasped the back of his neck. "God, I hope my father's not involved in this."

"From what you told me about the senator, I doubt it, Gray. Think about it. He knows this whole plot is centered around Denver. Do you really believe he'd do anything to harm Major Denver? Anything that could have ramifications for you and your Delta Force team?"

"You reassuring me about my family is a switch." He kissed her hard on the mouth. "Let's get out of here."

They took a taxi to a commuter airfield near the airport and, like magic, Senator Grayson Prescott's private jet awaited them.

They climbed the stairs to the plane and Gray poked his head inside the cockpit. "Keith? I'm Gray Prescott."

"Mr. Prescott." The pilot plucked off his headset and turned in the small space to shake Gray's hand. "Nice to meet you."

"Call me Gray." He tipped his head to the side. "This is Jerrica. She's traveling with us."

"Your father mentioned two passengers." Keith took Jerrica's hand in his. "Welcome aboard, ma'am."

Jerrica craned her neck over her shoulder to take in the cabin of the plane with its reclining seats, television screens and wet bar. "Wow, this is nice. Not what I expected."

"You two sit back and relax, and I'll have you in DC in no time."

When a woman in slacks and a blouse boarded after them and Gray stood to give her a hug, Jerrica's mouth dropped open. "You're kidding me. We have our own private flight attendant?"

Gray laughed. "My father is accustomed to certain amenities. Jerrica, this is Camille."

Jerrica shook hands with the other woman. "Is this an easy gig?"

"The best." Camille put a finger to her lips. "Don't tell anyone about it. I don't want Senator Prescott to get any ideas about hiring anyone else. Do you want anything before we take off?"

"I hate to be demanding, but I'd like a coffee." Jerrica reached for her seatbelt. "I can get it myself."

"Are you trying to put me out of work?" Camille winked and stashed her bag in one of the cabinets. "Cream, sugar? What about you, Gray?"

"Jerrica will have hers with lots of cream. I'll take mine black and if you have any of those breakfast sandwiches on board, we'll take a couple of those."

"I'll get the coffees, but you'll have to wait until we're in the air for the food. Those are Captain Keith's rules. Captain Keith, you want some coffee?"

Keith gave her a thumbs-up. "Yes, please."

Once they had their coffee, the plane took off. When it steadied and reached its cruising altitude, Camille brought them warm breakfast sandwiches, which Gray had ordered for her without meat.

As she bit into the English muffin, it crunched right before the melted cheese hit her tongue. She closed her eyes. "Mmm, remind me why I don't have a private plane."

"Because you're too stubborn to spend the money sitting in the bank." Gray raised an eyebrow in her direction. "Do you have enough in there to buy and maintain your own jet?"

She licked some cheese off her fingers. "I have no idea how much this all costs, but probably not."

When she finished her sandwich, Jerrica rested her head against the window and stared at the endless blue. Everything in her life felt far removed up here—all her worries, all her problems.

And she had plenty of them.

They touched down in DC after the hour-long flight, and Gray's father's car and driver met them at the airport.

In the backseat of the car, Jerrica smoothed her hand across the leather cushion and whispered, "Is this all courtesy of the American taxpayer?"

"No." Gray took her hand and drew it into his lap. "My father doesn't mix his private business with his government service, does he, Lawrence?"

The driver tapped the rearview mirror. "No, sir. I believe your father is the last honest man in Washington."

Almost a half hour later, Jerrica ducked her head to get a better view of the palatial house as the car rolled through the front security gates. "I guess honesty does pay."

Gray shrugged, as uncomfortable with his family's

wealth as she was with her multi-million-dollar settlement from the government.

When the car came to a stop, Jerrica combed her fingers through her hair and tugged her long sleeve over the tattoo that trailed onto the back of her hand, ending with a blue bird.

Gray squeezed her knee. "You don't have to do anything different, Jerrica. They'll like you just the way you are…or not. Doesn't matter to me."

"I know." She turned her head and kissed the side of his neck. "Big house."

"Yeah." He pushed open the back door before Lawrence could get out and open it for them. He did let Lawrence get their bags out of the trunk, as Gray waved at the man and woman standing on the porch.

Jerrica recognized Senator Prescott from the news—a handsome man going silver at the temples, the erect bearing of a soldier. Gray would look just like him someday.

The trim, stylish woman by Senator Prescott's side couldn't wait. She hustled off the porch and threw her arms around Gray. "It's so good to have you home. Just wish you had come straight here instead of taking a detour to New York."

"I had a good reason for that detour, Mom." He disentangled himself from her arms. "This is Jerrica West. Jerrica, this is my mother, Connie Prescott."

Gray's mom gave her a surprisingly firm handshake for such a delicate-looking woman. "Nice to meet you, Jerrica. Of course, Gray told us about you…before, so it's wonderful that you two reconnected."

As Jerrica returned the older woman's grip, she searched her face for signs of artifice, but the smile on Connie's lightly colored lips reached her sparkling blue eyes. Gray resembled his father without a doubt, but he had his mother's eyes.

"I'm so happy to finally meet you. I hope we're not inconveniencing you by dropping by like this."

Connie waved a hand behind her. "Look at this place. Does it look like it would be an inconvenience to house two more people?"

"Well, no."

"C'mon." Connie linked one arm with Gray's and the other with Jerrica's. "Time to meet the old man and don't worry, his bark's a lot worse than his bite."

As the three of them approached the man on the porch, Jerrica took a breath and dropped her shoulders. How bad could it be?

"Dad." Gray shook his father's hand, gripping him by the shoulder at the same time in a modified version of a hug. "This is Jerrica West."

The senator's eyes had lit up as they rested on his son's face, but the lines at the corners of those eyes deepened as he shifted his gaze to Jerrica.

She swallowed and stiffened her spine. "It's a pleasure to meet you, Senator Prescott."

"You can call me Scotty. Everyone does."

His handshake nearly brought her to her knees, but she gritted her teeth and gave as good as she got.

The corner of Gray's mouth lifted as his gaze darted between her and his father. "What is this, a stare-down? You can let go of Jerrica's hand, Dad."

He did, but he didn't release her from his laser-like focus.

"You know, if my son marries you he's going to have a lot of explaining to do on the campaign trail about your background and your connection to that business in New Mexico."

Connie smacked her husband's arm. "Scotty."

"That business in New Mexico? That was my family."

"Of course it was." Connie put her arm around Jerrica's waist. "Let's go inside and have some lunch, unless you want to go to your room and change."

Connie glanced at the hole in the knee of Jerrica's jeans and the different colored laces of her square-toed black boots. "N-not that you need to."

Jerrica climbed two steps and then turned to Scotty, her nose almost touching his. "And Gray has no intention of going into politics, so there's no need to worry about something that ain't gonna happen."

Scotty inclined his head as a muscle ticked at the corner of his mouth.

Gray threw back his head and laughed. "This is going to be a fun weekend."

Connie leaned her head against Gray's shoulder briefly and in a low voice said, "You have no idea."

Jerrica exchanged a look with Gray over his mother's head, but he just puckered his lips and aimed a kiss in her direction.

At least Gray had her back in this lion's den, but it could only get better after that rocky start…couldn't it?

Lunch turned out to be more informal than she'd expected in this house where she'd already caught sight of a cook, housekeeper and gardener.

Connie bustled around the kitchen pulling dishes out of the fridge and setting out cutting boards heavy with meats and cheeses. She stood back from the table, hands on her hips, surveying the feast. "Don't worry, Jerrica. Gray told us you're a vegetarian, and we have plenty of choices for you. I'm heading that way myself."

No drama marred their lunch, as Scotty peppered Gray with questions about his previous mission and Connie kept Jerrica entertained with a steady stream of anecdotes from her stint living in Manhattan and working in the fashion industry.

At the end of lunch, Scotty leaned over to Gray and whispered something in his ear.

Gray drew back. "You don't have to whisper, Dad. Anything you have to show me, you can show Jerrica—unless you're trying to hide something from Mom."

Connie raised her hands. "Nope. I know everything there is to know and couples shouldn't have secrets from each other, so you'd better bring Jerrica along with you."

Gray's eyebrows slammed over his nose. "Now you really have me going. What the hell are you two talking about?"

Bracing his hands on his knees, Scotty said, "This is more than just a secret, Connie."

"In thirty-three years of marriage, you never kept anything from me, Scotty. If you don't take Jerrica with you, I'll tell her anyway."

"When it comes to stubbornness, you took after your mother." Scotty jabbed a finger toward Connie.

Connie gave a genteel snort that flared the nostrils of her nose. "And when it comes to impatience, he takes after you. He's practically jumping out of his skin now, so you'd better show him…and Jerrica."

All this talk of revealing secrets had Jerrica wiping her damp palms on her jeans, and she followed Gray and his father out of the kitchen with a dry mouth.

Connie stayed behind, and Scotty kept his lips sealed as he led them through the massive great room to a set of French doors leading out to a patio area in full spring bloom.

The heady scent of the flowers almost made her dizzy, and Jerrica grabbed onto Gray's hand for support.

He squeezed her hand and nuzzled her ear. "I have no idea what this is all about, but I think my dad actually likes you despite your parentage. I think he was expecting you to be different."

Jerrica jerked back. "You're kidding."

"Not at all." Gray glanced up as they walked across the pool deck toward a grassy expanse. "Are you taking us to the back house?"

His father grunted in reply but never broke his stride.

"You have another house back here?"

"It's like a little two-bedroom cottage. My sister lived there for a while when she moved back here after college, and various employees have camped out there. Maybe they're giving it to us as a wedding gift and to keep you under their eye."

She jabbed him in the ribs even while her heart raced at his mention of a wedding. She hadn't even said *yes* yet. He hadn't even asked. She'd have to stay out of prison first.

As the little house emerged from a copse of trees, Scotty halted on the stone path that led to it. He dug into his pocket and pulled out a set of keys. He dangled them at Gray. "You can go on alone from here. I'll be at the house if anyone needs anything."

Gray cocked his head and snatched the keys from his father. "This had better be good after this cloak-and-dagger business."

His father pivoted away as only a military man could and marched back across the lawn.

Gray tossed the keys in the air and caught them. "Should we start guessing what's in there?"

"No. The cloak-and-dagger stuff, as you put it, has made me even more anxious."

When they reached the door of the house, Gray tried

the handle first and then shoved the key home in the lock. He thrust open the door and took one step over the threshold, shouting, "Come out with your hands up."

The click of a gun safety from behind the door prompted Gray to grab Jerrica and shove her behind him.

A bearded man, long hair brushing his shoulders, leveled a weapon at them as he stepped from behind the door. His dark eyes widened for a second, and the hand with the gun fell to his side.

"Is that an order, soldier?"

Chapter Fifteen

With the adrenaline still pumping through his body, Gray launched himself at his commander and threw his arms around the shoulders that weren't as broad as they had been.

"Rex! Major! I mean, sir."

Denver smacked him on the back a few times. "In the flesh."

"What are you doing here?"

"Probably the same thing you are." Denver shoved him aside. "Are you going to introduce me to the lady? I already know she's the infamous Jerrica West, and she's probably gonna save my life."

"Jerrica—" Gray circled his fingers around Jerrica's wrist and pulled her forward "—this is Major Rex Denver. Major, this is Jerrica West, Dreadworm hacker extraordinaire."

Denver took Jerrica's hand in both of his. "You can call me Rex—you both can, for now. I'm sorry this whole mess has put your life in danger, Jerrica."

"It's not your fault, Rex. Amit, my coworker, and I had already stumbled onto this before Gray showed up and we even had a clue what it all meant. If Gray hadn't come to New York, explained everything and protected us, I'm not sure where we'd all be right now."

"How close are you to figuring out the code?"

"We figured out the first level of the code, thanks to the wheel you sent Gray." Jerrica tapped her index finger against her temple. "But without understanding the secondary code—names, places, and so on—I'm not sure we can get much more out of it. We need to turn it over to someone who can decipher it, but I'm afraid to step forward, afraid to explain how I got the communications in the first place."

"Which is why you're here, right?" Denver raised his brows at Gray. "I'm assuming that's why you came to visit your parents. Having this code is not going to do you much good in Manhattan."

"That explains what we're doing here, but what the hell are *you* doing here? How'd you get into the country?"

"It's a long story and telling it would put too many people at risk, but I had to come in. I had to trust someone—other than you guys. Senator Prescott's on the Armed Services Committee, and, well, he's your dad." Denver studied the gun in his hand before shoving it in the back of his waistband. "I'm surprised nobody went to him before this."

"We didn't know who we could trust, if we could trust the people around him. You know my father—" Gray saluted. "By the book. I didn't even know if he would believe our story about an insider, a mole in our own government."

"I understand, but I think we have enough proof now. Cam was able to expose as fakes the initial emails that pointed to me. Asher figured out he was brainwashed at a government-run medical facility and used to implicate me. Joe put a stop to the lie that I had anything to do with that bombing in Syria. Logan and that young marine's sister were able to verify that something was amiss at the embassy outpost in Nigeria and Hunter was able to ID the terrorist group behind it all." Denver swiped the back of his hand across his nose. "You guys did good. You did more than I expected."

"We weren't going to let it stand, sir... Rex. We weren't going to sit by and allow others to smear your name."

"But it's beyond me, isn't it?" He leveled a finger at Jerrica. "This young lady right here can verify that fact— a terrorist attack on US soil, one that I got word about, one that I had started investigating with my sources in the field. I only had bits and pieces, but you tapped into the whole plan."

"Tapped into it but can't figure it out." Jerrica waved a hand behind her. "Do you think Scotty can help us with the rest?"

"Scotty?" Denver quirked an eyebrow.

"Oh, yeah." Jerrica crossed her fingers. "Me and him are like this."

Denver's laugh rumbled in his chest. "He's a tough nut, but he'll do what's right. He'll always do what's right, like you, Jerrica. Isn't that what Dreadworm's all about? Doing the right thing? Transparency?"

Jerrica's body stiffened beside him, and Gray draped an arm across her shoulders. "It looks like Olaf, Dreadworm's founder, has had a change of heart. He's been setting up his own staff, including Jerrica, to keep them from revealing the transmissions they uncovered."

"Is he working with the terrorists? The government?" Denver clasped both of his hands on the back of his neck. "The terrorists and some members of government are one and the same, aren't they?"

"M-my father was responsible for allowing Olaf back into the country. He already told me that Olaf was offered immunity and free passage back to the US in exchange for calling off Dreadworm, but Jerrica and I know he's working with someone else to keep the transmissions under wraps. One of Jerrica's coworkers at Dreadworm implied that whoever let him back in was the government mole."

Denver tugged on the end of his long beard. "Jerrica's coworker doesn't know much about how government works. Senator Prescott may have given the final order, but he didn't make that decision on his own. Hell, he probably wasn't in favor of the decision. We'll have to ask him what the official reason was for allowing Olaf back in without facing ramifications and who suggested it—that could be our mole."

Denver circled the room once. "What's the plan? You're going to crash your parents' big Memorial Day party with all the movers and shakers?"

"I'm going to be the bait." Jerrica raised her hand. "We think at least one of the government plotters will be in attendance. We think he...or she...will make a move once he sees me and Gray here, figuring that we either turned over the communications or are planning to do so."

"And if they don't make a move? If they play it cool?" Denver swept his hair back from his face and tucked it behind one ear.

"Then we'll make *our* move." Gray clenched his teeth. "One way or the other, this ends this weekend."

BACK AT THE main house in one of the many spare bedrooms, Gray stretched out on the bed. "I'm glad he's back, safe."

"He's not safe yet. Do you think he'll be okay hiding out here?"

"Nobody even knows whether Major Denver is dead or alive. I'm sure nobody suspects he's stashed away at a US senator's house. You heard him—my father even has extra security on the property, which won't look odd considering he's going to be hosting half of the government here in a few days."

"Is it going to be the good half or the bad half?"

"We've made progress for you to admit there *is* a good half." He patted the bed beside him. "You don't need to pace around the room. We're safe here."

Jerrica sank down next to him, but kept her feet firmly on the floor. "If we turn over the transmissions to your father, what's he going to do with them and will I get in trouble for having them?"

"My father wouldn't take any action against you, but it might be out of his hands."

"That's what worries me." She leaned back and rested her head on his stomach. "I need to crack the final piece that leads me to the computer generating the orders, and we need a date, time and location for this attack. I know it's in the reams of data I have. Someone just needs to make sense of it."

Gray massaged her temples. "We're close. It's going to be okay, Jerrica."

"There's still so much I don't understand about Olaf's involvement. He turned on Dreadworm to, what? Get back into the country and avoid prosecution? That doesn't seem like enough of a payoff to me."

"That's why I think it's more than that." He flattened the line between Jerrica's eyes with the pad of his thumb. "I think he's involved in the plot. It's his ultimate way of getting back at the government, the government he's been at war with for years."

"I suppose you're right." She rolled her head to the side to look into his eyes. "Maybe I can get to him. Maybe I can convince him to tell me who he's working with.

He can still get his immunity if he starts playing for the other side."

"I don't want you anywhere near him, Jerrica. We don't know what his motives are and even though you had a close relationship with him…once, he seems to have forgotten about that." He brushed the back of his hand across her cheek. "Come on. I'll show you the rest of the house before the hordes descend for the party."

"Hordes of politicians and government officials?" Jerrica rolled from the bed and flipped back her hair. "What could possibly go wrong?"

MEMORIAL DAY DAWNED with sunshine and promise. For the occasion, Jerrica shunned her customary black in favor of a colorful skirt and poppy-red top. A pair of sandals replaced the black boots, and she'd even had a pedicure the day before.

As she stood in front of the full-length mirror in the bathroom, wiggling her red toes, she smoothed the skirt over her thighs. If she had to come out as a Dreadworm hacker and get taken into federal custody, at least she'd try to look innocent.

Gray appeared behind her, wearing a pair of board shorts with the American flag emblazoned across them and a blue T-shirt that matched his eyes. Those eyes met hers in the mirror.

"You look…pretty, but don't think you have to change your style to fit in with these people."

"That's not it. First of all, it's too warm to wrap up in black jeans and boots." She stroked on some mascara and blinked her eyes. "Secondly, if I'm going down, I'm not going to look the outlaw part as they take me away in cuffs."

Gray rubbed her arms. "Nobody is going to take you away in handcuffs."

"Really?" She smacked the tube of mascara down on the vanity to her left. "Because it's time, Gray. I can't make any more progress on the code by myself. We have to turn it over to someone who can, to someone who can stop this terrorist attack, exonerate Major Denver and bring these rogue officials to justice. It's time for me to place my trust in the process."

He turned her around to face him and lightly kissed her lipsticked mouth. "Can you trust me, too? You're almost family. My father's going to do everything in his power to protect you—and as you've pointed out many times before, my father has a lot of power."

She snorted and then dabbed her nose with the tissue crumpled in her hand.

Gray swept her hair from her shoulder and pressed a kiss against her bare skin. "Let's pay another visit to Denver before we wrestle with the snakes at the party."

After a brisk walk, they arrived at the cottage. Denver opened the door before they could knock.

"I saw you coming." He snapped the door closed behind them and locked it, even though private security roamed the grounds. "Any news?"

Jerrica nibbled on her bottom lip. "I'm going to have Gray's dad point me in the direction of the most sympathetic FBI or CIA officer, and I'm going to come clean."

"I thought you'd come to that conclusion." Denver tipped his head toward Gray. "Do you agree?"

"I think Jerrica will be safer in federal custody—if that's the way it goes—than dodging terrorists and government insiders."

"Seems that we'll both have to put our faith in others,

Jerrica." Denver dragged his fingers through his long hair. "We're both on the line here."

"You haven't actually done anything wrong, though." She drove a thumb into her chest. "I have."

"I went AWOL, off the grid. That's not allowed for a soldier, no matter what the circumstances." Denver held up a glass of water to the window and peered into it as if looking into a crystal ball.

"What do you see in there?" Gray pinged the glass with his finger.

"Help. Reinforcements." Denver winked. "They're on the way. I can feel it."

"Well, you've been lucky so far." Jerrica squeezed the major's biceps. "I'm gonna stick with you and maybe some of it will rub off on me."

Gray rolled his eyes. "You're talking about Major Denver here. No luck involved. However he survived, however he got here, it had nothing to do with luck and everything to do with training and skill…and maybe a little badassery, and you possess all of those qualities, hacker girl, especially that last one."

"I got here because of you." She fluttered her lashes at him. "Plain and simple."

They all jumped at the knock on the door.

Gray peeked through the blinds. "It's my father."

"Then you'd better let him in. He does own the place." Denver strode past them and threw open the door. "Join the party, Scotty."

The senator's gaze darted to each face. "It's about time someone invited me to this party and told me what the hell is going on under my own roof."

Jerrica squared her shoulders and stepped in front of Gray's father. "I work for Dreadworm, and my coworker and I hacked into a clandestine database connected to the CIA's. We uncovered a plot involving an attack using sarin gas and blaming Major Denver, all engineered by dark forces within the government. We need help deciphering the code to find out the who, the when and the where."

Jerrica held her breath as Scotty took it all in with an unfathomable expression on his face. He finally blew out a breath and said, "It's what we suspected."

Denver and Gray erupted at the same time, talking over each other until Scotty held up one hand. "Not all of it, we didn't know all of it. I didn't know my son's girlfriend worked for Dreadworm and I didn't know about this database, but we've been receiving communiqués, threats from someone within the government to release certain prisoners, to take certain steps and approve certain agreements with countries that are all in our worst interests."

"Threats?" Gray rested his hands on Jerrica's hips.

He must've sensed she was about to keel over after her outburst.

Scotty dipped his chin to his chest. "Threatened as in, 'do these things or else.'"

"Or else what?" Denver wedged his hip against a table, crossing his arms. "Or else they release the sarin gas?"

"You got it, although we didn't know it was sarin. They threatened the leadership of the CIA, the FBI, the president himself."

"Was Olaf part of that deal?" Gray pinched Jerrica's waist.

"He was. The FBI has been working on several leads to track down who's behind this plan, using information unearthed by your Delta Force team. I know they believed their efforts to clear Major Denver were going nowhere, but we've had to be as secretive as the other guys. We don't know who to trust." Scotty leveled a finger in Jerrica's direction. "But we've never had computer exchanges between these people before."

Jerrica put a hand to her throat. "I have everything on my laptop, and my laptop is here. I-I can turn it over right now, if you want. The sooner the better."

"We'll have to wait until after the party." Scotty jerked a thumb over his shoulder. "The guests have already started arriving, and we don't want to alert anyone."

"I have a feeling Jerrica's presence is going to be an alert to someone. If anyone who's part of the plot attends this shindig, he or she might already know who Jerrica is."

"Let 'em try doing something in my house to my future daughter-in-law." Scotty's eyebrows formed a ferocious V over his nose, causing Jerrica to quake in her sandals and she wasn't even the target.

In fact, Senator Grayson Prescott wanted to protect her—his future daughter-in-law.

"Now let's get out there and play nice, or your mother's going to have my head on one of those silver platters currently displaying hors d'oeuvres too pretty to eat."

Scotty crooked his arm and motioned to Jerrica. She grasped his elbow, and Gray took her arm on the other side and brushed his lips against her ear. "I told you he liked you."

Jerrica floated into the party between the two Graysons. Gray's father hadn't called for her head when she'd made her big announcement. Maybe he could keep her safe—like son, like father.

Connie cut a path through her guests, who were already imbibing mimosas and Bloody Marys and selecting appetizers from the trays artfully deployed across the lawn, making a beeline for their little group, her fine features alight with fire.

She started speaking before she even reached them, her arms flung out to her sides. "I can't believe he had the nerve."

"Uh-oh." Scotty squeezed Jerrica's arm. "Someone must've brought a lady other than his wife or decided to wear white shoes."

"Can't be that. Memorial Day is when you're finally allowed to wear white shoes—if you really want to." Gray grabbed one of his mother's restless hands but she twisted away.

"You're both so funny." She shook a finger at her husband. "But you're not going to be laughing when I tell you what happened."

A murmur swept through the guests, rising and then falling to a whisper, the sound causing the hair on the back of Jerrica's neck to stand on end.

Scotty pinned his gaze to where the crowd parted and then spluttered. "Is the man out of his mind?"

Jerrica stood on her tiptoes to see the commotion. Her blood, racing through veins, turned ice cold as her eyes met the light blue ones of Olaf.

Chapter Sixteen

Jerrica grabbed Gray's sleeve. "What's he doing here?"

"That's what I want to know." Scotty took a menacing step forward, but Connie placed a restraining hand on his arm. "You can't toss him out on his ear in front of everyone. Assistant Director Collins brought him, along with the press clamoring at our front gate. You can tell him in no uncertain terms that Olaf is not welcome in my home, and I don't appreciate unapproved guests."

Gray made a sharp move and a half turn toward his father. "Collins, the assistant director of the CIA?"

"One and the same." Scotty's eyebrows formed a single line above his nose. "What do you think?"

"What do you think he wants us to think?"

Like a bird's, Connie's head swiveled back and forth, following the conversation between her husband and her son. "I don't know what you two are talking about, but Patrick Collins just brought the most notorious political figure of the day to my Memorial Day party…and I'm not happy."

"Plaster a smile on your face, Connie, and welcome your new guest." Scotty laced his fingers with hers and gave her a tug. "I'll explain everything later."

Jerrica licked her lips as she watched Gray's parents approach Olaf. "What should I do, Gray? Should I pretend I don't know he's behind the disruption at Dreadworm? Should I accuse him? Call him out? Denounce him publicly?"

"Let's play this by ear. Maybe Collins just outed himself as the mole, or maybe he doesn't realize we know about the plan."

"If Olaf told Collins, his good friend and savior, he knows." She tapped a passing waiter on the arm and snagged a mimosa. She downed half the drink and then snatched a couple of crab puffs from another tray and stuffed them into her mouth.

Did Olaf know she'd be at this party? He must've known. By the tilt of his smile when he spotted her, he had something planned—and it wasn't going to be pleasant. She had to find out about it before Gray did.

She patted her lips with a napkin. "Okay, let's hang back and watch what happens."

So many dignitaries crowded the lawn and the pool deck, half of them wanting to shake Gray's hand and discuss his political future with him, that it didn't take Jerrica long to escape Gray's realm and shimmy up next to Olaf.

She lowered her voice and rasped, "What the hell are you doing here?"

"It's my coming-out party. I'm here legally, and everything is above board. I'm free."

"What price did you pay? Or did someone else pay the price for you? Kiera? Her son? Major Denver?"

Olaf clicked his tongue, as a breathless woman headed their way. "I have so many fans wanting to speak with me, I can't talk right now. Meet me by the front gate in ten minutes. I have a proposition for you—you alone. Don't bring anyone with you, or…well, you know what could happen."

Jerrica's heart slammed against her chest, rattling her ribcage. She knew it. Olaf wasn't done with her yet.

She glanced over her shoulder at two men, their heads together with Gray's. They must be salivating over his potential as a political candidate—young, good-looking, connected, military. They obviously didn't know about the Dreadworm girlfriend who would totally and completely torpedo any chances he had at a career in politics—if he was still with her when he decided to throw his hat in the ring.

She ducked her head and scurried to the kitchen where controlled chaos reigned as the caterers moved in and out in a dance choreographed by Connie's chef.

Jerrica dug her elbows into the center island and buried her chin in her hands to wait out the ten minutes. Her mind raced as fast as the waiters whisking food out to the guests. She had an idea of what Olaf would propose, and her answer would be the one that would keep Gray safe.

Connie's chef gave her a nudge. "You're in the way— go socialize."

Jerrica gave the woman a half smile and slid out the door of the kitchen into the dining room. A few of Connie's guests bunched together, holding conversations in low voices. Gatherings like this must have a lot of hush-hush social interactions—like the one she was about to have.

She traipsed across the great room and out the front door, looking left and right. The Prescotts had created a path from the drop-off point outside the main gate to the side gate leading to the backyard. Most of the guests had already arrived and the parking valets lounged against the cars, smoking cigarettes and checking their phones.

Her sandals crunched the gravel as she made her way outside the gate to the guard shack in front of the property.

Her phone buzzed in the purse strapped across her body, and she checked the text message from Gray. She ignored his question and tapped the record button on her phone.

She scooped in a deep breath and rounded the corner of the guard shack. The branches on the bushes at the head of a trail that snaked into the woods bobbed and swayed, but nobody stepped forward.

Two seconds later, Olaf materialized on the path, his white-blond hair creating a bright spot in the foliage. How'd he get out here so quickly when she'd left him with an adoring fan?

Folding her arms, she dug her nails into her biceps. "What's this proposal?"

"So abrupt, after all we've been through together." He flicked his fingers at a bug flying in front of his face.

"I could say the same about you. Your attack on Dreadworm was so abrupt after all we've been through together. Or was it? How long have you been a part of this plan?"

"You know I don't reveal much of anything, Jerrica, even to you."

"What do you want from me?"

"It's easy, really. I don't want you to do *something*. I want you to do *nothing*. Do nothing with the information you hacked, so skillfully, I might add. I had assured my… companions that nobody would be able to break into that database I helped them create." He lifted his shoulders. "But I guess I created a monster, didn't I?"

"You helped them devise a means of communicating via computer and helped them with those emails implicating Major Denver."

He raised his hand. "That was I. Who else?"

"Why Major Denver?"

"Wasn't that a nice touch? Although in retrospect it was a mistake. We had to get rid of Denver somehow because he was onto the plan, but his setup was my idea. I thought I would be giving the finger to that Delta Force lieutenant who'd broken your heart. I had no idea he'd come crawling back to you. But then again…"

"What?" Jerrica barked the word so loudly, a startled bird took flight from a tree next to Olaf.

"Did Prescott really come groveling back to your bed because of your…charms? Or did he worm his way back into your affections to help his commanding officer?" Olaf brushed his hands together. "I guess we'll never know, but that doesn't concern me now."

"It's too late."

"What's too late?" Olaf's eyes glittered like chips of glass.

"I already told Senator Prescott about the database. He's going to make arrangements to have someone decode what I couldn't. It's over, Olaf."

"Oh, it's never over, Jerrica. You of all people should know that."

"How about me?" Gray materialized beside her. "*I'm* saying it's over for you. It's only a matter of time before those secret communications are decoded, and your plans to take over the government are finished."

"A matter of time. Yes, time can be our enemy or time can be our very good friend." Olaf placed his hands together and gazed into the distance over his fingertips. "At this moment, we have a drone loaded with a canister of sarin gas. Its destination? This lovely garden party."

"No!" Terror clawed through Jerrica's insides, as Gray reached for her hand. "And you're controlling it?"

"I do have control of it, but it's not operational…yet. We get what we want, that drone stays grounded."

"You people are insane." Gray lunged toward Olaf, but Jerrica grabbed his arm.

"Maybe, but we hold the cards." Olaf crooked his finger at Jerrica. "Come with me, Jerrica, and I'll tell you my proposal."

"She's not going anywhere with you." Gray put his arm around her and drew her close.

This time, she didn't melt into his body. She kept her frame stiff, her mind alert. "Anything you tell me, Gray can hear, too. Besides, you already told me to destroy the database I uncovered and the program I used to uncover it. That's not going to happen—I don't care how many drones you have coming. It's proof, and I'm not going to destroy the proof of who's behind this attack and why."

"Are you sure about that, Jerrica? All of it? I'm not done with my proposal, and I don't think you want your bodyguard, or whatever he is to you, to hear all your dirty little secrets."

A tremble ran through Jerrica's body, but she dug in her heels. "He can hear anything. Spit it out, Olaf. What's your proposal?"

"Destroy your work—it's not too late. You can disable anything you handed over to Senator Prescott, and I will deactivate the drone."

"What else? I know there's more."

Olaf spread his hands. "Or I'll turn in your father."

GRAY JERKED AND took a step back from the words that hung in the air between them. His arm seemed pinned across Jerrica's shoulders, but he shifted to the side to study her profile. "What's he talking about? Your father is dead, killed in the FBI raid on his compound."

"No, he isn't." Jerrica ducked away from his arm, taking a step closer to Olaf. "My father is not dead, Gray. He escaped and made his way to Guatemala. He's been hiding out there for years...most recently with Olaf."

Gray curled his hands into fists, not knowing whether to punch Olaf's grinning face or the wall of the guard shack behind him. "And you've known this how long? From the beginning?"

"I found out a few years after the raid."

"So, you knew when we were together...the first time."

"I did. I also planned to tell you this time."

Olaf snapped his fingers. "While I'd love to stand here and listen to you two work out your relationship issues, time is of the essence. That's the deal, Jerrica. You destroy your program, I'll call off the drone and nobody has to know about Jimmy James living in hiding—well, except the lieutenant here, but that's on you now."

Gray held his breath. No way would Jerrica put the country at risk for a father who'd put his own family in danger. No way would she put her relationship with her father over her relationship with him.

Jerrica puffed out a breath. "Deal."

Olaf crowed as Jerrica's response kicked Gray in the midsection. He almost doubled over, but he held himself erect. "You'll pay for this—both of you."

"Sorry, Gray, but this is my father we're talking about. I have to protect him against the government who harmed him, harmed us, my family." As she spoke to him, she turned toward him, a stranger to him now. Or maybe she always had been.

She blinked her eyes at him rapidly. "I'm going to leave with Olaf now. He'll help me stop the program, and he'll stop the drone. Once he and his forces take over the government, Major Denver will be exonerated. People will know he was used."

Was she signaling him? Olaf may have gotten the same idea as he moved forward to watch her.

"But we'll be living in a country held hostage by lunatics who want to do who knows what? Is that the country you want?"

She shrugged. "I don't care. This never was my country after I lost my mother and my brother."

Dragging her phone from her pocket, Jerrica said, "Olaf, I need assurances from you that my father is okay. He sent me an email the other night, so I know he was fine then, but I need to know that now."

Gray swallowed. She must've heard from her father the night her mood changed and she returned to her secretiveness.

"Text away. No harm has come to Jimmy. I've taken good care of him all these years…and you. Gave you a job you could've only dreamed of." He flicked one end of his scarf over his shoulder. "And then we get to work on your computer."

Jerrica looked up from her phone, her fingers still moving. "*Your* computer. I turned mine over already, but I can work on the program from yours. You do have your computer with you, right? You never go anywhere without your computer."

"Come on, then." Olaf waved a hand at Gray. "You'd better make sure your protector here knows that if anything happens to me, orders are in place to release the drone, and if he goes running back to his parents' party and tries to evacuate the place, the drone will be activated and if the gas doesn't kill these people, it will be released elsewhere. Do you want that on your conscience, lieutenant?"

"Go! Take her. You two deserve each other but if you think you and the other terrorists are going to stage a coup and run this country through threats, you haven't reckoned on the force of the US military."

"Hollow words, lieutenant, but good luck with that."

As Olaf led Jerrica into the woods and presumably to his computer, she twisted her head over her shoulder one last time and…winked and tipped her head down.

What the hell did that mean? His heart held onto the hope that Jerrica was playing Olaf, but his brain reasoned that she'd lied about her father. She'd lied about Dreadworm when he'd first met her. How many other lies had she told him? Had her body lied to him, too?

And how would she be playing Olaf? She couldn't overpower him physically. Perhaps she'd make a show of dismantling her program when she really had it backed up somewhere, but Olaf and his cronies still had a drone weaponized with sarin. The database implicating all the players wouldn't do them any good with that threat hanging over them.

As he turned to go back to the doomed party, the blood pounding in his eardrums, his eye caught a glinting object in the mulch on the ground. He took two long steps and scooped up Jerrica's phone, the one she'd been using to text her father. Had she received a response from him? She seemed to have forgotten she was waiting for one.

He turned the phone over in his hand and his eyes widened at the sight of a long, unsent text message. Had she forgotten to send it? Was her loyalty so strong for Olaf in the end that not even her father mattered?

Cupping the phone in his palm, he skimmed the message and then tripped to a stop. The message wasn't meant for her father; it was meant for him.

Chapter Seventeen

Gray rubbed his eyes and brought the phone close to his face.

Give me ten minutes to get onto Olaf's computer. Then evacuate the party. Watch who leaves first. My program holds the key to disabling the drone. Trust me.

He peeled his tongue from the roof of his mouth and ran it across his teeth. *Trust me.* Could he do it after all the lies?

If Jerrica were really playing for Olaf's team now, why would she want him to evacuate the party? Maybe she and Olaf wanted to take the plan to its fruition and stage the coup right now.

Telling everyone to leave the party would be a signal to make the drone operational. Maybe they had it planned so that nobody would be able to get out in time. His parents. Major Denver.

He worked his tense jaw back and forth. Jerrica had lied about Dreadworm, and she'd lied about her father—but nothing else. She'd been working as hard as he had to get to the bottom of this. She wouldn't throw it all away now.

He thought she'd been a stranger when she talked of

joining forces with Olaf and protecting her father, but when she'd turned and winked at him—she was the Jerrica he knew...and loved.

Trust her? Hell, yeah.

Checking Jerrica's phone for the time, Gray strode back to the house, the music floating into the driveway a strange accompaniment to the terror about to be unleashed—sort of like the orchestra playing on the deck of the *Titanic*.

As he charged into the great room, his jaw dropped. Five clean-cut men surrounded Major Denver, bearded and scruffy and smiling. "There he is. Prescott kept Jerrica safe, and she's ready to give us the goods."

His Delta Force teammates started forward and then stopped, the laughter falling from their faces.

Cam Sutton ate up the rest of the space between them and thumped him on the shoulder. "What's wrong, Prescott? We should be celebrating about now."

"Am I glad to see all of you." He glanced at the clock on the phone.

"You don't look it, bro." Hunter Mancini's dark eyes narrowed. "We were under the impression there was a nuclear attack planned, and your girl unearthed the real plan. I'd say that's a lot to be thankful for."

"Yeah, the real plan—sarin, a canister of it attached to a drone."

"My God." Asher Knight, still looking thin after his captivity, clasped the back of his neck with one hand. "These people are diabolical. Once Jerrica's intel is decoded, we'll know who's behind this?"

"I think we'll know a lot sooner than that." Gray tapped the phone where ten minutes had ticked away since Olaf left with Jerrica. "We have to evacuate this party—now. Keep an eye on the guests who are moving the quickest and most suspiciously."

"Wait." Joe McVie raised his hand. "Is this some kind of ploy to smoke 'em out?"

Logan Hess, his jaw set in a determined line, was already on the move. "Who cares? If Prescott says it's time to move, let's go."

Denver stepped into the fray, ready to lead, as always. "It's not a ploy, is it, Gray? Is that drone headed this way?"

"Not if Jerrica can help it, but maybe she can't. She's all alone with a maniac, and I let her go with him. I didn't trust her enough."

"Sounds like you trust her now and that's all that matters." Denver charged toward the patio and the pleasant scene about to be radically altered. "Let's get these people out of here, and watch out for suspicious behavior."

Major Denver took control of the situation, ordering his team to fan out among the guests to let them know a credible threat against the party had been received.

Gray took his parents aside and told them the truth. His mother handled the situation with aplomb and grace, making light of the news with her guests but ensuring that they gathered their things and left.

Gray eased out a breath as he noticed the majority of the guests on their way out without trampling each other. He scanned the skies for an incoming drone. The security detail had been notified of the plan, but ordered not to shoot down anything or try to intercept.

Then McVie signaled him, jerking his thumb toward the house. Gray made a stop to talk to his parents. "You two need to get out of here."

His mother dug in her heels. "I'm not being driven

from my home. If Jerrica thinks she can stop this thing, my money's on her."

"Dad? Talk some sense into her." Gray lifted his arms before joining McVie in the house.

What greeted his arrival in the great room caused him to trip over the track of the French doors. McVie and the others had lined up a handful of men and one woman on the large crescent-shaped sofa, a pile of cell phones and gas masks on the floor in front of them.

Sutton whistled through his teeth. "Talk about your suspicious behavior. We caught this bunch heading to the guard shack and a stash of gas masks. Convenient, huh?"

Patrick Collins, the assistant director of the CIA, aimed a polished loafer at one of the gas masks. "You'd better hold onto one of those yourself. We informed Olaf that the guests were being evacuated. He could send that drone anywhere now—a school, a hospital, a baseball game—and it's all on you."

"I could and I most certainly will."

All heads turned toward Olaf's voice, as he stepped down into the great room, Jerrica by his side.

She shot Gray a quick look from wide eyes, and then dropped her gaze to the floor.

Olaf patted the tablet he held aloft balanced on his palm. "I'll give you one more chance, lieutenant. You and your Delta Force men release my team here and no-body has to get hurt, nobody has to get gassed. But with the threat of our weapon still very much alive, we'll take control of the presidency, the government, and run things our way."

Gray shifted his gaze to Jerrica, who lifted her head and nodded once, a smile playing about her lips.

"Knock yourself out, Olaf. We have the FBI and mem-bers of the Secret Service on their way now to conduct the arrests of these individuals…and you." Gray pulled out his gun and leveled it at Olaf's head.

The man didn't even flinch. A slow smile spread across his pale face. "I don't think you want to do that, lieutenant. I already have the drone set up. Once my associate hears of these arrests, he'll know what to do."

"Let him try." Jerrica slipped the tablet from Olaf's hands.

Olaf choked. "What are you talking about, Jerrica? Y-you mean, you'd do it yourself? I can assure you, Prescott isn't going to allow that, either. He'll turn his gun on you just as easily as he did me."

"Nobody's going to do it, Olaf—not you, not me, not some shadowy associate—because it can't be done."

Olaf's face reddened, and his fellow traitors on the sofa began to murmur and shift uncomfortably.

"What have you done?" Olaf's icy blue eyes bugged out of their sockets as he turned them on Jerrica.

"You trained me well, Olaf. Now your servant is your master." Jerrica waved her hand in the air. "Did you really think I'd believe that database was so important to you if it contained just the names of the traitors? We'd learn all that information, anyway, when it wouldn't do us any good because you always had that secret weapon—the drone."

"Always had? *Have.* I have it." The veins stood out on Olaf's forehead and he wagged a shaking finger at the tablet in Jerrica's hands.

"While I was corrupting the database Amit and I uncovered, I was also using your tablet to figure out how to disable the drone." She smacked the tablet against Olaf's chest. "And I did."

Of course, Sutton was the first to hoot and holler, but the others followed suit.

Olaf sank to his knees, frantically tapping his tablet, his face getting redder and redder until it looked like that scarf was strangling him. Finally, he threw the tablet across the room and sputtered, "B-but your father. I'll rat him out. I'll turn him in. He'll spend the rest of his life in federal prison. L-look, I'll tell the FBI right now."

A swarm of dark-suited agents swarmed into the room, guns drawn, and Gray's Delta Force team gave way to them.

"Oh, well." Jerrica flicked her fingers in the air. "My father *did* break the law."

Epilogue

"Now, this is *my* kind of party." Jerrica wiggled her red-
polished toes in the water as she sat on the edge of the
Prescotts' pool, Gray beside her.

Martha Drake, Cam Sutton's girlfriend and the CIA
translator who'd been sent the initial emails implicating
Major Denver, sipped a sweating glass of iced tea. "I just
can't believe Patrick Collins, the assistant director, was
involved. Or, wait, maybe I can believe it. He never took
our investigation seriously, did he, Cam?"

"It wasn't just Collins. We couldn't get anyone to
take action. The setup against the major should've ended
there." Cam scooped up some water from the pool and
dribbled it on Martha's thigh.

"*You* can't believe it? How do you think I felt about
that?" Sue Chandler, Hunter Mancini's fiancée and the
only CIA officer present, motioned to their son on the
edge of the pool. "Jump!"

"Daddy. I want Daddy."

"Of course, you do."

Hunter used his powerful stroke to swim across the
pool. He patted his chest. "Right here, buddy."

"You can't jump yet." Asher Knight lowered his wrig-
gling daughter into a plastic inner tube while his fiancée,
Paige, held it steady. "Paige and I knew the plot had to

go all the way to the top. They'd gotten to the doctors in rehab. I'm just sorry I played into their hands."

Paige kissed him over their daughter's head. "That wasn't your fault, Asher, and the fact you discovered what was happening, despite your injuries, helped Major Denver even more."

Cam saluted. "That's right, Asher. We only hated you for a few weeks."

"At least my fellow volunteer at the Syrian refugee camp finally debunked the story of Major Denver being involved in the bombing there." Hailey Duvall, Joe McVie's girlfriend, slipped into the pool and ducked her head beneath the water, ruining a perfect hairstyle. When she popped up, she pointed a toe at Jerrica. "If you're looking for a few reputable charities to fund with your money, Jerrica, I can give you the info."

Joe came up beneath Hailey and lifted her in the air. "Run, Jerrica. She's going to turn you into a do-gooder like her."

"What I can't believe is the traitors were actually going to use sarin on American citizens. The nuclear weapons components stashed at the embassy outpost my brother was guarding must've been decoys for Major Denver." Logan Hess's girlfriend, Lana Moreno, rubbed some suntan lotion on her mocha skin.

"Let me do that." Logan smoothed the oil on her back. "Your brother is a hero, Lana. When is that baseball field going to be dedicated to him?"

"Soon." She grabbed Logan's oily hand and kissed it. "I just hope you're not deployed when it happens."

"I'll see what I can do."

All heads turned at the sound of Major Denver's voice. Cam waved his hand in the air. "The man finally shaved his beard and cut his hair, which actually makes you look older."

Denver threw a plastic football at Cam's head. "Watch yourself, son."

The major sat on the edge of a chaise lounge. "Did you all hear that the drone was located, thanks to Jerrica, and disarmed?"

"My father told us." Gray kissed the inside of Jerrica's wrist.

Martha pushed her glasses up the bridge of her nose. "I was happy to hear you and your fellow Dreadworm coworkers aren't going to face any charges."

"We cooperated fully and gave them evidence against Olaf in the murder of Klera Cramer." Jerrica shivered despite the warm sun on her bare back.

"Not to mention, you saved the country." Gray cupped her jaw with one hand.

"Hear, hear!" Major Denver raised his glass in the air, and the others followed suit.

"And our own Major Denver is not facing any charges for going AWOL." Gray raised his glass.

Sue swiveled her head left and right. "Looks like you're the only one not paired up, Rex."

"I'm good." He held up his hands. "The last thing I need right now is dates."

Denver jumped into the pool, splashing everyone and acting as a catalyst as the others followed him into the water.

As Jerrica shifted closer to the edge of the pool, Gray put a hand on her waist. "Do you know where your father is going to be imprisoned?"

"They haven't told me yet." She rubbed the end of her nose.

"I'm sorry it came to that."

"He's not. He was tired of looking over his shoulder, tired of kowtowing to Olaf. At least now I can visit him."

"Have I told you how amazing you are, hacker girl?"

"Just about a million times. It broke my heart when I saw the look on your face when you thought I'd sided with Olaf."

"I should've known better."

"Why? I never gave you much reason to trust me."

"You gave me plenty of reasons. Except…" He smoothed his hand over her thigh.

"Except what?"

"I don't think you've told me you love me since I stumbled back into your life."

"Oh, I'll have to remedy that right now because I do—with all my heart." She leaned over and touched her lips to his ear.

Just then, Cam grabbed her ankles and pulled her into the pool. "C'mon, we're ganging up on Denver. It might be our only chance while he's still feeling indebted to us."

Jerrica rolled onto her back and pushed off the side of the pool with her feet. She tilted her head back and shouted, "I love you, Gray Prescott."

After all, she didn't have to keep her love quiet anymore.

* * * * *

DEADLY COVER-UP

JULIE ANNE LINDSEY

Chapter One

Violet Ames drove slowly along the familiar winding roads of River Gorge, Kentucky, wiping tears and saying prayers. It had been years since she'd visited the rural mountain town where her grandmother raised her, and this wasn't the return trip she'd planned. Her version had involved an abundance of hugs and triple servings of Grandma's double chocolate brownies, but there wouldn't be any of that tonight.

Violet divided her attention between the dark country road before her and the sleeping infant behind her. Eight-month-old Maggie dozed silently in her little rear-facing car seat, having given up tears to fatigue only moments after the car exited the hospital parking lot. Violet rubbed her heavy lids and tried to stay composed, but it had been a tough day.

According to the midmorning phone call she'd received from River Gorge General Hospital, Violet's grandma, a seventy-eight-year-old widow, had fallen from a ladder in her barn and nearly killed herself. The notion was unfathomable. Grandma's barn was old and left unused after her grandfather's death many years back, so why was her grandma even in there? And why had she climbed the ladder? There was nothing to reach with it except an old hayloft housing a decade of dust.

Violet gripped the aching muscles along the back of her neck and shoulders with one hand, steering carefully with the other. She couldn't get her mind around the awful day. "What would have possessed her?" she whispered into the warm summer air streaming through her barely cracked window.

That was a million-dollar question, because no one at the hospital had a clue.

Her grandma, the only one who could explain what on earth she'd been up to, was lying unconscious in a bleach-and bandage-scented room, worrying her granddaughter half to death. She'd undergone surgeries for her broken hip and wrist and received sutures on her cracked head and a wrap for her swollen ankle. What she hadn't done was open her eyes.

Her doctor said she'd wake when she was ready, and he had faith that would be soon. He'd suggested Violet be patient.

Patience wasn't Violet's strong suit. In fact, she wanted to scream. Her grandma had been Violet's entire world before Maggie was born, and she knew it. Violet had made her promise to be careful with herself the year she moved from River Gorge to Winchester, nearly two hours away. And she had. "Yet here we are," Violet muttered.

She thumped the steering wheel with one palm as hot tears spouted anew.

Maggie started behind her, jostling the car seat's reflection in Violet's rearview. Violet couldn't see her face, but she heard the squirms and soft complaints as Maggie tried to find sleep once again.

Violet pressed her lips into a tight line, then wiped the new round of tears from her cheeks. They'd be at Grandma's house soon, where they could get a good night's sleep before returning to the hospital tomorrow, where hopefully they'd get some answers. Or better yet, find Grandma awake.

Soon the bumpy road grew steadily more uneven until cracked pavement gave way to sparse patches of dirt and loose gravel. Stones crunched and pinged beneath the tires and frame of Violet's little yellow hatchback as she maneuvered the final stretch to her former home.

A small smile pulled through her heartbreak as Grandma's farm came into view. Ghosts of her younger self on bicycles and horseback rushed down the drive to meet her, chased by the beloved hound dogs and yard chickens of her youth, sprayed with a garden hose held by her grandfather before he passed. Carried in Grandma's arms when her mother waved goodbye from the passenger seat of a station wagon driven by a man she barely knew.

Violet rolled to a stop in front of the old white farmhouse, nausea fisting in her gut and fat tears blurring away the world before her. She shifted into Park and climbed out to inhale the sticky night air. Summers in River Gorge were scorching hot with the constant threat of a thunderstorm. A volatile combination Violet had always loved.

She peered at her sleeping daughter. "This will be fine," she whispered. "Grandma will be fine." Unwilling to wake Maggie, Violet unlatched the entire car seat and hoisted it into her arms, baby and all.

With any luck, Grandma still kept a spare house key under the plant in the big red pot outside her dining room window.

Violet carried Maggie to the potted flower garden near the front steps and tipped the planter back with one foot. "Shoot." Nothing but bugs on the mulch-covered ground beneath.

She turned for the porch. All hope wasn't gone. Her grandpa used to keep a spare above the front door.

Grandma had hated it because she was too short to reach without something to stand on. Violet, on the other hand, hadn't had that problem since middle school when she shot up to five foot eight and a half and stayed there.

She slowed on the steps when she caught sight of the front door already ajar.

Could the paramedics have forgotten to lock up on their way out?

Had they even gone inside the house if Grandma had fallen in the barn?

Violet flipped the interior light on and swung the door wide. Maybe her grandma hadn't fully secured the door before heading outside to the barn, and the open door had gone unnoticed by the EMTs.

Eerie silence greeted Violet as she edged her way inside, trying desperately not to wake her daughter. She set Maggie, in her car seat, against the far wall, then pushed the door shut behind them. "Hello?" she called, as much from habit and manners as anything.

The fine hairs along Violet's neck and arms rose to attention. The couch cushions were all slightly askew and a small drawer in the side table was open. She double-checked that the television and DVD player were still there, then shook her head in a relieved sigh. It wasn't a robbery.

Violet rubbed the gooseflesh from her arms. Of course it wasn't. No one in town would bother breaking into her grandma's house. For one thing, everyone was perpetually invited in, and for another, it was a small town. Folks here knew her grandma barely got by on her grandpa's small pension. Besides all that, there was nothing to take that Grandma wouldn't freely give.

A small sound rose on the night air, perking Violet's ears and causing her to rethink her theory. Another little bump drew Violet's attention to the kitchen near the back of the home and jerked her heart rate into a sprint.

She pulled her cell phone from one pocket and dialed the local authorities before inching away from the darkened hallway, back toward the front door and Maggie.

"Hello," she whispered to the tinny voice answering her call. "I think there's someone in my grandma's house."

No sooner had she uttered the words than a hulking shadow erupted from the home's depths, bearing down on her fast with long, pounding strides. Violet screamed as his iron hands connected with her shoulders, knocking her end over end as he barreled past her and out the front door.

Maggie screamed in her car seat as the calamity of her mother's crashing body mixed with the loud bang of Grandma's front door hitting the wall.

Violet scrambled onto her hands and knees, then raced to Maggie's side. She climbed off the ground slightly bruised but wholly motivated to get her baby to safety. She wasted no time escaping the house with Maggie and locking them both into her car, engine running, while she waited for local authorities to arrive.

WYATT STONE DOUBLE-CHECKED his GPS as the quiet country road turned to gravel beneath his sturdy truck tires. He knew Gladys Ames lived on a rural property, but this was nearly isolated. No wonder she had been scared.

He drove with one hand on the wheel while he dug through a pile of papers on his dashboard with the other, fishing for a business card in decent condition. Normally, Wyatt was better organized, but his fledgling private security business had been growing legs faster than he could keep up or recruit a staff large enough to handle all the work, and that left Wyatt running on caffeine and determination more often than sleep and preparation.

A set of bobbing headlights appeared around the next pitted gravel bend and headed his way, demanding the lion's share of the narrow road and forcing Wyatt's truck onto the grass with two wheels. The sheriff's cruiser lumbered past at a crawl, leaving Wyatt to wait for the opportunity to forge on. Once he could, Wyatt pressed the gas pedal with a little more purpose than before. Gladys Ames had sent several messages to Fortress Security over the past few days, arranging for protection while she "handled some business," but Wyatt wasn't supposed to start work until tomorrow. So what had she gotten herself into that required a sheriff's presence since their last correspondence?

He slid his truck into the space behind a small yellow hatchback and climbed down from the cab.

A brunette with a baby in one arm and a half dozen assorted duffel bags dangling from her shoulders and hands froze at the sight of him.

It wasn't the first time a lone woman had looked at him that way. It wouldn't be the last.

His size and general appearance put most folks on edge, especially women. Certainly at night. Definitely alone.

Wyatt stopped moving.

"Ma'am." He tugged the curved brim of his worn-out Stetson and nodded. "I'm Wyatt Stone from Fortress Security, a private protection agency in Lexington. I'm here to see Gladys Ames."

This dark-haired beauty didn't speak or budge, though her arms must've been feeling the weight of her burdens. She was lean and tall for a woman, but Wyatt still had more than a half a foot on her. Like most people he met in this business, she looked incredibly vulnerable, breakable and scared. And he had a bad habit of looking dangerous, or so he'd been told.

Wyatt ran through a mental list of ways to get past this

beautiful guard dog without scaring her any further. He was there to help Gladys Ames, and a general web search had revealed her to be in her seventies. Definitely *not* this woman.

"I have a business card," he offered, "and a signed contract for services to begin tomorrow morning. I told Mrs. Ames I'd come sooner if I could. No additional charge, of course." Honestly, coming here straight from his last job had saved him five hours of traveling back to Lexington only to turn around and leave for River Gorge in the morning. He was going right past anyway. It made sense to start work a few hours early in exchange for an extra night of boarding.

The woman adjusted her baby on her hip and struggled with the cluster of bags hanging all over her. "Grandma hired you?"

"Yes, ma'am." Wyatt outstretched his hand, a new business card wedged between his fingers. "How about a trade? I take those bags off your hands, and you have a look at the card. Is Mrs. Ames inside?" He checked his watch, hadn't even thought about the time or a seventysomething woman's schedule. It was already after nine. "I don't want to wake her."

Tears sprang to the beauty's eyes and a small whimper puckered her rosebud mouth. "She's in the hospital."

Wyatt's senses went on alert. "Why?"

The woman slouched. Her face twisted in grief and agony. She made the proposed trade, then gathered her little girl more tightly against her chest, stroking her puffy brown curls.

Wyatt scanned the scene, impatiently waiting for an answer to his question. Had someone hurt his new client before he'd even gotten there? The road-hogging cruiser came back to mind. "Why was the sheriff here?"

"Grandma's in the hospital because she fell. Sheriff Masterson was here because there was a break-in. He dusted for prints and took some photos of the mess, but nothing was missing as far as I can tell. He made a report and said he'd follow up."

Wyatt stifled a curse and headed for the house as eight years of military training and a lifetime of natural instinct snapped into effect. "How badly was Mrs. Ames hurt? Was anything taken? Who found her when she fell? I need as many details as you have."

He let himself inside and unloaded the bags onto a tweed couch beside the door. He ran his fingers along the jamb and door's edge looking for signs of forced entry, then did the same with the windows before moving on.

The condition of each room grew progressively worse as he pushed deeper into the home. The television was untouched, and a small dish near the kitchen sink held what looked like a set of wedding rings. "This wasn't a robbery."

He turned to discuss the situation further, but the brunette hadn't followed him inside.

Wyatt strode back through the house and onto the porch. "Are you coming in?"

"I don't know."

He shifted his weight and locked restless hands over both hips. "I'm not here to hurt you. I'm here to protect Mrs. Ames, who assured me tomorrow morning was a fine time to start."

"Well, I guess she was wrong." The woman looked down at the card in her hand, as if she'd forgotten it was there.

"Tell me what happened." Wyatt moved to the porch's edge and lowered himself onto the top step. "I can't help until I know what I just walked into, but I assure you I *can* help."

Her eyes filled with tears again. "I don't know."

"You said she fell?" He highly doubted that was an accident, given her recent outreach to a security firm. "Is she going to be okay?"

"She's unconscious. Broke a hip and a wrist. She hasn't woken since the fall." The woman covered her mouth and nose with one trembling palm. A moment later, she stiffened her spine, wiped her nose and eyes against her arm, then locked both hands protectively around her daughter's back, seeming determined to be strong.

Wyatt pulled a handkerchief from his pocket. "Here."

"Thanks." She mopped her face and released a long, shuddered breath. "I'm her granddaughter, Violet, and this is my daughter, Maggie. I got the call this morning about her fall. We live in Winchester, so we came right out, and we were at the hospital all day, but she never woke up. I thought we'd stay here tonight, but when I got here…" She gave the house behind him a wary look.

Wyatt rested one boot on the step below him and stretched his other leg out. He'd been in the truck far too long, folded up like a clean pair of fatigues. "I'm sorry about your grandma." He worked his jaw, considering the unusual set of events. "What do you know about the fall?"

"Not much, and what I've been told doesn't make sense." Violet rubbed one hand over her forehead. She'd clearly had a horrible day, and his unexpected appearance wasn't doing anything to improve it.

"Tell me what you do know."

She rolled wide blue eyes back to him. "The hospital staff said she was on a ladder in the barn, but Grandma hasn't kept anything in there in years."

Violet swung her face away from him and squinted into the darkness beyond the house. Her shoulders squared, and her expression turned suspicious and hard. The visible heartbreak was replaced by something Wyatt knew well. Resolve. "Maybe it's time we see the barn," she suggested.

Wyatt dragged his six-foot-four and two-hundred-fifty-pound frame back onto its feet with a nod of approval.

He and Violet were going to get along nicely.

Chapter Two

Wyatt moved alongside Violet toward the big red barn behind Mrs. Ames's home. He worked to keep his thoughts on important things, like what Mrs. Ames had been afraid of when she'd hired him, and not things like whether or not the wedding rings in the kitchen belonged to the intriguing brunette at his side.

Violet stopped at the back porch, standing with Maggie under a small cone of light thirty feet from the barn. She waved a hand in Wyatt's direction, indicating he should go on without her. The look on her face said the sleeping baby on her hip was Violet's priority. "There's a pull string just inside the door that'll give you some light. Not enough to fill the whole barn, but it's something."

Wyatt gave the ladies a long look before reluctantly leaving them behind. He'd already cleared the perimeter. He didn't sense anyone else nearby. They would be fine, and he wouldn't be long.

A few steps into the barn, a thin beaded-metal chain bounced against his forehead. He tugged it and squinted against the sudden burst of light. As promised, it wasn't enough to explore the entirety of the cavernous structure, but it was all he needed. The ladder in question stood just a few yards away, blood staining the earthen floor at its base.

Wyatt accessed the flashlight app on his cell phone

and searched the ground more carefully, following a line of blood to the small puddle a few inches from the nearest ladder, making it obvious that someone had wanted people to believe she'd been on the rickety-looking structure when she fell, but that wasn't the case. She'd fallen where the line of blood began and had been moved to the ladder, where she continued to bleed until someone had found her. Aside from the blood trail, the dusty ground had been heavily trodden for an unused barn, probably evidence of whoever had discovered her and the emergency team who had taken her away.

"Do you see this?" he asked softly. His senses pinged like rapid fire. Violet's nearness charged the air between them. He didn't need to look to know she was there.

Violet gasped, then shuffled closer, having given up her hiding spot around the corner. "How'd you know I was here?"

"It's my job." And he had a feeling he'd sense her anywhere now that they'd met. Never mind the fact that the sweet scent of her so easily knotted his chest and scrambled his thoughts.

Training had surely played a part in his ability to track her movement without looking her way, but never in his life had he been so acutely aware of any woman, or so distracted by the question of where she placed her perfume. Did she dab it on her wrists, the curve of her neck? Along the valley between her breasts?

"Impressive," she said, sounding as if she meant it.

Wyatt had always been astute, but the army had honed his natural talents to a lethal point. Those skills had been incredibly useful as a soldier but were an unyielding burden as a civilian. Hearing every sound. Knowing every lie. Those were the reasons he'd rarely been at ease since his return stateside and the catalyst for opening his private security firm. That and the fact that he was good at what he did, maybe even the best. Wyatt read people, and he protected them.

Currently, Violet seemed to be deciding if she could trust him. The answer was a resounding yes, and he'd prove that to her with time. The shifting glances she slid between him and the open barn door suggested she was also wondering whether or not she could outrun him.

She could not.

Wyatt lowered the beam of his light to the stained floor. "Who found her?"

"Ruth," Violet said. "A friend of hers I ran into at the hospital. Grandma had invited her for lunch, but didn't answer the door, so Ruth looked out here and saw the barn door open."

Wyatt considered the new information. "Mrs. Ames broke her hip and wrist? Did she receive any injury that might have resulted in this kind of blood loss?"

Violet's skin went pale. "She hit her head. They gave her a bunch of stitches." Her free hand traveled absently to the crown of her long wavy hair, as if she might feel the sutures there.

A head injury explained the blood.

Wyatt extinguished the light and tucked his phone back into his pocket. "If your grandma was on the ladder when she fell, how do you suppose she hit her head only a few inches away from the base?"

Violet's brows knit together. Her attention dropped back to the shadow-covered floor. "She couldn't have."

"Right. With her body on the ladder, her head would've hit farther away, unless she fell headfirst from the loft, which would've done more than break her hip and wrist." He pulled his father's Stetson from his head and rubbed exhausted fingers over short-cropped hair. "I think she fell over there." He pointed to the wide start of a narrow line of blood, then swung his finger toward the ladder. "Someone moved her closer to the ladder, probably hoping whoever found her would jump to conclusions, which they did."

"So she didn't fall off the ladder."

"I don't think so, no."

Violet's beautiful face knotted. Her blue eyes snapped up to lock on his as recognition registered. "Grandma hired you because she thought she needed protection."

"Yes, ma'am."

"From who?"

He placed the beloved hat back onto his head. "She didn't say."

Violet's dark brows tented. "Do you think whoever it was might have done this to her?"

"That's what I intend to find out."

VIOLET WATCHED AS Wyatt grabbed the aged wood of the barn ladder and gave it a shake before climbing into the old loft. She'd never met anyone as big as Wyatt and watching him climb the ladder conjured memories of the giant on Jack's beanstalk. Her grandma was wise to choose him. If anyone could protect her, this would be the guy. Everything about him screamed military training. She recognized his rigid stance and searching gaze. She'd seen similar traits in Maggie's father, though the caution and compassion in Wyatt's voice had never been present with her ex. Violet's heart panged with regret at the unbidden memories rushing to the surface. She'd been naive to trust her heart so easily, and look where that had gotten her.

Maggie wriggled and Violet kissed her soft brown curls. She lifted a hand to shield her sleeping face from another round of dust falling from the loft. At least she'd gotten Maggie from the carnage of her train wreck relationship.

Awful as the love loss had been at the time, she'd gladly endure it again if that meant she'd get to be Maggie's mama.

Violet stepped away from the growing cloud of rustled dirt floating in the air. Soft scents of aged wood and dried hay slipped into her senses, sending a flood of nostalgia over Violet's anxious limbs. "I used to spend hours in that loft," she said, letting her voice carry to Wyatt. "Grandpa died when I was in middle school, and Grandma sold the animals, but I still came out here." Trying to feel near him.

The creaking boards went silent. Wyatt had stopped to listen. "What was up here then?"

"Just hay and me."

"What did you do?"

She smiled at the massive Wyatt-shaped shadow on the wall. He must've gotten his cell phone light out again. "Read. I was going to be a pilot like Amelia Earhart, or a Nobel Prize–winner like Marie Curie. Maybe a scientist like Jane Goodall." Violet had bored her grandma to death recounting all the things she'd learned up there.

"Are you?" Wyatt's deep tenor voice carried through the quiet air.

Violet chuckled, bouncing Maggie gently against her chest. "What? A pilot or Nobel Prize–winner or scientist? No. I'm a fifth-grade language arts teacher." As it turned out, Violet enjoyed telling others the things she knew more than she wanted to go off and do them herself. She only wished her grandpa had lived to see her with her class, sharing the stories he'd loved with them. He would've been so proud. And he would have loved Maggie.

Wyatt's steady footfall moved back toward the ladder. "There's a good-sized bare spot up here. Looks like either something pretty big was kept here or someone was clearing a spot for some reason."

"How would anything get up there?" That was the whole

conundrum, wasn't it? "Grandma couldn't carry anything up a ladder, especially something large." And they'd already established that she hadn't fallen from the ladder. She'd probably never even been on it.

Wyatt's long legs swung into view, and he returned to her side by way of the creaky rungs. "Take a look." He brushed his hands against his thighs, then turned his camera to face her. A picture of the dispersed hay overhead centered the screen.

"It looks like someone was just kicking it around to me," Violet said. "The whole floor is dusty. The space would be cleaner if something had been there long."

Wyatt rubbed the back of his neck, then the thick black stubble over his cheeks. "You're right. I should've seen that." He pressed his fingertips against heavy-lidded eyes. "I know you've had an awful day, and you're still deciding what to think of me, but can I trouble you for some coffee? I've got enough work to keep me busy a while, and I've been on the road all day."

Violet pulled her gaze to the open barn door and back. She'd checked out Wyatt's company website on her cell phone, using the business card he'd given her, while she'd waited briefly outside. Under the tab with details about the protectors for hire, she'd found photos of Wyatt. Posing in his dress greens. Running drills in fatigues. He seemed to be who he said he was. One founder of a private protection firm in Lexington. "What kind of work do you have to do tonight?"

He dropped his hands to his sides, then stuffed long fingers into the front pockets of his jeans. "I didn't see any signs of forced entry inside the home, so I'd like to replace the locks and dead bolts for starters, install motion lights at the front and back of the house, and add chains on the main entries."

"You're doing all that tonight?" Violet squeaked. Did he think that whoever had broken in and knocked her down might come back? A shiver coursed over her and she held Maggie tighter.

"Basic precautions," he said. "I've got everything I need in my truck, and a copy of your grandma's contract if you want to see it. Given the circumstances, I think she'd allow that."

Suddenly, the stranger before her seemed like the safer, handsomer of two unknowns. Violet was certain she'd sleep better with new locks and a trained military man under her roof. Besides, it was after ten already, and Maggie never slept past six. If Violet didn't get to bed soon, she wouldn't get much sleep.

Wyatt ducked his head. "I don't mind sleeping in my truck and starting tomorrow if that makes you more comfortable." He moved toward the string for the light and slowed for Violet to pass. "You've been through a lot today, and I've slept in that truck more often than my bed this month. I'd still like to get the new locks on first." His cheek ticked up in a lazy half smile before he shut it down.

Violet stopped to face him. She chewed her lip in indecision. "Why did Grandma choose you?"

"I'm the best."

Violet made a show of rolling her eyes, silently thankful for his efforts at levity given the day she'd had. "Humble, too."

Wyatt pulled the light string, delivering them into darkness as they made their way back outside. "I advertised strategically. Specifically to women's groups, yoga studios, churches that had events likely to be attended by elderly civilians. Word spread like wildfire. I suppose she found me that way."

Violet narrowed her eyes. "So you targeted women and old folks."

He nodded confidently. "Statistically they're the most common targets for violent crimes, harassment and stalking. I wanted to make a difference, not play bodyguard for some rich jerks."

Violet mulled the answer, impressed yet again. "You were planning to stay with Grandma while you're in River Gorge?"

"That was the agreement," he said. Wyatt matched his pace to hers as they walked back across the lawn to Grandma's home. "I have a week blocked off on my calendar for this, but I can stay longer if something changes. Mrs. Ames only said she had something to take care of, and she wanted the freedom to do it without having to watch over her shoulder." He grinned, sneaking a quick look in Violet's direction. "I was going to be her nephew, visiting from Lexington."

Violet rubbed the creases she felt gathering on her forehead. That cover story made Wyatt her relative, and it didn't say much about her, given the things she'd already thought about him. Like how nice he might look without a shirt. Or pants.

She turned her heated cheeks away.

It wasn't like her grandma to meddle, so Violet could only assume that whatever was going on had been dropped into her lap. *And it must be something big to force Grandma's involvement and require a bodyguard.*

She slowed at the front porch and turned to face Wyatt. "Will you be able to find out if her fall was an accident?"

"Yes."

"And if it wasn't, will you find out who hurt her?"

He dipped his chin in sharp confirmation. "I won't leave town till I do."

Violet evaluated the giant before her. He certainly seemed legit, and her grandma had chosen him. She'd even trusted him to stay with her while she did whatever it was that she was doing. "Okay," she said, resting her cheek on top of Maggie's head. "You can stay, and you don't need to sleep in your truck." She marched up the steps before she changed her mind. "I'll make up the couch and put on the coffee."

They went their separate ways then. Wyatt to his truck for his bags. Violet to set up a portable crib for Maggie in her grandmother's bedroom. She returned a few minutes later with a baby monitor and bedding to cover the couch.

Wyatt was already hard at work changing door locks in the kitchen. "I wouldn't have blamed you if you didn't let me in tonight," he said, attention fixed on the open door and his work.

"I wouldn't have cared," she said with a smile. If she'd suspected he was a danger to Maggie, his feelings would have been the least of her concerns.

Wyatt released a low chuckle. "Fair enough."

She started the coffee, then stuck a mug under the drip. "Cream or sugar?"

He shook his head in the negative. "Just the caffeine."

"Right." She carried the cup of coffee to her handsome handyman, then turned in a small circle, deciding where to begin remedying the mess left by an intruder.

She started with shutting cupboards and drawers, then moved on to clearing the counters. "What do you think Grandma was looking into that made her so afraid that she called you?"

"Well." Wyatt shut the back door and tested the locks before tossing a set of identical keys onto the counter and unearthing a chain system from his bag. "Could be anything." He lined the chain's casing against the door's edge and cast a look in her direction. "Did she say anything unusual to you lately?"

Heat crept over Violet's cheeks as she struggled to recall the last time she'd spoken to her grandma. "We don't talk as much as we used to. I've been busy since Maggie was born."

"How old is your baby?"

Violet chewed her bottom lip, debating how much to tell him about her life "Eight months. She didn't sleep for the first four, but she seems to be making up for it now."

He smiled.

"I can't complain. Even single moms need a break sometime, right?"

Wyatt's sharp brown eyes snapped in her direction. His gaze drifted to her left hand, then rose to her eyes. "Not married?"

"No. Never. How about you?" she asked. "Any children? Got a Mrs. Stone at home?"

"No, ma'am."

"Why not?" The words were out before she'd thought better of them. Then again, maybe this was the smart move. If he'd openly admit his inevitable defects, then she'd stop imagining the snare of electricity coursing between them at every turn. The fact that they were virtual strangers should have been enough to keep her from wondering what his hands might feel like on her hips or in her hair, but it hadn't. Maybe knowing he was a womanizer, gambling addict or married to his job would do the trick.

"I hear I'm a pain in the ass," he said, making the final few twists of his screwdriver. "Apparently, I'm cynical, distrusting and tenacious to a fault."

Violet laughed. "Comes with the job, I'd suppose."

"You're not joking." He slid the chain into the slot and tested the door. "I make my brothers crazy, and I've guarded their lives in combat. If they can't handle me, I'm not sure why anyone else would want to try."

Violet swept a pile of broken glass onto a dustpan and transported it into the trash. "How many brothers do you have? Any sisters?"

"No siblings." Wyatt frowned over his shoulder. "Sorry. I meant my brothers-in-arms. Sometimes I forget they aren't my blood, but we are undeniably family. Sawyer, Jack, Cade and I formed Fortress Security about two years after my military discharge. We've all tried to fit back into our civilian lives, but it didn't work for us. We're too far changed, and our particular skill sets don't translate well to civilian life." Wyatt packed up his tools, jaw clenched. "Eventually I decided to open a business where we could do what we've been trained to do. Guard and protect."

Violet's stomach tilted at the mention of his military service. "What branch did you serve in?" Maggie's dad was a marine.

"US Army Rangers." He seemed to stand impossibly taller as he reported the information. "Sawyer and Jack were, too. We met at Fort Benning." Pride puffed his chest and deepened his voice.

Violet found herself drifting closer, hungry to know more. "A security firm run by army rangers? Also impressive."

"It would be," he said, smiling, "but Sawyer's brother, Cade, was a jarhead."

Violet's mouth went dry. She didn't mean to judge an entire branch of the US military by the actions of one pregnant-girlfriend-abandoning creep, but the association was there nonetheless, roiling in her gut.

"We've all got our mottoes and taglines," Wyatt said, "but the bottom line for Fortress Security is honor first every time. Doesn't matter how you word it."

"God. Corps. Country. Family," Violet groused.

"Exactly."

Exactly. Violet set her broom aside and went to see what she could clean in the dining room.

Wyatt Stone might be kind, sexy and undeniably charming, but that marine motto had pulled her back to reality. The truth was that men like Wyatt would always put family last.

And that would never be good enough for Maggie.

Chapter Three

Violet woke on a gasp of air. Her heart caught in her throat as the faceless monster of her dreams vanished with the warmth of morning sunshine drifting through her grandma's bedroom window. The beloved scent of her childhood was everywhere, on the pillows and sheets, in the curtains and carpet. She took a long steadying breath of the floral dime-store perfume before peering over the bed's edge into her daughter's portable crib.

Maggie grinned around a mouthful of her toes, drool running down her chubby cheek. She released her foot instantly, reaching tiny dimpled fists greedily toward her mama.

Violet scooped her daughter into her arms and rolled back onto the antique sleigh bed for a long snuggle. "Today will be a better day," she promised. "We'll go see Grandma, and the doctors will say good things, and soon we'll be having breakfast with her instead of the enormous cowboy sleeping on the couch."

Maggie laughed and slapped Violet's cheek with one slobbery hand.

Ten minutes later, the Ames ladies were dressed in jean shorts and tank tops, prepared for another hot July day. Violet left her hair down, curling over her shoulders to her ribs, instead of pulled coolly into a ponytail. She told herself it wasn't for Wyatt's sake despite the already rising temperatures.

There was something about the way he'd turned those knowing brown eyes on her last night. The way he'd watched and listened to her, seeming to perceive everything, as if he could read her mind.

Given the handful of inappropriate things she'd fallen asleep thinking about, all starring him, she was thankful to be wrong about the mind reading.

Violet braced her shoulder against the curved wooden headboard and put her weight into shoving the bed away from the door. Barricading the room seemed silly by the light of day, but she wasn't exactly the best judge of men and inviting one the size of Wyatt to sleep over had seemed questionable after she'd come upstairs.

Doorway clear, Violet popped Maggie into a baby sling and headed silently downstairs to start breakfast without waking Wyatt. Six fifteen was early for anyone. It had to be an unthinkable hour for someone who had needed caffeine to stay awake at ten last night.

The beloved scent of fresh-brewed coffee met her in the stairwell as she descended into the kitchen, and Violet hurried toward it. Could Wyatt be awake already? And have had time to make coffee?

His bare back came into view a moment later, and she stopped to appreciate the way his low-slung basketball shorts gripped his trim waist, accentuating his ridiculously broad shoulders and thick, muscular arms.

"Hungry?" he asked without a single look in her direction. It was the second time he'd seemed to magically know she was there.

Violet moved casually into the kitchen, pretending not to have been ogling him. "I thought you'd be asleep."

Wyatt shuffled scrambled eggs around one of her grandma's iron pans and smiled over his shoulder. "I like to run before dawn. Watch the sun rise. Clear my head for a new day."

Violet gave a small laugh. "You've already been out for a run?" The only thing she liked to do before dawn was sleep.

"Sure. A run. A shower. Breakfast. I brought some aerial photos of your grandma's land with me in case I needed them this week, so I used them as guides and went around the property's edge. It worked nicely because I didn't want to go far from here without letting you know I'd be out. I wasn't sure when Maggie would wake."

Violet worked to shut her mouth. He remembered Maggie's name? She'd only introduced her once, and her baby had been asleep the whole time.

"Mrs. Ames has a nice setup here," he said. "Nearly fifty acres. Some of it is being farmed on the back side. Looks like she rents that to a local farmer. Everything near the house is incredibly peaceful, and there's a beautiful lake past the rose gardens."

Violet nodded. The rose gardens were her grandma's pride and joy. She raised blue-ribbon winners almost every year. The lake had always been Violet's favorite outdoor spot, especially in the summer. There was a nice breeze under the willows and when that didn't keep her cool, the shaded waters of the lake did.

Wyatt flicked the knob on Grandma's stove to Off. He shoved rich, buttery-scented eggs onto a plate and ushered them to the kitchen table, already set for two. "I helped myself to the fridge." A grimace worked over his face. "I hope that's okay. I plan to replace everything I used when I go into town. Just thought you'd be ready to eat once you woke."

Violet blinked. "Thank you."

He returned to the stove and levered fat strips of bacon from a second bubbling pan, then layered them on an oblong plate heavy with napkins to soak up the grease. "I grew up on a farm like this. Ours was a horse farm, but this place reminds me an awful lot of home."

"Good times?" she guessed by the wistful look on his face.

"Every. Single. Day." He tossed a red checkered towel over one shoulder and delivered the bacon to the table.

Violet's gaze traveled over his perfect chest to the jaw-dropping eight-pack abs below. A dusting of dark hair began beneath his belly button and vanished unfairly into his waistband.

"Oh." He looked down at himself. "Sorry. Bad habits." Wyatt disappeared into the next room and returned in a clingy black T-shirt. "Eat up. Big day."

Violet tried to hide her disappointment at the change of scenery and discreetly checked for drool. "What's on the agenda?" she asked, settling Maggie into the legless high chair clinging to the kitchen table's edge.

"I'm headed into town," Wyatt said, taking a seat beside Maggie with his loaded plate.

Violet turned for the counter and prepped a bottle of formula, then dug through her diaper bag for Maggie's favorite yellow container of Cheerios. "Breakfast is served," she said, delivering the pair to Maggie. Violet lifted her eyes to Wyatt. "What's happening in town?"

"I'm going to talk to folks," he said. "See what they have to say about your grandma and anything else that might be turning the rumor mill." He sipped his coffee and smiled at Maggie.

She threw a Cheerio at him and missed by a mile.

Violet went to pour a cup of coffee. Clearly, Maggie could hold her own.

Maggie's squeal of delight spun Violet on her toes.

Wyatt bit into a slice of bacon, utterly straight-faced while her daughter clapped and laughed.

"What are you doing?" Violet asked, enjoying the rush of pleasure at seeing her baby smile.

Wyatt chewed and swallowed slowly. "What?"

"Maggie squealed."

Wyatt glanced innocently at the pudgy-cheeked princess. "She did?"

Violet narrowed her eyes in a ruse of disapproval. "You know she did. You're sitting right beside her." She dropped her gaze to pull out a chair, and Maggie cracked up again. This time, Violet caught sight of Wyatt's pink tongue sticking out sideways before he pulled it back in. "Did you just make a face at my baby?"

"No, ma'am."

"I saw you make a face at her," Violet insisted, trying hard not to smile around the edge of her coffee mug. "You lied to me."

Wyatt slid serious brown eyes toward Maggie. "Snitch."

Maggie rocked and bebopped in her seat, eyes fixed tightly on Wyatt.

He wiped his mouth and set the napkin on the table beside his already-empty plate. "Okay. Truth? I've made several faces at your daughter this morning."

Maggie blew raspberries until spit bubbles piled on her chin.

"Oh!" Violet giggled. "Maggie!" She wiped her baby's chin and let the laughter grow. "I've never seen her do that before." A tear slid from the corner of one eye as she dotted Maggie's nose with the napkin. "What a nut."

Wyatt winked at Maggie before turning back to Violet. "What are your plans today? Do you want to join me in

town before we visit Mrs. Ames, or would you rather see
her first, then head into town afterward?"

The words were innocent enough, but they itched and
scratched at Violet's heart and mind. She'd known Wyatt
less than a day and suddenly it seemed as if they were playing house. *When were they visiting Grandma? When were
they going into town?* They. Violet, Maggie *and* Wyatt.

She took a moment to absorb the scene around her.

A handsome, attentive man had made her breakfast.
He'd made her daughter laugh, and he'd unwittingly made
Violet think of things that were impossible. Like a cute little nuclear family of her own. She felt so incredibly stupid.
The connection she imagined between herself and Wyatt
obviously boiled down to him being the first man who was
kind to her following Maggie's birth and nothing more. He
was simply being professional. He was there to do a job,
not fulfill Violet's fantasies. And she needed to get a grip.

Violet pressed a hand discreetly to her tummy, quash-
ing leftover butterflies. "No. Thank you." She couldn't
allow herself to think impossible things. It wasn't fair to
her or Maggie. And what was wrong with her anyway?
Since when was she so eager to have a man in her life?
Things were good already. "I think we'll visit Grandma
on our own," she said. "You can do what you need to do,
and we'll catch up with you later."

Violet pushed onto her feet and carried her still-full
mug and plate to the sink. With her back securely facing
the table, she squeezed her eyes shut and pulled herself
together. Lots of people made babies laugh. Wyatt wasn't
the first or the last, and she couldn't get attached to him
because of it. Much as she wanted a traditional family for
Maggie, the kind with a mommy and a daddy who kissed
goodbye and held hands while they watched TV, Wyatt
wasn't that guy.

She opened her eyes and straightened her expression before turning back to the duo making goofy faces at the table. "We should probably get going."

Wyatt tipped his head in that unsettling way, the one that made her feel as if he could see straight through her. "You sure you don't want me to come with you?"

"Yep." She pushed nervous fingers into the back pockets of her shorts. "We're fine, and we don't want to keep you from your work. The sooner we know what really happened to Grandma, the better. If she's awake when we get to the hospital, I'll call you so you can come by and talk with her in person."

His thick black brows knit together. "All right."

Violet pulled Maggie into her arms and posed her on one hip, then gathered her bottle and Cheerios in the other hand. "Have a good day."

VOICES OF HAPPY children rang through the speakers inside Violet's little yellow hatchback. The CD of nursery rhymes lightened her heavy mood as she fought through a fresh bout of worry for her grandma.

Sunlight streamed over the hills to her left, dashing the street in shards of amber and gold light. Puffy white clouds sailed in the brilliant blue dome above. It was a perfect day for a drive, and Violet had desperately needed to clear her head.

Putting some distance between herself and the sexy soldier guarding Grandma's home was just a bonus. She recalled seeing him pull up in his big black truck, check out the house and shuffle through papers on his dashboard. When he'd climbed out and stood as tall as a house, complete with cowboy hat and boots, her heart had given an irresponsible thud.

"Dumb," she muttered, taking another look at the rear-facing car seat in back. Maggie didn't need a daddy any more than Violet needed a boyfriend *or husband*.

The two of them were doing just fine on their own.

She smiled and returned her eyes to the road ahead. Flyers for the county fair waved and rippled on passing telephone poles, stapled beside missing pet posters and garage sale signs.

A half heartbeat later, her thoughts swept back to the shirtless man making her breakfast. Surely *that* wasn't part of his contract.

The gentle hum of an approaching engine edged into Violet's thoughts, erasing the memory of Wyatt seated beside Maggie at the breakfast table. The sound grew steadily louder, and Violet searched in every direction for the source of the aggressive hum.

Her little hatchback hugged the next curve, dropping low over a hill and into a valley just two miles from the county hospital. She forced her attention back to the road, but her roaming eyes returned to the rearview mirror with a snap.

A battered blue-and-white demolition derby car roared earsplittingly into view behind her as she crested the next hill.

Maggie's car seat rocked in frustration.

"Thanks a lot," Violet muttered at the mangled car racing closer in her rearview. She removed her foot from the gas to let the lunatic pass before they reached the next uphill curve and crashed. Violet's current speed was nearly fifty in a forty-five, and the sharp sway ahead was marked as fifteen miles per hour.

The wrecked car revved closer with an ominous growl. This time, the driver laid on the horn.

Beep!

The seemingly endless blast sent Violet's heart rate into

a sprint. She stuck her hand out the window and waved the guy to go around.

He didn't.

Instead, the attacking car roared closer until its entire front end was invisible in her mirror. *Beeeep! Beeeep!*

Maggie stirred, then began to wail at the continued horn blasts and growling engine.

Violet returned her foot to the gas pedal, pressing a little harder than necessary in an effort to put space between the other vehicle and herself. "Sh-sh-sh," she hushed Maggie, hoping to return her to a gentle sleep.

Maybe she could drive the speed limit as far as the next turnoff, then get away from the road-rager behind her. Or maybe he'd just pass her and move on when she used her signal.

Violet sipped oxygen and concentrated on the narrow two-lane road ahead.

The offending car dropped back a few inches, then charged forward once more, its hood half disappearing in the rearview.

Violet pressed the gas pedal and prayed.

Her death grip on the steering wheel grew painful as her little hatchback floated over the asphalt with a psychopath on its tail. Her fingers were snow-white and sore from lack of circulation.

The fifteen-mile-per-hour curve was coming up fast, and Violet was losing faith in her plan. She had to be able to slow down to take the next turn or pull over, but the beast behind her wouldn't allow it. She realized with a punch of fear through her chest that this could be the end. She could wreck her car with Maggie strapped helplessly in the back seat. The idea was almost too much for her to bear.

Maggie's desperate wails echoed through Violet's heart

and ricocheted off the walls of her racing mind until her vision blurred with fear and regret. They were trapped.

Beep!

Violet watched in horror as the assailing car dropped back, then lurched forward one last time. The reduced-speed sign flew past them, and Violet jerked her wheel.

Her little hatchback careered off the side of the road moments before reaching the steep bend and went skidding through the grass and gravel of a tiny church lawn and empty parking lot.

Beside them, the little white church stood alone at the base of the perilous curve.

The demolition derby car barreled onward, flying into the curve at high speeds and squealing its tires and brakes for several long seconds before the dreaded engine noise faded into the distance.

Violet pulled her keys from the ignition, then climbed out on shaky legs and unlatched Maggie from her car seat. Together, they moved to the church steps and sat, embracing and crying for so long Violet thought someone might find them and wonder if she'd lost her mind.

Maybe she had.

Frighteningly, she and Maggie had nearly lost so much more.

Chapter Four

Wyatt strode back into the blazing midday sun, adjusting his worn-out Stetson and squinting against the light. A trip to the local bar had proven equally as useless as all his other stops today. Wyatt had ordered a sweet tea for the sake of manners, then asked the motley lineup at the bar what they knew about Mrs. Ames. They'd all pointedly ignored him. Though it had been Wyatt's experience that small-town folks were occasionally tight-lipped when it came to outsiders, he'd usually had great luck with the men drinking their way through daylight. Local bars were the male equivalent of a beauty parlor for gossip and hearsay. Except not here. The handful of men who had bellied up to a beer and a shot glass at this bar had officially broken the mold. And just like the local diner, hardware store, mechanic and barber, no one had any news to share about Mrs. Ames.

Wyatt took his leave of yet another uncooperative group and headed back onto the street. He spun his key ring around one finger and took a long look in both directions. Where to next?

A sheriff's cruiser slid against the curb before he'd had time to decide. The cruiser's lights flashed. No siren. The man who climbed out was nearing fifty with narrow shoulders and a shiny star on his chest.

Wyatt tipped his hat and stepped aside, allowing the local sheriff room to pass on the narrow sidewalk. The town was a modern-day Rockwell portrait waiting to happen. So what had brought the sheriff and his flashers out? Wyatt paused, waiting to see where the local lawman would go. Had there been another "accident" like Mrs. Ames's? Or perhaps the bar patrons had reanimated and grown rowdy in Wyatt's absence.

The sheriff stopped in front of Wyatt and rested a palm on the butt of his sidearm. "Are you the stranger going door-to-door and making folks nervous?"

Wyatt glanced over his shoulder in search of a shady, bothersome guy.

No one was behind him. The sheriff was definitely talking to Wyatt.

"I don't think so, sir," Wyatt said. "I've been out enjoying your lovely town. Meeting folks. That's all."

The sheriff gave a long, assessing look. "Where did you come from?"

"Lexington," Wyatt answered, this time returning the scrutiny. Irritated, he crossed his arms and widened his stance. "You been sheriff long?"

"Long enough."

Wyatt smiled. "Someone reported me for being friendly?" He'd love to know who, but didn't have to ask to know the sheriff wasn't telling. Too bad, because whoever had made the complaint might also be the one with something to hide. A recent B and E for example, or maybe an assault on an old lady. "Is that a crime in this town?" Wyatt had spoken to a dozen locals, but he'd been careful not to ask anything too pointed. He'd asked if anyone knew Mrs. Ames, if they'd heard about her fall, and where he might get a good locksmith after the break-in. He'd already changed the locks, of course, but he'd hoped to read folks' expressions. See who was shocked by the news of a burglary and who already knew. Problem was that no one had paid any attention to him at all.

The sheriff sucked his teeth and grimaced. His stance was rigid, defiant, not at all welcoming or pleasantly confident. Wyatt pegged him for a bully. "What business brings you to River Gorge?"

"I'm visiting."

"Who?"

Wyatt homed in on the sheriff's features, the beating pulse in his throat, the dilation of his pupils. "Gladys Ames. Do you know her?"

The sheriff nodded. "I know everyone, but I've never seen you. Are you a relative?"

"No. Mrs. Ames is my girlfriend's grandma," he improvised. "I came to watch over her while she's here. Seems there was a break-in last night. You were there, right?" Hadn't Violet said it was a Sheriff Masterson whose cruiser had forced his truck into the grass on the narrow gravel road? "Got any idea who would've done something like that?"

A pinch of guilt tugged in his mind for announcing Violet as his girlfriend, but Wyatt wasn't about to tell the sheriff who he really was or why he'd come to River Gorge. Not considering the inquisition he was getting just for speaking to locals. For all Wyatt knew, the sheriff could be the reason Mrs. Ames needed his help in the first place. She certainly could have chosen to talk to the sheriff instead. And if he was being honest, the idea of being Violet's boyfriend wasn't a bad one. Which was confusing all by itself, because Wyatt didn't do relationships.

Sheriff Masterson cocked his hip. "Funny. Violet didn't say anything about a boyfriend when I spoke to her last night. She surely didn't mention anything about a man coming here to stay with her."

"Can you blame me? She was attacked inside her grandma's home. I couldn't stay away after that. Turns out I'm the overprotective sort." He straightened to his full height and locked his jaw, an intentional reminder that Sheriff Masterson might have the star, but Wyatt was there to protect Violet and Maggie. Anyone with different plans would have to go through him, and no one ever had. "Any leads on the break-in? Seems strange, doesn't it? Someone busts into an old lady's house, tears it up but takes nothing. She lives on a widow's pension. What was there to take? And the crime occurred on the same day she allegedly fell from a ladder." Wyatt furrowed his brow. "As the sheriff, that must send up some red flags."

"Crime happens everywhere. I'm looking into the break-in, but old ladies fall all the time." He gave Wyatt a more thorough look then, trailing him head to toe, lingering on his jacket, sides and ankles. Looking for signs of a weapon? If he had anything to say about the gun nestled against his back, or knife in his boot, Wyatt had a permit to carry concealed firearms and more training than the good sheriff could fathom for the knife. "Military?" he asked.

"Ranger."

The sheriff nodded; a rueful smile budded on his lips. "Violet know about that?" He snorted, clearly laughing at Wyatt. For his service? For his doomed pretend relationship?

Wyatt bristled.

A pair of women in fitted running gear came into view behind the sheriff, having rounded the corner from the direction of the local park. The taller, blonder one locked eyes with Wyatt. A coy smile curled the corner of her mouth. The petite redhead followed suit a moment later.

Wyatt smiled back.

Sheriff Masterson turned on his shiny shoes to follow Wyatt's gaze. He tapped the brim of his hat and smiled at the women. "Afternoon Maisey, Jenna."

The ladies slowed to a stop, still smiling at Wyatt. The blonde outright ogled him. Her hand bobbed up for a shake. "Jenna Jones," she said. "I don't believe we've met."

"Nice to meet you," Wyatt answered, taking her thin hand in his. "I was just asking the sheriff if he'd heard anything new about Mrs. Ames. She fell yesterday, then her house was broken into."

"No," the ladies gasped.

The blonde, Jenna, stepped closer, still holding his hand. "Mrs. Ames is the sweetest woman. I've known her all my life. Is she okay? I didn't hear about the fall."

The redhead looked at the sheriff. "Did he say someone broke into her house? Why would anyone do that? Do you have a suspect?"

Wyatt rocked back on his heels. Apparently his usual stops were all wrong in River Gorge. Normally, men spoke easily to him. Wyatt would break the ice on topics like sports, cars and military, then ask the things he really wanted to know. Around here that hadn't been the case. Maybe he should've simply gone jogging.

Jenna joined her friend then, turning to stare at the sheriff. "Are you going to answer her?" The tone was harsh and familiar. Wyatt doubted Jenna was related to the man; more likely they'd been former lovers or shared another form of history. Either way, she looked like she'd like to punch his face, and he looked like it wouldn't surprise him if she tried.

The sheriff sniffed. "I'm looking into it."

"Well, when you're done with that," she said, "maybe you could spend some time patrolling our streets. We just watched a demolition derby car run a hatchback right off the road by Devil's Curve. When are you going to do something about the morons using the county route as some kind of playground for their stupidity?"

Wyatt's heart seemed to stop. "What kind of hatchback?"

"Small," the redhead said. "Yellow, I think."

Wyatt's feet were in motion, pulling him away from the trio and toward his truck parked down the street. He turned to jog backward, needing to know but also needing to go. "Was anyone hurt?" He freed his phone and dialed Violet while he waited for the answer.

"I don't think so," Jenna said. "The car spun into the church parking lot, but it didn't roll and it wasn't hit. The beat-up old junker went sailing around the curve. A woman got out. She looked fine. We were on the towpath. It wasn't easy to see from there, but all the honking and engine roaring had gotten our attention. We caught the tail end of it all."

Wyatt's limbs ached to run. "When?"

"Maybe an hour ago."

"Thank you," he called, turning and diving into a sprint. The call connected and rang against his ear. *Pick up. Pick up. Pick up.* He willed Violet to answer his call. Prayed she and her infant daughter were okay. Kicked himself internally for letting her go off on her own when everything in him had said it wasn't safe. That whatever Mrs. Ames had gotten herself into wasn't over. He should have followed Violet, stuck by her, protected her.

It wouldn't happen again.

He yanked the driver's-side door open and swung himself behind the wheel. *Pick up.* He nearly screamed the words as he shifted into Drive and eased away from the curb.

His call went to voicemail.

VIOLET FORCED HER still-rubbery legs forward as she eased off the hospital elevator and down the long white corridor toward the nurse's station on her grandma's floor. Maggie was asleep in her arms, exhausted from crying after their run-in with a lunatic and his demolition derby car. The nurses were all busy when she finally arrived at the desk. Talking to visitors. Speaking on the telephone. Making rounds. None of the ladies in pastel scrubs made eye contact. When Violet had arrived yesterday, her cousin Tanya was one of the nurses. She was a distant cousin, ambiguously related, but neither she nor Tanya had ever questioned the connection. They'd been friends all their lives. Violet waited a long moment, scanning the area for an available nurse, before moving on, too eager to continue waiting. She wanted to see her grandma's face and take a seat someplace where she couldn't be run off the road. She'd try the desk again in a few minutes when the rush died down.

Violet hurried down the hallway to her grandmother's room. The sound of movement inside set Violet's heart alight. "Grandma?" She rushed through the open door and slid the curtain back with bated breath.

"Hello," her grandma's friend Ruth answered, "come on in." Ruth tidied her stack of playing cards, then cut and folded them together with a scissoring zip. She'd pulled a chair over to face Grandma's bed and appeared to be playing solitaire on her blankets. "No change," Ruth reported. Her tanned cheeks were spotted from too many decades in the sun, and her lips turned down at the corners, unhappy with her report. She doled out three cards and placed them near the foot of her bed. "I came after my morning chores." Her hair was pulled back in a severe bun, accentuating her sharp features and small green eyes.

Violet took the chair nearest Grandma's shoulder and

slid one hand over hers where it rested on the bed. Machines glowed and beeped on stands and poles nearby, monitoring her grandma's heart rate, pulse and oxygen levels. An IV dripped something into her veins. A wave of grief rolled through Violet and she forced the emotion down. Grandma wasn't gone. Grandma was a fighter. "Has the doctor been in?"

"Just Tanya," Ruth said. "She comes every hour or so to say nothing's changed." Ruth gave the cards a break and hooked one ankle over her opposite knee. A lifetime of hard outdoor work in River Gorge had left Ruth roughly the color of leather and likely a little tougher. "No news is good news."

Violet didn't agree. No news was maddening. She shifted Maggie in her arms and squeezed her grandma's hand. "Tanya was here yesterday when we got in from Winchester."

Ruth pursed her lips. "She's a good kid."

A twist of guilt wound through Violet. She and Tanya were the same age, twenty-six. Hardly kids. But Violet hadn't been here for Grandma. She'd left for college, and unlike Tanya, Violet hadn't come back. In fact, she'd visited less and less these last two or three years. She should have at least stayed the night at the hospital, shouldn't she? She rested her cheek against Maggie's head. No. She couldn't have stayed. She'd spent last night half fearing a second break-in and half curious about what the cowboy-for-hire on Grandma's couch might've done to anyone who'd try.

Her throat tightened at the memory of the fleeing intruder. He'd run straight for her. Broad palms plowing into her shoulders. He'd thrown her onto her backside in the space of a heartbeat. She'd found bruises on her back and elbows when she showered. Marks from where she'd crashed against the hard floors and rolled. Twelve hours later, a car had run her off the road. There was no way that was a coincidence. Even Violet's luck wasn't that bad. Her gaze ran back to her grandma's bandaged head. A near-fatal fall, a break-in, a psychotic road-rager, the hiring of a private security guy. That list definitely added up to something, and it wasn't coincidence. In fact, Violet needed to contact the local sheriff's department and make a report about the demolition derby car. Even if the driver wasn't found, it seemed like a good idea to document the strange and dangerous things happening around her. She'd considered calling the police from the church parking lot, but she and Maggie were too shaken, and the offending car was long gone. All she'd really wanted was to find respite somewhere with witnesses in case the car returned. Could the car's driver be the same man who'd been inside her grandma's home?

"Ruth," Violet began, turning back to Grandma's friend. "When you found Grandma yesterday, was the front door open to her home? Ajar maybe?"

"No." Ruth shook her head as if to underline the word. "I knocked. Rang the bell. Door was shut tight. Why?"

"Did you go inside?"

"Sure," she said. "Wasn't locked. Rarely is. I let myself in and took a look around. I called for her, but she wasn't there. I figured she'd run out to the garden to cut some roses, so I went around back. That was when I saw the barn was open."

"That's when you found her," Violet said.

"Yes." Ruth blinked emotion-filled eyes. "That's right."

"Do you have any idea why she was in the barn? Was she keeping something out there?"

"Not that I know of." Ruth raised a wide gray eyebrow. "Why?" She twisted in her seat to face Violet, a strangely parental look in her eyes. "Why all these questions? Did something else happen?"

Violet slumped in her chair, unsure how much she could say. It was impossible to know her limits without knowing what her grandma had been up to, but she was certain Ruth was a friend. Ruth had been part of Grandma's life long before Violet was born. Before Violet's mother, too. "Her home was broken into last night."

"What?" Ruth gasped. "Are you okay? Is the home? What did they take?"

Violet shrugged. "I don't know. Nothing seemed to be missing, but I haven't been here in a while." Honestly, she'd barely been anywhere since Maggie was born. These last eight months had boiled down to meeting her baby's needs and trying to calculate how many hours of sleep she might get each night. The answer to the second part was "never enough."

"A break-in," Ruth whispered, still clearly baffled.

"How has Grandma seemed to you lately?" Violet asked. "Was she okay, or was something going on with her?" Violet tipped slightly forward, begging Ruth to share something that might help her understand.

Ruth puckered her brow and stared at Grandma's slack face. "She's been a little on edge and distracted. I'd assumed that had to do with Mary Alice."

"What's wrong with Mary Alice?" Violet asked. She knew Mary Alice as well as she knew Ruth. Both women had been lifelong friends of Grandma's. They'd held Grandma together when her daughter, Violet's mom, had left, when her husband passed, and when she'd had to raise a grieving, rebellious granddaughter despite it all. "Is she…" Violet began, then halted. "Is Mary Alice…" She came up short again. Was there a nice way to ask if an old woman had died?

Ruth scrutinized Violet's struggle for words. "Mary Alice isn't dead, if that's what you were going to ask," she said after a few seconds. "She's got dementia, though. The symptoms have gotten a lot worse these last few weeks. She's slipping away fast, and the whole Masterson family has been a little grouchier than usual these days. The illness has taken a toll on everyone close to her, your grandma included."

Violet didn't know Mary Alice's family well, aside from the general knowledge small town living provided. Her husband had been the sheriff when Violet was young, and their son was sheriff now. Neither man was in the running for Mr. Congeniality, or the sort who'd show up at local gatherings, unless duty demanded it. "And you?" Violet asked.

Ruth gave a sad smile. "Someone's got to hold it together."

Tanya peeked her head through Grandma's open door and rapped her knuckles on the wall. "Knock knock." Her bright smile set Violet on her feet.

"Tanya." She met her cousin at the room's center and gave her a gentle hug, careful not to wake Maggie. "Any news?"

"Not yet," she said, rubbing Violet's arm when she stepped out of the embrace. "Dr. Shay says everything looks good, and we should be patient. Grandma will wake when she's ready. Until then, we just have to wait. She's been through a lot and it can take time to overcome an accident like this one. How are you and this little princess holding up?"

Violet stroked Maggie's back and her sleeping baby released a contented sigh. "We're okay."

"Good." Tanya smiled. "I'll be here as often as I can,

and I'll keep you posted if her condition changes. Grandma's tough, Violet," she assured. "She'll be fine."

Violet nodded. Grandma would find the strength to recover, and Violet would be there to help every step of the way. Until then, Violet needed to stick a little closer to the former ranger at Grandma's house. Violet had no intention of testing her luck with another burglar or demolition derby car, and she was certain he would have no problems handling either.

Of course, spending too much time with an attentive and sexy man like Wyatt Stone was going to pose a few problems of its own. Beginning with how to keep her undeniable attraction to him from blurring the lines of their reality.

Chapter Five

An engine roared outside the front window of Grandma's home. Violet jumped, still edgy from her run-in with the demolition derby car this morning. She'd called the police as soon as she got home and the woman who'd answered had promised to send an officer out to take the report, but she doubted any of the deputies would be racing to get to her.

Her heart sprinted and her palms grew slick as she moved carefully toward the front window to check the driveway. Maggie was asleep in her crib, but Violet could get to her and be outside in under a minute if she had to. She pulled the curtain's corner back with trembling fingertips, scolding herself once more for not taking Wyatt's suggestion to stick together today.

Relief washed through her chest at the sight of Wyatt's truck, back in the driveway. He was already making his way up the front steps in long, anxious strides.

Fresh terror rent Violet's heart as she took in his grim expression. Whatever had drawn that kind of fear on Wyatt's face was surely something for her to worry about. "Wyatt?" she asked, opening the door with an anxious tug. "What's wrong?"

His steps faltered a moment as his eyes landed on hers. "You're okay," he said, sounding half awed and half stricken. "Someone said a car fitting your vehicle's description was run off the road this morning. I thought for sure it was you. I tried calling. You didn't answer." His exacting gaze lingered on her face, her neck, her chest. "You're frightened. Breathing hard. Your cheeks are flushed. It was you, wasn't it?"

Emotion swept up from her core, taking her by surprise. "I called the police, then I worried that the car's driver would somehow know I tattled and come revving up the street looking for me. It's ridiculous. I know. I'm sorry I didn't answer."

"You need to save my number. When I call, I need you to answer."

Violet nodded. "Of course. I will next time."

"Did you get a look at the driver or the license plate?"

"No plate, and I couldn't see the driver through the tint and glare. It was crazy, though. He came out of nowhere," she said, hating the tremor in her voice. "He kept honking. Gunning his engine. Maggie was screaming."

Wyatt stepped closer and raised one tentative arm, an offering of comfort, hers to accept or deny. Violet hesitated. She didn't want to cry on a near-stranger's shoulder, but she needed the comfort, and she'd never see Wyatt again once this was over. So maybe she could be a little bit of a mess if she needed to be.

She fell against the strength of his chiseled chest and wrapped her arms around his back. His heart pounded strong and steady beneath her ear. His clothes and skin smelled of cologne and body wash, and Violet inhaled deeply.

A very long moment later, his arms circled her back, engulfing her, drawing her close in a powerful embrace. "It's okay," he said. "You're okay."

She rocked her cheek against his soft black T-shirt.

"Thank you. For being here. For coming to help Grandma and for staying now. I don't know what I would do here alone. I don't know if it's safe to stay, or if it's safer to go. If I leave, what happens to Grandma? If I stay, what might happen to Maggie?"

Wyatt curved his tall frame over her, lowering his mouth to her cheek. "I will protect you, your grandma and your daughter. You can trust me on that, and when I find out who is behind these violent acts, he will wish I hadn't."

Violet shivered. The words were flat and controlled, not spoken in anger, just statements of fact and strangely horrifying. Still, she wanted the promise to be true. "Thank you."

The bark of a police siren jerked her upright. She loosened her grip on him as she attempted to disentangle her arms from his waist.

Wyatt held her firm, locking his fingers against the small of her back. "I told the sheriff we were a couple," he whispered. "We shouldn't ruin the facade."

Violet tipped back, arching to study his blank soldier face and pressing their torsos tighter still. "What? Why?" Was that something he'd actually considered?

"He had a lot of questions," Wyatt said. "I ran into him in town, and I didn't want to out myself as private security."

"Right." She nodded. This wasn't about her. He simply needed a cover story. He didn't want to be her boyfriend. That was a fantasy she'd already let go too far. Besides, she knew firsthand that when men swept in to save the day, they were always gone in the morning. And Violet didn't need drama in her life. She needed stability.

The deputy marched in their direction, one hand at the brim of his hat. "Miss Ames?"

"Yes." Violet stepped away from Wyatt. She wrapped an

arm across her middle, defending against the coolness that settled in his absence. She shook the deputy's hand. "This is Wyatt Stone, my boyfriend." She cleared her throat as the last word lodged there awkwardly.

Wyatt took the man's hand smoothly and with confidence, as if it was no big deal for her to announce herself as his girlfriend and suggest all that the title might imply.

"I'm Deputy Santos," the man said, looking the couple over. "I'm here to make a report." His olive skin was the perfect accent to his shaggy jet-black hair and deep ebony eyes. "Were you both in the car when the incident occurred?" he asked Violet.

"No," Violet said. "It was just my baby and me."

Deputy Santos removed a small flip notebook from his shirt pocket and turned to an empty page. "Can you tell me everything you remember about the car, the driver and the incident?"

"Sure. I mean, it's not much, but I'll try," she said.

The deputy took notes as she described the incident from start to finish in as much detail as possible. His gaze rose from the paper when she described the car that had chased her.

Wyatt shifted his stance. "You know that car?"

The deputy returned his attention to the paper, finishing whatever he'd been in the middle of writing. "I can't say for sure, but I will look into it." He tapped the tip of his pen against the paper. "Anything else?"

Violet shook her head. "No. That's it." Something about the deputy put Violet on edge. He was hard like Wyatt, without the pretense of friendship.

He nodded, then turned to Wyatt. His gaze dropped briefly to the india ink tattoo stretching from beneath his shirt sleeve. "You serve?"

Wyatt dipped his chin sharply. "Ranger. You?"

Deputy Santos stood straighter. His stern expression eased. "I was Delta Force once upon a time."

Wyatt smiled. "It's nice to meet you." A strange vibe cropped up between the men. "Can I ask you something?"

Santos narrowed his eyes, cautious again. "You can ask."

"Did the sheriff's department get a call this afternoon about a man talking to folks downtown?"

The deputy's brow wrinkled in confusion. "About a man talking to people? What do you mean?"

Wyatt shook his head. "Nothing. Let me ask you something else. How well do you know the sheriff?"

Santos blew out a long breath. "Not well." He crossed his arms and widened his stance, seeming to consider whatever he would say next. "I got into law enforcement after the military. I came to River Gorge a few years back because I needed work, and this department had an opening. It didn't take long to see the Mastersons run this town. And that's fine. I don't want to run the town. I just do my job and skip the company picnics."

Wyatt bobbed his head. "Fair enough."

The deputy gave Violet a long look, then turned for the driveway. "The report will be available online tomorrow. First copy is free from the secretary at the station." He pried the door of his cruiser open and dropped behind the wheel. A moment later, he was gone.

Maggie's cries erupted through the baby monitor in the living room.

"Sounds like dinnertime," Violet sighed, checking her watch.

Wyatt opened the front door and held it for her to pass.

"Maggie's like a little hobbit, eating every meal twice." Lately, Violet couldn't seem to stomach more than coffee.

She hoped Maggie's continued interest in food was a sign that she wasn't as stressed out as her mom.

"Hey." Wyatt reached the interior steps before Violet. "Why don't I get Maggie, and you can start her dinner? Teamwork. Yeah?"

Teamwork? Well, that was a new one for Violet, especially in terms of childcare, though she absolutely wasn't opposed. "Okay. Thank you." Reluctantly, she headed for the kitchen, attention focused on the cries still registering through the baby monitor.

"What are you doing?" Wyatt's voice boomed from the little speaker in mock breathlessness.

Maggie hiccuped, then gave a shorter, softer complaint.

Wyatt groaned. "You're so heavy. I can barely lift you. Oh my goodness." He panted.

Violet smiled as she prepped Maggie's bottle and chose a jar of peas with carrots for her baby's midafternoon snack.

Maggie giggled, then complained, more softly still.

"Okay," Wyatt agreed. "I'll try again, but you have to help me."

"No!" Maggie yelled the only word she'd perfected.

Wyatt gasped. "What?"

Violet stifled a bubbling laugh. Maggie was every kind of cute, but Violet could already tell she was going to be a real pistol.

A moment of silence passed, then he laughed. "You didn't tell me you could talk. What else can you say?"

"No!" Maggie growled, then laughed.

"Wow." Wyatt's quick footsteps rocked down the stairs a moment later, and he had Maggie in his arms. "I don't mean to be critical, but your baby's kind of negative."

"No!" Maggie stated as if on cue.

Violet laughed. "That's her only word. Be nice."

Wyatt placed her in the high chair and put his hands on his hips. "You probably should teach her something else. What if someone comes by here offering a million dollars or free ponies?"

"No," Maggie answered, then squealed, utterly thrilled with herself.

Wyatt lifted one palm and shoulder as if to say she'd made his case.

Violet delivered Maggie's bottle and bowl of baby food with a smile. She took a seat at Maggie's side and began to spoon the veggies up.

Wyatt poured two glasses of iced tea and brought them back to the table with him, setting one before Violet and sipping the other. "I ran into the sheriff today."

"Yeah?" Violet lifted her gaze to him. "You asked the deputy about a call to the department. Was that true? Someone called the sheriff on you?"

Wyatt stretched his neck. "I don't think so, but that was what he claimed when he found me."

"Huh," she huffed, frowning as she stirred the pureed food. "He seemed fine when we spoke last night after the break-in."

"Do you know him very well?" Wyatt asked. "You grew up in River Gorge, right?"

"Yeah, but I don't know him well," she said, spooning another bite into Maggie's open mouth. "Grandma and I never had any reason to need the sheriff. I know his mother, but not him. Honestly, I hadn't had reason to speak with any of the local lawmen before today."

Wyatt set his tea aside, considering her words. "The sheriff seemed to know you."

"How so?" Curiosity flamed in her mind. "Did he say something?" Violet could only imagine the things the sheriff might have heard secondhand through the local grape-

vine, especially after Grandma and her friends returned
from Violet's baby shower last year. Violet had still been
reeling from the sting of rejection and fear of impending
motherhood, and she had been less than gracious when
asked about the baby's father.

"He seemed to imply you don't like military men."
Wyatt shifted his gaze to Maggie. "Her father served?"

Violet stiffened. "Yes."

"Was the sheriff right?" Wyatt asked. "You have something against military men?"

Violet dropped the little spoon, then scrambled to pick
it up, hating the anger and humiliation the thought of her
ex brought her. "Sheriff Masterson doesn't know anything
about me." She exhaled. She didn't want to talk about Maggie's father, but avoiding the topic would only make her
look more pathetic. Might as well get the story out and
over with, not that there was much to tell. "Maggie's dad
was a marine," she said. "I thought we were in love, and
he shipped out making big promises about our future. We
had a bit of a whirlwind romance, so I can blame myself
for that." She shot Wyatt a sheepish look. Whirlwind ro-
mances weren't something Violet normally participated in.
She tried to be much more levelheaded than that, but her ex
had been so persuasive, so charming. "We traded emails
for a while, but after I found out about the pregnancy, he
disengaged. Completely. Changed his number. Stopped returning emails. Maybe closed the account. I don't know,
but I gave him every opportunity to know her, to be part
of her life, even if I wanted to strangle him for breaking
my heart. He wasn't interested."

Wyatt appraised her with those careful dark eyes. "I'm
sorry," he said eventually.

"My heart was stupid, and I won't let it happen again."
She offered an apologetic smile. She always felt guilty for

speaking poorly about Maggie's dad, even if he was a big jerk for what he'd done. "At least I got Maggie out of the mess. I don't know what I'd do without her."

Wyatt made a sour face at her baby. "I don't know. She's pretty negative."

Maggie formed a wide toothless smile. "No."

Violet laughed as she wiped carrots off Maggie's sticky cheeks. "Are you sure this isn't just your natural effect on women?"

A deep belly laugh broke free from Wyatt's lips; it bounced in his chest and reached his eyes. "No. I'm honestly not sure at all." He turned the captivating expression on Violet and silence settled over the room.

"I'm glad you're here," she said. "And I don't have anything against military men. I'm thankful for each of you and for your service."

He watched her carefully, as if he was expecting something more.

Violet offered a handshake. "I'm glad to know you, Wyatt Stone."

He folded her hand in his. "It was my honor."

Their joined hands stilled. He'd held on too long and she'd let him. What did that mean? What would he think it meant? Violet pulled away, busying herself with clearing the high chair tray.

She didn't have to have something against Wyatt to keep her heart on guard. They could be friends. Work together. Help her grandma and then part ways. Nothing more. She rubbed her hands roughly against a kitchen towel, trying not to enjoy the way he spoke sweetly to Maggie at the table or the way she blew him kisses off the palms of her chubby dimpled hands. No. This wasn't permanent. Not even semipermanent. This was a flickering moment in her life, already on its way past.

WYATT FOLLOWED VIOLET off the back porch and into the sun. She'd said she needed some fresh air, and he couldn't bring himself to let her go alone. Not the way things were going down around her in this town. She'd tucked her baby into a circle of fabric and hung her off one hip like a purse. It was the weirdest thing Wyatt had ever seen someone do with a baby, but Maggie appeared happy. She kicked her bare feet and looked eagerly around. Violet kept a protective arm around her, but thanks to the construction of the sling, he thought, remembering what Violet had called it, Violet's hands were both free, too.

Violet stopped to admire her grandma's roses. Little stone plaques placed among the mulch identified the various bushes as county prizewinners. Wyatt didn't know much about flowers, but he could understand why these beautifully manicured plants had gotten so much glory.

"I think Deputy Santos knew that demolition derby car," Violet said, squinting against the sweltering sun. "There was recognition on his face at the mention of it, and how many cars like that one can possibly be in one small town?"

"Maybe," Wyatt agreed. He'd seen the look on Santos, too, but he had to be careful about assuming it meant anything more than surprise. "He seemed like an honest guy. He might make a good ally. After my run-in with the sheriff today, I'm sure he's got something against me, and he's the head honcho here. If he wants me arrested for interfering in his investigation, I'm going to jail. And I can't help you from there."

Violet paused, turning to face him. "So, he doesn't report to anyone? That's a lot of power in a little county like ours."

"It's a lot of power anywhere," Wyatt said. He shook his head. "Maybe my brothers are right when they say I'm cynical."

"Well," Violet said, "I think a little cynicism is warranted here. Something is definitely wrong. Someone hurt Grandma, broke into her home and ran me off the road. Then the sheriff said he got a complaint about you in town, but the deputy didn't hear about it. Makes me wonder if someone's holding something over the sheriff, maybe even keeping him from acting on valid threats and feeding him information on bogus ones. I think there's a good reason Grandma called you and not local authorities."

Wyatt rubbed his chin, struggling to stick with the facts at hand. "There could be a number of reasons she came to me instead. Maybe she felt she couldn't trust anyone here to keep her confidence, even the sheriff. In small towns, most people are connected somehow. News spreads. Could be that she needed more than a cop to watch her back. If she felt she was truly in danger, it's not as if a local deputy could move in with her temporarily. And I got the feeling, through her emails, that she might've wanted a little help looking into something because she asked about the agency's ability to research."

Violet played with Maggie's little hands as they walked, her gaze on the horizon, brow furrowed in thought. "Did you say my grandma wrote you emails? Did you keep them? Can I see them?"

"Sure."

Violet turned on her toes and headed back to the house.

Wyatt followed. "Are you getting hungry? You didn't eat anything earlier. There's plenty of vegetables in the garden, and I saw a grill on the rear porch."

Violet shot a skeptical look over her shoulder as she opened the side door to her grandmother's home. "You don't have to do any of that."

"I don't mind." The words came easily, congenially, and Wyatt realized he meant them. He liked the idea of cooking for Violet. "Here." They stopped in the kitchen, and he swiped through the emails on his phone before presenting the device to her. "These are all the emails I received from your grandma."

"Thanks." She set Maggie on the floor and handed her a large plastic block with a bell inside. "Okay." She accepted the phone then, lips moving slightly as she read the messages to herself, scrolling slowly. "I hate that she was afraid and didn't call me," she said. "I don't know what I could have done, but I wish I would've known. I feel so helpless."

Wyatt pressed a palm to her back, rubbing a small circle before pulling his hand away. He stuffed the offending fingers into his pocket. Violet wasn't his to touch. She was a client's granddaughter, and in a few days the mystery would be solved. She'd be back in Winchester, and he'd be in Lexington trying to forget the beautiful, smart and kind brunette who'd gotten under his skin from hello.

"Wyatt?" Violet turned to him, a strange expression on her face.

"What?"

"Grandma doesn't have a computer. So how'd she send these messages?"

The sudden roar of a massive engine split the afternoon air, stopping him from taking a guess. Glass shattered outside, and his truck alarm raged in response.

Wyatt raced to the living room and opened the front door. His truck lights flashed in protest at the apparent assault.

On the lane, a set of taillights fishtailed away, attached to the rear end of a blue-and-white demolition derby car.

Chapter Six

Violet dialed the police again, wishing she could put in a request for which officer would respond this time. Wyatt seemed to trust Deputy Santos, but she was leery of everyone today. She definitely hadn't liked talking to Sheriff Masterson on the night Grandma's house was broken into. He'd treated her with tamped-down hostility even then. Now she pressed her back against the front wall and peered outside. She watched as Wyatt stormed down the drive, then up the road a few yards in the direction the taillights had disappeared.

Maggie tugged on her leg, trying and failing to pull herself upright.

She scooped her baby into a hug and covered her in kisses.

"Violet," Wyatt's voice boomed through the window.

Violet jumped.

Outside, Wyatt stood, hands on hips, in the driveway. He'd shut the blaring truck alarm down, and was scowling at her little hatchback parked in front of his pickup. "You can come out," he said a little softer, though still loud enough to be heard from inside the home.

She opened the door slowly, then moved across the threshold as Wyatt lifted a cell phone to his ear. Maggie fussed on her hip, eager to be put down as Violet drifted

to Wyatt's side on autopilot. He asked someone on the
other end of his call to send a deputy back to his location.

Two police reports in one day.

In the quietest town on earth.

The sun heated Violet's skin, and the scent of prizewin-
ning roses wafted on the breeze. The nostalgia was thick,
but this wasn't the town she remembered.

The passenger window of Wyatt's truck was shattered.
Shards of glass glittered on the drive in tiny chunks.

"Hopefully Santos is back here in a few minutes," Wyatt
said, stuffing the phone into his pocket. "He can add this
to our growing list of assaults. It might make him look a
little more closely at the people in his town." Wyatt's hard
brown eyes swept from her face to the vehicles. "I'm sorry
you got the worst of it."

Violet followed his gaze to her hatchback. Her stomach
dropped as the damage to her little car registered. Six jagged letters were scratched into the paint of her driver's side.
GO HOME. "Oh my goodness." Her heart hammered and
her throat thickened. The letters stretched from wheel to
wheel. It was impossible to misinterpret the instructions.

GO HOME.

It was an order. It was a threat.

Who would do this? Why?

Wyatt wrapped one strong arm across Violet's back
and pulled her and Maggie against the hard-muscled vee
of his side. He rubbed her arm with his palm, creating heat
where goose bumps had risen despite the sweltering temperatures. "You can have it repainted."

She pressed a hand to her mouth, then nearly jumped out
of her skin when the *whoop!* of a deputy's cruiser bleated
behind her, already pulling into the drive.

Wyatt squeezed her a little tighter. "Great," he muttered.

Violet turned for a look at the new arrival. Not Santos, and not a deputy's cruiser.

It was the sheriff.

WYATT BRISTLED AS Sheriff Masterson climbed from his cruiser and moseyed serenely to their side, glancing only briefly at the damage to their vehicles.

"What seems to be the trouble?" he asked.

Violet made a strangled sound beneath the hand on her lips.

Wyatt tightened his fingers on her biceps, reassuring her he had this. "You got here awfully quick, Sheriff. I've barely disconnected my call to dispatch."

The sheriff's gaze drifted then, from Wyatt to Violet and Maggie. "I was in the neighborhood."

"Yeah?" Wyatt's voice deepened. He felt his muscles tightening to spring as he leveled a no-nonsense stare on the cocky lawman. "Any particular reason for that? Mrs. Ames's place isn't exactly on the beaten path."

"Seems you two need all kinds of help these days," he said, giving the vandalized vehicles a pointed look. "I figured I should keep an eye out."

"And yet you missed the culprit by only a few minutes." Wyatt rubbed his chin. "You probably got a good look at the car, though, since you were in the neighborhood. A blue-and-white demolition derby car." He raised his brows. "Sound familiar? It went hightailing out of here not ten minutes ago."

"Nope." The sheriff rocked on his heels and stuffed his hands into his pockets. "I didn't see anything on my way over except this pretty day."

Violet shifted, and Wyatt dropped his arm from around her, unwilling to hold her there if she wanted to go inside Instead, she rolled toward him, burying her face and hands against his chest, pressing Maggie to him with her. Wyatt's arms curled around them on instinct, making promises of protection he couldn't yet voice.

The sheriff took a few steps closer to the vehicles. "You certainly are having a lot of problems here. I'll make the report on this, but you've got to admit it begs a couple questions."

"Such as?" Wyatt pulled in deep breaths of clean country air and forced his temper into check.

"For starters," the sheriff said, moving past them to kick the front tire of Violet's car, "who'd you upset enough to do something like this? And why?" He squatted before the damage and dragged a finger along the deep lines. "Also gotta ask why you don't just take the advice here and go home." He creaked back onto his feet and shook his head. "Seems like the best way to protect that baby of yours is just get away from all this mess."

Violet tensed. She spun to face the sheriff. "Are you suggesting my baby is in danger? That the man who ran me off the road and vandalized my car might attack my infant? Is that what you're saying?" There was fire in her voice as she pulled her body away from Wyatt's, no longer afraid, no longer wanting protection. It was Violet's turn, her instinct, to defend what was hers.

Wyatt smiled at the sheriff.

The sheriff raised his palms. "No one said that."

"You implied it," she snapped. "And I don't like it. I'm staying here to see that my grandmother recovers from her fall. While I'm in River Gorge, I don't expect to be harassed and threatened. I expect you, the sheriff, to see to it that I'm not. Otherwise, what is your job exactly?"

Sheriff Masterson blinked long and slow. The fatheaded smirk fell from his lips.

Wyatt covered a laugh with a cough. He couldn't afford to lash out the way Violet had. He couldn't give the sheriff any reason to detain or arrest him, but the mama bear at his side had told the man where he could stick his thinly veiled threats, and Wyatt loved it.

The sheriff opened a notebook and took the bare minimum of information for his report, then left without a goodbye. He'd hooked mirrored sunglasses over his eyes, but there was no mistaking the downward twist to his lips. They'd really put him out by asking him to do his job.

Wyatt hated that guy.

He walked Violet inside and poured two fresh glasses of sweet tea. The others had grown warm and watered down with melted ice.

"What now?" Violet asked, drumming her thumbs against the kitchen table. "The sheriff obviously has no intention of helping us."

Wyatt rubbed his forehead. "I would have to agree with that assessment." He blew out a long breath and tried to refocus on something he could control. His investigation. "You said your grandma doesn't have a computer? Are you sure it wasn't stolen?" He retrieved his phone and checked the available Wi-Fi options. "I'm not picking up any networks." He moved through the rooms then, searching for signs of an internet cable.

Violet went to the old rolltop desk in the hallway and opened the filing drawer. "Grandma never had the internet while I lived here. I had a laptop for school, but I had to take it to the library or a café to get Wi-Fi." She sifted through the desk's contents for several minutes. "Nope." She waved a pair of white papers in the air. "These are Grandma's most recent phone and cable bills. Neither shows a charge for internet."

"Okay." Wyatt nodded. "I guess I can stop looking for a modem or router." He dialed the number for the body shop he'd passed in town, 555-BODY, and waited while it rang. "Let me see what I can do about our vehicles." He hung up partially satisfied. "I made arrangements for a new window installation and requested quotes for repainting your car, though I wouldn't recommend spending the money until we get to the bottom of whatever is wrong with this town."

Violet returned the papers to her grandma's desk, then leaned against the wall at its side. She stroked Maggie's tiny curls, her brow deeply furrowed. "Maybe Ruth has the internet. Grandma could've contacted you from Ruth's house." She pursed her lips, apparently not liking that explanation. "That reminds me," she said. "I saw Ruth again at the hospital, and she said she'd noticed Grandma hadn't been herself lately. She said she'd assumed it was because a friend of Grandma's has dementia and it's gotten a lot worse."

"I'm sorry to hear about her friend," Wyatt said. "What's her name?"

"Mary Alice. She's one of Grandma's closest friends, but a bit of a recluse." She dropped her palm onto a stack of novels piled on the desk.

"Oh!" Her eyes widened and her lips swept into a breathtaking smile. "I just figured out where Grandma used the internet."

AN HOUR LATER, Wyatt angled his truck into the lot at the local body shop and left his key with an attendant. The prices for repainting Violet's ten-year-old hatchback made buying a new one seem much more appealing.

Maggie had enjoyed a shaker of Cheerios on the drive over, and seemed ready for an adventure. Luckily, they had time to kill while the window was replaced, and according to Violet, the library wasn't far. She met him in the lot outside the body shop's office door, Maggie in a sling on her hip and a stack of her grandma's borrowed novels in her hands. "Ready?"

"After you." Wyatt scooped a hand through the air, indicating that she should lead the way.

They moved together along the narrow sidewalk. Traffic had picked up, and Wyatt walked closest to the curb, watching vigilantly for signs of trouble. Properties on both sides of the road were sprinkled with people. Some weeding flower beds, others rocking on a porch swing. Kids raced through sprinklers; others rode bikes with no hands or shot basketballs at netless rims bolted over closed garage doors. The occasional pickup truck trundled past, windows down and radio up.

"It's strange," Violet said. "Everything seems so normal from this perspective. It's exactly the way I remember this place, except that there's something bad circling us, and no one else seems to have a clue."

"It makes sense that no one knows what's going on," Wyatt said. "The attacks are pointed, and you're always alone when they happen. Whoever's doing these things wants to scare you away, not alert the whole town." He stepped into the street when the library came into view, then motioned Violet across. He moved like a crossing guard, watching both directions for signs of a blue-and-white derby car with an unhinged driver to appear.

"I guess," she said, arriving on the sidewalk outside the library. "I hate that Sheriff Masterson practically accused us of causing whatever problems we have. When will people like him stop blaming the victims?"

"People like him?" Wyatt asked. "Never." He followed Violet up the steps to a massive late-nineteenth-century building. Blue-gray clapboard covered the sides and a bright red door guarded the entry. A sign on the lawn declared the structure had once been home to the town's founder, built in 1864. A matching plaque beside the front door identified the historic estate as current home of the River Gorge Library.

Violet slipped inside and stopped at a large wooden desk. She stacked her grandma's borrowed novels into a tidy pile before her and smiled brightly at the woman behind the counter. "Hello, Mrs. Foster."

The librarian inched closer, gathering the books into her arms and squinting at Violet. She posed a pair of frameless glasses on the bridge of her nose and gasped. "Mercy!" She dropped the little pile of books onto the desk and pressed both palms to her narrow chest. "Violet Ames. It has been far too long. How are you? Come around here where I can see you."

Mrs. Foster met Violet along the side of the desk and hugged her tight. She leaned closer to coo at Maggie's face, then straightened for a look at Wyatt. "You must be the man I keep hearing about. Got some of the local women in a frenzy."

Violet barked a laugh.

Wyatt felt his cheeks heat stupidly. He offered her his hand. "Wyatt Stone. It's nice to meet you, ma'am."

She looked him over, then lifted her eyebrows at Violet.

Violet blushed. "Mrs. Foster, I was wondering if Grandma came in here recently to use the public computers?"

"Oh, yes. She's been here regularly for several weeks. How's she doing now? I heard she took a terrible spill. It's a shame. We get old, but we don't feel old. We do things we probably shouldn't."

"Like what?" Wyatt asked.

Mrs. Foster shrugged. "She was on a ladder in the barn, wasn't she? I threw my back out hauling Christmas decorations down from the attic last fall. I was laid up for two months. It happens. Lucky for her Ruth was there to find her. Living alone at our age is a dangerous business."

Violet chewed her bottom lip. "Do you know what she was using the computer for?"

"No." Mrs. Foster shook her head. "Recipes, I suppose. That's what I use them for."

"May I use one?" Violet asked.

"Sure thing."

Wyatt joined the women, winding through the aisles over creaky hardwood floors. Adult patrons relaxed on worn, antique-looking couches and armchairs arranged in little clusters. Children filled the floor space near the far wall, crowded around a woman in a cardboard crown reading from a tattered paperback.

"Here we are," Mrs. Foster said with a soft clap of her hands.

A bank of bulbous almond-colored computer monitors lined a series of tables. A hodgepodge of seating options stood in front of them. Mrs. Foster offered a stool to Violet, then dragged a rocking chair closer for Wyatt. "Here they are. Take as long as you need."

Wyatt stepped around the spindle rocker, certain he'd leave it in splinters if he tried to sit on it. "Do you know which computer Mrs. Ames preferred to use?" he asked. People were often creatures of habit, and he hoped that Violet's grandma was no different.

"Of course." Mrs. Foster smiled. "She liked this one. It has a nice view of the front window. A good choice if you ask me."

A good choice, Wyatt thought, *if you were watching your back and didn't want to be cornered or confronted in a public library.* He cringed. If only she had met her attacker at the library instead of alone in her barn.

"Very few folks use these anymore," Mrs. Foster went

on. "Everyone's got those smartphones and tablets. My great-nephew has both and he's in first grade." She looked sullen after uttering the words. "What's wrong with reading books?"

"We think Grandma was researching something," Violet said. "I'm hoping to find out what that was, so I can surprise her by finishing the job."

Wyatt moved in close to the machine and brought up the search history. "Do you keep a log of the users? Dates and times of use? The machine number? Anything like that?" If so, he could use the information to pinpoint what she was reading about online. From the looks of things, no one had deleted this unit's memory in a very long time.

"Of course. I'll be right back." Mrs. Foster hurried away in the direction that they'd come.

Violet stepped in close to Wyatt's side. "I didn't mean to say Grandma was researching anything. It just came out."

Wyatt forced a smile. "It's fine. Mrs. Foster seems nice, and you covered well."

The librarian returned with a clipboard. "I'm afraid I have to drop this off to you and run. Story time is over and Clary is being overrun with children demanding an encore."

They waited until Mrs. Foster had gone, then scanned the list.

"Wow," Violet said. "She's practically the only one on the list, and it looks like she came every morning for almost three weeks."

Wyatt scrolled through the machine's history, reviewing the links and pages that were visited each morning when Mrs. Ames was signed in. It was an unexpected list. "Was your grandpa a veteran?"

"Yes. William Ames," Violet answered. "Why?"

"She was searching military websites, Veterans Affairs

and national cemeteries with military interments." Wyatt felt the creeping feeling of spiders on his skin. The fine hair on his neck and arms raised in warning. Almost as if they were being watched. He gave the room a careful look, then turned back to the job at hand. "She was researching a man named Henry Davis. Does that name ring a bell? A relative maybe?"

"No." Violet played with Maggie's fingers and stroked her cheeks. "I've never heard that name before. Maybe he was someone she knew when she was young? A neighbor?"

"Not a neighbor. This guy was from Twin Forks." Wyatt considered that a minute. "Twin Forks isn't far from here. Maybe they dated?"

"I don't know." Violet puffed air into her bangs. "I wish she'd just wake up and tell us what is happening. We can't even be sure those searches have anything to do with her fall."

"True," Wyatt agreed, glad to hear her considering all avenues. "But the searches for my security firm are sandwiched between these every day for a month." He checked his surroundings again, hating the creeping sensation on his skin. "I don't know what it means, but I'm ready to get out of here. This guy, Davis, went missing nearly fifty years ago. Now seems like a strange time to start looking for him."

Violet's mouth opened. She shut it without saying whatever had come to mind. Maybe she was thinking the same thing Wyatt was. They needed to go.

"Hey." He stalled on a new series of other searches; this time Mrs. Ames had been researching a woman. "She was also looking for Mary Alice Grigsby."

Violet moved into the space at his side, staring at the list of websites and searches. "What about Mary Alice?

Grandma has known her all her life. What could there be to look up?"

"I don't know. There's nothing here. Just searches for her name, and this one has a year. 1968." He checked the area for eavesdroppers and lookie-loos again. "I'm deleting the browsing history on this computer in case anyone comes in here asking the same questions we did. Henry Davis might be a lead, or it could be nothing, but considering the past few days' events, I'd rather cover our tracks."

"Agreed." Violet moved to the children's area and selected a few board books for Maggie, then went to check out.

Mrs. Foster greeted them. "Did you find what you were looking for on the computer?"

Wyatt leaned forward to fabricate a nonspecific cover-up, but Violet spoke first.

"Yes." She nodded, overly emphatic and oddly perky. "It looks like she really did want a kitten. I knew she had to be lonely living here by herself. She's been researching tabbies and local humane society adoption drives. I think I'll pick up a kitten for her and surprise her when she wakes up."

Mrs. Foster beamed, scanned the board books, then returned them to Violet. "That's so delightful of you. I wish my grandkids were as thoughtful. There now. I've put these on your grandma's library card. See you in two weeks?"

"Absolutely." Violet handed the books to Wyatt, then hurried back outside with him on her heels.

"Smooth," Wyatt said, more than a little impressed by her ability to think on her feet.

"Thanks. Now we just need to find out who Henry Davis is and why Grandma has been researching him all month. No problem." She rolled her eyes to emphasize the sarcasm, and Maggie laughed.

Wyatt pressed his cell phone to one ear. "I'm already on it."

A SHORT WALK for ice cream and the reading of a few board books on a park bench later, Wyatt received news that his window was fixed. Violet waited with Maggie outside the body shop office while he paid and collected his keys. The unsettling sensation of being watched hit her, sending chills across her skin and making her impossibly more antsy.

"Ready?" Wyatt asked, crossing to the driver's-side door.

Violet jumped. She'd been scanning the streets in search of the reason for her chills and missed his reappearance from the office. "Yes."

They climbed inside, ready to return home and process what they'd learned from the trip to the library.

Wyatt checked his mirrors and eased onto the road, then cast a wayward glance in her direction. "Everything okay?"

She rubbed the gooseflesh from her arm. "Just paranoia, I think." She watched the road, examined drivers in passing cars and searched the shadows of darkened alleyways as they made their way through the small downtown.

Soon, the buildings fell away, and they were back on the county road leading away from town and the hospital, toward her grandmother's house. The view was magnificent. The country in full bloom. Mountains lined the horizon. Forests reached into the heavens. And there with them, below the cloudless blue sky, were chasing squirrels, soaring birds and the occasional deer standing just inside the tree line at the roadside.

Violet watched the meandering river that cut through the valley below as the road sloped constantly lower, plummeting down the mountain. Her heart gave a painful thud as the deadly curve where she'd been run off the road came into view. She'd been going the other way, climbing up the hill, but she knew the curve, and just being near it tightened her limbs and jaw.

Wyatt slowed the truck and veered toward the shoulder. "Was that guardrail always busted like that?"

Violet leaned forward, straining for a clearer view. "No. I don't think so."

Wyatt pulled the truck onto the road's gravelly edge, stopping parallel to the torn and twisted guardrail.

Violet's eyes widened as a little red pickup came into view below, a wake of broken trees and flattened grasses stretching up the hill behind it.

Wyatt hit his flashers. "I'll be right back."

Violet watched in horror as he dashed over the mountainside to the truck, nearly standing on its crushed nose at the base of the ravine, just feet from the winding stream.

He pulled his phone from his pocket and caught it between his shoulder and ear while he wrenched open the driver's-side door.

"Someone is still in there," Violet whispered, realizing there was no other reason for Wyatt to open that door. Fear and panic lightened her head and heated her cheeks. She rolled down her window. "Can I help? What can I do?" she called.

Wyatt shook his head and raised a flat palm in her direction, indicating she should stay put. The low tenor of his voice carried in a mumble to her ears. He gave their location. The truck's description. Then the details of the driver. White female. Sixties or seventies. Deceased.

Violet opened her door. She gathered Maggie into her

arms and inched along the road's edge, suddenly terrified of being alone. Memories of the angry, roaring derby car slicked her palms and beaded sweat along her neck and forehead.

She took a few steady steps past the broken guardrail, keeping to the more level spaces between trees. Before she'd intended, she found herself at Wyatt's side, peering at the familiar female driver of the little red truck. Sickness coiled in Violet's core as the unseeing green eyes of her grandmother's friend Ruth stared back.

Chapter Seven

Wyatt rocked slowly on the front porch swing, fighting the memories of finding a nice old lady dead just hours earlier, and waiting for a return call from Sawyer at Fortress Security. If folks who knew Mrs. Ames were going to start turning up dead, Wyatt needed to get to the bottom of this mess fast, and Sawyer was the best man he knew at digging up buried information. Sawyer hadn't been a civilian as long as Wyatt, and he was having a tougher time adjusting, probably one more reason research jobs were his specialty. He got lost in them and frequently came out knowing more about his subjects than the people themselves. Sawyer was also excellent at reconnaissance. He was a ghost, and that was exactly what Wyatt needed. With Sawyer on the job, Wyatt could keep his focus on Violet and Maggie.

He stretched his long legs, pushing the silent swing back, then letting it glide forward once more. Shadows played on the horizon. Crickets and bullfrogs chirped and croaked in the distance. Lightning bugs rose from the grass. He listened closely to the night, picking up immediately on the sound of Violet's soft footfalls inside. The muted thuds of her return trip down the steps after putting Maggie into bed. Her daughter's jabbering voice carried softly through the baby monitor, presumably in Violet's hand.

"Hey." She opened the front door, toting the little white monitor.

Wyatt dropped a palm on the swing beside him. "Need a break?"

She accepted easily, setting the device on the armrest at her side. "Maggie's taking all this in stride," she said. "I could use a lesson."

"It helps when you have a strong mom to shelter you from the storm." Wyatt moved his arm across the swing's back, letting his hand dangle over Violet's shoulder. He fought the urge to drop it around her. Keeping up the pretense of their fabricated relationship in public was one thing. Touching her whenever the urge struck was downright unprofessional.

Violet stared into the night. "I can't believe Ruth is gone."

Wyatt considered offering a few words of comfort, but came up empty. What had happened to her grandma's friend was awful and the timing was incredibly worrisome.

"I think she was probably on her way from visiting Grandma," Violet said, "and I can't help wondering if that's why she had the accident. What if she was purposely run off the road?"

"The sheriff is looking into it," Wyatt said. "We'll know more soon."

Violet turned fearful blue eyes up to him. "That could have been Maggie and me."

The monitor at Violet's side glowed brighter. A series of tiny arching lights circled the speaker, illuminating with Maggie's every babble, responding to the decibel and urgency of her calls. At the moment it was slow and tired baby talk.

Despite the tense mood, a smile pulled at Wyatt's mouth. He couldn't help it. He'd love to know what that little nugget was yammering about. "She's got to be beat," Wyatt said. "It was a hot one, and she spent plenty of time in the sun."

Violet gathered her hair into a loose ponytail and sighed. "Nearly ten thirty at night, and it's still a hot one." She released her dark brown locks, and they fell over her shoulders once more, releasing an intoxicating vanilla scent before landing briefly on his hand, then sliding away. "Any word from your partner?"

"No. Not yet." He dared a look into her tired, defeated eyes. "We will figure this out." He tapped her shoulder with his dangling hand. "That's a promise."

Violet pursed her lips. "Okay." She pulled her feet onto the swing and tucked them beneath her, erasing the bit of distance that had existed between their bodies. Her head fell against his shoulder.

Wyatt's heart expanded at the gesture and her answer. *Okay.* Those two syllables suddenly meant everything. There was no doubt in her tone. No question. Just *okay.* She trusted him to fulfill his promise, and he would. His heart gave a powerful tug, and a fresh realization knocked him over the head like an anvil. That juiced-up protective instinct, the urge to touch her, comfort her, see her smile…the desire to make Maggie laugh, to be near her, to be with them both… Wyatt had begun to think of these ladies as if they were *his* to protect. Not just as if it was his job to keep them safe, but as if he was protecting what was already his.

"I put on some coffee," she said. "I doubt I'll be able to sleep. Not after a lunatic marched right onto the property to carve up my car. So I thought I could stay downstairs with you, keep watch."

Spend the night with him? That was her offer? Wyatt struggled to organize his thoughts. "You should sleep. You're exhausted, and Maggie needs you to bring your mommy A game." He forced a smile. He doubted Violet would accept the advice for her own good, but he had a feeling she'd do anything so long as it was for Maggie. "I'll keep watch."

"What do you think will happen if I don't *go home*?" She deepened her voice on the final two words, a mockery of the vandal's voice, Wyatt assumed with a grin.

"You can, you know," he said. "I can handle things here if you think you'd be safer at home." He hated the words, but they were true and already out of his traitorous mouth.

"I've thought of leaving," she said. "I've tried to guess what would be best for Maggie, but I can't. Something awful is happening here, but what if whoever is behind all these terrible things thinks I know something I shouldn't? What if he thinks I've uncovered what Grandma knew? Or that she'd told me what she was up to before her fall? How can I be sure her assailant will just let me go home and forget about it? What if his goal is to separate me from you? Will I be in more danger without your protection?" Her blue eyes pleaded with Wyatt for answers. "I don't want to be the naive little woman who runs headlong into trouble only to discover she was safer here all along."

Wyatt's heart broke for her. He hated the fear in her eyes and the questions he couldn't answer. He hated that criminals and evil existed in the world. It was the very reason he and Sawyer had founded Fortress Security.

The lights on the monitor flickered, glowing brightly as Maggie squealed. The sound was momentarily audible through the home's open front door as well as the little speaker. The lights dimmed, and she gave out a long weary groan.

Violet straightened slightly, shifting away from Wyatt. "She's okay. I call this portion of the bedtime routine 'singing herself to sleep.'"

Wyatt listened more closely to the strange moaning sound. Not crying, but not babbling. Just a low stretching lament. "You might consider voice lessons," he suggested.

Violet elbowed his ribs playfully. "First she's too negative for you, and now she can't sing? I think your expectations are too high, Wyatt Stone."

"I've heard that before," he admitted. His gaze returned to the little monitor. How had a man left this woman and his sweet baby? A military man. A man who was supposed to live by a code of honor. It wasn't right, and yet if that's who the guy was, maybe it was best he wasn't around to influence that little girl. She deserved better. They both did.

"What?" Violet shifted at his side, frowning.

"Nothing." Violet's ex was none of his business. Wyatt pulled his gaze away from the monitor, fixed it on her sincere blue eyes instead.

"Something," she pushed. "What were you thinking? Be straight with me. I need to know what's going on here. All of it. Not the filtered version, either. If you know something you haven't told me…" She trailed off. "Please."

"I'm sorry Maggie's daddy left," he blurted. "That's all I was thinking, and I know it's none of my business."

Her brows rose.

Wyatt groaned inwardly and braced for her rebuff. He wasn't great with words or timing. Being a straight shooter was perfect for military life, but it was a continuous train wreck as a civilian. "I'm sorry. You asked."

Violet shifted again, putting as much space as possible between them on the small swing. An inch. Maybe two; given the swing's size and his, it was a miracle to find as much space as she did. "Thanks, but we're fine."

"I can see that. I still hate that he left." Wyatt rubbed his palms down the thighs of his jeans. "It's not right, and I can't understand it."

She studied him. "I was reckless with my heart. That's on me."

Wyatt bit his tongue, forcing his mouth to be still before it got him into trouble. What had happened to Violet wasn't her fault, but he doubted he could convince her otherwise. Violet was strong. Determined. Maggie was lucky. And Violet's ex was a full-fledged idiot.

Violet deflated, rolling her back against the swing. She ran the pads of her thumbs beneath her eyes.

Was she crying? His gut fisted. Had he done that? "Hey." Wyatt planted his feet against the porch boards, stopping the swing. "I didn't mean to be rude. I just think you both deserve better."

"It's not you," she said. "The last two days are catching up with me. That's all." She heaved a sigh, then dropped her hands onto her lap. "I want to see Grandma again tomorrow. I wish I'd asked Ruth about Henry Davis. Maybe Grandma told her something useful." Maybe that was the reason Ruth's family was now planning a funeral.

Wyatt offered a remorseful smile. "I'll drive this time."

"All right."

"About what you said earlier," Wyatt began, "we don't know if you and Maggie will be safer by staying or going, but if you stay I can promise not to leave your side."

"If we stay, will it keep you from your investigation? Finding out who did this to Grandma should be your first priority. Not us. We're extra. Not what you negotiated in the contract."

He lifted his cell phone from the armrest beside him. "This is all I need. If there's a cell tower, I can work. And Violet?"

"Yeah?"

"I don't give a damn about that contract."

She smiled. "Okay."

His phone buzzed against his palm with an incoming text. "See?" he said, smiling as he lifted his phone. "Work." He swiped the screen to life and read the message from Sawyer.

"What?" Violet sat taller, apparently seeing the shock on his face.

"When I spoke with Sawyer earlier, he wondered if your grandma had been researching on behalf of her friend with dementia. Sawyer's grandpa had Alzheimer's, and he said those patients often recall things far in the past as clearly as, or more clearly than, things that happened yesterday. He thought maybe Mary Alice had asked your grandma about something, and your grandma went to look it up."

Violet puckered her brow. "That's possible." She motioned to the phone in Wyatt's hand. "But why do you look like the phone is burning you?"

Wyatt reworked his expression. "I asked Sawyer to look into Mary Alice Grigsby, and he learned that she was married later the same year Henry Davis went missing."

"So?"

"Her married name is Mary Alice Masterson."

AIR WHOOSHED FROM Violet's lungs. She'd known Mary Alice's last name, but Wyatt hadn't. "Of course." Why hadn't she made the connection before? "Mary Alice is the sheriff's mom." And Grandma's friend. "Is it possible Mary Alice told Grandma something meant to be a secret?"

"Maybe," Wyatt said.

Violet's thoughts whirled. Was Mary Alice's relationship to the sheriff relevant to the derby car or Grandma's accident? To Ruth's death?

Wyatt's phone buzzed again. "Email," he said, motioning her to move in closer. He flicked his thumb over the screen and opened the new message.

Breath caught in her throat at the subject line. *Henry Davis.*

Wyatt clicked the link in the message, rerouting them to an article from the neighboring county's newspaper dated 1968. A twenty-three-year-old soldier, Henry Davis, was presumed AWOL when he didn't return for duty after a brief leave. His last known whereabouts was a concert in Grove County.

"River Gorge is in Grove County," Violet whispered. She set her head back against the top wooden slat of the swing when she finished reading. Her heart kicked and spluttered in her chest as facts from the seemingly irrelevant article played in her mind. Nothing made any sense. Not even the gentle giant seated beside her, more worried about her comfort and safety than the mystery at hand. She'd overheard him earlier, telling his partner that he couldn't manage the research this time. He'd said Violet and Maggie were his priorities, and he hadn't called Maggie "the baby" or "Violet's daughter," the way most people did. He'd called her Maggie and Violet loved the way it had sounded. Wyatt, a virtual mammoth compared to her tiny daughter, saw Maggie as a person. Not an accessory to Violet. Not a possession to be protected or managed. A person. Violet saw that same truth manifested in Wyatt's actions. He worried when she fussed, and he made silly faces to calm her when she was mad. He was kind and loving.

Violet gripped the knotted muscles over one shoulder and squeezed. She couldn't afford to care about Wyatt's kindness. She couldn't take it personally. He was a nice man who was doing his job. Violet was a single mom who needed to get her head straight about what was real and what was fantasy. Having a family for Maggie, like the one Violet had never had—that was fantasy.

She excused herself, opting to stew over her naivety alone. Forget the coffee. She needed to rest and reboot her tired mind.

Hours later, sunlight drifted through the parted curtains, waking Violet with a start. Dust motes danced and floated on the air above her head, suspended like iridescent confetti. A smile touched her lips. Her gaze darted to the alarm clock on the nightstand. It was after eight. Maggie must've been as tired as her mama. She never slept past six. The baby monitor was dark. Powered off. Violet rolled onto her side for a look into the pop-up playpen.

Maggie was gone.

Violet was on her feet. "Wyatt!" She bulleted down the steps toward the kitchen. Slowed quickly by the familiar sounds of nursery rhymes and Maggie shouting, "No!" As the kitchen came into view, so did her daughter, head thrown back in laughter.

Wyatt waved a spatula at her from his place at the stove. "Eggs and toast again. I'm a one-hit wonder."

Violet padded over the cool linoleum floor to stand beside Maggie's high chair. She kissed her head and caught her breath. "The monitor was off. She was gone." Her fingers curled against the table. For a moment, she'd thought the worst. Forgotten there was someone else in the house. Someone good.

"She was babbling and chattering on about nothing for a long while," he said. "When you didn't jump right up like yesterday, I assumed you needed the sleep." A mass of deep lines ran over his forehead. "Was that wrong?" Wyatt's dark gaze shifted from Violet to Maggie, then back once more. "I didn't mean to scare you." Color ran from his face and a look of discontentment settled where congeniality had been moments before. "I thought you'd hear us as soon as you woke. Hear her laughter. Start your day with some extra sleep and a smile."

Violet rubbed her eyes. "No. It's fine. I guess." Was it? She had no idea. No one had ever helped her before, and Wyatt was practically a stranger. Right? Maybe she'd been right to push the bed against the door on that first night.

She shuffled to the coffeepot and poured a large mug of steaming clarity. Though she wasn't sure how much it would take to make this visit to River Gorge any less confusing than it already was. "Did you learn anything new about Henry Davis?" She rested her backside against the countertop and sucked hot coffee into her system.

"Not yet. I asked Sawyer to check his military records. It looks like he never went back after his leave. Could have gone AWOL intentionally. Lots of folks didn't believe in the war then. He could've assumed a new identity and vanished. Whatever happened was permanent. Sawyer said Henry's parents eventually had him declared legally dead, so they could have a memorial service. Sawyer's going to try to contact his next of kin and see if anyone has heard family gossip about what might've happened to him. His folks are long dead now, but there could be children, nieces, nephews, siblings."

The landline rang, and Violet jumped. She rubbed the goose bumps off her arms. "Maybe that's the hospital," she said, hurrying to the wall to answer. "Hello?"

"Um, yes," a shaky female voice began. "Violet?"

"Yes. This is Violet."

"Oh, good. Well, this is Mrs. Foster." She paused. "From the library. I have those other books you requested."

"I didn't request—"

"Yes, that's right," Mrs. Foster cut her off. "They're here now, so you should come on down and pick them up."

Violet's gaze swept the room, landing on Wyatt's blank face. "Now?"

"Yes. Now would be fine, dear."

Violet felt fear pool in her stomach and fix her feet in place. She'd been awake for ten minutes and already something else was wrong. "I'll be there as soon as I can."

"Darling?" Mrs. Foster added hastily, a bit louder this time. "Bring your friend."

The line went dead and Violet whirled on Wyatt. "That was Mrs. Foster. We need to go to the library. Now."

Chapter Eight

Violet hurried up the steps to the library. It was barely 9:00 a.m., and the library wasn't slated to open until ten, but the lights were all on inside. She cradled Maggie in her sling as she jogged, heart and mind sprinting with concerns for what awaited her beyond the historic red door.

Mrs. Foster met them at the threshold, swinging the door wide and motioning Violet and Wyatt inside. "Thank you for coming." She pressed the door shut behind them and slid the lock into place. "I'm sorry I behaved so strangely on the phone, but I was worried, and I didn't know what else to do. Now that I've had a moment to relax, I wonder if I've wasted your time."

"What worried you?" Wyatt asked. "And for the record, you can call anytime."

"Yes," Violet agreed. "It's no trouble for us to be here. What happened?"

Mrs. Foster wet her thin white lips. "Sheriff Masterson was here this morning when I arrived at eight. I came early to tidy up and restock shelves. It's too hard to get to it once we open. I won't have any help here until afternoon." She splayed thin fingers over her collarbone, a tremor playing on her narrow frame.

Violet inched closer. "You don't look well," she said, sliding a steady hand down the librarian's arm, shoulder to elbow. "Can I get you some water? Would you like to sit down?"

Mrs. Foster nodded, then moved to the nearest table and took a seat. "I'll be fine. Like I said, I've surely overreacted. After what's happened to your grandma, and now Ruth, I can't help feeling as if I'm living in an episode of *The Twilight Zone*."

Violet took the seat across from Mrs. Foster, then set Maggie on the floor, keeping an eye on her as she crawled to the nearest chair and tried to pull herself up. She'd dressed her little princess in a red-and-white-checkered sundress, complete with lace-rimmed socks and ruffles across the little white bloomers beneath. All she needed was a pair of cowgirl boots to complete the outfit, but Violet had forgotten them, rushing through her routine to get to the library. It was okay, she assured herself. The pediatrician had said babies learning to stand and walk do better in bare feet than in soled shoes. Of course, Maggie wasn't walking yet, but she tried getting onto her feet at every opportunity.

Wyatt crept along with Maggie staying a step behind as she moved chair to chair, grabbing hold and failing to get completely upright before moving on. "Why was Sheriff Masterson here?" he asked Mrs. Foster. "You say he was waiting for you when you arrived?"

"Yes," she said, then frowned. "Well, no. I didn't mean the current Sheriff Masterson. I meant the former one. Tom Sr. That man was sheriff so long I think I've gotten the title in my head like it's part of his name."

Violet glanced at Wyatt. "Mary Alice's husband was the sheriff before her son, but I've never met the man."

"Well, you haven't missed out on anything," Mrs. Foster said. "If you've met Tom Jr., then you'd know apples don't fall far from their trees." She folded her hands on one knee, crinkling the material of her simple brown-and-white print dress. "They're both about as friendly as an alley cat, but Tom Sr. is harder. He's always made me nervous, and he seems to have taken up drinking, which made it worse this morning. I imagine life's been tough on him since Mary Alice was diagnosed with dementia, but it's barely 9:00 a.m." She fiddled with her skirt, looking suddenly sad. "It was rough on everyone when Mary Alice's slow decline took a plummet last month. We all knew it was coming, of course. That's the nature of the disease, but how do you prepare for something like that?" She shook her head sadly.

Violet's heart broke for Mary Alice and all the folks who loved her. "What did Mr. Masterson want today?"

"He wanted to come inside and take a look at the computers, so I let him. I'm not even sure if I could have said no. He was the sheriff for years. Decades. When I smelled the gin on his breath, I got worried. Then I thought about how odd it was for him to come this morning asking about the same thing you did yesterday. Especially since your grandma and his wife are so close, and one is ill and the other is in the hospital. Maybe I read too much Agatha Christie. I don't know, but the timing, and the way he showed up here for the first time ever, as far as I know, and two hours before we open, set off my internal alarm bells." She scrunched her face. "That's silly, right?"

"No," Wyatt said. "It's perceptive and smart."

Violet scooted to the edge of her seat. "He asked about the same thing we did? Do you mean my grandma?"

"Yes." She wrung her hands.

"Did he say what he was looking for, specifically?" Wyatt asked.

"No. He just wanted to know if Mrs. Ames had used the computers and if anyone else had come in asking about her. I said no to both." Her cheeks darkened in humility. "I don't normally lie."

Violet offered a small smile. "It's okay. You were scared and alone with a man who'd clearly been drinking. Anyone would have acted out of character in that situation."

Mrs. Foster lowered her eyes. "Thank you for saying that."

"It's true," Violet assured. "What else can you tell us?"

"Not much. I asked him how Mary Alice was doing. He said fine. When he asked if your grandma had been in to use the computers, I told him she'd fallen and was in the hospital. He didn't respond to that. He just marched on past me and flopped onto a chair at one of the computers. That was when I called you."

Wyatt took another small side step, following Maggie around the table. "Did you know Mary Alice and Tom before they were married?"

"Loosely," she said. "I met Mary Alice at a bonfire in Potter's Field. It was a big hangout in those days. We stayed friends for a little while after that. As long as we could, I mean."

"Any reason it didn't last?" Wyatt asked.

Mrs. Foster let her gaze fall briefly to the floor, clearly uncomfortable rehashing other folks' personal stories, yet still visibly unnerved by her morning run-in with the former sheriff. She pulled her attention determinedly back to Wyatt. "Once she was married, things changed. She'd longed to be out of her parents' home so she would be free to do what she wanted, but moving in with her new husband was worse. When they returned from their honeymoon, he practically isolated her. Once they had children, she barely left home. Most of her friends moved on. We still chatted when she came in for new books each week. I enjoyed that time very much, but it was always limited. He was always outside waiting in the car. Your grandmother hung on, though. She refused to let Mary Alice slip away into isolation. After the dementia diagnosis, your grandmother was practically the only person Tom would let in the door."

Wyatt crossed his arms. "Sounds like the Mastersons have been in power a long time. Let's hope neither man is behind all the lawbreaking."

Maggie made it to Violet's chair and grabbed her mom's calves, trying and failing to pull herself upright. Violet lifted her onto her lap for a kiss.

Wyatt relaxed his stance and turned his full attention on Mrs. Foster. "May I take a look at the computers again? I'm not sure what there is to find, but I'm curious about what Mr. Masterson looked up while he was here."

"Help yourself," she said with a flip of one wrist. "I'm just glad he's gone. His son came to pick him up a few minutes before you got here. I'm not sure how he knew where to find him, but he removed him through the back door service exit. I suppose it would've been embarrassing to be caught hauling your drunken father away from the library at eight thirty in the morning."

Maggie wiggled, and Violet set her back onto the floor. She flipped immediately into a crawl and headed off in the direction Wyatt had gone.

"Mrs. Foster?" Violet asked, a new question popping into mind. "Does the name Henry Davis mean anything to you?"

Mrs. Foster paused. She frowned. "It sounds vaguely familiar. I'm not sure why."

"He's a military man from Grove County who went missing in 1968. He was twenty-three at the time."

"Oh my. That would make him my age now." She cupped one palm over her jawline. "No. I can't place the name. I'm the wrong person to ask. I didn't get out of River Gorge often as a young woman. Is he still missing?"

"I'm not sure."

Wyatt's head appeared to bob over the aisles of books as he strode back into view. Brown eyes deep in thought. He'd dressed in low-slung jeans and a fitted gray T-shirt that accentuated his body in knee-buckling ways. The set to his jaw made Violet want to run her finger along it, maybe also her lips. "There were no recent searches on any of the computers," he said. "Makes me wonder if he might've come in just to check the search history like we did."

Mrs. Foster looked ill. She let her hands fall onto the table. "I didn't watch. I wanted to put some distance between us, so I went to the desk and called you. It just didn't feel right, him being here like that."

Violet leaned across the table and squeezed Mrs. Foster's fingers. She understood the unsettling feeling, the uncertainty and fear, not knowing if there was real danger or if she couldn't trust her instincts anymore.

"What do you think he wanted?" the librarian asked. "What's all this about? First you, then Tom. It isn't about buying your grandma a cat."

"No." Violet offered a sad smile, though she was unwilling to tell Mrs. Foster any more than she absolutely had to. There was no reason to drag her into Grandma's mess any further than they already had. She lifted her gaze to Wyatt's grim expression. Was it too late?

"Where's Maggie?" Wyatt asked. He twisted at the waist, examining the immediate area. "Can you see her?"

"No." Violet slid her chair away from the table, nearly toppling it in her haste. Her heart lodged instantly, painfully, in her throat. "She went after you."

Wyatt spun on his boots and launched into a sprint,

heading back in the direction he'd come. "I don't see her," he called. "She's not here."

"Maggie!" His voice boomed over the rows of book-laden shelves.

"Oh dear." Mrs. Foster went toward the front door. "I'll check behind the reference desk."

Violet forced her leaden feet into action. She ran the length of the long room at half speed, ducking to peep under tables and slowing to peer down each empty aisle. "Maggie?"

Wyatt fell into step at her side a moment later. "She's not in the back. Not near the computers, in the bathrooms or activity space."

"Maggie!" Violet hollered, more loudly, more desperately. She raked shaky fingers through her hair, gripping her skull and trying to think. "She's a baby. She can't have walked away."

"Right," Wyatt agreed. "She's not tall enough to reach doorknobs, and there are no more open doors. The library isn't open yet, so there are no patrons to take her, and there's nothing to get hurt on." Wyatt ticked off perfectly good reasons for Violet to remain calm. "So let's split up and start again."

"She's not here," Violet said, rubbing the heavy ache in her chest. "We've already looked. Something's happened to her. She's in trouble. I feel it. I know it! Maggie!" She turned in a slow contemplative circle. The back door stood silently before her. "Mrs. Foster said the sheriff took his dad out this way."

"She can't open that," Wyatt said. "Even if it's unlocked."

"Yeah?" Violet sprinted for the door. "And what if someone took her?" She thrust her weight against the heavy door, and it burst open. Unlocked.

No, Maggie definitely couldn't have opened the door,

Violet thought as she squinted against the sun in search of the sheriff or maybe the blue-and-white derby car, but an adult could have.

A red-and-white-checked sundress scuttled swiftly through the distant grass.

"No!" Violet flew from the door, hitting the parched earth at a run. "Maggie! No!"

Her baby was closing the distance to the sidewalk and headed for a very busy street.

Chapter Nine

"Maggie!" Violet raced for the road, adrenaline forcing her forward faster than her legs could keep up. Her feet tangled and she fell, jamming her palms against hard, unforgiving earth. "Stop!" Tears streamed from her eyes as she regained herself. The plea was little more than a choked cry and she pushed her shaken frame upright. "Stop!"

Maggie slowed to look over her shoulder. The skirt of her little red-and-white dress fluttered in the breeze.

Violet was back in motion. "Baby, wait! Wait for Mommy!"

Maggie smiled. She turned back for the road, drawn to a plastic bag caught on a manhole cover and billowing like a balloon. The bag vanished and reappeared, repeatedly crushed by passing cars, only to reinflate with the next warm dose of wind.

"Maggie!" Wyatt's voice blasted through the air. He flew past Violet in long steady strides. "Whoa now." He skidded to a stop between Maggie and the road.

Violet froze in place. Her frantic mind nearly collapsed in relief.

Wyatt swept her baby into his arms and carried her back to Violet, easily delivering the beautiful child to her mother.

"Thank you." Violet sobbed against her baby, cuddling

her, snuggling her. "I'm so sorry," she cried. "I shouldn't have taken my eyes off of you. I love you so much. I'm so very sorry."

Maggie whimpered and squirmed, then let out a heart-breaking wail.

"Oh my goodness." Violet wiped frantically at her face. "Now I've scared her." She groaned. "Shhh. It's okay." She bounced Maggie in her arms and fought the powerful wave of emotion pushing against her barely held composure.

A strong arm curved around her back, offering strength where she had none. Wyatt nudged her toward the library. "This wasn't your fault," he said. His voice was thick with promise and resolute determination. "You had no reason to worry. You couldn't have known." He moved slowly, stead-fastly, at her side, matching his pace to her much slower one. "Let's take a minute. Get some water. Then I think it's time we pay Mary Alice and Tom Masterson Sr. a visit."

Violet swallowed hard. Her tongue felt swollen and sticky. She could definitely use a glass of water, but she wasn't sure she was ready to see Tom Masterson. If he had anything to do with what had happened to Maggie, he might be the next one in the hospital.

Wyatt helped her back into the library. He explained what had happened and warned Mrs. Foster to be care-ful. He got directions to the Masterson home while Vio-let calmed Maggie and herself with interchanged lullabies and Lamaze breathing. Her heart swelled with thanks and appreciation for him by the second. Not just for saving her daughter, but for being strong when she couldn't. For keeping a level head and for trudging forward to learn the truth and stop this criminal when Violet only wanted to run and hide.

She fastened Maggie into the five-point safety har-ness of her rear-facing car seat, then checked the belt a dozen times for security before joining Wyatt on the pickup's front bench. "I can't believe that just happened," she croaked, still strangled by residual fear. "Who would do something like that? To run me off the road or scratch up my car is one thing. That's a hands-off crime. A jerk move. But to creep into a building with three adults and steal a baby." She smashed her mouth shut, unable to voice the rest aloud.

To carry an infant away from her mother and leave her alone and unprotected, where anyone could hurt or abduct her. Where any manner of horrific fate awaited her.

The image of her baby nearing the busy downtown street flooded fresh into her mind. A hot tear rolled over her cheek. "It's pure evil."

Wyatt slid a large calloused hand across the seat between them and gripped Violet's fingers. He didn't speak. He just held tight, pulling cautiously into traffic, his trusty Stetson tipped low on his forehead.

Violet curled her fingers in response, gently squeezing him back.

WYATT SLID HIS truck against the curb outside a well-maintained craftsman-style home on Ridge Road. Mrs. Foster wasn't able to recall the exact address, but she'd described the place to a T, right down to the American flag waving proudly over the broad front porch. "Ready?" he asked Violet, in no hurry to release her small hand.

"Not at all," she said, slowly unfurling her fingers from his. "I have no proof that the man who lives here took my baby and left her outside the library, but I still want to slug him. Hard. And a lot."

Wyatt fought a smile. "Me, too. But you're right. We have no idea what really happened, so we can't make assumptions, and we need to go at this gently. Search for answers, not revenge. Not yet," he added. Though he certainly wouldn't be opposed to a little painful restitution for whomever had taken Maggie.

Violet turned heated eyes on him, frowning deeply. "Fine. But if he's behind this, I'm hitting him. I don't care if we find out today or on Maggie's sixtieth birthday."

Wyatt extended a fist her way to lighten the mood. "I accept those terms."

She bumped her tiny hand against his, then lifted wiggling fingers in the air.

Wyatt laughed. "Okay. Get out. That was too corny to happen in my truck." His smile grew as he watched her. The strange and unfamiliar tug returned to his chest and gut. He admired her, he realized. He was proud of the way she stood up for herself and fought for her daughter, and for the way she kept moving forward when others would've fallen down.

Violet opened her door with a straight face. "I was the Queen of Corn once, you know?"

He joined her outside the vehicle as she loaded Maggie into her sling. "Still are, I think."

Maggie drooped against Violet's side, having exhausted herself crying.

"No. I was the actual Queen of Corn. I rode on a float in the Harvest Day Parade and everything."

"Good grief." Wyatt feigned horror. "You can't keep things like that bottled up. They'll fester."

The screen door of the home creaked open on heavy springs, then snapped shut, drawing their attention to the porch ahead of them. A frail-looking woman in a housecoat and curlers shuffled out. She carried a bag of yarn to the nearest rocker and lowered herself slowly into it, resting the bag at her feet. She positioned a set of giant needles on her lap, then tugged a fuzzy blue strand of yarn from the bag until it lay limply over her legs.

Wyatt dipped his head to Violet's ear. "Is that Mary Alice?"

"Yes." Violet paused, watching the woman. "She used to be so plump and vibrant," she whispered.

The woman began to rock and knit. She hummed tunelessly as she worked, oblivious to the pair standing on her sidewalk.

Violet slid her arm beneath Wyatt's and curved her hand around his biceps. She led him to the woman's front porch steps, but stopped short of climbing them. "Mary Alice?"

The woman's hands froze, stilling her busy needles. She lifted her head first, then moved milky blue eyes in search of Violet.

Wyatt shrugged off the willies. Obviously, the woman was ill, but the look on her face was distant and haunting. Besides that, he couldn't see into her home despite an open door. The rooms were cloaked in shadow thanks to a bright morning sun. It would have eased Wyatt's nerves to know where drunk Tom Sr. was at the moment. Passed out, hopefully. Wyatt didn't like the idea of walking into potentially hostile territory without a better plan than ask questions and see what happens. Still, how could they plan for this? A conversation with a woman suffering the way Mary Alice was?

"Hello," the woman said. She seemed to reanimate after a long moment of studying Violet. "It's a beautiful day."

"Yes, it is," Violet said. "How are you feeling?"

"Oh, very well, thank you. I'm knitting a blanket for Tom. It gets cold at night, you know?"

Violet slid her eyes toward Wyatt.

He could practically hear her thoughts. It had been a low of eighty-three degrees last night. He'd slept in as little as possible with every window open. Mary Alice was confused. Not exactly a great interviewee, but he nudged Violet to keep going. Confused or not, Mary Alice was all they had to go on at the moment.

She turned a bright smile on the older woman. "I hope we aren't disturbing you. Is Tom home now?"

Another sign Violet could read minds. Wyatt looked to Mary Alice, needing the answer to that question.

She went back to work on her blanket. "No. He's at work. He takes afternoon shifts so he can be with me and the baby all day."

Wyatt rubbed a palm across his forehead, collecting beads of sweat along the way. There were so many things wrong with her statement. She thought she had a baby? That her husband was at work, not retired? And apparently she also wasn't clear about the time. Barely 10:00 a.m. Not afternoon or evening.

Mary Alice lifted her gaze suddenly and affixed it to Violet. "Is that your new granddaughter, Gladys?" she asked. "Shame your daughter ran off on her like that. Better for Violet, probably, but tough on you." She shook her head, looking forlorn.

Violet loosened her grip on Wyatt's arm.

Mary Alice thought Violet was her grandmother? And Maggie was Violet?

Wyatt covered her hand with his, keeping it there. He gave her fingers an extra squeeze for reassurance. He felt guilty for being exposed to secrets he hadn't asked for, but Violet should know he'd never pass judgment. He didn't care who had raised her or why. He was there for her and Maggie.

Violet lifted a palm to shade the sun from her eyes. "I'm Violet," she said. "This is my daughter, Maggie, and my boyfriend, Wyatt."

Wyatt's shoulder's squared at her proclamation.

Mary Alice went back to humming.

He dropped his hand away then, stunned by the real-ization that he'd become impossibly, unprofessionally at-tached to Violet and her baby.

Violet released him in turn, wrapping her arms around her sleeping baby instead. "Mary Alice, do you remem-ber Henry Davis?" she asked flatly, obviously ruffled by Mary Alice's mention of her mother.

Mary Alice raised a death glare in response. "I told you to never say that name. It was a secret. My secret. Not yours. You aren't supposed to talk about him."

"I'm sorry," Violet stuttered.

Wyatt tented his brows, unsure what to say to that or what her fevered words had meant.

"I didn't mean to say it," Violet went on. "I forgot. Please forgive me?"

Mary Alice jerked her chin woodenly up and down. Her knitting needles jammed and poked at the yarn, no lon-ger working in peaceful harmony or with a skilled grip. "I told you not to say it. I told you never to tell anyone. Have you told him?" She flickered an angry gaze toward Wyatt.

"No," Violet promised. "I swear it. I only came by because I'm having trouble remembering things, and I thought you could help me."

Wyatt shifted his weight, leaning and peering around the home in each direction, listening for signs Mr. Mas-terson was on his way to break up the chitchat and kick them off his property.

Mary Alice's angry expression faltered. "Me, too," she said.

"It's hard." Violet sighed long and loud. "I hate it."

"Me, too."

"If only I could remember about Henry Davis," she said.

Mary Alice threw her yarn down at her feet. "I said stop it."

Violet started. She leaned closer to Wyatt, as if the old lady might become a threat.

He leaned into her, supporting her. "Go on," he whispered, "you've got this. Rewind a little and take it slow."

She straightened with a long exhale. "Sorry," she apologized again. "I keep forgetting. I don't mean to."

Mary Alice's eyes widened. She hunched forward, resting bony elbows against her thighs. "You haven't forgotten where you put it? Have you?"

"It?" Violet asked. "I think I have. Do you know where I put it?"

"No!" Mary screamed the word. She jerked upright and paced the porch, tugging at her clothes. "You said you'd keep it safe. You promised! And now you've lost it?"

"I don't know," Violet pleaded. "I can't remember what it is. I might know where I put it. What was it? Tell me," she urged.

Mary Alice stopped to look more closely at Violet. She examined Maggie, then Wyatt.

He wondered what she saw. Mary Alice was the first person he'd encountered in a long while who was a complete and unpredictable mystery to him. Sadly, probably also to herself.

She lifted the material of her housecoat, stared at her hands, the porch, the sky. Then she dropped her face into waiting palms and sobbed. "I don't know what's happening."

"Mary?" A deep tenor exploded into the air. "Mary?" The thunder of racing footsteps underscored the bellow. "I'm here. I'm coming." The screen door whipped open again, sending Mary Alice against the railing with a squeal.

A tall gray-haired man with broad shoulders and lean build pulled her into his arms. He rocked her clumsily. Probably still drunk from the morning gin, Wyatt assumed. "What's wrong, honey?" he rasped. His drooping lids shaded red-rimmed eyes.

"I don't know," she said. Her words were muffled against his chest. "I can't remember."

The man straightened, taking notice of Wyatt, Violet and Maggie. "Who are you? What are you doing on my property?" His red pocketed T-shirt was torn at the sleeve and slightly askew. His faded blue jeans hung low on his hips. The hems puddled around bare feet, too long without a belt and shoes. "Did you do this?" he barked. "Did you make her cry?" His meaty hands rolled into fists against Mary Alice's back.

His words were fired quickly, but sloppy from drink. He narrowed his eyes on Maggie. His mouth opened again, but he didn't speak.

Shocked, Wyatt thought. *He recognizes Maggie.*

Wyatt fought the urge to lash out, to force Violet and Maggie into his truck and come back to get answers from this man privately and by force. "Sir," he began calmly instead. "I'm Wyatt Stone. This is my girlfriend, Violet Ames, and her daughter, Maggie. We're in town because Violet's grandma was in an accident. She's at the hospital now. Been there a couple days."

Mary Alice wrenched in her husband's arms. "What?"

"My grandma fell," Violet said. "I don't know how she fell, but she's not waking up." The pain in her voice was a punch to Wyatt's chest.

Mary Alice's eyes seemed to clear. She lifted her chin, searching her husband's face. Mary Alice was back in the moment.

Tom Sr. registered the change in her, as well. He gripped

her forearms firmly and lowered himself until their eyes were level. "What did they ask you? What did you say?"

"Nothing," she gasped, tugging uselessly against his hold. "I don't know."

"Why were you yelling? Crying?"

Mary Alice pulled free. Stunned, she lifted her fingers to her dampened cheeks. "I was crying?"

"Damn it!" Tom yanked the door open and forced her inside. "I've told you never to talk to strangers. What if they'd come to hurt you?"

"Why would anyone want to hurt her?" Violet asked.

He curled his lips into a snarl. "Don't tell me how to manage my wife. Get off my property. You've got no cause to be here." He marched to the edge of the porch, rage glowing in his eyes.

Violet inched back, her expression livid, presumably from Tom's declaration of "managing" his wife. "We came to see Mary Alice."

"Why?" he demanded. "She's not well, and you're harassing her. I ought to press charges."

Violet scoffed. "What kind of charges?"

"Harassment! For making her scream. For making her cry. She's not well, and you're scaring her."

"You're scaring her," Violet snapped back.

Wyatt pressed forward, mimicking Tom's movement and body language. He angled himself to shield Violet and Maggie from the lunatic on the porch. He'd had enough of Tom's yelling. "We didn't mean to upset her, Mr. Masterson. We only came because we know how close she and Violet's grandma are."

Mary Alice watched through the screen door, her palms pressed to the mesh on either side of her face. "I want to see her," she said. "I didn't know she was hurt. I don't understand what happened. I need to see she's okay."

"Shut up, Mary," Tom said, sounding tired.

"We don't know what happened, either," Violet said, stepping around Wyatt's shoulder, putting herself back in Tom's line of sight. "She's not okay."

Tom roared in frustration. He smacked the wall beside the front door, sending Mary Alice back a step. "Go sit down," he said. "She's an old lady who fell off a ladder. That's all."

"That's all?" Violet challenged.

Mary Alice's eyes brimmed with unshed tears as she returned to the screen, glaring at her husband.

"Yeah," he groused, "that's all."

Mary Alice spun away, slamming the front door behind her.

Tom braced his hands on his hips. He rolled his shoulders and widened his stance. "Come back here again, upsetting my sick wife, and I'll have a restraining order issued. Now, for the last time. Get. Off. My. Property."

Violet turned away, starting for Wyatt's truck in quick, easy strides.

Wyatt stared at Tom a while longer, assessing, challenging. Waiting to see if he'd blurt something useful in a fit of agitation.

He didn't.

"Have a nice day Mr. Masterson," Wyatt drawled, slow and intentional. "Probably be seeing you around soon."

Wyatt didn't know how or why, but he was sure Tom Sr. had something to hide. Wyatt's gut suggested it was something Tom would hurt anyone to keep covered. Violet's grandma. Ruth. Violet. A baby. Even his own wife if necessary.

Wyatt gave the Masterson home a long look as he pulled away, hoping Mary Alice didn't take any questionable falls before he figured things out.

Chapter Ten

Violet sipped iced tea and watched the dimming daylight from her grandma's back porch, thankful Wyatt had insisted on coming home before hurrying over to the hospital. She hadn't realized at the time how much the day's events had worn on her, but she felt it now, even all these hours later. She'd even fallen asleep sitting up at the kitchen table while Maggie took an afternoon nap. Violet smiled against the rim of her glass, enjoying the sight of Maggie on the porch at her feet, gnawing on her favorite plastic pony. She couldn't seem to decide which she enjoyed more, cuddling the bulbous pink horse or biting its head.

The back door opened and Wyatt appeared, filling the frame as he passed. "You ladies doing okay out here?"

Maggie stopped to smile a moment before going back to work on her pony's rounded ears.

Violet did her best to look at ease, though she doubted he'd believe the facade. Wyatt seemed to see past everyone's smoke and mirrors, his mind always at work, processing, evaluating. He studied people when they spoke, watched their hands as they moved. If only she'd had more insight when it came to love. She might not have spent the first half of her pregnancy crying tears of heartbreak over Maggie's father's rejection and the second half angry she'd been so stupid. She might've even known that he wouldn't matter at all once she saw Maggie's sweet face in that delivery room. After that, Maggie was the only thing that had mattered. She couldn't help wondering if Wyatt saw past all her other pretenses, too. Did he know the way her traitorous heart flipped and floundered at the sight of him, or the way he appeared in her fantasies? First the dirty ones, then lately, the ones about being a family?

Wyatt tilted his head, zeroing in on her in his trademark style, sending gooseflesh up her arms and coiling a spring in her stomach.

Violet cleared her throat. "Pull up a chair. There's a beautiful view, but it's going fast."

Wyatt lowered his large frame onto the porch beside Maggie and made a goofy face at her.

She squealed.

His cheek kicked up on one side. "I doubt this view ever goes bad."

Violet fought the blush warming her cheeks. Lines like those weren't helping her quest for clarity. "Any luck with your research?"

"No. I've put Sawyer on it, though, and he's excellent at finding things that others have tried to bury." He locked his jaw and averted his gaze. Frustrated? Violet tried and failed to read him the way he seemed to so easily read her.

"We can ask a few questions at the hospital," she suggested, wishing she had more to offer. "I wish I knew what Grandma had planned while you were here. I'd happily pick up the torch for her if I could find it."

Wyatt adjusted his long legs, bending one knee to his chest and dropping the opposite foot off the porch's edge. "You and me both."

Wyatt had spent the day hunched over his laptop, using his cell phone hot spot for internet service. He'd researched Henry Davis, the Masterson family and Violet's grandparents. So far, he hadn't found a clear link between the Mastersons, the Ameses and Mr. Davis. "I'd like to know what Mary Alice thinks she gave your grandma," he said. "She lost her mind when she thought it was lost, whatever it was."

"I know," Violet said. "I figure that's what the burglar tore the house up looking for, but I haven't seen anything unusual around here. Just Grandma's stuff and now a bunch of our luggage."

They needed Grandma. "Feel like going for a drive?" Violet asked.

"Hospital?"

"Yeah. I know someone would have called if anything had changed," Violet began.

"But you'd like to see her," Wyatt finished. "I don't blame you."

Maggie shoved her toy against his hand. "Po."

Wyatt raised a brow. "Pony?"

"No!"

Wyatt laughed. "Come on, short stuff." He pulled her into his arms and stood fluidly, then offered a free hand to Violet. "Might as well make that trip now and get as much as we can out of evening visiting hours."

"Thanks." Violet ignored the electricity climbing her arm to her chest as Wyatt pulled her onto her feet.

The hospital was quieter in the evening than it had been during Violet's previous morning visits. She supposed folks had already headed home for dinner by now. It was after seven and they'd be kicked off Grandma's floor at eight.

Violet veered across the hall to the nurses' station when she spotted Tanya's blond head tilted over a computer screen. "Excuse me, nurse?" she said sweetly.

Tanya lifted her face. "Yes?" Her smile doubled at the

sight of Violet. "I hoped I'd see you tonight." She rounded the desk and pulled Violet into a hug. Her pale blue scrubs had tiny American flags on them. "How are you doing? I'm sorry I missed you yesterday. I'm covering so many shifts this week, I don't know which way is up."

"Don't forget to rest when you can," Violet warned.

"Always the mama," Tanya said. Her brows lifted. "Where is Maggie?"

Violet looked behind her. "There." She pointed across the wide hall where Wyatt was doubled over at the waist, gripping Maggie's tiny hands in his as she attempted to walk. Her dimpled arms stretched high over her head as she swung clumsy legs out before her.

Violet laughed softly. "She's barely managed to pull herself up," she told Tanya. "I think it's safe to say he's getting the cart before the horse over there."

"I could be training the next Ninja Warrior," Wyatt said, clearly eavesdropping. "An Olympian, a professional bull rider or..." He swung her into his arms and made a gravely serious face. "What do you want to be when you grow up?"

She clapped and smiled proudly, showing off both of her new bottom teeth.

He headed for Violet and Tanya. "She's undecided. I don't think we should rush her."

Violet rolled her eyes, utterly enjoying Wyatt's ease and comfort with Maggie. "Wyatt, this is my cousin, Tanya. Tanya, this is Wyatt."

"Ah," Tanya said. "This is the boyfriend folks have been talking about."

"Nice to meet you," Wyatt said.

Tanya gave him a long once-over.

"Anything new with Grandma?" Violet asked, forcing Tanya's attention off of Wyatt's fantastic torso.

"No. Nothing, but the doctor thinks she's through the

worst. He expects she'll be waking up soon. There's no physical reason that she wouldn't."

Violet's shoulders drooped in relief. "Really?"

"Yeah. It's just a matter of time now. Everything post-op looks really good. Grandma's strong, Violet," Tanya said. "She'll get through this, and she'll probably have one heck of a story to tell."

Violet's smile grew. "No doubt."

The desk phone began to ring and Tanya frowned. "I've got to get that, but I'm on shift until eleven, so don't worry about the posted visiting hours. I'm not about to kick you out." Her gaze turned back to Wyatt as she changed directions.

Violet felt a sliver of jealousy. Fake boyfriend or not, she was beginning to feel extremely, illogically, *stupidly* attached.

"Tanya?" Wyatt asked, stalling her cousin's retreat.

"Yes?"

"Do you know Mary Alice Masterson?"

"Sure. She's a good friend of Grandma's."

"How's she doing?" he continued. "We've heard she took a turn for the worse recently. Any idea what happened there?"

Tanya lifted a finger, then grabbed the phone long enough to put it on hold. "Mary Alice has been struggling for a long while," she told Wyatt. "She came in a few weeks ago after a fall in her kitchen. The doctors ran a bunch of tests that showed her dementia had significantly advanced. They recommended Mr. Masterson look at nearby assisted living facilities, but he was determined to keep her at home, so no one pushed."

Wyatt frowned. "He didn't have to take the doctor's advice? Do what was best for Mary Alice?"

"No. He's in good health and retired, so he can be with

her all the time," Tanya said. "If her needs become too much, he can hire an in-home nurse or look into facilities then. Moving can be confusing for patients in Mary Alice's situation, and the transition can be tough. Each family has to make decisions based on their own timelines and abilities."

Wyatt's lids drooped. "Right."

Tanya smiled. "Sorry. I've got to take that call."

Violet leaned against his side. "Of course." She led the way to her grandma's room and settled into the chair beside her bed, then quietly whispered the story of everything she and Wyatt had seen, heard and experienced since she'd first received the call about her accident. Some people believed that coma patients were aware of the things going on around them. Violet hoped those people were right. "If you hear me, Grandma, I need you to wake up and tell me what all this means." She stroked hair off her grandma's forehead. "We need you," Violet whispered. "And I'm scared."

Wyatt's palm slid protectively over her shoulder, offering his peace and confidence.

Violet tipped her tear-dampened cheek against his finger, accepting the offer.

WYATT OPENED THE passenger door to his truck and waited as Violet fastened Maggie into the rear-facing car seat. Her dark curls were wild from static electricity. He waited while Violet climbed inside, then shut the door behind her. It had been a long day. One of many, but possibly his worst so far. Not knowing where Maggie had disappeared to this morning, then seeing her headed for a busy road... Wyatt's stomach fisted at the memory. A wave of nausea rolled through him as he climbed behind the wheel. He wasn't sure how Violet hadn't completely lost her mind.

He could see the way it had worn on her, but she kept moving forward.

The silence in the truck was deafening. The night around them, suffocating. Violet's troubled expression reflected in the glass of her window.

"Want to talk about it?" he asked.

"I wish she'd wake up," Violet said. "Grandma's the key to all this, whatever this is, and she needs to wake up." She fiddled with the fraying hem of her shorts. "I have a theory. Want to hear it?"

"Of course." He caught her gaze briefly before refocusing on the dark road.

Violet wet her lips and angled her body toward him in the shadows. "I think Mary Alice said something that didn't sit well with Grandma, so Grandma started asking questions. I think whatever it was bothered her so much she couldn't just let it go or chalk it up to Mary Alice's confusion and nothing more. And I think it has something to do with Henry Davis."

Wyatt couldn't disagree. Violet's idea was as good as any he'd had, but hers worried him. If Violet was right, it would be dangerous for her grandma to wake up. Whoever had hurt her before would likely be back to finish the job.

"And I think Mr. Masterson knows Mary Alice has a big secret," Violet went on. "I think her condition scares him because there's no way of knowing if she's forgotten it completely or if she's five seconds from announcing it to the mailman. He keeps her under his thumb so she doesn't tell, and the stress is getting to him. That's why he's drinking at eight in the morning, and that's why he wants me to go home."

"You think Mr. Masterson drove the derby car?" That was something Sawyer could research. Even if the car wasn't registered to Masterson, Sawyer could look at Masterson's local network, his friends and neighbors, and find the link if one existed.

"I do, and if I'm right, he knows he's in trouble. Either Grandma's going to wake up and take him down, or I'm going to uncover Mary Alice's secret while I'm looking for answers about what happened to Grandma."

"It's a solid theory," Wyatt said. "Maybe it's time we focus on the derby car. Find out who's behind the wheel, and we find out who wants you gone. Then we can figure out why." The car had no plates, but Wyatt had gotten a decent look at it as it sped away from the house. There had to be a register, photograph or something they could use to link the car to an owner.

"Thank you," Violet said. She sank straight white teeth into her bottom lip and turned wide blue eyes on him. "I'm glad you're here."

Wyatt forced his gaze back to the road. Remembering his place in her presence was harder all the time. He was too attached. Too attracted. He'd been hired by her grandmother to do a job, and so far he was failing. He'd gotten distracted playing house and entertaining ideas he hadn't had in a very long time. He wasn't husband or father material. If he ever had been, the military had carved it out of him. Even if he had heard the granite shell of his heart cracking when Maggie offered him her favorite pony. Even if Violet had trusted him to hold and comfort her. Even if he thought being loved by them might be all he needed to become the man he'd started out to be, it wouldn't matter if Violet didn't want another soldier in her life. Because no matter how long Wyatt lived or how many years eventually separated him from his active service days, he would forever be a ranger. There was no separating the two.

Blue and white flashers illuminated the darkness behind him, pulling him back to the moment.

"What?" Violet twisted and turned on her seat, craning for a look through the rear window. "Is that for you?"

"No." Wyatt eased his foot off the gas and drifted closer to the berm, providing the deputy with ample room to get around him on the winding country road. "I'm not speeding. I'll just get out of his way."

The cruiser stayed on his tail several seconds more, then added a siren to the flashers.

Violet scoffed.

Wyatt pulled over. He got out his driver's license and truck registration, then stacked them with his license to carry a concealed weapon. He powered his window down and waited. Fingers gripping the wheel at ten and two, he caught the cards between his fingertips.

"This is ridiculous," Violet complained. "They haven't done enough to scare and harass us? Now we're going to get run off the road or pulled over every time we get in a vehicle?"

A bright light hit the side of Wyatt's face and he grimaced. "Everything okay, Officer?"

Deputy Santos turned his light on Wyatt's hands. "Points for being prepared."

"What seems to be the problem?" Wyatt asked. "I'm sure I wasn't speeding."

Deputy Santos shone his light on the pieces of identification. "This is your truck?"

"Yes, sir. Bought it new the same month I was discharged."

"Any reason this truck might've been reported as stolen?"

Wyatt felt his jaw drop. He snapped it shut. "No, sir." Wyatt had worked damn hard for the money to buy this truck, and the vehicle had practically been his second home since opening Fortress Security. Yet someone had said he'd stolen it? His grip tightened on the wheel.

"Do you have a concealed weapon with you now?" Santos asked.

"Yes, sir. I've got a piece at my ankle and another in the glove box."

"Any reason for that? Two handguns seems like a little overkill for your average weekday evening."

"You'd think," Wyatt muttered. He locked eyes with the deputy, weighing a major decision. Had he been right about him? Was he a potential ally?

"He's protecting Maggie and me," Violet answered suddenly. She leaned across the bench for a better look at the deputy.

Santos shifted his weight, returning the IDs to Wyatt. "I'm glad you've got someone here to help you feel safe, Miss Ames. I'm just not sure this is a two-gun town." He worked up a smile, possibly an attempt to lighten the mood.

"That's not what I meant," she said.

Wyatt leaned over the door frame, making the decision to confide in someone who could possibly help them and hoping the quick background check he'd run on Santos revealed all he'd needed to know. "Okay, here it is. I'm not her boyfriend. I'm a personal security agent from Lexington, hired by her grandma just days before the woman took an unexpected fall that's put her in a coma. Now I'm here to find out what had her so scared that she felt she needed outside protection instead of just contacting the local sheriff and his crew."

Santos rocked back on his heels. He looked toward his car, then up the road before returning his attention to Wyatt. "Go on."

"You know as well as I do that in the few days since I came to town, Violet's been run off the road, I've been accused of harassment, my truck got a busted window, her car was scratched to hell with the clear message, 'go home.' The house has been burgled, her baby was set outside and left alone this morning near a road. We found her ten yards from a busy street, and now my truck has been reported as stolen. I've got reason to be extra cautious. It feels like a two-gun town to me."

Deputy Santos narrowed his eyes, then swore beneath his breath. "I'll contact dispatch, let them know the truck is clear."

"Thank you."

Santos rubbed his forehead. "I'll pull up the reports on Mrs. Ames's fall and see if anything seems off."

Wyatt tipped his hat in appreciation and the deputy was gone.

Violet watched as he drove away. "Do you think he'll tell anyone?"

"No, but we need someone in law enforcement who will stick up for us if we're right about the corruption." He eased onto the road and smiled at Violet, hoping to look more confident than he felt. "Try not to worry."

She peeked over her shoulder at Maggie, then settled back in her seat. "That's not going to happen."

Wyatt divided his attention between the road before him and the darkness reflected in his rearview. He pressed the gas pedal with a little more purpose. The sooner they were home, the better.

"Who do you think reported your truck stolen?" Violet asked. "Can anyone do something like that?"

"I don't know." His attention returned to his rearview.

Another car had pulled in behind them at the last crossroads, and the silhouette, though masked by the blinding headlights, looked a lot like another deputy's cruiser.

The blue and white lights began to spin on top before he could tell Violet to be prepared.

"You're kidding," she grumbled, twisting for a better look at the lights.

Wyatt pulled over, gathered his identification and put his hands where they were easily visible once more. "It's fine," he assured her. "We're less than a mile from your grandma's house. We'll head straight there from here and call it a night."

She crossed her arms and frowned. "This is ridiculous. How can they get away with this?"

"They're just doing their jobs."

"This is not okay," she said. "Someone lied to the sheriff's department for the sole purpose of causing you trouble."

Sheriff Masterson strode up to the window and sucked his teeth. "License and registration."

Wyatt handed him the papers he hadn't had time to put away since his last stop.

Sheriff Masterson glanced at them, uncaring. "You want to step out of the vehicle for me?"

"Sir." Wyatt spoke before touching his door handle. "I handed you my license to carry a concealed weapon, and I have a gun on my person."

The sheriff pulled his chin back and rested a palm on the butt of his sidearm. "Are you planning to use your weapon tonight, son?"

"No, sir."

"Then get out."

Wyatt cast a look in Violet's direction. "Be right back. Stay in the truck."

"Come on," the sheriff urged, impatient.

Wyatt moved to stand outside his truck, keeping a respectable distance from the sheriff. The air was warm and thick around them and filled with night sights and sounds. Stars, fireflies, owls and crickets.

No witnesses.

The sheriff stared. "I got a notice that this vehicle was stolen. You know anything about that?" He pointed his flashlight into Wyatt's eyes.

"Yes, sir. Your deputy just pulled me over for that five minutes ago. He read the registration I gave him. This is my truck."

The light moved away and Wyatt blinked furiously, bringing the sheriff back into view. His face was masked in a disbelieving look. "Are you giving me an attitude?"

"No, sir. I'm explaining."

"*Com*plaining sounds more like it," the sheriff said, cutting him off. "Do you have a problem I need to know about?"

Wyatt bit down hard on the insides of his cheeks. He couldn't let himself be baited. He needed to get Maggie and Violet to safety.

"I hear you visited my mother today," the sheriff continued. "How'd that go?"

Wyatt squelched a groan. The conversation had taken an ugly, and probably unavoidable, turn. "Not well."

Sheriff Masterson nodded. "My dad told me all about it when he called asking for a restraining order. You want to tell me what you were doing over there bothering my sick mama?"

"Violet and I were paying a respectful visit to her grandma's best friend. Nothing more. We thought she might want to be updated about what happened to Mrs. Ames."

The sheriff crossed his arms. "Dad says you made her cry. Seems to me you're a nuisance. A harbinger of trouble. Have you considered taking your vandal's advice and seeing your way back out of town?"

Violet's head and shoulders popped through the open driver's-side window. "We are not leaving town until we know my grandma's okay. Period. I don't care what else happens. You know," she seethed, "as far as sheriffs go, you're pretty horrible at your job."

Anger flashed in the sheriff's eyes, and he took a step toward Wyatt's truck. "You shut your face. No one asked you, you—"

Wyatt thrust himself between the sheriff and Violet. "Watch it now. You want to think before you finish that sentence." His blood boiled and his fingers curled into fists at his sides. "And you'd be best to find a respectful tone when you speak to her again."

The sheriff took a step back. He looked at Wyatt's steaming face, then at the fists, still clenched tightly on both sides. "Are you threatening me?" He reached for the cuffs on his belt and shook his head. "Threatening an officer gives me cause to haul you in."

"That's crap!" Violet said. "That's an abuse of power."

Wyatt turned to stare at her. He moved his head in a tiny warning. "Keys are in the ignition. Call Fortress. Talk to Sawyer. He can be here in an hour. Lock up tight until he gets here. Trust him when he does."

The cuffs pinched, cold and angry around Wyatt's wrists as Sheriff Masterson crammed them on, yanking each arm behind his back. He forced Wyatt to the cruiser, then pressed his face against the warm hood to pat him down. He removed the gun from Wyatt's ankle strap.

Sheriff Masterson clucked his tongue as he towed Wyatt upright. "I sure hope Miss Ames and that baby are going to be okay without you."

"Son of a—" Wyatt yanked himself around and towered over the sheriff. "You keep your hands off her."

"Another threat? You're on a roll tonight, huh, big guy?"

"If anything happens to either of them before I get out of these cuffs, I'm going to hold you personally responsible, and I won't care how long you want to lock me up when I'm done with you."

The sheriff's face was bloodless as he pushed him back. "Go on. Get in."

Wyatt dropped onto the cruiser's back seat, anger roiling in his chest. He nodded to Violet as the cruiser passed her window.

She pulled his truck into line behind them and took the turn toward her grandma's home.

Wyatt prayed Sawyer could get to River Gorge before the next bomb fell.

Chapter Eleven

Violet drove Wyatt's beast of a truck right onto Grandma's lawn, pulling as close to the front porch as possible before shifting into Park. She'd dialed Fortress Security while Sheriff Masterson had crammed Wyatt's face against the hood of his cruiser, then explained the night's events to Sawyer. The engine of his vehicle had growled through the line as she spoke.

Sawyer was on his way.

Still sitting in the truck, Violet noticed how the head-lights flashed over ruined rows of Grandma's prized roses, and her heart lodged in her throat. The mulch was littered with red and white buds, pink petals and whole yellow flowers, all chopped and crushed into the ground. The re-maining stems were headless, thorn-covered sticks, stand-ing broken and naked in the moonlight.

It was a silly thing to care about in the big scheme of things. They were just flowers. Only plants. But it was *another* threat. And it hit home hard. Whoever had done this knew how important the roses were to her grandma. And it only solidified Violet's opinion that Mr. Masterson was the villain in this story. Not good news since she doubted his jerk of a son would ever arrest him, short of catching his father in the act of murder. Maybe not even then.

In the morning, Violet would talk to her grandma's doctors about moving her to a facility outside Grove County, somewhere the Mastersons couldn't reach her.

Anywhere but here.

Violet scanned the dark yard once more, thankful they'd left the porch light on. "One," she whispered, steadying her nerves and checking her rearview. "Two." She gripped the handle at her side. "Three." Violet popped the door open and jumped out. She flung the cab's back door open and hoisted Maggie's car seat from the cradle, baby and all. Then she shut both doors with the flick of a wrist and bump of a hip. They flew onto the porch in three long strides. Violet juggled her sleeping baby in the heavy car seat while trying to work the key into Grandma's new lock. Her clumsy hands and fraying nerves made the simple task nearly impossible.

"Come on," she scolded herself as fear crawled all over her.

The night sounds seemed to close in on her. The wind was an ominous whisper in her ear, a chill along her neck.

She wrenched the door open and slammed it shut behind her with a whimper, securing the dead bolt and chain before checking the other doors and windows. "All clear," she whispered to herself, repeating Wyatt's confident phrase. The home was all clear. And she and Maggie were alone.

Violet scrubbed a heavy hand against her quivering lips, then forced her feet into motion. She tucked Maggie safely into her crib, then returned to the first floor to put on a pot of coffee. Next, she lowered her grandpa's old rifle from its ornamental spot above the fireplace and loaded the heirloom with ammunition. Violet hadn't had any target practice in a decade, but if someone came close enough to hurt her or Maggie, she wouldn't miss.

Her mind raced, cluttered with the awful day's events. Losing Maggie at the library. Watching Wyatt be forced away from her. Her heart even ached for Grandma's roses. Violet had helped her choose the plants. She'd shoveled mulch and kept them watered each night as the sun went down. She'd tended them dutifully and with love until her last day in River Gorge. After that, she'd enjoyed Grandma's calls to her college dorm room, updating her on the blooms. She'd been ecstatic to learn Grandma had won prizes for them at the county fair, and she'd been honored when Grandma planted a bush of white roses in Maggie's honor following her baby's birth. That tribute had meant the world, and now those buds lay scattered among the mulch, angrily trampled by whoever had committed the crime.

Two mugs of coffee later, a set of headlights flashed over the front window, and Violet raised Grandpa's rifle. She marched slowly to the living room and peeled back the curtain. An old-model Jeep Wrangler sat in the drive behind her car. No driver.

She dropped the curtain and pressed her back to the wall, counting silently to settle her nerves, then she looked again. A man dressed in all black stood just outside the glass.

Violet clamped a hand over her mouth to keep from voicing her shock.

"Miss Ames." A slow Southern drawl slid under the door and around the window frame, smooth as molasses and warm as fried chicken. "I'm Sawyer Lance. You can put the weapon down. I believe you invited me here."

Violet stayed out of sight, but kept the rifle in clear view of the window. "Show me some ID."

The man positioned a small white rectangle in his fingertips and extended his arm toward the window. "Sawyer Lance," he repeated. "Fortress Security."

Violet peeked.

His hair was sandy and overgrown, his beard thick and unkempt. His fitted T-shirt and jeans gripped every muscular plane of his body. He wasn't as big as Wyatt, but he was close and twice as scary. The Fortress Security business card in his hand had his name embossed in black letters.

"Do you have a photo ID?"

He snorted, then bent at the waist peering through the glass, hands cupped at the sides of his face for a better view. "Are you kidding me?"

"Come on," she demanded, waving the rifle's barrel. "Show me, or get off my grandma's property."

He mumbled under his breath, then wrenched upright and fished a wallet from his back pocket. "I would like to state for the record that you're implying I'm not me, which means someone is out here impersonating me and in possession of my business card. Furthermore, you are suggesting someone has gotten the best of me, taken my cards and vehicle and left me behind." He turned a military ID in her direction. "I realize you do not yet know me, but trust me when I say that ain't ever gonna happen."

"Where's your driver's license?" she asked, stalling. Wyatt had told her to trust Sawyer, but opening the door to another stranger was proving tougher than she'd imagined.

"Expired while I was overseas."

Violet inhaled deeply and opened the door.

Sawyer walked in. He dropped a black duffel on the couch and scanned the room. "How many people in the house?"

"Two," Violet said. "My baby, Maggie, and me. Well, now you, too."

"How old's the baby?"

"Eight months."

He nodded. "You were right not to trust me. I could've been dangerous, but I'm not."

She felt her brow furrow. Her gaze lingered on his scarred face. The angry puckered skin of a newly healed burn marred the area over his left eye.

Pale blue irises studied her as she studied him. He kicked his cheeks up in a sudden grin. "I mean, I'm not dangerous to you, but I definitely am dangerous." He waltzed through the room, heading for the kitchen. "Where's the baby? How many rooms on each floor? How many entrances and exits?"

Violet struggled for words and tried to keep up. She answered as many questions as she could while he checked her work, testing the door and window locks, then exploring the home in detail. "Why haven't you gotten a new driver's license?"

"I just got home. Newly discharged."

"How new?"

His smile dropped. "New enough. Where would you like me to set up for the night?"

"Wyatt slept on the couch."

"Sounds good to me."

Violet squirmed, the need to be hospitable warring with her desire to run upstairs and drag the bed in front of the door again. "I'll get you some coffee." She turned for the kitchen without waiting for a response.

Sawyer followed.

Violet's chest constricted as she poured two mugs, recalling the way Wyatt had done the same just hours before. Where was he now? Why hadn't he called? What was Sheriff Masterson doing to him? Would Wyatt have an "accident," too?

She rubbed her eyes as tears threatened to form.

"You must really hate coffee," Sawyer said.

She jerked her gaze to meet his. "I hate that Wyatt's

stuck in jail when he didn't do anything wrong, and I don't know what's happening to him."

"He's fine." Sawyer set his mug aside and began unloading a laptop from his shoulder bag.

"How do you know? Have you spoken to him?"

Sawyer stopped to stare. "Have you met him? Trust me. He's fine."

She flopped onto a vinyl padded chair at her grandma's kitchen table and pinched the bridge of her nose.

"You guys are close?" Sawyer asked.

"He's the only person I trust," she said defensively, hoping Sawyer couldn't see straight through her, too.

"Well, I'm going to try not to take that personally," he said, logging on to the laptop and typing in a password. "Where's your Wi-Fi?"

"No Wi-Fi. Wyatt's using his phone as a hotspot."

"Great." The tone of his voice made it clear Sawyer didn't think that was great at all. He extended long, lean legs beneath the table and stretched his neck slowly, tipping his head over each shoulder.

The phone rang before Violet could tell him to suck it up. She strode to the wall and lifted the receiver. "Hello?"

"Violet Ames?" a man asked. "This is Roger at River Gorge General Hospital."

"Yes," she answered breathlessly. "This is Violet. What's happened? Is my grandmother okay?"

Sawyer stilled. His eyes lifted, focusing wholly on her.

"I'm sorry to say she's taken a turn for the worse. We're calling the family in now."

Her heart sputtered. "What?"

"You should probably make your way back here," he said. "I'm sorry."

Nausea rocked Violet's gut as she hung the receiver back on its cradle. "My grandma isn't going to make it," she said, barely believing the words. "We were just there. She was doing great." *Someone's done something to her.* Bile rose in her throat at the thought.

"I'm sorry to hear that." Sawyer slid a key ring across the table in her direction. "Take the Jeep. No one here will recognize it. I'll stay and watch over Mandy."

"Who?"

"The baby." He pointed up the staircase. "Your daughter."

"Maggie."

He nodded. "Unless you want to wake her. Then I'll just hold down the fort. Whatever you want."

Violet worked her mouth shut. She didn't want to wake Maggie or leave her with a man she'd just met who couldn't even remember her name. She also didn't want to take Maggie back out on the road when who knew where the next disaster would occur.

Wyatt's words echoed back to mind, strong and assured. *Lock up tight until he gets there. Trust him when he does.*

She turned her eyes back on Sawyer. He was a mess. Scarred face. Bruised knuckles. Messy hair, matted beard. He looked more like the problem than the solution, but Wyatt trusted him, and she trusted Wyatt. Violet took the keys from the table. "Maggie shouldn't wake up before dawn. Don't touch her if she does. Just call me on the number I called you from earlier. I'll be home in an hour. If I'm not, I'll be in touch again."

He gave her a limp salute.

"Keep her safe," she ordered.

"That I can do all day."

VIOLET RAN THE length of the empty second-floor hallway to the nurse's station. Tanya leaned against the desk, speaking to another nurse in patriotic scrubs. Her eyes widened at the sight of Violet.

"Sorry I took so long," Violet said. "Have they moved her? I just realized I don't even know if this is the right floor anymore." Was she in another ward now? Critical care or wherever patients go to... Her throat ached and she couldn't swallow. She worked to collect a full breath and some of her senses. "What can I do?"

Tanya looked as if Violet had grown a second head. "What are you talking about?"

"Grandma," Violet answered, frustrated and suddenly uneasy. "Someone called to tell me to get down here."

"Why?"

Violet's limbs went limp with confusion. "Something went wrong. The hospital was calling in the family."

"What went wrong?" Tanya asked. "Grandma's the same as she was when you were here before." Her eyes turned suspicious. "Who did you say called you?"

"Roger." Violet turned toward Grandma's room. "Roger from River Gorge General Hospital."

Tanya shook her head slowly in the negative. "I don't know anyone named Roger, and I've been here all night."

Violet burst into motion, racing for her grandma's room and praying that the phone call she'd received was a mean joke and not a threat on her grandma's life. Her shoes skidded over the highly polished floor and ground to a halt outside her door. "Grandma?"

The curtain was pulled around the bed, making her grandma invisible in the dimly lit room.

"Grandma?" Violet's skin heated. Her stomach knotted. Her tongue seemed to swell in her mouth as she hit the light switch and dived for the drawn curtain. Terror seized her chest as she whipped the flimsy curtain back.

Grandma's face was serene and waxen as it had been

during visiting hours, but the rolling tray used for mealtime had been positioned over her middle.

Tears stung Violet's eyes as she took in the gruesome message before her.

The tray's faux-wood finish was covered in crushed rosebuds and petals. A note lay among the destroyed blooms, stained with color from their petals.

Your baby or your grandma, Violet? You can't protect them both.

48 hours and the clock starts now.

Chapter Twelve

"Oh my goodness!" Tanya rushed in from the hallway and dashed to Violet's side. "Who did this?"

Violet spun on her. "Who was in here last?" She pulled her phone from her pocket and dialed Sawyer. He needed to check on Maggie immediately.

"No one," Tanya said. "I looked in on her when you left, then turned out the light and went on my rounds." She dragged worried eyes back to the roses. She lifted a shaky hand toward the note.

"Don't," Violet warned, shoving her hand away. "Don't touch it. There could be fingerprints there that will help us know who wrote it."

Tanya shoved her hands into her pockets and rocked back on her heels. "Why aren't you freaked out? What's going on? What aren't you telling me?"

Violet lifted a finger to indicate that she needed a minute, then she reported the incident to Sawyer and demanded he check on Maggie. Once she knew her baby was safe, she called the police. Dispatch took a report and promised to send a deputy, but Violet couldn't promise to wait. Her heart was being torn in two. She needed to be with Maggie, but Maggie had Sawyer, an armed, trained security agent and former army ranger. Grandma had Tanya, but someone had already gotten past her once. Though, to be fair, Violet hadn't been completely honest with her cousin about how much danger their grandma might be in. Maybe what she really needed to do now was confess. Coming clean with all the details might give Tanya an advantage, not put her at risk the way she feared. Maybe not knowing was the bigger risk.

She turned to Tanya. "We need to get Grandma out of here. She needs to be moved to a facility outside this county as soon as possible. I was coming to make the request first thing in the morning."

Tanya narrowed her eyes and crossed her arms. "Why?"

Violet weighed the notion. On the one hand, sharing details with Tanya could put her in danger. On the other hand, at least Tanya wasn't a baby or in a coma. She could help, and she deserved to know what was happening to their grandma. "I think someone connected to the sheriff's department, maybe even the sheriff or his dad, has been harassing me since I got here, and I think whoever is doing this is the same person who hurt Grandma."

Tanya's eyes widened. "She fell."

"Sure. After she was knocked down."

"Off a ladder," Tanya corrected.

Violet shook her head slowly in the negative. "And the man I was here with earlier isn't my boyfriend. He was hired by Grandma to protect her, but she didn't have a chance to tell him why. She was already here by the time he got to her place."

Tanya dragged her gaze from Violet to their grandma and back again.

Violet thought she saw an argument forming on her cousin's lips. Yes, everything she'd just said sounded crazy. It was crazy. And it was all true.

Tanya wobbled to the guest armchair and collapsed onto it. She slid her attention to the letter on Grandma's tray. A threat and a countdown. "Okay," she said. "I'll talk to the doctor first thing in the morning and tell him she needs to be closer to you because you're her preferred caregiver. Then I'll call every good facility in the neighboring counties to see which ones have a bed available."

Violet wrapped her in a quick hug. "Thank you." She stepped back with an apologetic frown. "I can't stay here and wait for the deputy. I need to get home to Maggie, and I think I might stop by the sheriff's department on my way. He might be corrupt or he might not, but the whole force can't be. Maybe making a scene down there will get an honest deputy's interest piqued."

She posed her phone over the bed and snapped a half dozen pictures of the gruesome floral scene, then moved the rolling tray as far as possible from her grandma.

"What should I do?" Tanya asked. "I don't want to leave her, but I'm the only one on the floor for another twenty-five minutes. I need to be at the desk."

"Call security," Violet said. "Get someone up here to sit with her until a deputy arrives, but don't let a deputy in here by himself. There's something off about this case and the sheriff's department. I've got no real proof. Just a lot of coincidence and intuition."

"Intuition." Tanya bobbed her head, clearly shocked by the night's turn of events and the metric ton of mess Violet had just dumped on her. "Honey, that's the best tool in any woman's arsenal, and it's good enough for me."

Violet passed the receiver to Tanya from the phone beside Grandma's bed, stretching the spiral cord across the distance. "Here. Call security, but don't leave until someone gets here to take your place and remember what I said about the sheriff's department."

Tanya accepted the receiver, then pressed a few buttons on the handset. "Be careful."

Violet hesitated. "Don't tell anyone what I just told you. Do your best to act as if I didn't."

Tanya nodded.

Violet took the stairs to the parking lot, unable to stand idly waiting for the elevator and unwilling to let her anger fizzle before unleashing it on whoever would listen at the sheriff's department. How many times did she and her family have to be threatened before the sheriff did something about it? How could she believe he wasn't involved when he didn't seem to care what was happening to her? Wasn't that his job?

She climbed into Sawyer's Jeep and mashed the gas pedal to the floor. She nearly leaped from the vehicle when she arrived at the sheriff's department, fully primed with adrenaline and a thirst for justice.

The front door was flung open beneath her heavy hands and she marched to the front desk. "I'm here to see Sheriff Masterson," she told the gray-haired woman staring back at her. "My name is Violet Ames, and I'm not leaving until I do."

"What's this about?" the lady asked.

A door opened nearby and both women turned to look. The smug-looking sheriff walked out, trailed closely by a brooding Wyatt. The men slowed at the sight of Violet. Wyatt regained himself first, then closed the distance to her side. He slid his hands over hers and pulled her to him. "Thank you for coming so fast," he said loudly, then much more softly, "Let's go."

She stiffened. "No. Someone threatened Maggie and Grandma. *Again*. My *baby* and *comatose* grandma," she seethed. "I came to talk to the sheriff." Her voice grew louder with each word, and several faces turned in her direction.

Sheriff Masterson went to stand with the gray-haired

lady on the other side of the desk. "Is there a problem, Miss Ames?"

"Yes," she barked, drawing more attention as planned. "Someone in your town has repeatedly threatened and endangered my baby, my grandma and myself." She faced the screen of her phone to him and flipped through the photos taken at the hospital.

His jaw locked.

"What are you going to do about it?" Violet demanded. "She can't exactly leave town like you keep suggesting I do, now can she?" *Barring that hospital transfer I just requested.* Violet's nose and eyes stung with barely tamped-down emotion. The week's buildup was quickly reaching a tipping point, but she couldn't afford to look weak. She needed the sheriff to see her as strong. Unwavering. She steadied her breathing and plowed ahead. "And what kind of policy is that anyway? Anyone having trouble ought to just leave town? Then you can boast about how safe your county is? No crime here."

Wyatt pulled her against him and buried his face in her hair. "We need to go." He lifted his mouth to her ear. "Now."

Violet's will wavered. Wyatt's warm breath on the delicate skin of her neck and cheek had distracted her, defused her. She grimaced at the sheriff. "You need to help me. Help my grandma." She cast her gaze to all the other men and women in uniform watching her mental breakdown. "We have forty-eight hours."

She turned and let Wyatt lead her away.

WYATT STARTED SAWYER's Jeep as Violet buckled in. "It was smart of you to take this vehicle. No one knows to look for you in it, and Sawyer keeps his glass tinted to the legal limits. This time of night, it'd be impossible to know who was driving."

Violet wrapped her arms around herself tightly and stared at the sheriff's department as they passed through the lot. "What happened in there?"

"Nothing. They left me in a room alone the whole time. By the time I got a young deputy to allow me my phone call, they let me go. I called Sawyer, but pretended I was speaking with a lawyer."

She frowned. "You called Sawyer? Not me?"

"You were supposed to be with Sawyer. When he told me you were at the hospital, I thought I was going to have to walk there."

Violet rolled her eyes. "That's five miles away."

Wyatt eased onto the road and hooked a right toward Mrs. Ames's house. "So? You were there, and it's not like Sawyer could come and pick me up. He said he was instructed not to touch the baby, and he didn't have the keys to my truck anyway."

She looked his way. "So the sheriff hauled you all the way to the department just to leave you in a room and do nothing? No threats or grand inquisition? Nothing? What was the point?"

"Because he can?" Wyatt guessed. He'd assumed it was a typical bully's lesson. He's in power, so Wyatt must concede. He'd also considered it might be another warning.

"Did you see the photos I showed Sheriff Masterson?" Violet asked.

"Yeah." Wyatt caught her eye then. "It wasn't the sheriff. He never left the station. I could hear his big mouth in every room for almost two hours. Giving orders. Making stupid jokes. Watching a game on television in the break room. He didn't have time to get to the hospital after taking me in."

Violet let her eyes drift shut, then turned her face away. "Maybe he pulled us over on his way from the hospital."

"Maybe, but we were also on our way from the hospital, so he would've had to be fast with the note and roses."

She pressed the heels of her hands against her eyes.

"We will find out who did this," Wyatt vowed. "I know I've said it before, but it's true, and I need you to trust me."

Violet's lips twitched, but the smile never formed. "The monster ruined her rosebushes."

"I'm sorry." The photos had been tough to see, especially the note. The devastation in Violet's eyes had sliced straight through him. "Those were her roses left at the hospital?"

She nodded, eyes glossy with unshed tears.

Wyatt reached out and pulled her as close as the seat belts would allow, then gripped her small hands in one of his and squeezed with promise. He released her when he pulled into her grandma's drive. The Jeep's headlights washed over the destroyed rosebushes and Violet's tiny car. The little yellow hatchback sat at an awkward angle. The two tires farthest from the house had been slashed, probably with whatever had been used to destroy the roses. "You didn't tell me about your car. I think it's having as rough a week as you are."

Violet wrenched upright and clamped her hands onto the dashboard. "I didn't even notice that earlier. I've barely looked at my car since it was carved up." She pounded her foot against the floorboard. "As if the paint job wasn't going to break the bank, now I need two new tires."

Wyatt forced a tight smile. "Maybe if you leave it sitting out here long enough someone will just take it and your car insurance will replace it with a whole new one." He met her outside the passenger door and walked her to the porch, maneuvering around his truck in the front yard. "Were you drunk when you parked my truck like that?"

"No."

She laughed, and the hardened shell of Wyatt's heart cracked a little further. "Well, you might consider retaking the parking test, 'cause you missed the driveway by about twenty-five feet."

She laughed again, this time taking his elbow in her hand as they climbed the steps.

Wyatt stopped short of opening the door, knowing it was the last time they'd be alone before he faced Sawyer and a long night of research. "Come here." He pulled Violet to his chest and wrapped her in his arms. To his great pleasure, she hugged him back.

More than that, she melded herself against him.

Wyatt's heart thundered and his hands slid over her narrow back, and he enjoyed the feel of her more than was remotely acceptable for their situation. He pressed one palm to the curve of her spine, fingers splayed over the thin material of her shirt, and drifted the other into the plane between her shoulder blades. "I'm sorry I wasn't with you at the hospital tonight." His voice was low and thick. Guilt had nearly consumed him as he'd sat in the empty room wondering if she and Maggie had made it home safely. "I'd promised to stay with you, to protect you. Instead, I let that menace bait me into saying the wrong thing."

"You were defending me," she whispered, turning her beautiful face up to his. "I was honored."

Wyatt pursed his lips. "I was stupid. Impetuous. I should've found another way to make him back off without causing us to be separated. If something had happened to you or Maggie…" The words stopped coming. He couldn't bear to finish the sentence.

Wyatt moved one palm to cup Violet's jaw. He let the

pad of his thumb caress her cheek. Logically, he knew what he was doing was wrong and unprofessional and that she should tell him where to stick his grabby hands, but the look in her eyes was electric and the magnitude of that pull was enough to make him brave. Wyatt lowered his head. Closer. Breathing her in and waiting for the will to knock it off. This wasn't the job. And he wasn't that guy who'd take advantage of a stressed-out single mom who probably just wanted something safe and normal to hold onto amid all the danger surrounding her this week.

Violet rose onto her toes, arching her back and trailing her small hands over the curves of his chest to his shoulders. The unmistakable heat of desire darkened her eyes.

A low, needy moan rumbled through him as his nose lined up beside hers, seeking, testing. Tasting her sweet breath as it washed over him. Feeling the heat of her body pressed to his.

Her mouth was *right* there, waiting to be taken by him.

The home's front door swung open beside them and Violet sprang from his hold.

Sawyer stared out. "I heard you pull up like ten minutes ago. What are y'all doing out here? Is this a private discussion or are you about ready to get in here so we can get to work?"

Violet hung her head and darted inside, hiding her pink cheeks behind long brown hair.

Wyatt took a minute to pull his thoughts together and remind himself that he loved Sawyer, and he didn't really want to knock him out right now. "Thanks for coming."

"Anytime." Sawyer locked the door behind Wyatt, then followed him into the kitchen.

Violet was already at the table, hands folded and looking mighty guilty. Wyatt tried not to think too long or hard about why. "Did Maggie wake while I was away?" she asked.

"Nope." Sawyer dropped onto the chair positioned at the end of the table. "But she shouted, 'No!' so loud I thought someone had gotten in through an upstairs window. I was halfway to her room when I heard her snoring."

Wyatt grinned. That chubby-cheeked princess was a riot. He could imagine Sawyer ready for battle, tearing up the steps to defend the baby, only to see she was telling someone off in her dreams. *Probably me*, he thought wryly.

"That was about all I heard from her," Sawyer said. "What about you, Stone?" he asked Wyatt. "How was jail?"

"Super."

Violet tapped her phone's screen as the men spoke. A moment later, she set the device aside. Both men's cell phones buzzed. "I sent you copies of the photos I took at the hospital. Just in case the scene goes missing. I have proof. Tanya saw it, too. What should we do now?"

Sawyer flipped through the photos. "Are these the roses from right outside?"

"I think so," Violet answered. "Some jerk was real busy tonight."

Wyatt itched to go to her, to comfort her. Would she really have let him kiss her? Did she want him to? And had he seriously not jumped on that opportunity? He felt his brows pull together. It had been the right thing to do. Hadn't it? It would have been wrong to let her confuse her appreciation for his protection with real feelings for him. Right?

Sawyer dropped his phone on the tabletop and shot a pointed look at Wyatt. "Small-town cover-up?"

"Yeah. Seems that way. Problem is going to be finding out who is covering for who. Binds run deep and tight in a town this small."

Sawyer expelled a long puff of air. "Nothing truer than that, and the way I understand it, your main suspect is the former sheriff." He rocked his chair back on two legs. "That's no good."

"Nope," Wyatt agreed.

"And that guy is the current sheriff's daddy, yeah?"

"Yeah."

Sawyer performed a long, slow whistle. "Doesn't get tighter than that."

No, it didn't. Wyatt shifted in his seat. "The cover-up theory is only a theory. We have no idea what's been covered up or why. Not even a guess."

Sawyer set his chair down with a thud. "Violet's grandma needed protection for some reason. Now her granddaughter and great-granddaughter do, too. Are you thinking this all started with something big?"

Wyatt nodded. "I doubt anyone would bother trying to run folks out of town over something small."

Sawyer did another whistle. A short, slick burst this time.

Violet rolled her head over one shoulder and fixed her gaze on Sawyer. "Any chance you've got some new information on Henry Davis?"

He tapped his pointer fingers along the worn Formica tabletop like drumsticks. "I'm working on it."

"What about the derby car?" Wyatt asked.

"Still working."

Wyatt scraped his chair back and went to the refrigerator for a bottle of water. "I'd like to know what kind of thing would motivate a person to threaten an old woman and a baby." Just the thought made his blood boil. He pressed the cold bottle to his forehead, then against the curve of his neck. "It's got to be something huge. Theft? Embezzlement? Gambling debt?"

"Why does it have to be about money?" Violet asked. "Maybe it's a case of identity theft or fraud. Maybe Sheriff Masterson helped Henry Davis disappear when he didn't want to go back to war, and Mary Alice's dementia makes it likely she'll forget that was a secret."

Sawyer stroked his ratty beard. "Maybe the sheriff isn't really a Masterson. Maybe the missing soldier is really his daddy and that kind of truth come to light would besmirch the family name."

"Besmirch?" Wyatt asked. "Really?"

"Hey, I know things," Sawyer said.

Wyatt smiled.

Violet flipped through the photos on her phone. "That note said I have forty-eight hours. I don't have any reason to think this will be sorted by then, so I told Tanya I want to move Grandma out of the county."

The men turned to face her. Neither spoke.

"Tanya said she'd talk to the doctor first thing tomorrow morning, then reach out to some facilities in search of an open bed. The note-writer was right. I can't protect them both. Unless Maggie and I move into Grandma's room at the hospital, I can't be in two places all the time. Maybe moving her into another county and putting her safety in the hands of another police or sheriff's department will help remove some of the danger."

Sawyer tented his brows. "Good idea."

Wyatt agreed with the move. Mrs. Ames would be safer somewhere outside the potentially corrupt sheriff's jurisdiction, but Wyatt wasn't so sure about Violet and Maggie. "I think you should stick with us until we know who's behind this. Going off on your own could be dangerous like we talked about." As long as he didn't do anything else to get himself hauled off to jail again, he'd never let Violet or Maggie out of his sight.

Violet yawned. "Let's see what Tanya has to say after breakfast." She rubbed her eyes. "I can try talking with Mary Alice again tomorrow."

Wyatt moved to stand beside her chair. "I don't know. I've heard the words *restraining order* more times than I'd like today. I think we'd be wise not to push the old man." He gave his partner a long look. "Maybe you can give Mary Alice a shot. No one knows you yet. Maybe take a walk down her street, see if you see a nice old lady on the gray-and-black craftsman-style porch with the American flag."

Sawyer smiled. "Ask her about the missing man from five decades back? Sounds good."

Violet yawned again.

Wyatt offered her his hand. "How about we move this to the living room? It's more comfortable in there, and I've already seen you fall asleep at this table today. Why not mix it up a little?"

Sawyer chuckled. "You're still a thrill a minute, I see."

Violet accepted his hand, then leaned against his side as they made their way back to the front room. She settled on the love seat and tucked her feet beneath her. Wyatt took the cushion on her right.

Sawyer sat on the floor, back resting against the couch, a clear view of the front window and door on one side, the hallway, kitchen and rear exit on the other. Wyatt knew because he'd spent his recent nights seated there, too, pushing the same few seemingly useless puzzle pieces around in his head.

Mary Alice, Mr. Masterson, a missing GI from 1968 and Violet's grandma.

In other words, a dementia patient, a drunk, a missing person and an old lady in a coma.

Basically, they had nothing and less than forty-eight hours to find out who'd written that note.

The clock was ticking.

Chapter Thirteen

Wyatt's eyes snapped open. He'd fallen asleep talking to Sawyer, trading theories and exploring the difficulties of investigation in a small town where the sheriff was angry and shady. He woke to the muted thuds of wood on wood. The warbled words of a voice on the morning air.

Sawyer rose to his feet across from him and crept down the hallway toward Mrs. Ames's kitchen. He'd heard it, too.

Wyatt blinked, forcing his eyes into focus. His mind had fixed on a distant sound.

The back door opened and shut softly.

Wyatt eased away from Violet. She'd tipped against him during the night, set her cheek on his shoulder and an open palm on his chest. "Shh," he soothed, detangling their warm bodies.

Violet's eyes cracked open, her expression mired in sleep. "Where are you going? Is it Maggie?"

"No." Wyatt stretched to his feet and collected his sidearm and holster from the table, securing them to his belt. "She's asleep. Stay here."

The sound came again, this time followed by a whistle.

Violet scooted to the edge of her cushion. "What was that sound?"

"Sawyer went to see. That was him whistling."

Her blue eyes cleared immediately. "A warning?"

"Nah," Wyatt said. "That whistle is more like, get out here and see."

"I'll get Maggie."

They parted ways in the kitchen, Violet taking the steps to the second floor and Wyatt moving through the back door and into the yard beyond.

Sawyer stood just inside the barn where Mrs. Ames had fallen, both hands on his hips. He nodded at the loft above. "There's our noisemaker. What do you suppose that's about?"

Wyatt stepped forward, peering into the cavernous structure, drawn to the continued thuds and murmuring. "Hello?"

Sawyer joined him, arms crossed. "Wonder how long she's been up there."

"She?" Wyatt asked.

"The old lady."

The loft boards rattled and Mary Alice appeared, pacing closer and closer to the edge. "Where is it?" she asked. "Where is it? Where did you put it? Where did it go?"

"Mrs. Masterson?" Wyatt asked, drawing her attention to the barn floor below. "What are you doing up there? Be careful. You're at the edge. Step back." Faint rays of amber-and-gold light filtered through the space between boards. Tufts of hay fell from the loft. Wyatt craned his neck for a better look at the uninvited guest. "On second thought, why don't you come on down here and tell me how I can help?"

"Not until I find it!" she yelled. Her features hardened in a look of sheer defiance. "Where is it?" She spun away from the edge, but slid on the loose hay and stumbled. Her arms flew wide, grasping at air. "Oh!"

Wyatt shot forward, racing to the place where she would land if she fell. "Be careful!"

Mary Alice regained her balance and stared down at him through the space between loft boards. "Who are you?" she asked. "Why are you here?"

"I'm Wyatt Stone. A friend of Mrs. Ames. I'm here to help you."

Mary Alice stilled. Her ruddy cheeks went white. She tipped precariously forward, lowering her nose toward the boards at her feet. "Did she tell you about him?"

"Yes," Wyatt lied. "She trusted me with the truth. You can, too."

She straightened then, shuffling back from the edge. She pressed narrow, wrinkled hands over her mouth and sobbed. "I'm so sorry."

Maggie's sweet babbles reached Wyatt's ears before Violet made it into the barn. "What's happening?" Violet asked, moving into place between Wyatt and Sawyer.

"There's an old lady crying in your loft," Sawyer explained.

"Why?"

Sawyer pointed a silent finger at Wyatt.

"It's Mary Alice," Wyatt explained. "She's looking for *it*."

Violet stepped back, one hand against her forehead, seeking the woman overhead. "Mary Alice? Are you okay?"

Dust sifted through the boards overhead, fluttering to the earthen floor. "Gladys?" Mary Alice inched closer, her eyes puffy from tears. "Is that you?"

Violet frowned. "Does Tom know you're here?"

"No." She shook her head vigorously. "Of course not. You know I'm not supposed to leave."

Wyatt rubbed a hand through his hair. "I've got to call the sheriff's department. She's clearly confused, and her husband's probably worried." Much as he'd like to take advantage of having the woman alone for questioning, it wasn't right. She needed help he couldn't begin to give.

"Or he's drunk again," Violet grouched. "How about you call the sheriff, and I'll talk to Mary Alice? Maybe this is a blessing in disguise. I'd hoped to speak with her again."

Wyatt turned away, dialing the department. "Good luck. You'll probably only have about five minutes once I make the report."

"What?" Mary Alice called. "What are you saying, Gladys? Did you tell him? Did you tell that man about Henry?"

"Of course not," Violet said.

Wyatt darted forward, hoping to salvage the lie. "It's okay. I've already told her you trust me and she can, too."

Violet puckered her brow. "Oh."

"Liars," Mary Alice cried. "Everyone lies. I lie," she said. "I've lied all my life. I don't want to anymore."

Violet struggled with a wiggly Maggie, who'd nearly turned herself upside down trying to get to the floor. "It's okay," she promised. "I don't blame you. You can always talk to me when things get hard."

Wyatt finished his call and pulled Maggie into his arms. He tipped his head toward Mary Alice. "Keep going," he told Violet. "I've got princess."

She wet her lips and moved toward the ladder. "I'm sorry you're upset, Mary Alice. I never meant to upset you."

"You shouldn't have told," she said. "It wasn't your story to tell. I want the box back now."

"Okay." Violet turned victorious eyes on Wyatt. "What box?"

He motioned with one hand. "Keep going," he whispered.

Mary Alice didn't respond.

Violet reached for the ladder. "Can I come up? We can talk privately."

Wyatt cringed. That wasn't what he'd meant. He swept a hand out to stop her and missed.

Her fingers curled around the wood.

"No!" Mary Alice screamed.

Violet jumped back, rushing toward the center of the barn where Wyatt stood, looking up as Mary Alice continued to scream. "Sorry! I won't come up. I'll stay right here."

Mary Alice gave Wyatt a long questioning look. "Are you here to arrest me?" she asked. Her gaze stuck to the sidearm on his hip.

"No, ma'am. I'm not here to arrest you." He cocked his head and trod lightly. "Why would I do that?"

"Because I kept his things," she said. "Hid them. Then gave them to Gladys, and now they're gone."

"They're in the box you're looking for?" he asked.

Mary Alice moved into view at the loft's edge then crumpled to the loft floor. "Yes." Her housecoat puddled around her as she lay in the hay, as if she'd disintegrated before his eyes and the ugly brown material was all that remained.

"Who do the things in the box belong to?" Violet asked.

"Mary Alice!" Mr. Masterson's voice boomed in the distance.

Wyatt spun in place. Shock and curiosity rushed in his mind.

Had someone from the sheriff's department told Mary Alice's husband where she was, or had he already been on his way looking for her? If so, then why had he assumed she would be here? Did he know that his wife had given Mrs. Ames something to keep for her?

The distant cry of a siren crept into the barn with them.

Backup was coming, and Wyatt was willing to bet the first cruiser on the scene would be driven by the sheriff, Mary Alice's son.

Mr. Masterson plodded through the open barn door. His shadow stretched ominously before him. "Where is she? What did you do to her?"

Mary Alice sat up, revealing herself. "Here I am," she croaked, running the sleeve of her housecoat under her nose. Her sullen expression was caught somewhere between desperation and hopelessness. "Take me home."

Mr. Masterson stomped into the room's center. His blue T-shirt was untucked, and his blue jeans needed a belt. He hadn't tied his boots or combed his hair, and the heady scent of beer lingered on his breath. "Get down here. What are you doing up there? You know you aren't supposed to leave."

She swung trembling legs over the loft's edge and shimmied on her stomach, searching blindly for footholds on the creaky ladder. "I'm sorry. I didn't mean to."

"You didn't mean to walk out the front door while I was sleeping?" he groused. "Didn't mean to walk all the way over here without telling anyone? You didn't mean to climb into that loft? Didn't mean to scare me half to death? To defy my rules?"

Mary Alice began to cry again. She stopped her descent, her frail body jackknifed over the loft's edge.

"Easy," Wyatt warned both Mastersons. "Mary Alice, please take your time and be careful coming down. Mr. Masterson, watch yourself. I'm getting a good idea of how you treat your wife privately, and it isn't going to fly here."

"Is that a threat?"

Wyatt crossed his arms and squared his shoulders in answer.

Mr. Masterson scoffed. "I've got dogs who know better than to push me. Are you smarter than my dogs, son?"

Wyatt bit the insides of his cheeks. The metallic taste of blood filled his mouth, pulling him back from the edge of saying something that might land him back in jail. He couldn't afford to give the sheriff a reason to take him away again, and threatening the man's father seemed a sure way to do exactly that.

The arriving siren peaked, then silenced outside the barn. The sheriff strode into the tension moments later, evaluating the scene before rushing to his mom's aid on the ladder. He whispered to her, calming her and helping her slowly to the ground. He lifted furious eyes to his father. "Dad? You want to explain to me what the hell happened here?"

Mr. Masterson stared at Wyatt, teeth gritted.

"I'm sorry," Mary Alice said. "I was only looking for his things."

"Whose?" Wyatt repeated his earlier question.

"Henry's." She cupped a hand over her lips and flipped her gaze to meet her husband's. "I think I should lie down."

"I think you should shut up," he muttered, ripping her roughly from their son's hands. "Let's go."

The sheriff followed closely behind his parents, looking more like a sullen boy than a man in charge of an entire county's safety.

Wyatt shadowed them, both sickened and aghast at the twisted family dynamic he'd watched play out.

"I shouldn't have kept his things," Mary Alice whispered loudly as they approached her husband's truck. "I just wanted to return them to his people. It's the right thing to do."

"Shut. Up!" Mr. Masterson stopped and gave her arm a firm tug. His eyes were bright with rage.

"Dad," the sheriff warned.

Mary Alice whimpered and jerked away.

Mr. Masterson wrenched the passenger door open and nearly tossed her inside.

"Where are we going?" she asked, fumbling to right herself on the bench. "To the well?"

Mr. Masterson slammed the door. His eyes slid shut for a long beat.

The well meant something to him. But what?

His son closed in on him. "I'm heading to your place from here. I won't be ten minutes behind you."

Mr. Masterson climbed behind the wheel without another word and reversed down the drive.

Violet slid into place at Wyatt's side, tucking Maggie safely between them. "That was all kinds of disturbing," she said softly.

Sheriff Masterson turned to gawk, as if he'd somehow heard her. He tipped his hat and scowled. "Take good care of your grandma, Miss Ames. Ladies get old and bad things start to happen."

VIOLET'S HEART THUDDED roughly in her chest. Had the county sheriff just threatened her grandmother? In front of witnesses? Was he insane? She set Maggie in the grass with trembling hands, then dialed Tanya's cell phone, praying her cousin was at the hospital.

"Hello?" Tanya answered.

"How's Grandma?" Violet blurted. "Is security still with her? Have you spoken with the doctor?"

"Violet?" Tanya asked. "Are you okay?"

"I'm fine. A little shaken, but how's Grandma?"

"She's fine. There hasn't been any change."

"And the doctor?" Violet pressed.

"He hasn't been to this floor yet, but it's still early, and he's got patients on floors one and five, as well. I'll call as soon as I know more about the transfer. Okay? Right now, I need to make my rounds."

"What about security?"

"There's a man outside her door now. A new one will come when the shift changes."

Violet breathed a little easier. "Okay. Tell me as soon as you talk to the doctor about Grandma's transfer." She disconnected and turned to Wyatt, who'd swept Maggie off the ground when she'd crawled straight to him. "What was the name of that body shop you took your truck to?"

"R.G. Auto Body."

Violet tried to focus on the larger problem and not on the fact that her baby was getting too attached to a man who would soon be gone. "I want to get my tires replaced. I want to know Maggie and I can leave if we need to."

Wyatt shared the number, then played with Maggie while Violet made arrangements to have her car towed to the shop.

She wasn't sure if River Gorge was safe or if it was better for her to just go home to Winchester, but one thing had become abundantly clear. Violet needed a way to get Maggie out of town in case of emergency. She needed an escape plan, and a car with two bad tires wasn't going to get the job done.

Violet paid the tow truck driver when he came for her car, then went inside to check on Maggie and the guys.

Wyatt moved away from the window where he'd been watching her and went to stare over Sawyer's shoulder at a series of topographical maps spread over the kitchen table. Maggie's body was limp in his arms. Her head was cocked back. Her eyes closed in slumber.

Violet slipped in close and removed her baby from Wyatt's strong arms. "I'll put her to bed, then be right back."

"Take your time," he said.

Sawyer grunted, a pen between his teeth.

Violet slipped upstairs and tucked Maggie into her crib, then nearly leaped back down to see what they were doing with those maps. "What are the red marks for?" she asked. Had something happened while she was outside making arrangements to get her broken car fixed? "Are those local maps? River Gorge? Grove County?"

"Wells," Sawyer answered.

Violet dragged her attention from Sawyer to the maps, then fixed it on Wyatt. "What?"

"Mary Alice asked her husband where they were going in such a hurry. She asked if they were going to the well, and Mr. Masterson nearly stroked out in response."

"Everyone in town has a well," Violet said. "What are the maps for?"

"Everyone has a well," Wyatt said, "but they don't go to them. They are a resource, not a destination."

Sawyer spun a map in her direction. The page was marked over with blue ink. "The circles represent abandoned wells in this county. Some have probably been decommissioned by the state. The rest should be boarded over, but accessible. I'm going to pay them all a visit once I finish mapping them."

Violet turned the page back to face him. "There must be dozens. These marks are spread all over the county, and some of them are in the middle of nowhere. How will you even get there?"

Sawyer lifted one foot off the ground and gave it a wiggle.

Violet rolled her eyes. "That will take forever. I only have thirty-six hours."

"I'll drive to as many as possible, then hike to the rest."

Violet fought the frustration knotting in her muscles.

It was all anyone could do. More than most, and Sawyer was ready. She needed to hope it was enough. "I need some fresh air."

Wyatt opened the back door for her as she passed. "Feel like taking a walk?"

Desperately. Violet pursed her lips. "I don't know. I just put Maggie down."

"I've got her," Sawyer said. "Babies love me. Especially Mandy."

"Maggie," Wyatt and Violet corrected in near unison.

Sawyer laughed. "I'm just yanking your chains. Go walk. Let me work."

Violet pulled in a deep breath, then grabbed the quilt off the back porch's swing on her way down the steps.

Wyatt fell into stride beside her with two bottles of water in one big hand. He offered one to Violet, then took the quilt from her and tossed it over his shoulder.

"Thanks." Violet accepted the water, then slid her free hand around his elbow as they walked.

Wyatt turned a careful smile on her. "We got off to a rough start this morning, but it's been a good day. Mary Alice said the box of things she's looking for belonged to Henry."

"She had to mean Henry Davis," Violet said. "There's no way there's a second Henry in this mess."

"I assumed as much, given your grandma's internet searches, and now we know the Mastersons visit a local well for some reason. Based on Mary Alice's tone, it's not a good time when they do. If we're lucky, Sawyer will find the well she was referring to, maybe even find the box and get this mess wrapped up by nightfall. Then that note won't matter. We'll know who wrote it before the forty-eight hours is up."

"It's a lot of wells."

"We've already got a plan in place, so he won't need to search them all. He'll be methodical and efficient with the ones he does."

Violet's mind raced as the torrent of emotions whipped through her. Fear for herself and her family. Sadness for Mary Alice and hers. Hope that this new revelation would be the one to break the case. And something else. Something warm and strange and new when she thought about the way her hand felt on Wyatt's strong arm, or the way he'd held her on the porch last night. For a moment, she thought he might want to kiss her, too.

Violet had sworn she'd never date another military man. Her ex had pridefully put service to his country above everything else, and when he learned he was having a baby, he'd dropped her like the plague. As far as she knew, he was still proudly serving his country. Her heart still stung for Maggie's sake. Violet knew what it was like to not know her father. It stunk. But maybe her ex was the exception and not the rule. Maybe all her fears of being hurt again, of seeing Maggie lose another male figure in her life, were keeping her from taking a chance on something amazing.

She glanced his way and caught him staring.

Or maybe she was a silly-hearted dreamer who wanted impossible things. Like a real, true, toe-curling, ballad-worthy love.

Wyatt slowed at the sight of the lake beyond Grandma's field. "Is this where we're headed?"

She cleared her throat and nodded. "Yeah." She hadn't really had a plan when she'd walked out the back door, but the lake was a good place to be still and think. Behind them, her grandma's barn and home were distant red and white dots. Had they really walked so far already?

Wyatt spread the quilt on the ground.

Violet lowered herself onto it, enjoying the mix of sun and shade as a warm breeze jostled the limbs of a mighty oak overhead.

Wyatt took a seat beside her, his brown eyes searching. "I'm glad Sawyer's here," he said finally.

She smiled. She wasn't sure what he'd been going to say, but she hadn't considered that Sawyer would have anything to do with the conflict wrinkling his brow. "Oh yeah?"

Wyatt reached for her hand and pressed his palm to hers, twining their fingers and looking as guilty as any man she'd ever seen. "I'm glad he's here because I've let myself become distracted. I've gotten too involved and become too emotional to do the job I need to do."

Violet rolled her eyes, trying not to overthink the meaning behind his words. "Yeah. You seem like a real wreck."

"I am." Wyatt pulled their joined hands to his chest, soulful eyes still searching hers. "I wanted to kiss you last night."

"Why didn't you?" The question had formed and presented itself before she'd thought better of it.

Wyatt wet his lips, unmoving, unspeaking.

Violet waited, her gaze locked on his. The fear of rejection cresting anew.

He dropped his attention to her mouth, sending her insides into a spin.

"Wyatt," she whispered. "Say something."

He lifted a suddenly heated gaze to her eyes. "I was being a gentleman."

"And now?"

Wyatt slid a steady hand against her jaw, long fingers caressing her cheek, his broad thumb brushing over her bottom lip. "Now I'm just a man." He lowered his mouth to hers slowly, purposefully, never releasing her from that steady gaze.

The electricity she'd felt at his side or standing toe-to-toe on the porch was nothing compared to the power that coursed through her when his mouth moved against hers. Caressing, searching, giving. Her limbs were soft with pleasure, and longing circled in her core. It was the kind of kiss Violet had always wanted, but had never before experienced. The kind that made women half crazy with desire until they believed anything was possible.

Even a real, true, toe-curling, ballad-worthy love.

Chapter Fourteen

Violet hated to leave the lake behind. Things felt different there, more hopeful and less tragic. Take that cheek-pinkening, heart-pounding kiss for example. That was the power of the lake. Unfortunately, that sweet moment couldn't last. A clock was ticking back in their reality, and finding whatever Mary Alice had been looking for was top priority.

Wyatt matched Violet's pace on the way back to the house. She tried not to stare at his conflicted face or ask him about his thoughts. It had been her experience that the person asking often didn't like the answer, and Wyatt hadn't spoken since breaking off their kiss. He'd looked at her for a long moment with mind-melting intensity, then suggested they should get going. Not exactly what she'd been thinking at the moment, but she supposed it was nice of him to take her mind off things for a while.

He delivered Grandma's quilt to the back porch, then opened the door for her to pass.

Violet offered Sawyer a smile, then went straight upstairs for a shower. A cold one.

She managed to re-dress and blow-dry her hair into soft, cascading waves before Maggie woke from her nap. Violet told herself the extra swipes of mascara and lip gloss had nothing to do with the big brown-eyed man in her kitchen.

She checked her finished reflection in the mirror and did her best not to recall the feeling of Wyatt's skilled lips on hers. She doubted her mouth would ever be the same. Or her heart, for that matter.

Maggie made a soft noise, drawing Violet's attention to the crib where her baby simply rolled over and continued to sleep peacefully.

Violet left the bedroom door open on her way out. She tugged the hem of her black cutoffs and adjusted the neckline of her baby blue satin tank top on her way back to the kitchen.

The men looked up when she arrived.

Wyatt's jaw sank open.

Sawyer gave an appreciative nod. "Welcome back."

"Thanks," Violet said, pleased with the responses, especially Wyatt's. "How's it going?"

Wyatt worked his mouth shut and clapped a hand on Sawyer's shoulder. "We split the list of wells into groups by location. Sawyer's going to take the farthest set first, then work his way back toward town. You, Maggie and I will drive past some of the closer locations and see if any are visible from the road. I've got a feeling the wells most easily accessible have been completely decommissioned by now, but it's worth a look. I figured we can help eliminate some possibilities before we go to the hospital."

"Hospital?" Violet asked. "I want to see Grandma, but you must have plenty of research to do while Sawyer is well-hunting. I don't want to slow you down." How much time did she have left now? Could she even be sure the one who'd written the note would truly wait two days before doing whatever awful thing he had planned next?

"We can do both," Wyatt said. "I'll make time."

Sawyer stood and arched his back in a deep stretch, showcasing an undeniably fit physique. His lids drooped over crystal-blue eyes as he straightened. He was probably devastatingly handsome beneath the shaggy hair and beard, but Violet suspected he hid just as much behind the cocky grin and aloof facade as the disheveled-chic look he was rocking. She'd thought of asking Wyatt about Sawyer's story more than once, but she'd kept the question to herself, certain Wyatt would take his friend's secrets to the grave, whatever they were.

"I'm taking the truck today," Sawyer said. "If someone gets hauled off to jail again, it might as well be me."

Wyatt smiled. "Might as well."

Thirty minutes later, they were all on their way out. Wyatt locked the front door behind them as their little tribe dispersed. Sawyer on his way to investigate abandoned wells. Wyatt, Maggie and Violet to perform a little drive-by reconnaissance on their way to the hospital.

She watched thick green foliage blur past her window and a pair of small white clouds sail across a perfect blue sky. If only her thoughts were half as clear as that sky. "What if the sheriff finds Sawyer on private property and does something irrational?" she asked. A few gruesome possibilities jolted into her mind. "At least you had me as a witness when he went bonkers before."

"Sawyer's fine. Sawyer is vapor," Wyatt said. "No one sees him unless he wants them to." His jaw set and he cast Violet a dark look before sticking his attention back to the road. "The sheriff won't find Sawyer."

"But what if he does? What if he tries to hurt him? There's no one around to stop him from doing anything crazy."

Wyatt slid mischievous eyes in Violet's direction. "In that highly unlikely scenario, I'd be more worried about the sheriff's safety than Sawyer's."

Violet felt her brows rising over her forehead. "You're

saying Sawyer's dangerous?" A memory swept to the fore-front of her mind. Hadn't Sawyer told her as much the night they'd met? *I'm not dangerous to you, but I defi-nitely am dangerous.*

"I'm saying he's been through a lot, and a cocky small-town sheriff isn't going to get the best of him."

Violet considered his words. Sawyer had also said he was newly discharged. She didn't know how long he'd been enlisted, but it didn't take a professional to see that he'd been through some things. "Is he okay?"

"No," Wyatt answered flatly. "Sawyer's highly trained and severely post-traumatic, so I'm hoping for everyone's sake that no one around here ticks him off."

A chill slid down Violet's spine as she let that sink in.

Wyatt slowed at the next crossroads. A giant wooden sign stood reverently near the corner.

Violet focused her attention on the cracked and peeling white paint instead of whether or not she'd been reckless to leave Maggie alone with Sawyer earlier.

A series of black block letters splayed across the chip-ping paint, spelling the words *Potter's Field.*

Wyatt crawled to a stop beside the sign. "Did the librar-ian say she met Mary Alice at Potter's Field?"

"Yeah, and according to my grandpa, it used to be a hangout for vagrants and hippies," she said with a chuckle. "He loved to tell stories about the whole place being cov-ered in tents and young travelers making love, not war."

Wyatt wheeled the Jeep in a new direction, traveling the length of the field. He watched Violet with a broad smile. "Wonder what the librarian was doing here."

Violet laughed. "Who knows? She was young then, too."

Wyatt rolled to another stop on the desolate country road. He peered across the cab and out Violet's window at the lush green land. "This might've been a wild hang-out fifty years ago, but all I'm seeing today is soybeans."

"Times change, I guess," Violet said. "Maybe we'll have better luck looking for the wells." Her phone rang and she turned the screen to face her. "It's Tanya," she said, the familiar bud of panic pushing through her too-temporary calm. "Hello?"

"Hey," her cousin's voice was pert and chipper.

Violet sighed in relief. Not bad news then. "Hey," she said. "What's new?"

"Well, the doctor has given us the green light to move Grandma. He says she's stable, and her vitals are strong, so there's no reason to keep her here if you'd prefer to move her to another facility. There are four within an hour's drive from here. You could stay at her place and make the commute if you wanted, at least until school started. That way, we'd both have easy access to her, and I'm sure she'll wake any day now, so we don't even have to think long-term like that."

Violet stilled. She didn't want to upset her cousin, but Tanya seemed to be missing the point that Grandma was in danger. What was she thinking by suggesting they move her to a place nearby? "That's great news, but I think we need to get her farther away from here than an hour's drive, and I definitely can't stay at her place. It's not safe, and I need to get back to Winchester."

Silence gonged through the phone.

Violet looked to Wyatt, who gave a stiff dip of his chin and orchestrated a three-point turn on the empty road, directing the Jeep toward the hospital.

Violet mouthed the words *thank you*. Sometimes it was as if Wyatt could read her mind. It was helpful at the moment, and utterly humiliating when he caught her daydreaming. About him.

"We'll be there soon," Violet said. She could hear Tanya breathing softly through the line, though she hadn't spoken in several long seconds. "I don't want to take Grandma away from you. I know your schedule will make it hard to see her, but we need to keep her safe until this is over." Violet's heart pinched. The ever-ticking clock said that wouldn't be long now. One way or another.

"I know," Tanya said. "I just wish she'd wake up."

"Me, too."

The CB radio on Sawyer's dashboard crackled. A fuzzy male voice rattled out a list of acronyms, then directed an ambulance and available unit to a too-familiar address.

Wyatt jammed the gas pedal, fishtailing over the asphalt.

"That's Grandma's address," Violet said, stunned.

Something bad was happening there. Again.

Violet gritted her teeth against a load of horrendous thoughts and possibilities. "Tanya," she said. "I've got to go."

WYATT PARKED SAWYER'S Jeep on the gravel lane outside Grandma's house and jumped out. He hauled Maggie onto one hip before shutting the doors.

Violet met them at the front bumper. She passed Wyatt's phone back to him. "Grandma's in the hospital. We're here, and Sawyer's in the field. So who needs an ambulance?"

She'd sent a series of text messages to Sawyer via Wyatt's phone, confirming his safety and whereabouts while Wyatt piloted the Jeep. Sawyer sent a selfie of himself on a rope in rappelling gear and wearing a miner's hat. She'd presumed he was inside a well, but he didn't add a caption to the photo, and she didn't ask. Wherever he was, it wasn't Violet's grandma's place.

An EMT jogged in their direction as they moved up the

rutted drive on foot. He stopped outside the closed doors of an ambulance.

"Excuse me," Wyatt called. "This is my girlfriend's grandma's house. We're staying here while Mrs. Ames is in the hospital, but it's just us." He lifted his gaze to a pair of EMTs guiding a gurney toward the barn. "So what's going on?"

Violet curled a warm hand around his elbow and leaned against his side.

The young man pulled the ambulance's back doors wide. "We received a call about an elderly white female…"

His answer was cut off by the approach of a blaring siren and sound of skidding tires on gravel.

"What the hell is this?" Sheriff Masterson yelled, stomping his way up the drive from the newly arriving vehicle. The lights on top of his cruiser continued to spin behind him.

The EMT paled. "I'm sorry, sir, but she appears to have fallen from the hay loft."

"Who?" Violet asked. "You haven't told us anything, and it's starting to scare me."

Wyatt didn't need to wait for an answer. He'd heard him clearly before, *an elderly white female*. There was only one person that could be.

A pair of men in matching EMT uniforms hustled toward the open ambulance bay with a loaded gurney.

Mary Alice Masterson was strapped aboard.

Mr. Masterson followed them, hands shoved deep in his pockets, gaze fixed to the ground.

The sheriff's hard eyes went round. "Mama?" He shoved his way to the woman's side and gripped her hand in his. "She's going to be okay," he said, shooting an icy look at each EMT.

The grayest of the EMTs forced a tight smile. "The

sooner we get her to the hospital, the more we'll know more about her injuries."

Sheriff Masterson fell back a step. Tears formed in his eyes as he stroked her gray hair. "Okay." He accepted the answer and allowed the men room to load his mother into the bay.

"Would you like to ride with her?" an EMT asked.

It was unclear if he'd meant to address Mary Alice's husband or son. They stood side by side now, glaring at each other.

"No, thank you," the sheriff ground the words out. "I'll take the cruiser, and Dad can ride with me."

Violet turned to Mr. Masterson. "What was she doing back in the barn?" Her voice was low and careful, but she held him in her stare. "You just took her away from here."

His jaw clenched and released, but he didn't speak.

Violet nearly vibrated with frustration at Wyatt's side. She turned her gaze on the sheriff. "No one's been in that barn for years, and now your mother was the second woman to fall from the hayloft this week. Don't you think that's a strange coincidence?"

Sheriff Masterson narrowed his eyes.

Wyatt pulled her against him. "I think we'd better go inside." The Masterson men looked as if they were close to a brawl, and Wyatt didn't want any part of their family feud. Not with Violet and Maggie so close by.

She dug her heels in briefly, but allowed him to walk her to the front door.

They watched from the window as the father and son climbed into the sheriff's cruiser and drove away.

Violet dropped the curtain and reached for her baby, who went to her with a smile. "I think that man just shoved his sick wife out of Grandma's hayloft, then called an ambulance to pretend it was an accident."

The same thought had crossed Wyatt's mind. And something more. "It might not have been an accident she wound up there this morning, either."

"You don't think she slipped away like he said," Violet guessed, passing Maggie to Wyatt. "You think he let her come here earlier so that when he did this we would all say, 'Oh, yeah, she was just up there ranting earlier.'"

"Maybe," he said, "or we could've interrupted his plan the first time."

The former sheriff was a fox in old man's clothing if Wyatt had ever seen one. He was sure of it. Problem was, his son wasn't going to dig into this. If his mom died, he'd go down in local history as the guy who arrested his dad for murdering his sick mom. The great Masterson legacy of Grove County would be ruined.

"That's really disturbing," Violet said. "You know what else I think?" Her face lit as she brushed past him on her way to the home's rear. "I think Mary Alice is the most honest Masterson we've met, and she believes a box of Henry Davis's things is in that barn. Maybe we just haven't looked in the right place yet."

Chapter Fifteen

Wyatt joined Violet in the barn, curiosity winding through
him. Was she right? Had they simply missed something
each time they'd been out here?

She took Maggie from his arms and began rocking her
hips the moment her baby was nestled against her. "If I had
something important to hide, I'd put it someplace no one
would look. This seems like the perfect place, and Mary
Alice obviously agrees." Violet's hand was protective on
Maggie's head as she moved, holding her baby close.

"Can't hurt to give it another look," Wyatt said, watching the Ames ladies drift through filtered sunlight in the
dusty old space.

"Let's split up," Violet said. "I'll start on that end. You
start here."

Wyatt smiled as she walked briskly away. He'd spent
years commanding troops of battle-weary men, but lately
he was the one taking orders. Mostly from a brown-haired
beauty and her baby.

He couldn't help recalling the news that Mary Alice had
let slip that day on her porch. Violet's mom had run off and
left her. Maggie would certainly never have to worry about
that or wonder if she was loved. That fact was written all
over her mother's face and etched into everything she did.
A useless thread of anger curled in him when he thought

of anyone who'd willingly leave their child behind. Another reason he was glad he didn't know Maggie's father.

Violet moved slowly along the far wall, dragging her fingers over the aged wood. Sunlight blazed through a second-story window, backlighting her silhouette and emphasizing the tantalizing shape beneath her sexy tank top. At her height, and in those shorts, her trim, tanned legs seemed to go on forever, and his gaze traveled the length of them to the hem of her cutoffs, then the images arrived unbidden. Her legs across his lap. Her legs around his hips.

Wyatt swallowed a groan and forced his head to turn away. Never had a woman so easily derailed his focus. If the Mastersons weren't eventually the death of him, he had a sneaking suspicion Violet Ames soon would be.

He traced a path along the barn's perimeter, taking his time but seeing nothing he hadn't on his previous trips inside.

Violet's soft voice carried on the air as she sang to Maggie.

Wyatt dared another look in their direction, and his heart tightened. He admired her dedication to her daughter and her grandma. It was clear that family meant everything to her, and that meant everything to Wyatt. The idea of having Violet and Maggie in his life permanently rushed over him like a freight train. It was a dogged and unrelenting notion these days. *What if she wants that, too?* The kiss she'd leveled him with by the lake hadn't helped. The more time he spent with her, the more time he wanted.

Unfortunately, it didn't matter that Wyatt's family and friends would love Violet and Maggie, or that they would be safe, adored and happy with him. Right now, all that mattered was that he finish the job he'd started with as much integrity as possible. He needed to keep his carpooling, pancake-burning fatherhood fantasies out of it. Violet needed a professional security agent to protect her. So that was what she would get.

"Wyatt?" Violet called.

He moved immediately toward the beacon tugging at his core. "Yeah?"

"Look." She crouched on the floor beside Maggie, who had already begun to crawl to him.

Wyatt scooped her up and kept moving. "What do you have there?"

"I'm not sure." Violet slid her fingertips along the floorboards with sheer concentration on her brow. "There's a knothole here, but the more I look at it, the more it seems man-made. There was a big wooden storage unit here when I was young. I suppose the hole could've been caused by moving that."

Wyatt worked the phone from his pocket and turned his flashlight app on the boards, where Violet worked diligently to get a fingerhold.

The light scattered, reaching deep beneath the wood.

He tented his brows is disbelief. "There's a room down there."

Violet rolled back on her haunches. "You're kidding. I was only hoping for a small compartment with the mystery box inside. Is it a root cellar? Tornado shelter?"

"Let's see." Wyatt set Maggie aside with a kiss, then passed his phone to Violet. "You work the light, and I'll see if I can get in there somehow."

Together, they found the hinges, camouflaged within the floorboards. The trapdoor rumbled open with a long, lamenting groan.

A puff of pride filled Wyatt's chest at the shock on Violet's face. "You've got a good eye. I'm not sure I'd have noticed this if I walked over it a dozen times."

She pulled Maggie onto her lap. "Thanks."

He gauged the small drop, then braced his hands on either side of the opening. "No problem. Now, keep that light going."

"Wait! You aren't going down there, are you?"

Wyatt jumped into the hole. "Yep." He lifted his arm overhead. "Not deep." He reached a hand up through the hole. "Mostly dirt."

"See anything?"

"Nah. Can you shine the light around me?"

Violet tapped his phone against his head. "You're too big. You're blocking everything."

Wyatt took the phone and shuffled around the cramped space, using the narrow beam as his guide. He checked the floor, walls and boards overhead until a yellowed cigar box appeared, tightly wedged in a nook above him. Without the light he would have only seen an empty cellar. Would've walked right by it just like the carefully carved knothole in the floor.

Wyatt set the box on the barn floor near Violet and Maggie. He hoisted himself back out of the little room and secured the trapdoor behind him. "You want to do the honors?"

Violet caught him in her warm gaze. "No."

Wyatt smiled. He flipped the box's lid open, exposing a set of someone's personal belongings: an antique watch, dog tags from the 1960s and a worn leather wallet.

"Henry Davis?" Violet asked.

Wyatt turned the box around for a better look at the metal tags. "Yeah." He shifted onto one hip and pulled a handkerchief from the back pocket of his jeans. He didn't want to disturb the missing man's things, but he had to know if the wallet was his, as well. He used the thin cloth to open the bifold. A Kentucky driver's license confirmed the owner of that item, as well. "Henry Davis."

Violet released a shaky sigh.

Wyatt helped her to her feet, box tucked carefully beneath his arm.

"I was hoping the box contained some old love letters," she said, dusting off her baby and her backside. "Something personal that Mary Alice didn't want her husband to see. This is much more unnerving."

She was right. A man didn't just leave his wallet and dog tags behind. Unless he left in a hurry or didn't want to be found.

"What do you think this means?" she asked.

"Nothing good." Wyatt led the way back to the house and locked them inside when they got there. "I need to let Sawyer know about this. He might want to change his search based on our find."

Violet set Maggie in her high chair and offered her a shaker of Cheerios. "In what way?"

"Well—" Wyatt dialed Sawyer's cell "—when he left, he was looking for anything out of the ordinary. Nothing specific. Maybe a box." He mimed the cigar box's size with his palms.

"And now?"

Wyatt pressed the phone to his ear. The icy slick of instinct sliding like a shiv into his gut. "Now I think we're looking for Henry Davis."

VIOLET TRIED NOT to panic as Wyatt drove Sawyer's Jeep off the road and onto the unplowed area alongside Potter's Field. Sawyer had insisted they come out and meet him when Wyatt called to tell him about the cigar box. He hadn't said why, but she had a solid guess that whatever it was wouldn't be good.

Wyatt parked the Jeep beside his truck in a clearing of dirt and gravel, then waved to Sawyer in the distance.

Violet climbed down, heart hammering, throat thick.

She freed Maggie from her car seat and slipped her into the baby sling positioned across her hip and adjusted a white eyelet bonnet over Maggie's soft brown curls, tilting the brim until Maggie no longer squinted against the sun.

Coming out here to see what had Sawyer so wound up hadn't been Violet's first choice, but staying home alone was so far at the bottom of her list she couldn't see it. So she'd decided to suck it up and go for the drive.

"Took you long enough," Sawyer yelled, closing the space between them. "I hope you brought me some water."

Wyatt tossed him the bottle he'd brought along from Grandma's fridge, then waited as Violet made her way to their sides. "Okay. Gang's all here. What did you find?"

Violet braced herself for the answer. *Not Henry Davis's remains. Not Henry Davis's remains,* she chanted internally.

"See for yourself." Sawyer turned and marched around the back side of a row of stately evergreen trees. "For starters, these pines are about fifty years old," he said.

Violet wrinkled her nose. She nearly laughed out loud. "And?"

"And I figure they were planted to hide this." He ducked under a line of barbed wire and walked to the edge of a circle made of bricks and covered in plywood. "Every other well I've visited today has either been decommissioned by the state, or is covered in rotted, dilapidated, ancient plywood. Every other well has been long forgotten."

Wyatt lifted the wire for Violet to duck beneath. "This is also covered in plywood."

"Correct." Sawyer's crystal eyes twinkled. "But this is covered in nice, well-maintained plywood, and it's also the only abandoned well in the county that sits on a property owned by Old Man Masterson." He nodded slowly as

Wyatt cocked his head. "Now ask me when he bought this lovely landlocked parcel."

"Fifty years ago?" Violet guessed.

"Round about," Sawyer answered. "This property is landlocked. It's no good for home building and it's junk for hunting, so why buy it at all? Why plant those trees in front of this well? And why is this the only well that hasn't been decommissioned by the state? Why is it covered in good, solid plywood?"

Violet stepped through the fallen and crunchy pine needles on the ground, nausea ripping at her insides.

Wyatt circled the well, then took one large step away and circled again, tracking his gaze across the ground. Searching.

Sawyer hiked a foot onto the new plywood and cast his attention around them, taking in the larger picture. "We're at the edge of the property, but a barbed wire fence is set up about thirty feet out, making its own perimeter with the well at the center. No-trespassing signs are nailed to the corner posts."

Violet gave the now-distant Potter's Field a long look. "Maybe the previous sheriff bought this property to stop all the wild parties. My grandpa ranted about what a nuisance the folks were in Potter's Field and about all the litter they left behind."

Sawyer gave the adjacent field a curious look. "I think the sheriff could have kept folks off that land without buying the property next door. Besides, no one has ever lived here. They can't. No road frontage. This would only be good for farming, and no one's farming it." He nodded toward the neighboring soybean rows. "They're farming right up to it, then that's it."

Wyatt ducked into a squat about ten feet from the well and gave a worrisome whistle. "Sawyer?"

Sawyer's head jerked in Wyatt's direction. His frame went on alert. "Yes, sir." He jogged to his friend's side.

Something in Wyatt's voice had the same effect on Violet. Her limbs were wooden. Her feet heavy. Wyatt had found something, and she was certain it wasn't anything good.

"What is it?" Violet's heart took off at a runner's pace.

Wyatt extended his palm at her like a crossing guard. "Wait."

He looked up as Sawyer approached. "This looks like an old land mine. That can't be right, can it? Surely no one would…"

The distinctive *click* beneath Violet's shoe stopped his sentence along with her heart. Whatever her foot had landed on, it didn't belong in an empty field. It wasn't more pine needles. Not a fallen branch. Or a pine cone or debris.

"Don't move," Wyatt warned, his handsome face pale with shock and fear. He straightened slowly, carefully, as if he were the one about to take his last breath instead of her.

She could see it written in his stance, his sad, almost sickened gaze. Violet had also found a land mine.

"No!" Maggie said, clapping her hands at the sight of Wyatt headed her way.

Tears pooled in Violet's eyes, stinging her nose and blurring her vision. "Wyatt," she sobbed. How could she have been so careless?

"Shh," he cooed, examining her feet as he crept closer.

Both men approached with caution. Knees slightly bent, arms forward, eyes wide. They came at her in a vee, moving in from opposite angles, as if they were cornering a wild animal.

"Be very still," Sawyer said. "Don't move your feet." He dropped into a crouch before her and moved the parched grass.

A choked warble escaped her tightening throat.

"No!" Maggie jerked forward again, nearly throwing herself from the baby sling, nearly forcing Violet's weight to shift fatally on the aged mine plate. "No!" she sang, chubby fists opening and closing, wanting Wyatt as he neared.

Despair clawed through Violet's chest. She saw the truth in Wyatt's eyes. There was no saving her, but she wouldn't accept this fate for Maggie. Her heart rent in two at the possibility that this was the end for her daughter. It couldn't be. Not now. Not like this. Not Maggie.

"Wyatt," Violet cried. "Save my baby."

Chapter Sixteen

Wyatt couldn't respond. His mind worked overtime, scrutinizing the situation, recalling the other mine he'd just seen. Considering its age. Potential instability. And the possibility it would go off simply because Violet had stepped on it, instead of waiting for the pressure to release.

Sawyer inched past him. He took Maggie into his arms, then dipped his chin at Violet. His cool blue eyes locked on Wyatt. "I'll get her away from here. Try not to be too stupid."

Wyatt flickered a look in his friend's direction. "Stupid is a matter of opinion."

"Wyatt." Violet's voice was a desperate quivering mess. "Go with her. Stay with her."

"Give me a minute," he said slowly. His mind raced through probabilities and calculations. With Sawyer and Maggie out of the way, he had an idea that might not kill them both. It wasn't a great one, but they were out of time for those.

"Please," Violet pushed. "Take care of Maggie. I can stand here until I know you're long gone. She doesn't have to see, and she won't remember. It's okay. Just, please, go. Protect her."

The pain and sacrifice of her words seared through him. "Remain calm," he said, inching away.

"She's going to be orphaned. Just like me. But I'm okay because I was loved. Tanya will take her. Tanya will love her."

Wyatt paced away, his hardened heart reduced to mush. "Do not shift your weight off that plate."

"I won't," Violet vowed. "Make sure my baby knows I loved her more than I've ever loved anyone or anything. More than she can possibly imagine." Tears rushed down her cheeks, dripping over her lips and falling freely from her chin and jaw.

The Jeep's engine revved to life. "Hey, Stone," Sawyer called through the open window, his voice clearly carrying over the long distance. "What's the plan?"

"Take care of my baby!" Violet screamed, hot eyes flashing at Sawyer. "Get out of here!"

Wyatt raised his hand to Sawyer. "Back up about a hundred yards." He turned to Violet. "Do you trust me?"

"What?" She wiped her tears and watched him with keen curiosity. "What are you doing? Why did you stop? Why aren't you leaving?"

Wyatt backed up another three steps. "Do you trust me?" he repeated.

"Yes."

He lowered into a sprinter's stance. "Then don't fight the impact," he said. "Just let it happen."

Violet's chin swung left, then right. "No. Get out of here! Protect Maggie!"

"One," Wyatt said.

"No! You'll be killed!"

"Two."

"Wyatt!"

He launched forward on angry, determined legs, propelling himself through the grass at top speed, barreling toward the woman he loved. He would not let her die. Would not let her sweet baby become an orphan. Not now. Not ever. And not on his watch.

He lowered his frame to reduce his center of gravity on impact, planting his hard shoulder into her soft middle and tossing her easily with him through the air. Their bodies collided with the smack and crunch of flesh and bone.

The explosion that followed was teeth-rattling. Wyatt's ears rang, and dirt and debris rained over them in hunks and patches. Sticks, rocks and chunks of earth pelted them as they bounced against the hard ground and rolled to a stop at the barrier of pine trees.

Violet's scream was silenced upon impact.

Wyatt's vision blurred as he struggled to pull his lids open and set the world straight once more. Images of battlefields from his past mixed frighteningly with the one thing that mattered in his present. Violet. He pulled himself into the moment, forcing memories away and his body onto bruised and bloodied forearms. "Violet." His voice was foreign to his ears, too low and gravelly. The blurry image of her swayed before him. His head pounded and ached. His heart took a deep cutting blow when she didn't answer. "Wake up," he ordered, but her arms lay limply at her sides, face rolled slightly away, eyes closed. She was motionless save for the shallow rise and fall of her chest and a blessedly still-beating heart.

Wyatt scrambled to her, forcing his vision to clear and reaching for her sweet face.

A thick smear of crimson covered her exposed cheek and ear. The unmistakable shape of a flat gray stone was visible beneath her head, scattered over with pine needles and long brown hair. "No." He forced himself onto his knees. "Violet," he demanded. "Violet!" He'd taken the brunt of the blast with his back as they flew. She should have been okay. Wyatt searched her throat for the heartbeat he needed to feel, slow but strong.

"Wyatt?" Sawyer's voice registered nearby. He appeared then, darting through the trees to Wyatt's side. Maggie cried on his hip, arms reaching for her mother, but Violet didn't stir. "Do you want an ambulance out here?" Sawyer asked.

"No." Wyatt curled a motionless Violet into his arms and pushed himself onto aching legs. "I don't want the son of a bitch responsible for those mines to know we found his hiding spot. You protect Maggie. I'll get Violet to the ER, then we'll come back here tonight, find out what's hidden in that well." Wyatt's long purposeful strides ate up the distance as they tracked through the woods, back to their vehicles, away from the well and the booby traps around it. "We're going to need help from outside this godforsaken town if we want justice served."

"You want me to hunt down that deputy?" Sawyer asked. "Santos?"

"No. Take Maggie home and guard her with your life," Wyatt instructed. "I'll be there as soon as I can. Then we'll figure this out together."

"Yes, sir."

The drive to the hospital was excruciating. Every dip in the road and jostle of his frame hurt bone deep. Worse than that, his constant prayer for Violet's eyes to open wasn't answered.

He left his truck outside the emergency room entrance, doors open, engine running.

"We need help," he called as the glass doors parted. Violet's motionless body lay over his arms. Blood from her head clung to his shirt and skin. "Help us!" he demanded, using the full power of his deep tenor to command attention.

A man in a white coat turned his way, followed by a pair of nurses. The trio snapped into action, rushing to his side.

"What happened?" the doctor asked.

"I'm not sure," Wyatt lied. He hadn't taken time to think of a proper story on the drive over, and he didn't want to tell them about the land mine. He and Violet had escaped the worst of the explosion. Their injuries were mostly a result of their graceless landing. Besides, once the sheriff knew they'd been so close to his well, Wyatt was sure whatever had been hidden there for fifty years would be moved immediately. "We hit our heads when we fell," he finally said. "She landed on a rock. She's bleeding."

The doctor pulled Violet's eyelids open and shone a light into them while the nurses ran for a gurney. Together, the team strapped Violet down and wheeled her to a station stocked with supplies. A nurse started an IV drip. The doctor checked her vitals. They administered triage to her cuts, scrapes and bruises. The questions came rapid-fire as they worked. "How long has she been unconscious? How far did you fall? Where were you when it happened?"

Wyatt claimed that they had been hiking, enjoying the view from a significant height when the trail gave way along the edge. They fell a great distance, tumbling over rocks, limbs and roots.

Soon, Wyatt was pushed back and a curtain was pulled around them as they worked.

Wyatt collapsed onto an empty chair against the wall. He bent forward at the waist, catching his face in open palms and doing his best to hold himself together.

The sounds and scents of the hospital crept into his scrambled thoughts, taking him back overseas. Flashing memories of other terrifying times. Other injured loved ones. He pressed his fingers hard against his temples, forcing images of war from his mind.

"Looks like a slight concussion." The doctor's voice was back. Close again.

Wyatt jerked onto his feet, blinking away the past and pulling the moment at hand back to light. "Will she be okay?"

The doctor hugged a clipboard to his chest. "Sure. She's suffered extensive lacerations and contusions, but they'll heal. The bruised ribs will take time." He grimaced. "It's as if she hit a tree on her way down. We put something in her IV for the pain and stitched her head."

"Thank you." One hot tear blazed a trail over Wyatt's icy cheek. He took the doctor's hand in his and shook it hard. "Thank you."

The doctor kept hold of his hand. "She said not to let you leave without an exam."

"She's awake?" He dragged the doctor toward the curtain.

The doctor caught Wyatt's elbow in his free hand. "Not until I take a look at you."

Wyatt kept moving. He had nearly a foot and probably fifty pounds on the little man beside him. "I want to see her." He ducked through the barrier and felt a mound of tension roll away.

"Hey," she said softly. Her head was wrapped in white gauze. Her arms were spattered with bandages and dark with bruises.

"Violet." He stroked hair from her cheeks. "I'm so sorry."

She batted glossy eyes. "You saved our lives."

Wyatt lifted her small hand to his face and a hot streak swiveled over his cheekbone.

"Hey." Violet wiped the single tear away. "We're okay," she whispered. "Because of you."

Wyatt leaned over the silver bed rail, gathering her in

his arms and burying his face in her soft brown hair. It wasn't the right time to tell her that he loved her, but he'd never been so sure of anything in his life, and he would tell her one day soon. What she did with the information was up to her. Nothing would diminish that truth.

Violet peeked over his shoulder, sweeping her gaze through the room. "Where's Maggie? I want to see her. Is Sawyer in the waiting room?"

"No. They aren't here, but they're safe. He won't let anyone hurt her."

The doctor cleared his throat. "I'd better have a look at you."

Wyatt spun around. He'd nearly forgotten they weren't alone. "Go for it." He squeezed Violet's hand, unwilling to let her go. There was so much he wanted to say, but the timing was awful, and the emotions were raw and new. He wasn't sure where to start. He could see a future with Violet and Maggie. The kind his folks had with him. The kind he'd given up on when he joined the service. A near decade of army life had changed him. Hardened him. But Violet and Maggie were changing him back. Excavating the man he'd started out to be.

Her hand curled over his wrist as the doctor moved into view, flashing his penlight into Wyatt's eyes. "Will you check on Grandma when the exam is finished?" Violet asked. "Maybe ask Tanya to come down here if she's on duty? I need to get those transfer papers filled out." She lifted an apologetic face to him as the doctor stepped away. "Maggie and I can't stay. It's just too dangerous to be here any longer than is absolutely necessary."

Wyatt pressed a kiss to her forehead, inhaling the sweet scent of her and making a memory he hoped would last. "It's okay."

He gave the doctor another two minutes to finish his

job before shaking him off. "Thanks," he said then, interrupting the instructions he'd heard a dozen times before. "Aspirin. Ice. Rest. Water. Got it."

Wyatt rode the elevator to the second floor in search of Violet's cousin Tanya and a quick visit with her grandma. He focused on his marching orders instead of the fact that accomplishing these tasks meant saying goodbye to Violet and Maggie.

A man in a hospital security uniform leaned his elbows on the nurse's desk, flirting with a young blonde. The chair outside Violet's grandma's room was empty.

"Hey," Wyatt complained. "Why aren't you watching room two fourteen?"

The man tented his brows at Wyatt, taking in his battered appearance. "She's fine. Old Sheriff Masterson's in there with her."

Wyatt swore. He hopped into a painful jog and rushed through the door to her room.

Mr. Masterson leaned over the comatose woman, his lips moving near her ear.

"What are you doing here?" Wyatt snapped. "Get away from her."

Mr. Masterson looked Wyatt over with a mischievous smile. "Well, what on earth has happened to you?"

Wyatt ground his teeth. "Get out."

Mr. Masterson crossed the room and stopped inside Wyatt's personal space. The old man was tall and broad. Bold and cocky. "You think I'm old," he said. "You think I don't know what you've been up to, but this is my town, and I don't miss a thing."

Wyatt stood firm, squaring his shoulders and locking his jaw. "Stay away from this family."

"Believe me. I tried." He tossed a glance in Violet's grandma's direction. "Some people just won't listen."

"Knock knock." A smiling man in a gray suit, tie and glasses appeared in the door. "I hope I'm not interrupting anything. I'm Dr. Fisk. I've come to check on our Sleeping Beauty over there."

"I was just on my way out," Mr. Masterson said. "I've got lots to do today." He tipped his hat to the doctor, then left Wyatt with a withering smile.

Wyatt turned to face the frail-looking woman in the hospital bed. The clock was ticking, and he had to get her out of there before Masterson had a chance to finish what he'd undeniably started.

Chapter Seventeen

Violet sat on her grandma's living room floor, filling plastic totes with memories and praying they'd all get out of River Gorge alive. She wrapped a framed photo in newspaper, then set it on a stack of photo albums in another nearly full container. "I know I can't take everything, but it feels as if anything I leave is doomed for destruction."

Wyatt watched from the couch where he bounced Maggie on one knee. "Pack as much as you want. There's plenty of room in my pickup's bed, and I've got no problem renting a box truck if that's what you need."

"Thanks." Violet's head ached nearly as much as her body, but she'd never complain about anything as trivial as a headache again. Not after what she, Wyatt and Maggie had just been through. "The doctor said we can move Grandma tomorrow after breakfast. Whatever isn't packed by then can just stay. Meanwhile, this is a good distraction." Violet had nearly lost everything a few hours ago and the hollow feeling left behind in her gut felt like a warning. "I don't care what Grandma was looking into anymore. It's not worth dying over, and I just want to get her out of here before tomorrow night when my forty-eight hours are up."

Wyatt set Maggie on the floor, then lowered himself down beside her. "I'm sorry that you were ever in danger," he said, leveling her with sincere brown eyes. "None of that should have happened once I got here. I've failed miserably at that, but I won't leave without making sure whoever is behind these attempts on your life and your grandma's is arrested, even if it is the Mastersons."

Maggie patted Wyatt's jean-covered thigh and beamed up at him.

The look in his eyes was unfathomable, and Violet's heart twisted hard.

"What are you up to?" he asked Maggie.

Maggie leaned closer, grabbing tiny fistfuls of his cotton shirt, and pulled herself up to stand.

Violet's heart soared. "Oh my goodness."

Wyatt's eyes stretched wide. "Look at you!" He caught her under her arms and lifted her high into the air, weaving her over his head with a rumbling belly laugh before delivering her to Violet's hands.

She kissed her baby and hugged her tight. "Big girl," she sang. "You did it!"

"No!"

Wyatt snorted. He cupped the back of her head in one big hand and planted a kiss on her forehead. "Nice work, cowgirl."

Maggie clapped.

Violet's heart melted. She didn't want to separate them. Maggie had responded so profoundly to Wyatt's attention from the very start. She'd never seen anything like it, and it killed her to think this was the end. "You don't have to stay here, you know," she offered. "Grandma would understand, and she wouldn't want anyone to die over this."

Wyatt gave a tight smile. "I won't leave your side until you're settled in Winchester, but after that, I'm coming back to River Gorge to finish this. Your grandmother deserves that much, and so do you."

"It's not worth it," Violet said, firming up her tone. "Staying here is a bad idea. The Mastersons aren't right.

We all need to leave. I'm not even sure Grandma will be safe in the new facility. I keep thinking of all the ways Sheriff Masterson could find out where we went and how easily he can get to us anywhere we go." She snuggled Maggie closer before returning her to the floor where she could practice her new trick again. "I don't know how to keep them safe, and it's terrifying." The awful note she'd found at the hospital had said as much. She couldn't keep everyone safe. She was only one person, and now she was injured and slow.

"You're right to leave," he said.

"Maybe. But you're here. Anywhere else I'll be on my own."

It was a conversation they'd had days ago, and the right answer wasn't any clearer now than it had been then.

Sawyer's Jeep growled up the drive to Grandma's house, country music rattling the windows before he killed the engine.

Wyatt rose to let him in.

Sawyer sauntered inside with a smile for Violet. "The guy at the body shop says your car will be finished in the morning. They've got the tires in stock, and they're planning to get them mounted and balanced when they reopen. I caught him on his way out for the night."

Deputy Santos climbed the porch steps and followed Sawyer inside.

Violet hadn't even heard a second vehicle over Sawyer's music. "Deputy Santos?"

Wyatt extended a hand to him, looking utterly unsurprised as always. "It was nice of you to come."

Sawyer clapped the deputy on his back. "He just wanted to make sure we're all doing okay after that near-death experience y'all had."

Deputy Santos cocked a brow. "What near-death experience? I'm here because you told me there had been another break-in."

Sawyer lifted his shoulders in an exaggerated shrug. "I lied. But you're already here, so you might as well come on in and hear about our day."

Wyatt locked the door behind them.

Violet pulled Maggie onto her hip, then led the men into the kitchen. Every step sent a current of pain and nausea through her. "Can I get you a cup of coffee?" she asked the deputy.

"No. Thank you." He looked to Sawyer, then Wyatt. "What's this about?" He scanned the room, stopping briefly on Wyatt's banged-up face before landing on Violet's bandaged head.

She touched the gauze nervously. "I have a slight concussion," she said. "I was nearly blown up today." She slid Maggie into her high chair and posed her plastic pony on the tray.

Santos rubbed his stubble-covered cheeks and chin. "All right, I'm listening."

Wyatt deposited the cigar box of Henry Davis's things on the kitchen table. "We found this hidden in the floorboards of the barn out back."

Sawyer moved in closer. "The barn where all the old ladies keep taking suspicious spills." He passed the deputy a pair of latex gloves.

Santos opened the lid.

Violet poured herself some coffee, then began to talk. She explained everything they'd learned since last speaking to Deputy Santos. "So you see," she concluded, "if we're right about the sheriff and his father, we're going to need your help."

Santos swore. He ran a hand through thick black hair, then shut the box lid.

Sawyer produced a thumb drive from his pocket and

offered it to their guest. "Everything you need to locate the well is on there. Several geographical and aerial maps and a copy of the deed to the land. Plus, all the notes Wyatt's made while visiting your lovely town."

Santos rolled his shoulders and rubbed his forehead. "I'll take a look. See what I come up with, but I've got to tell you, I've felt followed since that night I pulled you over. I'm pulling threads and being quiet, but it's slow work."

"We don't have time for slow, Deputy," Violet said. "I've got less than a day." She walked the deputy out, then watched as the cruiser's taillights disappeared into the night.

Sawyer lingered in the kitchen with Maggie.

Wyatt moved to stand behind her at the window. Heat from his skin burned through the soft fabric of her pajama top. She dared to lean back, and he accepted her weight easily, winding strong arms around her middle. "How are you doing?"

Their reflections stared back at her, and she loved what she saw there. Trust. Appreciation. Desire.

"Right now?" she said, finding a smile amid the pain. "Pretty good." Violet let herself have this moment. She wasn't ready to say goodbye to Wyatt, but he would soon be gone nonetheless. She rested her head against his chest, still admiring the view of their reflections.

"I won't leave your side until I know you're safe. I promise you that, but right now you should probably get some sleep. Big day tomorrow."

Violet turned in the small cocoon of his arms and clasped her hands behind his back. "What if I'm not ready to say goodbye to you?" she asked, feeling brave and arching against him for a better look at his face too high above hers.

Surprise flashed in his eyes, followed closely by pleasure. "Yeah?"

"Yeah."

He leaned forward, dropping his forehead against hers. "Then don't."

Sawyer arrived to wreck the moment, Maggie in his arms, pulling firmly on his ratty beard.

Violet rolled her head in his direction without letting Wyatt go.

"What?" Wyatt asked, tightening his hold on her.

"There's something else," Sawyer said.

Violet eased her grip on Wyatt. For a moment, she'd had hope. Grandma was being moved out of town tomorrow. A local, and hopefully honest, deputy was helping them look into things. Wyatt didn't want her to say goodbye.

And now Sawyer had arrived with bad news. She could feel it in her already achy bones.

"What?" Wyatt repeated, his voice deeper now.

"I got something on that demolition derby car you asked me to locate. I found one matching the description registered for the county fair about ten years back. An online article linked it to a man now in his eighties. I stopped at his place to ask about the car while I was out fetching Santos for you. Nice fellow. Confused though. He thought the car was in his outbuilding." Sawyer set Maggie on the floor and crossed his arms. "The man hadn't been out there to look at it in about eighteen months. He had a stroke, and he lives alone."

Violet considered the new information. "You think someone stole it. Anyone could've been behind the wheel."

Sawyer tipped his head side to side. "Possibly. Though Mary Alice Masterson frequently drove him to his medical appointments and did some shopping for him every week before she got sick. They knew each other when their kids were young."

Violet dropped her arms to her sides. "So Mr. Masterson probably knew about the car and that the car's owner would never miss it if he borrowed it. It's been him trying to get rid of me all along."

Wyatt rubbed a stubble-covered cheek. "You should've seen Masterson's face at the hospital. He knew when he saw me that I'd likely come head-to-head with one of his land mines, and he didn't even blink."

"Well," Sawyer said, "the good news here is that we've got nightfall working for us. He won't be able to get out there and mess with whatever's in the well until dawn."

Violet's adrenaline spiked as fear shot through her once more. "You aren't planning to go back out there tonight, are you?" Memories of her misstep and the telltale *click* of the land mine rushed to mind. She recalled perfectly the weight of Maggie in her arms. The terror on Wyatt's face. The all-encompassing pain that had taken hold of her as she'd struggled to find consciousness after the blast. "You can't."

Sawyer didn't answer.

"Tell him," she instructed Wyatt.

Violet's cell phone rang, instantly changing the direction of her panic. Tanya's number centered the screen. "Hello?"

"Violet?" Tanya asked, a tremor in her voice.

The urge to be sick nearly overtook her. Images of Mr. Masterson with a pillow pressed to her sleeping grandma's face or introducing something deadly to her IV pushed their way into mind. "Yes?"

"She's awake!" Tanya chirped. "Come on. She's asking for you. I have to do my rounds, but you should come!"

Violet was on her feet in a second, immediately swaying under the nausea and pain of her too-quick movement. "Grandma's awake."

Wyatt steadied her, then pulled Maggie into his arms. "I'll drive."

Sawyer walked them to the truck. "I'm going to gather my gear and see what's in that well."

Violet bobbed onto her toes and kissed his cheek. "Be careful," she said. "I doubt complaining will stop you, and I've got to go, so please, please watch yourself."

Sawyer turned a megawatt smile on Wyatt. "Your girl just kissed me."

Wyatt wrapped an arm around Violet's shoulders and shook his head. "Don't get any ideas."

"I can't keep the ladies away."

Violet let herself enjoy the flutter of butterflies in her chest as Wyatt easily accept Sawyer's accusation that she was his girl.

He opened the passenger door to his truck. "I figure all the bad guys recognize Sawyer's Jeep by now. That ruse is up. Might as well ride in style again."

She buckled in with a smile. Scents of earth and leather, cologne and spearmint clung to the cab's interior. Violet had to admit, she liked Wyatt's ride a whole lot better than Sawyer's.

Wyatt transferred Maggie's car seat from the Jeep, then tucked Maggie into it and snapped her five-point safety belt. He climbed behind the wheel and dragged his palm over the dash as if to welcome himself home. "Let's go meet Grandma."

VIOLET RAN AHEAD inside the hospital and called the elevator.

Wyatt trailed behind, seemingly in no hurry with Maggie in his arms, though his incredibly long strides delivered him easily to her side before the shiny doors were fully opened.

Violet fell back a step at the sight of the elevator car's passengers.

Sheriff Masterson and his father stepped out and

rounded the corner away from them without speaking. The sheriff's face was red and knotted. His father's was a mask of disgust.

A woman in a gray pantsuit stepped on board ahead of Violet and Wyatt. Her name tag said Hospital Administrator. "Four, please."

Violet pressed the button, an idea forming in her mind. "The sheriff and his father were just here," she told the administrator. "They looked devastated. I hope Mary Alice hasn't taken another turn for the worse."

The woman gave Violet a curious look. "Are you friends of the family?"

"Yes," Violet improvised. "All my life, especially my grandmother and Mrs. Masterson."

"Oh." The administrator turned to Violet. The deep remorse of her disposition raised gooseflesh on Violet's arms. "I'm sorry to be the one to tell you, but I'm afraid Mary Alice is gone. She had an awful fall earlier, and in her current condition she just wasn't able to recover. Absolutely tragic. I'm very sorry for your loss. If there's anything I can do to help the family, you'll let me know?"

Violet wobbled her head in what she hoped resembled agreement. Then she slid her hand into Wyatt's. Mary Alice Masterson was gone. Would her grandma be next?

Wyatt squeezed her hand in reassurance, probably reading her thoughts as usual.

When the elevator opened on Grandma's floor, they darted out, hurrying hand in hand down the hall.

The empty chair outside her door sent the ugly images back to Violet's mind. Where was the hospital security she requested? Had the sheriff sent him away? If so, she could only imagine why and to what end. "Grandma!"

Violet skidded to a stop at the sight of her grandmother tilted up on her hospital bed. Wyatt slowed behind her.

A man in a hospital security uniform poured water from the pitcher on her bedside table. "Look at that, Mrs. Ames, you've been awake less than an hour and you already have company," he said, handing the cup to her. "I'll be right outside if you need me."

Grandma's eyes brimmed with tears that fell easily as she stretched her arms toward Violet. "Get over here."

Violet embraced her grandma, who kissed her cheeks a dozen times.

She touched the bandage on Violet's head with soft, careful fingers. "Oh, no." She slid teary eyes to the man standing at Violet's side. "Mr. Stone?"

Wyatt offered his hand. "Yes, ma'am. It's nice to finally meet you."

Emotion raced over her pale face and gathered on her brow. "You know what's happened, then?"

"No," Violet said. "Not really. We have guesses, but everything has been a real mess."

Her grandma examined Wyatt, taking him in head to toe. Her attention lingered on Maggie snuggled tightly against his broad chest. "Maggie?" she asked, with utter awe. She motioned Wyatt nearer and stroked Maggie's chubby legs when he reached the bed rails. She beamed at her great-granddaughter and tugged gently on her socked feet. "She's perfect."

"Thank you," Violet said with evident pride. "We're going to stay with you for as long as you need to heal, but right now I need to know what you know."

Grandma dragged her gaze from Maggie to Violet with a solemn nod. "It started when I had lunch on Mary Alice's porch last month," she said. Her brow furrowed. "How is she? Have you been over to see her while I've been out?"

Violet looked to Wyatt. She felt the words backing up in her throat.

"She's gone," he said, filling in the tragic blank. Regret clung to his handsome face. "I'm sorry. I know she meant a lot to you."

Grandma swallowed hard. "How did it happen?"

"She fell from your hayloft."

Grandma covered her mouth with one thin hand, then rested back against the bed. "Fell," she scoffed.

"Grandma," Violet pressed, hoping she wouldn't ask about Ruth next. Violet's heart couldn't take delivering more horrific news, and she wasn't sure Grandma was in any condition to accept more. Besides, they were all in danger, and that needed addressing immediately. "We really need to know what you know."

Grandma wiped the tears from her cheeks with trembling fingers. "Mary Alice spent our whole meal obsessing about a man she knew a long time ago. I only met him once, but Mary Alice was involved with him briefly before he went to war."

Wyatt shifted Maggie in his arms and patted her back gently when she began to wake. "Henry Davis?"

"That's right." She nodded slowly. "You found the box."

"Yes, ma'am," he said. "It's safe now."

"Good."

"Go on," Violet said, squeezing her grandma's hand.

"Mary Alice got involved with Tom after Henry was deployed. According to Mary Alice, he and Tom had words when Henry came to see her while he was on leave. That didn't surprise me. Tom was just a deputy then, but he was always a bully. Their son isn't much better." She looked from Violet to Wyatt. "Anyway, the rest of her story got gruesome from there. At first, I chalked it up to the dementia stealing her reality. Then I found just enough information online to make me wonder."

Violet's palms grew damp as she prepared for the rest of the story. "Mr. Masterson killed Henry Davis, didn't he?"

Her grandmother sighed. "I think so. Mary Alice said Henry fell. Tom punched him, and he went down, but he hit his head on the well near Potter's Field and never got back up. She said Tom didn't want to go to jail over something that was an accident, so he tossed Henry's body in the well and neither of them spoke of it again. When she gave me that old cigar box, I knew I was in deep."

"I'm so sorry," Violet said.

"I didn't want to bring her story to authorities without basis, so I decided to try to back it up first. Then I'd contact someone outside the county sheriff's department for help."

"That's when you called Wyatt," Violet said.

"Yes." Grandma's composure cracked. She pulled a tissue from the box on her bedside stand.

"Reaching out for help was smart," Violet said. "Mr. Masterson is a mess. I think he's the reason you're in here, and now I'm certain you're lucky to be alive at all."

"Well," her grandma said, touching the bandage on her head, "seems like I wasn't as smart as I'd thought." She pressed a fresh tissue to the corner of one eye. "Mary Alice wanted that man's family to have his things and to know what really happened to him. She said they needed to know he wasn't a deserter, and she wanted him to have a proper military burial."

Wyatt cleared his throat. "I can see that he's interred properly."

"Thank you," Grandma whispered.

Violet pulled in a deep breath. Now they just needed to get Grandma in front of someone who could find justice for Henry Davis before anyone else wound up dead.

Chapter Eighteen

Wyatt's phone buzzed in his back pocket. He slid the device onto his palm and puzzled at the number on the screen. Local, but he didn't recognize it. "Wyatt Stone," he answered.

"This is Deputy Santos," the man said. "I think we need to talk."

Violet was on her feet, instinctively reaching for Maggie as if she could somehow sense the tension bunching in Wyatt's muscles.

Her grandma grabbed the bed's metal rail, straining closer. "What's wrong?"

Wyatt turned away, angling his torso for some privacy. "Where?" he asked Santos.

The deputy heaved a troubled sigh. "I don't know. There probably isn't an ideal location in this town."

"You found something?" Wyatt guessed. If the deputy believed them about the former sheriff, then they had an ally, and that was all they needed. That and maybe Henry Davis's remains. Wyatt wasn't sure Mrs. Ames's retelling of a dead woman's tale would be enough, especially considering Mary Alice's mental state at the time of the revelation.

"I took those things you gave me to a coffee shop at the end of my shift," Santos said, "and I gave them a long hard look. I had to admit the story was compelling, so I headed back to the department, thinking I'd slip onto my computer and look for more details in the cold cases. When I got there, my bottom drawer was unlocked. I never leave it unlocked. My files were askew. Key was in my pocket."

"Meet us back at the Ames house," Wyatt said. "Mrs. Ames woke from her coma tonight, and she filled in all those blanks we talked about."

"Yep." Santos disconnected.

Wyatt gave the trio of Ames ladies a long look. What was safest for them? All of them? "Violet, why don't you and Maggie stay here this time? You'll be safe. There's security at the door. Witnesses everywhere."

"No way." Violet stood with Maggie.

Wyatt lifted a palm. "I'll see what Santos found, then give you a call on my way back. I won't be long, and it will give you more time to visit with your grandma."

"No." She kissed her grandma's cheek. "I want to hear what Santos has to say. We can come right back after."

Grandma nodded. "Go. You're both safer guarded by him and all that military training than by me and my broken hip."

Tanya cruised into the room with a balloon and pink plastic bag. "There you are." She hugged Violet, then tied the balloon string to the arm of the guest chair. "I clocked out early so I could run down to the gift shop and get you these before the shop closed." She upended the bag onto Grandma's legs. Magazines. *The Rose Parade. Garden Delight.* And *Country Lady.* Tanya's smile dimmed as she took in the faces around her. "What?"

"We have to run back to Grandma's place and check on something," Violet said. "Stay with Grandma?"

Tanya smiled. "Of course."

"I'll call if we learn anything significant," Violet said.

"I'll try to come back tonight, but if Maggie falls asleep, I'll let her." She shifted her attention to her grandma, wishing for all the world that she could pull up a chair and stay with her every minute until she knew they were all safe. "Either way, I'll be back here first thing tomorrow to get you moved."

"Moved?" Grandma asked.

Tanya waved a hand. "I'll fill her in."

Violet nodded. "I'll see you soon, Grandma."

Wyatt took her hand and headed for the parking lot.

"THANK YOU," VIOLET SAID as the bright hospital lights faded into the night behind them.

Wyatt glanced her way, his profile strong and confident. "For what?"

"For letting me come along," she said. "For not fighting me on it. I know you want to protect me, and you wanted me to stay at the hospital."

Wyatt's sharp eyes narrowed. "I want to protect you, not control you."

Violet smiled, then set her hand atop his fingers where they rested on his thigh.

He turned his palm over, gently twining his fingers with hers. "Honestly, I can do a better job looking after you if you're with me anyway, and this should be a quick meeting. No danger included. I was probably overreacting. Seeing danger where there isn't any. I think my run-in with Mr. Masterson earlier has me spooked."

"Well, hopefully Santos has something good, and this will be over by morning." Gratitude swelled in Violet's chest. She was glad for Santos's help. Thankful her grandma was finally awake and that there was security stationed right outside her room. Thankful also for not one but two of Fortress Security's finest looking after Maggie and her. Things were definitely looking up.

She scanned the peaceful night, enjoying the moment until something caught her eye in the mirror. Violet tensed at the distant glow of emergency flashers and her stomach knotted.

"Fire truck," Wyatt said, a smile curving his lips. "For a minute I thought I was being pulled over again." He eased onto the berm so the bleating truck could blow past. A moment later, Wyatt repeated the maneuver to allow an ambulance the space it needed on the narrow road.

"That's not good," Violet said, attention glued to the flashers disappearing up ahead. "Wyatt?"

Wyatt swore. He'd seen it, too.

"They're going toward Grandma's house."

Wyatt pressed the gas pedal. Hard.

Violet's head clung to the seat. Her muscles clenched. Her chest pinched. "What if something has happened to Sawyer?"

Wyatt tossed his cell phone from the cup holder. "Call."

Violet scrolled through his contacts and hit Call. The phone rang slowly, time ticking at half pace while she waited. "Voice mail."

Wyatt's grip tightened on the wheel. "Sawyer's good. No one could've gotten the jump on him."

Sure, Violet thought. *He also has a quick temper and obvious PTSD.* An assailant didn't need to surprise him as much as provoke him, and she imagined the sheriff would see any response of Sawyer's as justification for firing his weapon.

A pair of deputy cruisers appeared up ahead, coming at them from the opposite direction, sirens on and flashers illuminating the sky. They, too, took hasty turns in the direction of Grandma's house.

"Holy," Wyatt whispered as the flames came into view. Violet's gut gave a mighty heave.

The smoke was black and thick. The flames cut through the starry sky. Grandma's driveway and the street out front were clogged with emergency vehicles and officials in a multitude of uniforms. Firefighters were posted on the lawn, directing water from great white hoses. EMTs waited by ambulances. Deputies stared openmouthed at the shooting flames.

Violet sat motionless in her seat, horrified and sickened at the sight of her childhood home going up in flames. All the mementos that she'd so carefully packed for tomorrow's move. Gone. The kitchen where she learned to cook. The bedroom where Grandpa read her stories and tucked her in at night. Everything she knew about her mom, wherever she was. Gone. Gone. Gone.

Wyatt opened her door and pulled her out with a hug. His trademark Stetson was low over his eyes. "I'm sorry about the house, but I sure am glad no one was here."

Violet nodded woodenly. The acrid scent of smoke stung her eyes and burned her throat. Heat from the inferno blew in waves over her skin. "I'm going to try Sawyer again."

Wyatt went around to collect Maggie. He returned a moment later.

"Voice mail," she said once more.

Wyatt moved toward the nearest ambulance. "Maybe an EMT will fill us in."

Violet followed, praying silently for Sawyer's safety.

Then the unmistakable outline of his Jeep came into view, parked between emergency vehicles. "Wyatt," she whispered.

Wyatt swore under his breath. He straightened his hat,

then passed Maggie to Violet. "Hey!" he called, jogging closer to the home.

A nearby fireman turned in his direction. "I think there's someone in the house."

The man started at the sight of Wyatt with Violet on his heels. "You need to get back, sir, ma'am. Maintain a clear distance. It's not safe."

Wyatt bristled. "I think my buddy's in there. His Jeep's in the drive."

The fireman shook his head. "Structure's not sound. We haven't found anyone inside, and I'm pulling my men out."

The sharp cry of a siren turned the little crowd toward the road.

The sheriff's cruiser rocked to a stop in the center of the road. He moved solemnly on foot in their direction. His flat expression rattled Violet's nerves. He didn't care that her family home was on fire. Didn't even look surprised. "I'm afraid you two need to step away from the home and let these men work."

Wyatt stalked toward him. "What have you done?"

An upstairs window shattered, and Wyatt spun in the direction of the sound. "What was that?" He looked briefly at Violet with hope in his eyes.

What if Sawyer was trying to get out? She'd thought so, too.

Wyatt scanned the scene, then burst into a run, disappearing into the smoke.

"No!" Violet screamed. "Wyatt!"

Maggie cried and bucked in her mother's arms.

"Shhh. Sorry. Sorry." Violet bounced gently, rocking and cooing to the baby as she moved slowly back from the raging heat. "Do something," she demanded of the sheriff and fireman, both staring blankly at Wyatt's silhouette as he vanished into the smoke engulfing the land around her home.

The fireman smashed the button on his walkie-talkie. "We've got a man heading into the building at the east first-floor entrance."

Static crackled back.

Violet's stomach knotted. Maggie's continued cries shredded her mama's heart into pieces. "Shh. Shh. Shh." She tried unsuccessfully and wished she could cry, too.

"Captain," a male voice rattled through the line. "House is empty. We're heading out back. See if we can save the barn."

The fireman gave Violet and Maggie a long, regretful look. He depressed the walkie-talkie button once more. "Watch for the civilian on your way out."

Violet closed her eyes and sent up desperate prayers for both Wyatt and Sawyer.

"Ma'am," the fireman said, forcing Violet's eyes open once more. "He might've gone around back. Maybe he saw something we didn't. My men are headed there now. We'll know soon enough."

Violet nodded, wiping tears on her wrist. Seeing what others didn't see was kind of Wyatt's shtick.

She stepped back farther, contemplating a seat in Wyatt's truck, away from the drifting smoke, when a gunshot rang out. "What was that?"

The sheriff's face turned in the direction of the sound, but he made no move to acknowledge it.

"Hey!" Violet yelled over the crackling fire, rushing water and endless chatter of a dozen emergency responders gathered on the lawn.

He pointedly ignored her, looking instead at the other stupefied faces around them.

"Was that a gunshot?" the fireman asked.

The sheriff shook his head. Negative.

"Liar!" Violet shoved the sheriff with days' worth of anger. "Do something!"

The sheriff stumbled back, caught off guard by her outburst. "It was probably the snap of burning wood."

The fireman wrinkled his brow. "Sounded like gunfire."

"Ammo in heat," the sheriff said.

Violet felt the tears come again as she stared into the thick smoke, watching each returning fireman arrive empty-handed. No casualties. No Sawyer. No Wyatt.

"Fire's out," an emerging man explained. His hair was gray, and his helmet was tucked beneath his arm. "Circle up."

The fire crew moved toward him, away from the home and closer to their truck, turning their backs on her and Sheriff Masterson.

Violet listened while they made plans to minimize the damage from the home's inevitable collapse.

The deputies tipped their hats before climbing back into their cruisers.

The EMTs packed up and rolled out.

Violet watched the smoke.

An eternity later, a silhouette appeared in the haze, wearing the cowboy hat she knew so well.

Violet moved toward Wyatt, drawn like a magnet. She took a wide path in his direction, steering clear of the firefighters in their huddle and slowing when the rear corner of her grandma's house came clearly into view. She avoided the thickest smoke, angling past a patch of shrubs and trees in the side yard, hyperaware of Maggie on her hip and the reaching tendrils of smoke as it slithered over the ground.

When the figure grew clearer, a handgun became visible in his grip.

The fine hairs on her arms and neck rose to attention.

Something was off in his stance, the tilt of his head, the sinister feel in the air. Violet pulled to a stop.

The figure advanced, removing itself from the shadows. *Mr. Masterson.* She took several steps back, keeping a distance between them.

Her toe caught on something.

Someone groaned.

"Wyatt?" She dropped beside the man at her feet. "Oh my goodness! What happened? Are you okay?" Masterson's gun flashed back into mind.

Blood soaked the side of Wyatt's shirt and seeped low into his waistband. She *had* heard a gunshot earlier.

"You shot him," she cried.

Wyatt's eyes fluttered open and rolled. "Go," he croaked. "Run!"

Violet jerked upright. *Run.* Get help. "Okay." She turned for the fire truck just beyond the patch of trees.

"Ah ah ah." The silhouette with the gun stepped into clear view, Wyatt's Stetson perched on his head. "Time to go," the former sheriff told her, rearranging Wyatt's hat on his head.

Violet stumbled back. "No. I'm not leaving him."

He pointed the gun at Violet. "Are you sure? Because I won't ask again."

Sickness coiled in her gut. Would he really shoot her? Holding a baby? She turned in search of help. The fire truck blocked her view of the firefighters. "I'll scream," she threatened.

"Scream and I finish him off right now. How about that?" He lowered the barrel to Wyatt's head and pressed it hard to his skin, rocking Wyatt's forehead back.

Wyatt tried to roll onto his stomach, tried to push onto his knees despite the blood pooling everywhere. He made a swipe for Masterson's feet, but he smoothly stepped aside.

"Ma'am?" a male voice called, presumably the fireman she'd spoken to earlier. "You back here? Everything all right?"

Mr. Masterson cocked the gun.

"I'll go," she whispered, then followed the direction of Masterson's gun to a side-by-side vehicle parked in the trees a few feet away.

Violet cuddled Maggie to her chest as the off-road vehicle gunned to life. At least the fireman looking for her would find Wyatt now. At least he still had a chance.

Chapter Nineteen

Wyatt dragged himself onto his knees and forearms, coughing and wincing with each pull and tug of his wound. He'd been shot before, but the pain of seeing Violet and Maggie forced into Masterson's hands was worse than anything he'd ever known.

"Help!" a fireman called, racing to Wyatt's side. "Help!" The man snapped into action, immediately evaluating his injuries and rousing assistance from his team.

Wyatt listened as they spoke in familiar acronyms and medical terms. His vitals were good. His heart rate was high, but what did they expect? He'd been shot and seen the woman he loved abducted along with the baby who'd stolen his heart.

"It's a through-and-through, but you're going to need an ambulance," the man said. "What happened?"

Wyatt gritted his teeth against the pain. "Masterson shot me."

Wyatt had seen someone in the haze of smoke and raced to get his hands on the guy. He'd hoped it was Sawyer, but would've settled for capturing the arsonist. A gunshot had stopped him short and planted him in the grass where he'd blacked out until Violet tripped over him.

Anger pooled in his core as he recalled the way Masterson had spoken to Violet, the way he'd grabbed her and forced her away.

"The ambulance is on the way," someone said. "It hadn't gotten far, and they're turning back now."

"Call Deputy Santos," Wyatt said. "I don't need an ambulance. I need to get to Masterson before he kills them." He fumbled his phone from his pocket and dialed Santos himself. "Stitch me, so I can go."

"Santos," the deputy answered on the first ring.

"He's got the girls," Wyatt said, his head light from pain and blood loss. "Meet me at the well."

"We're already on it," Santos said. "I've got your man with me. We're changing direction now. Give us twenty minutes."

Wyatt disconnected with a prayer. He hoped to hell the old man was headed to the well with Violet and Maggie. Wyatt wasn't sure where else to look for him, and every second mattered.

The hands of the fireman cleaning his wound stilled. His face wrinkled in confusion. "Who did you say might kill them?"

"Masterson," Wyatt groaned. "The sheriff's dad."

The man scanned the area. "The sheriff was just here. Where'd he go?"

"Probably after his dad." Wyatt shot a pleading look to the man with gloved hands on his side. "If you give me the suture kit, I'll do it myself."

The man opened the kit with a frown. "The ambulance is only a few minutes away. I haven't done this in twenty years, and that was in the field in Fallujah. The scar I left behind was monstrous."

"Did your patient live?" Wyatt asked.

The man's face twisted into a proud smile. "Yes, sir."

Wyatt gave a stiff dip of his chin. "Get started."

VIOLET DRAGGED HER FEET as Mr. Masterson shoved her forward through the trees toward the old well where she'd nearly been killed not long ago. Her muscles were rigid with fear as he forced her along. Terror clenched her heart and stole her breath with each and every footfall. "You don't have to do this," she pleaded as the barbed wire perimeter came into view. Chunks of earth were tossed and scattered where the explosion had occurred. Her tongue swelled and her mouth dried. "I won't say anything to anyone. I swear it."

"Shut up," he said. "Keep moving."

Violet's chest constricted and burned. "I know that what you did was an accident," she croaked. "You were young and scared. You panicked. Anyone would have done what you did in that situation."

Masterson hoisted the barbed wire for her to duck underneath. "Would you?"

Violet bit her lip, unable to take another step. Sheer panic stopped her pitiful momentum. She couldn't cross that line, and the lie Masterson wanted to hear just wouldn't come. She wouldn't have done what he did. She would have gotten Henry Davis help, or at least tried. She would have carried her accidental victim in her arms if needed to try to save his life. She would have confessed everything and prayed for forgiveness.

Yes, accidents happen, but what Masterson had done wasn't an accident. Maybe when Henry Davis fell and hit his head, but not after Masterson threw him down a well. Not after he hid the lie for fifty years. He'd watched while Henry Davis's family searched for him. He'd let the reporters call him a deserter. Masterson had even sworn his own wife to silence, isolated her so she had no one to tell.

No. Violet wouldn't have done what Masterson had done.

"That's what I thought," he said. "Now duck under this

wire, or I'll take your baby and let her crawl around again, test her luck on my minefield."

Violet tightened her hold on Maggie. "You're the one who put her outside the library. You left her alone. She could've gotten into the street. She could have been killed!"

"That was the idea," he said, waving the gun at her baby until Violet ducked under the wire as he'd commanded. "With a tragedy like that in play, you would've lost all interest in digging up my secret. But, oh no, you just keep coming." He cocked the pistol and pointed it at Maggie. "Hurry up. Get over here or I shoot."

Violet turned her hip away from him, putting as much distance as possible between the psychopath and her baby. The well was covered in shadows, and she had no intention of going one step closer. "Please. Just let us go. She can't testify against you, and I won't. For her sake."

Masterson blinked as headlights flashed through the night, bouncing across Potter's Field and illuminating the abandoned well. Violet's stomach twisted at the sight. The plywood covering had been dragged away. Masterson had prepared for this. He wouldn't stop until she and Maggie were down there with Henry Davis.

Mr. Masterson grimaced at the open well. "What the hell?"

Sheriff Masterson appeared in the flood of light, breezing through the field in their direction. "Dad!" The sheriff ducked under the barbed wire and stepped carefully in his father's direction. "You're out of control. You burned that woman's house down."

Mr. Masterson turned a feral expression on his son. "Get back, Junior. I did what I had to do, just like I always have. You don't need to be a part of this."

"I'm the sheriff," he screamed. "Of course I'm a part of this. And you need to stop." He rested a palm on his sidearm, eyes wide, bewildered and crazed. "I can't let you do this. Not again."

Violet took a tiny step back. She positioned Maggie against her chest and secured her in a bear hug, preparing to run.

"No, you don't." Mr. Masterson's hand snapped out and caught her by the arm. "Let's go."

Violet jerked away from his grip. Stumbling for footing, she tripped over herself and fell heavily onto her backside. A barb from the fence ripped through the tender skin of her side. Maggie wailed as they thudded against the ground.

Violet clutched her baby to her chest. "Please don't do this."

The sheriff stepped forward, gun in hand. "Dad." There was warning in his eyes.

Masterson yanked Violet onto her feet and gripped her to his side. "I've told you to butt out. You'd be wise to listen. Your hands are clean."

"Hardly." Wyatt's voice was salve to Violet's frantic heart. He stepped into view behind the sheriff, a gun in one hand, the other palm pressed against his bloody side. "Put the gun down, Masterson. Let her go."

The sheriff made a disgusted sound and turned on Wyatt. "Get over there with them before I toss you down the well myself. This is family business."

Wyatt sidestepped the sheriff, unfazed by the threat and splitting his attention between the armed men. "We know what you've both done," he said. "It took fifty years, but the truth has caught up with you."

Mr. Masterson scoffed. He looked at his son. "Put these three down, and it's over. That's all we've got to do."

"No." Wyatt shook his head. "Not at all. You see, your wife told Violet's grandma everything. She found out the story was true and called my private security firm for protection while she turned you both in. She's awake now. She told us the story. My man's been down your well." He nodded toward the yawning hole only a few feet from Violet and freshly uncovered.

Wyatt eased through the headlights, stepping carefully into position near the line of trees, forming the third tip of a small triangle with the Mastersons. "We know Henry Davis's body is in that well. We know you bought the property to protect your secret. You drove the demolition derby car used to run Violet off the road and visited the Ames home to vandalize our vehicles." He swung his eyes to the younger man. "We know you broke into Mrs. Ames's home after one of you tried to kill her. You left a threatening note for Violet at the hospital. Reported my truck as stolen. And your father set that fire tonight."

The Mastersons exchanged heated glares.

Wyatt's steady tone was at odds with his pale skin. Beads of sweat gathered along his forehead and at his temples. "Now you're going to pay for your crimes."

Mr. Masterson dug his fingers deep into Violet's hair and forced her forward, bent face-first over the gaping well. "I don't think so."

Maggie wailed and clung to her mother's chest above the seemingly endless black hole.

"Stop!" Violet cried. "Please. No."

Behind her, a gun went off, and the fingers in her hair loosened.

Mr. Masterson released her with a jolt, nearly toppling her into the open well. He dived at his son in a rage. "You took a shot at me?"

Violet fell against the well's brick edges, landing hard on one hip before scurrying back from the hole. She stopped short as the land mines returned to mind, and she sobbed against her sweet baby's crying face, curving her shoulders over Maggie where they sat on the treacherous earth.

Before them, Wyatt wrestled with the sheriff, both angling for a dropped sidearm, presumably the one that had gone off moments before.

Mr. Masterson stalked toward them, gaze intent on the dark ground. His boot connected with Wyatt's blood-soaked side and sent him rolling across the grass.

Violet winced at the sight of the gruesome connection. She pressed Maggie tighter to her chest, using her hands to shield her baby's eyes from all the ugly sights.

Wyatt was on his knees in a second, face red and fists curled. He jolted forward, connecting his shoulder to the old man's middle, the way he had saved Violet's life earlier. Mr. Masterson grunted as the air whooshed from his lungs, and he landed with a hard thud and a desperate groan.

The sheriff flew at Wyatt, but was deflected with a well-aimed punch to the gut. Sheriff Masterson doubled over in pain and was rewarded with Wyatt's elbow against his neck and shoulder.

Wyatt twisted the sheriff's hands behind his back and used his cuffs against him.

Mr. Masterson creaked into a sit, rasping in pain. "You can't win," he said. "That man is the sheriff. No one will believe you, and the buck stops with him." He raked his hand over the dark ground in search of his fallen pistol, then pointed it at Wyatt.

A new set of headlights flooded the scene. The vehicle rocked to a stop several yards away, while the faint wails of emergency vehicles whirred to life somewhere in the distance.

Violet watched in confusion as a coroner's van pulled in and took its place beside the sheriff's car. A deputy's cruiser and two ambulances followed.

Mr. Masterson lowered the weapon.

"Hello, Sheriff Masterson." Deputy Santos's voice flowed from a backlit figure moving through the blinding headlights. "Wyatt, Miss Ames, I'd like you to meet Sam Culley, Grove County coroner."

Sawyer appeared in the light, having climbed down from the passenger's side of the coroner's van. The incoming trio stopped at the edge of the barbed wire perimeter, clear of the mines.

"About time," Wyatt groaned, shoving off the sheriff's back. He dusted his palms and nudged the cuffed sheriff with the toe of one boot. "Did you know that in the great state of Kentucky, only the sitting coroner can arrest the sheriff?" he asked. He turned a cheery smile on Mr. Masterson. "Turns out the buck doesn't stop here."

Deputy Santos shined a heavy flashlight on the ground, stepping carefully toward Mr. Masterson to relieve him of his weapon.

Sawyer skulked toward Wyatt, gaze fixed on the ground. "You think I'm slow, but I had to go get this guy out of bed." He motioned to the coroner, now reading the sheriff his rights from the safety of the perimeter fence. "He doesn't even live in this town. And we followed Santos over here, who drives like my great-grandmother."

Santos shot him a look. "Shut up."

Wyatt shook Sawyer's hand in one strong pump.

He snatched his Stetson off the old man's head, then headed straight for Violet's side.

Violet's sobs were stifled for Maggie's sake, and her heart was fit to explode. The incredible rush of relief and anticipation of being in Wyatt's arms once more was nearly painful.

"Are you okay?" Wyatt hoisted her up with one arm

and took Maggie from her with the other. He cuddled them both to his chest. "I thought I'd be too late."

Maggie snuggled instantly against him. Her cries had faded to grateful whimpers.

Violet knew exactly how her daughter felt. In Wyatt's arms, everything was okay and anything was possible.

VIOLET AND WYATT sat in the stiff chairs of the hospital waiting room while Maggie toddled speedily across the floor. It was hard to believe that nearly a year had passed since Violet had gotten that terrifying call. The one that told her Grandma was in a coma. The one that had changed her life in every possible way.

"How are you doing?" Wyatt asked, concerned as always about Violet's comfort, well-being, ability to rest and every general whim.

"Perfect," she said, feeling the depth of truth in the word.

Wyatt grinned. "Good." He pulled Maggie onto his lap as she stumbled against his legs in a windmill of chubby arms and giggles.

Grandma cruised through the doorway a moment later, an expert on her cane. The months of physical therapy following her accident had left her in better condition than she'd started, and the overall experience had given her a new lease on life. She didn't even mind the cane. "Am I late?"

Wyatt and Maggie greeted her with hugs and cheek kisses. "Nope."

"Excellent." She took a seat at Violet's side and patted her arm. "I've got things all set at home. All I need now is your little miss."

Wyatt raised Maggie in the air. "Here she comes," he

said, flying his sweet girl like an airplane to her great-grandmother's lap.

Grandma kissed Maggie's nose, then raised her eyes to the soldier who'd saved all their lives. "Trial's over. Did you hear?"

Wyatt nodded. "We did. The prosecuting attorney called after breakfast."

"He called me, too," Grandma said, looking pensive but satisfied.

Violet tried to smile, but she had too many mixed emotions to manage it.

According to the attorney, Mr. Masterson was found guilty for the murders of Henry Davis and Ruth, for the attempted murder of Grandma and Wyatt, the abduction and attempted murders of Violet, Maggie and his wife who fell from Grandma's barn but later died from complications of her already diminished condition. Along with about a dozen other things. Sheriff Masterson was found guilty for his role and participation in the extensive cover-up and everything that had involved.

It was hard to be happy about the verdict, even with justice served, when so many people had lost their lives.

"Mrs. Stone?" A nurse called from the waiting room door, her eyes settling quickly on Violet.

Warmth rushed through her, as it always did at the sound of her name with Wyatt's. There really wasn't anything greater than being loved by him. And to think she'd tried to swear off military men.

He was on his feet in an instant, reaching for her. He hoisted Violet easily onto her very swollen feet and smiled. "Beautiful."

She rolled her eyes and rubbed the base of her aching back. She'd gained thirty-six pounds and was shaped like a whale, but he never stopped insisting she was perfect.

She slipped her hand into his and shook her head at the man who'd saved her life in every way possible. Her handsome, courageous, honorable husband. "I love you."

He leaned down to kiss her, and her knees nearly buckled with pleasure. As usual.

Grandma clapped her hands together. "That's our cue, Miss Maggie." She set Maggie on her feet, stood and took her hand. "We'll meet you at my place for lunch and the big news," she told Violet and Wyatt. "Your family was already starting to arrive when I left."

Grandma's place was now just down the street from Violet, Wyatt and Maggie. Grandma had collected the insurance money from the fire, sold her land and gotten a cottage in Lexington while she finished recovering from last year's fall. The cottage was warm and inviting with less upkeep and maintenance than the farm had required. More time for things that mattered, like family, she'd said as she signed the papers. She'd even planted a rose garden in the backyard.

Wyatt and Violet kissed Maggie and Grandma goodbye, then followed the nurse to an ultrasound room.

"Have you decided?" the nurse asked. "Would you like to know the gender of your baby?"

Violet smiled up at her husband. "Absolutely."

The whole family was gathering for that news as they spoke, and Violet couldn't wait to start her next adventure with the man she knew would never let her go.

* * * * *

JOIN US ON SOCIAL MEDIA!

Stay up to date with our latest releases, author news and gossip, special offers and discounts, and all the behind-the-scenes action from Mills & Boon...

 millsandboon

 millsandboonuk

millsandboon

It might just be true love...

MILLS & BOON

THE HEART OF ROMANCE

A ROMANCE FOR EVERY KIND OF READER

MODERN

Prepare to be swept off your feet by sophisticated, sexy and seductive heroes, in some of the world's most glamourous and romantic locations, where power and passion collide.
8 stories per month.

HISTORICAL

Escape with historical heroes from time gone by. Whether your passion is for wicked Regency Rakes, muscled Vikings or rugged Highlanders, awaken the romance of the past.
6 stories per month.

MEDICAL

Set your pulse racing with dedicated, delectable doctors in the high-pressure world of medicine, where emotions run high and passion, comfort and love are the best medicine.
6 stories per month.

True Love

Celebrate true love with tender stories of heartfelt romance, from the rush of falling in love to the joy a new baby can bring, and a focus on the emotional heart of a relationship.
8 stories per month.

Desire

Indulge in secrets and scandal, intense drama and plenty of sizzling hot action with powerful and passionate heroes who have it all: wealth, status, good looks…everything but the right woman.
6 stories per month.

HEROES

Experience all the excitement of a gripping thriller, with an intense romance at its heart. Resourceful, true-to-life women and strong, fearless men face danger and desire - a killer combination!
8 stories per month.

DARE

Sensual love stories featuring smart, sassy heroines you'd want as a best friend, and compelling intense heroes who are worthy of them.
4 stories per month.

To see which titles are coming soon, please visit

millsandboon.co.uk/nextmonth

MILLS & BOON
MEDICAL
Pulse-Racing Passion

Set your pulse racing with dedicated, delectable doctors in the high-pressure world of medicine, where emotions run high and passion, comfort and love are the best medicine.

MILLS & BOON
Desire

Indulge in secrets and scandal, intense drama and plenty of sizzling hot action with powerful and passionate heroes who have it all: wealth, status, good looks… everything but the right woman.

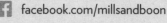